Kingmaker
Andrakis Book Two

30th Anniversary Edition

Tony Shillitoe

First published in 1992 as Kingmaker by Pan Macmillan.
Re-published in 2006 as Maker of Kings by Altair Australia.
Republished in 2024 as Kingmaker on Amazon.

Cover art by Kirsi Salonen
http://www.kirsisalonen.com

ISBN: 978-0-6458658-3-7

For Graham Phillips, who gave me good advice that brought Andrakis to life, and to the tireless work of Roxarne Burns, Jane Palfreyman and Linda Funnell, who all saw the same vision and believed in it.

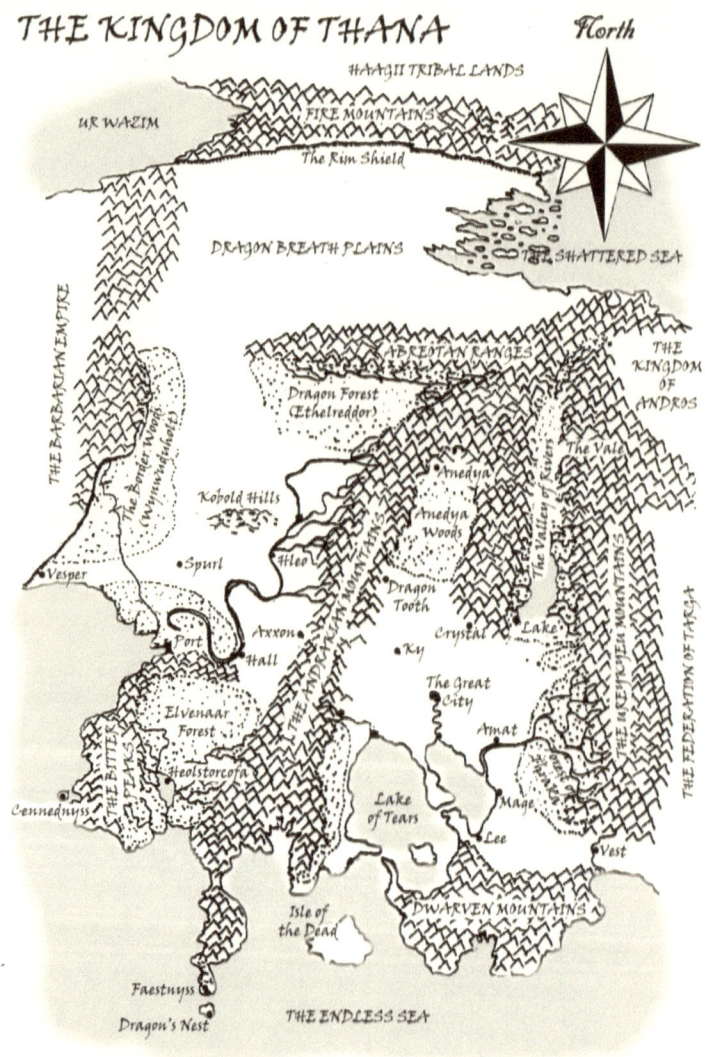

THE KINGDOM OF THANA

North

HAAGII TRIBAL LANDS

UR WAZIM

FIRE MOUNTAINS

The Rim Shield

DRAGON BREATH PLAINS

THE SHATTERED SEA

THE BARBARIAN EMPIRE

ABREOTAN RANGES

THE KINGDOM OF ANDROS

Dragon Forest (Ethelreddor)

The Vale

The Border Woods (Wyfynwilden)

Kobold Hills

Anedya

Anedya Woods

The Valley of Kings

Vesper

Spurl

Hleo

Dragon Tooth

Crystal

Lake

THE ANDRAETON MOUNTAINS

Port

Axxon Hall

Ky

The Great City

Amat

THE LAKE VAETHA MOUNTAINS

Elvenaar Forest

Heolstorcofa

Mage

THE FEDERATION OF TARA

THE BITTER PEAKS

Cennednyss

Lake of Tears

Lee

Vest

Isle of the Dead

DWARVEN MOUNTAINS

Faestnyss

Dragon's Nest

THE ENDLESS SEA

RANU KA SHEHAALA

North

KAL DENN

NYEDENA MARKESH

UZ ERHAAG

• Tul Et Hazier

UR WAZIM

Tul Ur

Yul Ur

BATTEN ILYA'ESTA

Tul Batt •

Tul Irandus •

• Tul Ji-nya

Tul Haruk •

• Tul Adena •

• Tul Ira

Tul Markesh •

BATT JI'NYA

Tul Ka Arik •

• Tul Fez-ur

Tul Maheem

Tul Ilya'esta •

Tul Arat

Tul Kareb

Tul Ranu •

Yul Ithrandur

BATT ITHOS

Tul Methaa •

MIHRANTZ (The Great Ravages)

Tul Ethta •

Tul Ef-ur

Tul Kal

Tul Lemet

Vesper

Spurl

Tul Kebur

Tul Yom Nir

Tul Ithos

Port

Tul Oozek

Tul Shadak

UR SHADU

Tul Arik

Tul Shadu

"The essence of holding absolute power over a man is in convincing him of your trustworthiness and friendship, while you sow seeds for his self-destruction. Nothing is more satisfying than to watch a victim perish through his own ignorance."

from Destinies Determined,
a treatise by Chancellor Ki of Andrakis

One

A dark figure slipped over the castle wall and perched delicately beneath the parapet, secreted in its shadow. For several moments, the figure and shadows were one – silent, motionless – as two soldiers passed above, their lanterns afraid to pry too deep into the night. The figure waited for the soldiers to move beyond earshot before sliding effortlessly down the fifteen-span stone face to the lip of the cliff.

A chill breeze touched his face. He flinched and listened. The night brooded. Pale moonlight lit the white ribbon road thirty spans below, and flickering lights winked in the Great City, south of the cliff. Everything seemed normal. After a cautionary glance up, at the dark parapet, the figure dropped over the edge, down the rocky cliff face, to the silent road.

The King's Way was deserted. Though raucous revelry rose from the throng in the Inn of Dragons, and light spilled from doorsills and windows, few people were travelling the thoroughfare. Jerome moved quietly, noting unusually dark doorways and gaps between buildings with the practiced eye of a Guildsman. He'd been given a simple test – steal an item from the Great King's castle – a mission he accomplished without drama. He clutched the fine silver goblet, pilfered from the Great King's servant kitchen, beneath his leather jerkin. The goblet was his key to the Guild's title of Master Thief, but he was a master of his art, and he deserved the title. He sidestepped a large pool of light, radiating from an open doorway. There was little risk of being stopped by the Great King's men this time of night, but a Master Thief takes no chances, he reminded himself, even if most of the Great King's Haardrishii, the elite Kingdom warriors, were being marched to war.

Laughter tumbled from the doorway, as he passed in

darkness on the opposite side of the street, and he saw motley figures hunched over a table, and knew fellow thieves were scattered in there to relieve the merchants and mercenaries, caught in rigged gambling games, of unnecessary monetary baggage. He wasn't one for that caper. He couldn't grasp the complexities of card sequences or loaded bone dice. He was an active thief, at home scaling walls, or scrambling silently through sewers and tunnels. That was why he was so good.

Insecurity still irked him. He glanced over his shoulder, but the street was quiet. Two figures sauntered across The King's Way, further up, and disappeared through a brief portal of light when a door opened. A knot of men lurked in a dark archway near the Inn of Dragons, but he knew who they most likely were. No. Something else wasn't right. He could feel it in his bones. He paused, and moved on, his ears trained on the street behind him.

A little way down the street, he stepped into a doorway and watched the pool of light he'd passed. No one appeared. He waited. A rider trotted into view and rode by – a mercenary – a lone warrior looking for hire in the Great King's war. The rider wasn't what he sensed in the darkness. He waited a few more moments, before he stepped into the street to continue. Maybe he was being overcautious. The test was almost over. It had been too easy. Perhaps the Guild had another test for him. No. No one was good enough to follow him undetected. He perfected that art. As a Master Thief, he'd be called upon to train others because he was the best at his trade. He doubted even the Guild Master could successfully track him, without being noticed. Yet, he was uneasy.

He reached the alley he was seeking, and turned in. As he slid from view off The King's Way, he sprinted and slipped into a dark gap between two buildings. If he was being followed for certain, he'd discover who it was this time. He waited. The King's Way was deserted. Jerome relaxed, but kept his pale blue eyes trained on the alley's entrance. Patience: the best thieves knew patience was their prime skill. Impatient thieves were soon dead thieves. He'd lived too long in the game to be anything less than patient. He listened to the rhythm of his heart, silently counted the beats, and watched.

A tall figure, cloaked, barely visible, except to Jerome's trained eyes, appeared in the alley entrance. The figure stopped and peered into the gloom. Jerome concentrated on controlling his breathing, maintaining silence. Hesitation – and then the figure advanced. Jerome's fingers tightened on the bone haft of his dirk. The stranger passed and headed along the alley toward the river. With steady, deliberate movement, Jerome emerged from his hiding place and followed.

The narrow alley wound between dark structures, turning back on itself, at intervals, but Jerome knew it like the back of his hand. He played in it from childhood, so it was easy for him to follow another person at a reasonable distance without losing his quarry. Yet, when he edged around the third turn in the alley, the figure was gone. Surprised, he faltered, searched the inky confines, but nothing registered, beyond a wall of black buildings and the soft sound of the river water lapping against the bank. A cold shiver ran up his spine. Something terribly sinister was unsettling his world. All senses on edge, he eased away from the corner, gently stepping back to begin his retreat. Hands gripped his throat.

His head throbbed. His throat felt cut inside, afire with scratching, burning pain. A hard surface pressed against his nose, chest, and legs. His tongue was swollen and sore, and he tasted dust. He heard shuffling feet – light footsteps. He couldn't move his arms, or his hands, because they were bound. He was face down on a floor. He opened his eyes, to find it was pitch black. Someone moved again, closer. He tried to bend his legs, to stand, but they were also tied. He was helpless. He tried to recall the last events – the alley, darkness, hands tightening on his neck, fear – but even thinking hurt. Footsteps scraped beside him. He tensed.

'Leoht!' a voice commanded.

The wall of night dissolved as a soft glow lit the floorboards. Jerome blinked, letting his eyes adjust. He bent his knees to begin a roll, to bring him to face the disembodied voice, but a heavy foot pushed on his back and pressed him against the floorboards. Pain stabbed through his head.

'Don't struggle,' the voice ordered.

It was soft, cold, compelling, and fear flashed through Jerome's spirit. He'd never heard the voice before, not in the Guild.

'That's right, Jerome, you don't know me. But I know you. I know everything about you.'

Jerome shivered. For years, as a thief, he fought fear and won time and again. A Master Thief ignored fear. But suddenly he was afraid – very afraid – afraid of the voice, the cold voice.

'Fear's terrible, isn't it?' said the stranger. 'You feel it now, eating at you. Good. You should be very much afraid of me, Jerome. Power is based on fear. I learned that a long time ago. The more fear one creates, the greater the power one wields. It's a simple law. And I'm the most powerful individual you'll ever know, Jerome. So be afraid. Savor your fear. Let it ooze through you. It's the last emotion you'll experience in life: fear, gut-wrenching fear.'

Panic overwhelmed him. What was happening? Was this part of the Guild's game? Were they testing his courage? Why couldn't he place the voice? Unless the Haardrishii had him. No. The Great King's black-armoured soldiers didn't orchestrate clandestine entrapments. They preferred open and honorable confrontation with the Guild in their policing role. But the voice perplexed Jerome because it was vaguely familiar – someone he knew, but not from the Guild. He was convinced this assault was part of a test. It had to be.

'You're mine to use now, Jerome. You're no longer your own man. I am you,' the voice coldly informed him.

Yes. He understood what was happening. It was the test,

the Guild's test. Summoning every effort, Jerome forced his emotion to obey his will. Fear? No. He could leap that hurdle. They had frightened him, but he was going to be a Master Thief, and no trick or terror would prevent that. He concentrated on his voice. No quavering. He'd show them courage. Yet why did his tongue feel swollen, his throat violently sore? His head ached and ached. With supreme effort, he whispered to the floor, 'I know the game, and I'm not afraid.'

A hand wrenched his shock of blond hair, and the foot lifted from his back, so that his face was jerked up to gaze into his antagonist's eyes. Jerome squinted to make out the stranger's visage and stiffened with shock. He was staring into the sharp Aelendyell features and grey oval eyes of A Ahmud Ki, the Great King's Advisor.

'This is no game, Jerome,' A Ahmud Ki hissed. 'Your mind is mine. You've taught me the secrets of the Guild, the watchword, the doors, the tunnels. You've served me well. It's a pity you can't be there to see the outcome. That's the unfortunate price you must pay. That's your destiny.' Jerome's eyes widened with renewed confusion as he watched the wizard's face melt, and change, until he was staring at his own features on the face of A Ahmud Ki.

'Where is he? We want the Advisor now! Where is he?' Great King Thana heaved his paunch forward in the seat of his golden throne, leaning ominously toward Chancellor Rheims, while Rheims, at the foot of the throne steps, fidgeted with the hem of his dark green cloak and shuffled nervously like a mantis whose world was disrupted by inquisitive children.

'My Royal Liege, your Royal Advisor is not available at present,' he warily replied, sensitive of the Great King's mounting displeasure.

'Not available?' roared Thana, his purple robe flaring to accentuate his annoyance. 'Not available when We order him to attend?' Rheims watched the Great King's face redden as he puffed with anger. Since the news reached the Great City of the massacre of two of the Great Armies' Wheels at The Rim Shield, Great King Thana was increasingly unsettled and irritable. He broke into public fits of rage, sobbed in the privacy of his chambers, and perpetually blamed everyone at the King's Table for advising him to send his Great Armies against the Haagii. Rheims, terrified the Great King would rail against him, quietly tried to placate his Lord's demeanour. 'We want the Advisor,' Thana reiterated. 'Where is he?'

Rheims shook his head. 'His servant informs me he is still recuperating from the injuries he sustained when he was conducting an experimental spell.'

Thana eased into his throne and rubbed his pudgy nose. 'It's been four weeks, a month that he's refused to attend Our pleasure. Is he frightened to face Our wrath for his foolish advice? Is he as cowardly as all the other fools who sit smiling at Our Table?'

Rheims waited patiently. None of the Lords were really frightened of the Great King. Of them all, Rheims knew the Great King's Advisor, the strange wizard with Aelendyell features who mysteriously arrived from Targa bearing the news of the Dragonlord's return, would be the least concerned by Thana's fit of pique. The wizard was already a law unto himself in the castle.

'We'll tolerate his impudence no more. Fetch him, Rheims. We order you to drag him before Us, if necessary!' Thana bellowed. He banged his pudgy fist against the soft metal edge of his throne to emphasize his frustration, and winced with pain.

Rheims made a tentative step onto the first throne step. 'Are you hurt, my Liege?' he inquired.

Thana screwed up his face and glared. 'We've given you an order!' he hissed through his teeth. Lord Rheims bowed low, quickly turned, and scampered from the Throne Room. The Great King watched the Chancellor's retreating back, until he disappeared from the Throne Room, while he rubbed his fist, wishing he had more sense than to hit things.

He shifted his weight in the throne, readjusted his griffin-shaped crown, and stared across the empty Throne Room at tapestries decorating the far walls, depicting vast ancient battles, his ancestor Aian Abreotan wielding his flame sword, slaying dragons.

The world had come full circle. The Dragonlord was back. Two Wheels of his Great Armies, ten thousand warriors, half his Kingdom's soldiers, were slaughtered beneath The Rim Shield, the Haagii were marching into the northern plains again, and terrified messengers arrived in the Great City crying that dragons were coming south with the Haagii. He was the Great King. He was Aian Abreotan's descendant. He had to stop the Dragonlord. It was his duty.

Thana clenched his fists, until the knuckles whitened, and beat them against his forehead. How could he triumph? There was no Aian Abreotan in his castle, no flaming sword forged by the Dwarven and wrought with the magic of the Elvenaar, and his finest soldier, High Lord Mara, was slain with his Wheels at The Rim Shield. Who remained? Who would replace Mara? Who would drive out the leather faced Haagii marauders flooding into his Kingdom? Who could he trust to keep the Dragonlord from him? He was alone, surrounded by weak fools who would perish like eggs beneath the Dragonlord's crushing foot, and he, Great King Thana, thirty-seventh descendant of Aian Abreotan, would suffer the vengeance of the Dragonlord in the place of his long dead ancestor. It was all so unfair.

Lord Rheims left the marbled arch, leading into the castle's gardens, and stepped into the thick jungle greenery. Birds fluttered through overhanging boughs, flashes of crimson, lemon and brilliant blue, their song turning the castle grounds into a magical paradise. The Royal Advisor had embellished the Royal Gardens with his magic, but Rheims distrusted magic. Wielders of magic were unpredictable. There were few of them in Thana's Kingdom, save Lord Waeron Ardath the Royal Drycraefter, and the Aelendyell ambassadors, but the Royal Advisor had started a school of Apprentices, since arriving, and their numbers were growing. The proliferation made Rheims uncomfortable because the Apprentices formed a private army within the castle walls for the Royal Advisor – a force Rheims perceived as a potential threat to the Kingdom. Great King Thana was too blind to see what was happening within his stronghold, because he was so afraid of the mounting threat from the Haagii.

The Royal Advisor's black tower rose like a polished rod from the profuse greenery. Four of A Ahmud Ki's Apprentices sat on the gravel foreground to the tower, their legs crossed, and eyes shut in intense concentration, and they made no show of acknowledging Rheims' presence. He studied their shaven heads and grey woollen smocks and wondered how their training allowed them to close out the world so readily and easily.

At the tower's base, he paused to stare upward. There were no windows, no door, no visible seams; nothing but solid black stone. The first day the tower appeared, the Great King and his attendant lords came to the gardens to marvel at the Royal Advisor's magical construction, and even then Rheims spied danger in a being who could create such a structure, with little time or effort, but he couldn't warn Thana because the Great King didn't want to listen. His mind was full of dragons and Dragonlords, fears carefully and shrewdly planted by the new Royal Advisor.

There was nowhere to knock. Rheims stood before this tower, on the insistent orders of the Great King, every day since the news arrived that Lord Mara's forces were routed. Everything, including the advancing Haagii armies, pointed to Lord Mara's death, and the death or capture of ten thousand Kingdom warriors. Thana had every reason to worry.

Pak, A Ahmud Ki's nondescript servant, stepped through the tower wall, as if it was insubstantial. The familiar magical illusion always irked Rheims, and he was certain he would never get used to it. Pak's pleasant but bored expression gave Lord Rheims the predictable answers to his questions even before he asked them. They were the same questions he asked every day, and Pak would give him the same tired answers.

'Greetings, Lord Chancellor,' said Pak, with his customary deferential nod. 'I trust you are well?'

'I'm well, thank you,' Rheims replied. 'You know why I am here again.'

'Yes, my Lord. Unfortunately, my master is still not fully recovered, and cannot grant the Great King audience. Is there a message I can pass on?'

Rheims studied the man. Pak was nothing special to look at. Neither tall nor broad, neither short nor fat, his beard was cropped close to his skin, and he wore a simple grey leather jerkin and leggings, with a short sword thrust through his belt. His head was shaved bald, in the manner of the Advisor's Apprentices, and only the man's glittering dark eyes exposed his intelligence. Rheims wondered why the Advisor chose to set his trust on so ordinary a being.

'Yes,' Rheims replied, after a moment's hesitation. 'Tell the Royal Advisor the Great King has been more insistent in asking after him, and will no longer tolerate excuses. There is a meeting of the King's Table, scheduled for three days' time, to decide what must be done next. Tell the Royal Advisor that Great King Thana orders him to attend.'

Pak nodded, and stepped back, disappearing effortlessly through the ebony wall.

Rheims remained where he was, flanked by silent Apprentices beneath the cool shade of the trees. This is another world, he thought, as he looked around. There are secrets here, secrets about the Royal Advisor locked in the place he's created. What would the secrets reveal? Would the answers be less pleasant than the questions? Rheims shuddered involuntarily and squinted up at the circling blue sky above the dark lip of the tower. He felt as if he was being watched. He'd completed the Great King's task. Time to return to the comfort of the castle rooms. For all their beauty, he hated these gardens.

Two

If the spell worked as it should, he had all the knowledge he needed of the Guild's secret ways. The shape-change spell he acquired in the realm of Targa, the federation of sorceresses east of Thana's Kingdom, enabled him to copy Jerome's features and pass for him physically. But the greatest value remained in the mind spells he synthesized from the magic of the Ranu Ithosen and the Targan sorceresses, spells that enabled him to search and learn his victim's innermost memories. He not only looked like Jerome, he carried the thief's thoughts and knowledge. No one would suspect the Royal Advisor was prowling through the heart of the Thieves' Guild. He adjusted his thin black cloak and turned the handle.

His eyes quickly adjusted to the inky blackness. The room, part of an old wooden storage shed attached to the rear of a ramshackle house, was formerly owned by a bankrupt and long dead merchant. Jerome entered the Guild stronghold by this room, through a well-oiled trapdoor, hidden beneath an old packing box by the wall, opposite the entrance. He made for the place and lifted the solid box that formed part of the trapdoor. A crude wooden ladder descended. Soft scratching from behind a disordered pile, in the near corner to his left, made him freeze. He waited, until he heard something shuffle, and a muffled cough. Someone else was in the room. With all the skill he could muster from his youth in the Aelendyell forest, ears and eyes trained on the source of the sounds, he lowered the trap lid. Nothing stirred. He stepped back from the box and crouched against the wall. He heard another muffled cough. With extreme care, he eased along the wall toward the pile, until he could peer over the lower part at who or whatever lay behind it, and saw a heat shape bunched into the pile of rags and boxes, a small one – a child. The child coughed again, violently, and curled into foetal warmth, pushing deeper into the rubbish. The child was asleep and hadn't seen him after all.

He relaxed, but he recalled the sick and hungry men, women and children lingering outside the gates of the Palace Ithrandyr Shadu when he was in Ranu Ka Shehaala. They were wasted lives. Leiksha Ithrandyr Shehaal, omnipotent emperor of Ranu Ka Shehaala, for all his power and wisdom, wasted his full potential. So did the inept fat fool who called himself Great King of this land. Both allowed poor people, like this child, to live without purpose or use. Even the forest-bound Aelendyell, his hated kin, had more sense. No one suffered poverty in the forests. Caring for Aelendyell childlings was the common responsibility of every Aelendyell adult. In the human cities he visited, children were left to scrounge and die, and were useless. When he held supreme power, as he was destined to do, he'd leave no waste. All his servants would be useful, and when their worth was expended, they would be consumed. No waste. The child stirred again and coughed. A Ahmud Ki leaned away from the pile, returned quietly to the trapdoor, and descended.

At the base of the ladder, tunnels led three directions. A Ahmud Ki recalled the memory he acquired from Jerome and turned to follow the left passage. Darkness still enveloped him, but his Aelendyell heat vision prevented him from running into walls.

Several paces on, a lantern swung before his eyes. Dazzled, he adopted a defensive stance, ready to incant a spell, only to be greeted by a torrent of laughter from the lantern-bearers.

'Ho! Jerome the Wall is returned somewhat tetchy from his adventure.' More laughter.

A Ahmud Ki rubbed his eyes and blinked. At least four figures were crowded in the passageway behind the lantern, but he couldn't discern facial features in the blinding light.

'Creeping around The Maze in the dark is a bit risky ain't it?' said the voice holding the lantern. Grinning yellow teeth glistened beside the light – a face, rough beard – an earring.

13

Jerome's memory rolled through A Ahmud Ki's mind. 'At least it's possible for me, Gordon, you son of a whore,' he replied. Jerome knew this man well: a member of the Guild's Eyes and Ears, the security watch set to catch intruders in The Maze. A Ahmud Ki judged Gordon's reaction to his response very carefully. He didn't have Jerome's voice and expression, only the face, and mastering personality traits required time and patience, two commodities he abandoned in favour of expediency. If the thieves spotted too great a difference, he had to be ready.

Gordon laughed, and clapped A Ahmud Ki on the shoulder. 'Airs and graces in the voice now as well, is it? You mongrel breeder! One trip to the Great King's joint and he thinks he can speak right proper to boot. Pah! Password?'

'There isn't one tonight,' A Ahmud Ki snappily replied. 'You couldn't remember it, if there was one.'

More laughter met the jibe. 'Too much lip from you, my friend,' Gordon warned good-naturedly, 'and I'll steal that coveted prize you've worked so hard to bring back from the castle.' Gordon held up the goblet, that Jerome had stolen to prove he'd been inside Thana's castle, before A Ahmud Ki's surprised eyes. Raucous laughter erupted from everyone in the passage. A Ahmud Ki quickly composed himself, threw an indignant look at Gordon, and held out his hand. 'Never before have I got the best of you, Jerome the Wall, but tonight I've done it, and with one hand while the other held a lantern!' Gordon guffawed with delight. 'Ho, this will make a merry tale in the tavern!' He slipped the goblet into A Ahmud Ki's hand and pressed him on the back. 'Get along with you, Master Thief. Go see the Guild Master. But remember Gordon has taught you a lesson as well,' he chuckled. 'And here, take a light, lest you fall foul of some ill-mannered vermin in The Maze, like this lot,' he added, gesturing at his grinning companions as he handed a lantern to A Ahmud Ki.

Further along the tunnel, A Ahmud Ki reached a crossroad. He turned left. The passage ran through several low-ceilinged rooms, empty of people, but filled with crude wooden seats and tables. Doors opened off each room, presumably to sleeping quarters. His encounter with Gordon had gone well enough, though his voice obviously failed. Jerome must have had a sense of humour, a touch of arrogance, going by Gordon's responses. He would remember that. Letting Gordon filch the goblet was a mistake, although Gordon's glee at his success suggested the move wasn't too out-of-the-ordinary. Nevertheless, A Ahmud Ki doubted he could pass a close inspection from these humans. So long as he got to his destination; that's all that mattered.

He wound through passages, up and down rough-hewn stairs, and it reminded him of his first journey, under watch, and blindfolded, after stumbling accidentally into The Maze from the Dragonlord's lair in Targa. He regretted releasing the Dragonlord from his tomb, not because of the devastating war that resulted, but because he squandered his opportunity to acquire the Dragonlord's awesome powers, the Fifth Ki of magic. When Mareg Dru'artha Sutnavanistra burst from his sarcophagus, released from the glyph imprisoning him, A Ahmud Ki leapt for his life into a portal mirror that brought him to a cave, deep beneath Great King Thana's city. In his search to escape, A Ahmud Ki entered the Deep Cave in the Thieves' Guild maze, where thieves captured him, but he was fortunate in convincing Guild Master Orrin to release him.

His purpose in returning was twofold. The Guild was an undeniable power in the Great City because Thana's soldiers, even his fearful Haardrishii, were unable to curb the Guild's nocturnal and illegal activities. The Guild flourished, despite the Great King's war against the Haagii, and whoever controlled the Guild controlled most of the Great City, with a veritable army of professional thieves and assassins. That was a power A Ahmud Ki sought.

But a richer prize lay hidden in the Guild's coffers – the tomb of an ancient Dragonlord, buried beneath the Deep Cave. If he had free access to that treasure, what secrets of magical power could he not unlock for himself? The Fifth Ki

– the Ki he never knew existed before the Targan sorceress, Lady Tarnyss, caused him to unleash Mareg Dru'artha Sutnavanistra from his prison – would open to him. He would possess all Five Ki – all five sources of magic – and be the most powerful being since the beginning of Time.

So engrossed was he in thought, he failed to notice others staring at him, as he passed them in the passages. Only when a hand pushed firmly against his chest, to stop him, did he remember where he was. Barring his way were two burly ruffians, seasoned street brawlers with battered faces and broken noses. They blocked access to a door. 'You got business with anyone here?' one ruffian grumbled, through his bushy moustache.

A Ahmud Ki searched Jerome's memory. He had to be outside the room where the Master Thieves met. 'Out of my way,' he warned. 'I'm here to see the Guild Master.'

The men moved forward, the first pushing A Ahmud Ki roughly against the wall. 'You don't give no orders here. Understand that?' He pushed harder against the wizard's chest. 'Understand?'

Anger welled in A Ahmud Ki. No one pushed him, no one, but he remembered his purpose and concentrated on control. 'If you ease up, I might let you off lightly,' he quipped, adopting a demeanour more suitable for Jerome.

The ruffians stared hard at him, murder glinting in their eyes. These men are assassins as well, he realised. They could kill him, here and now, without even considering a purpose for it. The shorter one released pressure on A Ahmud Ki and grinned. 'Well, since you've been so generous,' he said gruffly, 'I'll make an exception this time. I'd hate to stand in the way of so important a nobody. What's your business?'

'I'm finishing a test,' A Ahmud Ki replied, pretending to straighten the jerkin under his cloak. He lifted the stolen goblet into view, carefully exposing the royal rampant griffin engraved on its silver surface. 'An important test.'

The goblet attracted the guards' attention and the taller man bent to the door handle. 'Begging your 'umble pardon.

Can't 'old up royalty now, can we?' he said with deliberately clumsy elocution. 'Be entering as you may, sire.' He grinned and winked at his companion, and A Ahmud Ki forced a thankful smile as he walked between the two thieves.

The room was surprisingly small, almost an antechamber. An ash-laden fireplace filled the right wall, a door led left, and a low bench sat against the opposite wall. A Ahmud Ki searched Jerome's memory for a clue, and discovered he had never been beyond the door into the room. As he sat on the bench, he rationalized that, if Jerome hadn't been a Master Thief, there was no surprise to discover there were parts of the Guild's stronghold he hadn't been privy to. Little matter: he had to be close to the Guild Master. He searched his recollections of The Maze, but couldn't visualize much, except that the Guild Master spoke to him in a small room.

A turning doorknob interrupted his thought. The door to his left opened, and a sullen man entered, wearing a dusty grey jerkin and pants. 'You're Jerome the Wall?' the man asked. A Ahmud Ki nodded. 'You've completed the test?' Again, A Ahmud Ki nodded. The man paused, before saying, 'The Guild will see you now.'

A Ahmud Ki followed his guide into a larger room that was smoke-filled and poorly lit by a solitary lantern. Figures clustered around a wooden table at the far end, and coals of a dying fire glowed behind them. They were animated, intently pursuing an argument. He resisted his desire to peer into their thoughts, lest anyone sense his prying and expose his disguise, but he was curious, nonetheless.

His guide whispered into the ear of a man, at the right-hand end of the table, and the man turned to A Ahmud Ki. Recognition lit the stranger's eyes, but he made no effort to communicate. Instead, he elbowed the figure to his left to get his attention. The head turned, and A Ahmud Ki saw a woman. Her hair was hidden beneath a cap, but irascible tufts of orange stuck out defiantly, and wattles of fat rattled beneath her chin. Her sharp green eyes noted every detail about him. He was also aware of another figure beginning to

17

stand, to his left, and everyone turned to stare at him. The standing figure moved into the light, and A Ahmud Ki identified Orrin's weathered face taking his measure. Deep set, dark eyes glinted in the flicker of lanterns. 'Who's this man?' Orrin demanded.

The man who first turned to face A Ahmud Ki replied, 'Master Orrin, this is Jerome the Wall.'

'You know him?' Orrin asked.

'He's known. He served under my apprenticeship, a time ago.'

The speaker had a scar running across his chin from his right cheek. If he knew Jerome well, A Ahmud Ki had to be especially careful, because he hadn't mastered Jerome's voice, and this man could expose a fraud. That would complicate his purpose tonight, a complication he didn't want. He sifted through his store of Jerome's memories, until a name, Tarek, attached itself to the man's features. Tarek taught Jerome the art of garroting.

'Why is he here?' Orrin asked, closing on A Ahmud Ki.

They were waiting for his reply. 'I've done the test,' he replied. Hoping to divert attention from his voice, he reached inside his jerkin to withdraw the goblet, and put it on the table.

Tarek reached for the goblet, but the woman snatched it up. 'Fine piece, indeed. Make a lady a lovely present!' she chortled mischievously.

'You ain't no lady, Patti,' quipped Tarek.

'You wouldn't know a lady if you was knocked down by one,' she retorted.

'And that'd be a fine enough pleasure for you, Tarek,' a third party guffawed. General amusement greeted the comment.

'Enough,' said Orrin, commandingly. 'To the matter at hand.' He squared up to A Ahmud Ki, and looked directly in his eyes, and A Ahmud Ki was oddly conscious of Orrin's broken, flattened nose, the product of countless street brawls. 'To earn the right to be called Master Thief, Jerome the Wall, you must display skill, courage, and intelligence.'

The Guild Master reached for the goblet in Patty's plump fingers. 'This is your proof?' he asked. A Ahmud Ki nodded. 'Nothing more?' Orrin prompted. A Ahmud Ki shook his head. Master Orrin remained staring, deliberating, and the pause made A Ahmud Ki wonder if Jerome had failed in some way to fulfil his test. Or was Orrin beginning to suspect something else was amiss? Orrin turned away, tossing the goblet casually up and down in his right hand, his back to A Ahmud Ki. 'Wait in the other room,' he abruptly ordered. 'The Guild will consider your case, Jerome.'

A Ahmud Ki closed the door, as he stepped out of the room. Had Orrin seen through his ploy? Unlikely. To be Guild Master of the Thieves Orrin had to be an exceptional man, but not good enough to second-guess me, A Ahmud Ki decided. Being forced to wait was more likely standard Guild procedure, in case anyone had reason to bar the rise of an aspirant to Master Thief. How many enemies had Jerome made? Unlikely very many. He seemed well known in the Guild, but not notoriously so – unless there were secrets Jerome hadn't known. The trick was to get the Guild Master alone. Clearly, the Guild was the highest contact an individual could have with Master Orrin. His power would have come at someone's expense, and others would hunger for his position. Orrin protected himself with numbers. A Ahmud Ki noted that ordinary Guild members feared one-to-one meetings with the Guild Master. Jerome had associated that event with potential death, or at least ultimate disgrace. Master Orrin ruled by fear. Clever. A Ahmud Ki remembered his meeting with Orrin after he appeared in the Deep Cave.

'You have looked upon the face of the Guild Master of Thieves,' Orrin said. 'This face holds your life.'

Orrin was the supreme power here, which made it illogical for Jerome to ask for a personal audience with the Master of the Guild. There was only one way to ensure the meeting occurred.

A Ahmud Ki visualized the Guild meeting room where Jerome's promotion was being decided. Two doors led out. One must open into a cavity, behind the wall of the room in which he currently stood. He moved to the wall at the right of the low bench. Passing was risky when he had no image of his destination point on which to focus. *If the space beyond is a corridor, and I project too far? If it is a steep stairwell?* I've risked coming this far, he decided, so he whispered the incantation and pressed against the wall.

Light flickered from a rusty lantern beside a door, six spans away. A dishevelled figure lounged against the wall, and the figure seemed to disregard A Ahmud Ki's abrupt appearance, until the man's eyes focussed. He jerked to his feet. 'Where in Teka's name did you come from?' he spat, astonished, fumbling for his dagger.

A Ahmud Ki smiled, pointed his index finger at the thief, and uttered a single Aelendyell word, 'Hildegicel!' A gleam of metal shot from the wizard's fingertip and punctured the man's vest. The thief opened his mouth in disbelief, stared at blood beginning to pump from his wound, and toppled forward, his dagger tumbling harmlessly to the floor. A Ahmud Ki tried the door and found it locked, but a brief search through the dead guard's pockets produced the key. He opened the door.

Three burning lanterns hung from the ceiling, a polished elmoak table on a large mat filled the centre, a bed squatted in the far left corner, and tall cupboards stood at the right. Shelves ran along the remainder of the right wall, and a tapestry of a riotous inn scene covered most of the left wall, nearest the door and beyond the bed. *If this is the Guild Master's room,* A Ahmud Ki decided, as he surveyed it, *then Orrin keeps himself comfortable.* A Ahmud Ki found a pottery mead jug on the table. He picked it up, returned to the corpse, propped it against the wall, and arranged the jug to give the impression the thief was drunk. *Not exactly original,* he mused, as he masked a little of the blood on the dead man's jerkin, *but there wasn't time to be tidy.* He straightened and concentrated, weaving his hands about his body to dispel his altered shape as Jerome the Wall. Restored, A Ahmud Ki shook his dark robes, pleased to be rid of the unclean thief's appearance, and re-entered Orrin's room to wait.

The wizard waited a long time before footsteps approached the door. Someone paused in the other room. A jug smashed against the floor and low curses were mouthed, the door swung back on its hinges, and Orrin strode angrily into the room. He stopped when he spotted a dark figure sitting at the far end of the table, and his hand grasped the hilt of his dagger. 'Who are you?' he demanded.

A Ahmud Ki enjoyed hearing the thin edge of fear in Orrin's question. In answer, he stood and lifted his cowl to expose his silver Aelendyell locks. Orrin gasped and faltered a step backwards. 'The Guild Master recognises me,' A Ahmud Ki said with a smile.

'I should have slit your throat the night we had you here as Jonn of Targa,' growled Orrin, his eyes flashing defiance.

'You should have,' A Ahmud Ki said softly, 'but you made a mistake.' He sensed the Guild Master adjusting his feet, strengthening his balance, as he eased the dagger from his black leather belt. 'Aren't you curious as to why the Great King's Advisor is paying you a visit, before you try to kill him?'

Orrin's hand froze. 'Why are you here?'

A Ahmud Ki grinned. 'The Guild's getting sloppy. It needs a new Master.'

Orrin scowled at the wizard's sarcasm. 'Who?' he retorted. 'You?' He spat on the floor, with contempt. 'Before you could even lay claim to such a title, you'd have to prove your worth, and then deal with me. There are better than you who failed, and they were true Master Thieves.'

'Could any of your so-called 'betters' have got through your Maze, and your minions, to meet you, face to face, undetected?' asked A Ahmud Ki quietly. 'Even you couldn't do that.' Orrin's face quivered with anger. 'Dealing with you,' A Ahmud Ki added, 'will be mere child's play.'

The Guild Master's hand blurred into action and his silver dagger flashed through the air – and stopped, short of its target, hanging mid-air before A Ahmud Ki's heart. Stunned by the vision of the floating dagger, Orrin's anger dissolved into fear. His eyes widened, as A Ahmud Ki's hand passed over the dagger, without touching it, making its deadly point rotate toward him.

'I take it,' A Ahmud Ki mocked, 'that's your best effort?' A flick of the wizard's finger, and the dagger flew past Orrin's ear, embedding in the edge of the open door. Orrin dived, and rolled to his feet, and he came up holding a second dagger. 'Impressive,' A Ahmud Ki noted, sarcastically. He motioned toward the Guild Master, palm upward. Orrin felt air punched from his chest, as he slammed against the shelves on the wall. He crumpled to the floor amid a flurry of falling artefacts. He fought to regain his breath and staggered to his feet. 'Had enough?' asked A Ahmud Ki. Exasperated, Orrin charged, but A Ahmud Ki sidestepped, allowing the Guild Master to crash into his bed. 'You must be tired, if you're so desperate to get into bed,' the wizard quipped.

Orrin rolled back to his feet, glaring, breathing heavily. 'You're a dead man, Advisor,' he puffed. 'A word from me, and a thousand thieves will come down upon you, and you'll die a grizzly death.'

A Ahmud Ki laughed, but his expression became menacing as he leaned forward to stare into Orrin's face. 'If I utter a certain magical word,' he hissed, 'you'll die a thousand grizzly deaths, over and over, forever.'

Orrin recoiled, ashen-faced, and stumbled back onto his bed, dropping his dagger. He swallowed hard, looked up into A Ahmud Ki's piercing, dark eyes, and asked, 'What do you want from me?'

Three

Pak struggled toward the long oak table, weighed down with his burden of books, and placed them before his master with an audible sigh. A Ahmud Ki lifted his eyes. 'Are there more?' he asked.

'These are all I could find in the Great King's library, Master Ki,' Pak dutifully replied. 'No others mention Dragonlords, except those scribed in the time of King Aian Abreotan. There are very few manuscripts before then, and most are riddled with mildew, and written in strange tongues.'

'Fetch them.'

'But they are unreadable, Master.'

A Ahmud Ki glared at his servant. 'Don't presume to compare your limited judgmental skills with mine.'

Pak immediately abased himself. 'I apologize for my foolish statement, Royal Advisor. I meant no comparison with one so mighty and all-knowing.'

A Ahmud Ki waited, holding Pak to the floor with his will. A servant this useful would be hard to come by, but Pak had limitations. Ambition was always a price for intelligence. How much is this one learning while he scrabbles around, doing my bidding, A Ahmud Ki wondered? 'You are excused,' he said. 'This time.'

Pak rose and bowed his shaven head. 'Thank you, Master Ki.' He turned to leave.

'After you've brought me the texts, I want to speak with Peret,' A Ahmud Ki instructed.

'Yes, Master,' said Pak. He hesitated, in case the wizard had more to add, but A Ahmud Ki turned to his reading, silently dismissing his servant. Pak bowed and withdrew.

A Ahmud Ki studied the open volume. The page was a stilted longhand entry by a dead scribe named Estra. 'Long will there Peace be upon the Land after the Fall of Evil, and then thievish Change will creep through the People's hearts until they no longer remember the former times of Glory. Then will He come again, not as a Shadow but as True Fear.' A Ahmud Ki read quickly. Estra mentioned no one and no place by name, but he wrote stoically of a dreadful creature destroying all things. The motif appeared in many texts written during King Aian Abreotan's reign, the warrior who defeated the Dragonlords in the time of the Dragon Wars, a thousand years ago. Tapestry images, from the sorceresses' hall of learning in Targa, clouded his mind as he read. Visions of Abreotan's flaming sword severing dragon necks danced before his eyes.

He thumbed through more books, searching furtively for passages on Dragonlords. Some texts referred to Abreotan banishing them, some said he slew them, and others claimed he imprisoned them with their own magic so they could never return to this world. A Ahmud Ki at least knew the answer to that mystery. Already he had inadvertently released Mareg Dru'artha Sutnavanistra from his shackles within the Inner Sanctum of Targa. Where were the others imprisoned? One was trapped beneath the Deep Cave. Now that Orrin was his pawn, he could access that prison, without running the gauntlet through the thieves' Maze. Secrets of the Fifth Ki were buried there, and all he had to do was work out how to control and harness the imprisoned Dragonlord's power. One text must surely explain or record how Abreotan subdued and imprisoned the Dragonlords. One text had to hold an answer.

A second motif featured in the texts. Prophets wrote of the rise of a being beyond their times. Some called the resurrected being 'the Dark One', others 'the Dragonlord', others simply referred to 'He' without naming the being. A Ahmud Ki was part of a prophecy being fulfilled. He first learned that from Karrilyon, his Ithosen mentor in the land of the Ranu Ka Shehaala, many years beforehand, and later, in Targa, witches, and members of the sorceresses' Order, spoke of him as the harbinger of disaster. So, a dark power would rise, but the second motif was to do with the

Dragonlord's downfall.

'There shall rise One, bearing a two-edged sword and the mark of the moon, and that One shall slay the Dragonlord.'

'In the Time of Darkness, Light from the Moon shall lead the way, and He of Evil will fall, slain by the Moon's flaming sword.'

'There shall be two who seem as one, but the true bearer will carry the sword again, and a new King will slay the Dragonlord.'

The messages of the different writers were ambiguous, open to interpretation, like the words of all prophets. A Ahmud Ki recalled there were Aelendyell texts prophesying a time of Darkness would return, but the texts were brief, garbled, and obscure. Still, he pondered, holding one heavy volume open, prophecies were potent in the right hands at the right time. At least fifteen scribes referred to a similar prophecy. With a Dragonlord loose, he had the perfect opportunity to increase his power in the Great City and the Kingdom by sharing the prophecy widely, and engineering its fruition.

Footsteps interrupted his reading. He looked up to see a grey-robed Apprentice entering; Peret. Peret prostrated himself on the stone floor, his bald pate shining from the daylight spilling through the windows, and A Ahmud Ki waited, as always, asserting his authority, before speaking. 'Irand shadu arat shehaal,' he said, his Ranu greeting echoing in the reading room.

The Apprentice raised his face from the floor, eyes averted, to reply, 'Irand shadu arat shehaal, Master Ki. What is your will?'

'Rise, and approach,' A Ahmud Ki instructed. 'Pak informs me that you're almost healed.'

Peret rose, and glanced at the pile of texts surrounding A Ahmud Ki, as he replied, 'Yes, Master,' surprised by the Royal Advisor's unexpected interest in his health.

'Good,' said A Ahmud Ki. 'I am pleased. I have need of you.' He straightened. 'When I searched your sleeping mind for details of the battle on The Rim Shield, I came upon a fascinating memory of a warrior who saved your life. I'd like you to tell me about him.'

Peret nodded. Nothing escapes the Searching Eye of the Great Master, he reminded himself, not even thought. 'He was a Runner for one of High Lord Mara's Wheels, Master, but he was different. He wore his black hair in a ponytail, and the others referred to him as a guardian.'

'What was his name?'

Peret searched his memories of the desperate retreat through the grey dust of Dragon Breath Plains. 'Andra.'

'How did he save you?'

'High Lord Mara ordered us up the road, with his retinue, to view the battle from the top of The Rim Shield. That's when everything changed. Dark clouds rolled down from the Fire Mountains, and creatures with fire in their jaws swept across the skies, burning everything. The Haagii poured down the road toward us. We tried to fight them with our magic, but there were too many. Terima and Kalin and Ustras fell, and so did Lord Mara. Only Nim and I remained. And then Nim fell. I heard a battle cry, and this warrior was among the Haagii, his sword sweeping them aside as though they were a mere inconvenience. When two Haagii cornered me, somehow he slew them as well, and we escaped to join the others.'

'Impressive, in a small way,' said A Ahmud Ki. 'But you recalled something special about his sword.'

'Yes, Master,' replied Peret. 'There was no blood on its blade.'

'Perhaps his blows were quick and clean.'

'No, Master,' Peret insisted. 'He cut through leather armour like butter. There was blood over everything, except on the blade. And he often plunged deep.'

A Ahmud Ki raised an eyebrow. A warrior single-handedly accounting for numbers of Haagii? A magical sword? He flicked his eyes over a piece of text under his hand. 'Did this warrior have distinctive marks on his face, or hands?'

'No,' Peret replied, but then he remembered Andra's face, serious and drawn, as they struggled across the grey desert, desperately trying to reach the distant green horizon and water. 'Wait. He had a scar on his cheek, cusp-shape, like a crescent moon.'

A Ahmud Ki remained calm, but inwardly he felt ice melt in his stomach. The old prophecies mentioned the mark of the moon. Could the old scripts hold true? 'Where is this warrior now?' he asked.

Peret looked down. 'Dead, Master.'

A Ahmud Ki looked up. 'Dead?'

'Yes, Master,' Peret replied, sensing his master's disbelief. 'He perished at the edge of the desert, the night before we were found by the villagers. His friends were too weak to bury him. We left him where he lay.'

A sardonic expression crossed A Ahmud Ki's face. This Andra is dead? How could that be possible? Is Peret lying? he wondered. He used a mind spell to search Peret's memory, and saw a vision of a warrior, dehydrated and lying in the grey dust of Dragon Breath Plains, his exhausted and distraught companions bent over him. Peret wasn't lying. He accurately described what he had seen. The pony-tailed warrior with the crescent scar was dead. Peret's memory of his scar was hazy, limited, but the mark seemed to be nothing more than a whitish disfigurement ironically torn in the shape of a crescent moon. A Ahmud Ki had read the texts referring to the prophecies thoroughly, but none had specifically described the extent, position, or even true shape of the moon symbol. He imagined something more impressive than a forlorn blemish. Besides, if this Andra was dead, and he had little doubt that it was true, the scar was nothing more than coincidence. He grinned. 'Dead. Fascinating,' A Ahmud Ki said to himself, before returning his attention to the Apprentice. 'What happened to his sword?'

'The giant one with red hair, Claarn, took it,' Peret explained. 'He said the sword would be needed when the Haagii invade the Kingdom.'

A Ahmud Ki leaned back on his chair, and folded his hands together across his stomach, ruminating on the situation and its possibilities. His knowledge of sword crafting was limited, but he did know of certain metal smiths capable of fashioning exceptionally sharp blades that might cut as cleanly and efficiently as the sword Peret described. There was a possibility the sword had some minor magical property, as Peret believed. If not, he could embellish it with minor magic to make it appear an arcane weapon. The sword had the beginnings of a reputation among the survivors of The Rim Shield massacre, and, if he built on that platform, perhaps he could create a hero of the dimensions illustrated in the ancient prophetic scripts. Then he could create a living vision of the old prophecy and use it as a vehicle for his ascension to power in the Kingdom. His hero would bear the mark of a full moon, and ancient arcane runes on his face, for all to see and believe he was the Saviour, the one warrior, described in the prophecy.

Peret concentrated on remaining motionless, awaiting his master's instruction as Apprentices were trained to do. Patience, concentration, and obedience: the Three First Principles of Learning that Master Ki taught. Failure at any one meant dismissal from the Advisor's lessons.

A Ahmud Ki moved his hands to his chin and broke his silence. 'I want the sword,' he said, in an even tone. 'Go to this giant with the red hair and tell him the Royal Advisor wishes to see the sword for himself. Bring it to me.'

Peret bowed. 'Your will be done, Master!' he snapped obediently, and quickly withdrew, his bare feet whispering across the floor.

A Ahmud Ki watched his Apprentice leave. Peret was lucky to be alive. Only a handful, fifteen, all near death, had stumbled out of the grey dust of Dragon Breath Plains to bring the terrible news of the Great Armies' slaughter at the hands of the Dragonlord's host. Fifteen. One Apprentice. Such was the power of the awesome enemy that promised to descend upon the Kingdom under Mareg's command. Peret glimpsed that power, so he was invaluable to A Ahmud Ki, because, through his memory, A Ahmud Ki could see what the Dragonlord was creating. He could learn.

All too logical! A Ahmud Ki slapped the cream parchment onto the oak table, sat back, and ran his hands through his silver locks. He grinned and shook his head, partly with satisfaction, partly with disbelief, and looked at the unrolled, soiled parchment on the table. Why else would the Great King's castle sit atop a plateau, which thrust out of the surrounding plains of Ky, when there was no geological reason for the plateau to be there in the first place? He laughed aloud. 'Me, A Ahmud Ki, unable to recognise the obvious!'

Pak watched his master's curious outburst with wry indifference, aware he might not be invited to understand why the Royal Advisor was amused. His task was to skim through the texts piled before him, searching for details on Dragonlords, no matter how minute or vaguely related. They had been reading silently for a long time because darkness was gathering outside. 'Shall I light the lanterns of the library, Master?' he inquired.

A Ahmud Ki turned, a broad grin creasing his handsome features. 'No, Pak. This will be sufficient.' He cupped his hands, whispered a command, and a magical sphere of energy spread its soft, warm light through the room. Released, the sphere floated toward the high ceiling, and hovered. 'That's far more efficient,' he said, with satisfaction. 'Come here, Pak.' Pak left the text he was reading, and shifted to A Ahmud Ki's table, where the Royal Advisor pointed at a yellowed parchment. 'Do you recognise what that is?'

Pak looked closer. There were lines and words forming shapes and patterns. 'A map, Master Ki?'

'Of what?'

Pak studied the parchment. Words inked near the centre read, 'King Aian Abreotan's High Fortress of Andrakis'. Architectural plans detailed the design of a castle, the buildings, and the library where they stood at that moment. 'This place, Master?'

A Ahmud Ki lifted the document and held it to the light.

'Yes, this place; all this place, even parts we didn't know existed. Look closer.' He ran his finger along lines on the map. 'Here, in that wall to our right, behind the bookshelves. See that? A secret passage. And here. Beneath the Haardrishii stables. A shaft leading down to the city. Here. Another passage. A longer one, with steps dropping deeper into the plateau. And here's another secret room. Behind the chamber of the Great King's bedroom.' He dropped the map to his side and spun. 'This whole structure is riddled with secrets. We've seen only a tenth of what it holds.' He lifted the map to study it again. 'I wonder how much that fat excuse for a king knows of this?'

He checked the plans, and strode to the bookshelf, which, according to the old map, hid the entrance to a secret passage from the library. He filed through the books. Most were covered with a layer of fine dust, suggesting they hadn't been moved in a long time. He searched behind half a dozen larger, leather-bound volumes, and his fingers touched a loose panel, in the stone between the shelves. 'Pak!' he called. Pak joined his master. 'Push this.' A Ahmud Ki showed Pak the panel and stepped aside. No point taking risks, he silently decided.

Obediently, Pak pressed the panel. An audible click came from behind the wall, and a grinding rasp, as stone moved on stone, and the wall and shelves parted to reveal a dark, musty entrance.

A Ahmud Ki peered in. The air was stale and cold. Cobwebs lined the passage the few spans. Evidently, no one used this passage recently. Good, very good, he thought. He stepped back from the entrance. 'Close it,' he ordered. Pak obeyed. The wall and shelves returned to normalcy.

When Pak turned, he found A Ahmud Ki poring intently over the map, his smile growing by the moment. 'What is it, Master?' he ventured. Asking a question was bold – he knew that – but something in the Royal Advisor's manner suggested there was nothing to fear in asking at that moment.

'He's here. Right below us,' A Ahmud Ki said cryptically.

'Who, Master?'

A Ahmud Ki laughed again. 'The Dragonlord,' he explained. 'Right here. The Deep Cave sits at the edge of the plateau. Abreotan entombed one Dragonlord right beneath his own fortress, in the catacombs and caves of the plateau which the Dragonlord created.' A Ahmud Ki paused, before continuing. 'I wonder if the Thieves Guild really know how close their Maze runs to the castle's maze of tunnels? I must ask Orrin when we next speak.' He moved away from Pak, and the table, and gathered his robes. 'I can have the Fifth Ki,' he said with finality, 'and this map shows me how to get it.'

Four

Lord Rheims watched the Great King pace the length of the King's Table, his hands locked behind his portly back, his sparse tufts of hair catching the light from the shining lanterns burning along the wall. Thana had become increasingly agitated in the days since the survivors of The Rim Shield massacre returned to the Great City. Fifteen remained of the ten thousand sent against the Haagii; and they all described being overwhelmed by an army of incomprehensible numbers, and dragons searing the earth with tongues of flame. The Dragonlord sent the survivors back with a simple message: he would come.

Sweat glistened on Thana's shiny forehead and beaded in the palms of his clenched hands. He turned to Rheims in a whirl of green and black robes. 'We are tired of waiting. Go. Call them in.'

Rheims bowed his grey insect head and scuttled to the double doors that opened into the Throne Room where the waiting Lords gathered. 'His Royal Highness orders the King's Table to assemble!' he announced, with all the officialdom he could muster, and stood aside to let the Lords enter.

Lords Gerran, Eustice and Kerry led the party in, chatting amicably about internal trade affairs. Gerran's boyish face was full of gaiety, as he laughed at Kerry's witticisms. Eustice waddled between them, interested, but failing to do more than smile in response. Behind them, the Royal Drycraefter, Lord Ardath, entered beside Haephus, the High Priest of the Holy Order of Teka, Goddess Protector of the Great City. Next came the stocky figure of Surdrok, head of the Haardrishii. Surdrok kept to himself. Rumours he'd been a particularly ruthless member of the Royal Assassins were evident in his presence. Last to enter was the dark-robed Lord Nisus, the man responsible for Thana's safety. He oversaw the Royal Assassins, and only he knew if the rumours concerning Surdrok were true. Each Lord took his place in the green high-backed chairs at the King's Table. From the windowless walls, tapestries and paintings, depicting the conflict between King Aian Abreotan and the Dragonlords, stared down at the assembly.

Thana moved to the head of the dark oakwood table, and frowned at the company, his hands fidgeting nervously with the edge of his gilt chair. 'Where is the Royal Advisor?' he asked, glaring at his Chancellor. Rheims peered into the Throne Room, hoping to find the tall figure of A Ahmud Ki there, but only the Palace Guards were present, rigid at their posts. 'Where is the Royal Advisor?' Thana bellowed.

Rheims turned sheepishly to the Great King. He didn't want to be honest quite now. 'He appears to be late, Your Royal Highness,' he replied, faltering.

'He cannot say he has not been told. You informed him of Our meeting?'

'Yes, My Lord,' Rheims confirmed. The Chancellor clutched his spindly fingers.

'Then he dares to defy Us again?' the Great King complained. In a fit of exasperation, Thana wrenched his chair from beneath the table, and it toppled to the floor. Rheims left the doors and rushed to pick up the Great King's chair. 'We will not tolerate this impudence, not from anyone!' the Great King yelled. 'We created a Royal Advisor to advise us. And now he presumes he can ignore Our orders at will! We will not have that!'

As Thana span to face the Lords, he was aware they were staring at a space to his immediate left. Perplexed, he turned to discover what held their attention. A Ahmud Ki bowed. 'As ordered, my Royal Lord, I am here,' the Advisor said with an amicable smile.

Thana was momentarily stuck for words, so A Ahmud Ki took the opportunity to move to his seat at Thana's left hand. The Royal Advisor gave a cursory glance at the other Lords, and nodded to Surdrok, who returned the nod, before he sat. The Great King glowered at A Ahmud Ki – no one sat but the Great King until invited – but the Advisor seemed

33

oblivious to the tension surrounding him, and Thana lost the courage to confront him. The remaining Lords looked at each other and at Rheims. The Chancellor appeared embarrassed. 'Oh,' he gasped, and with greater conviction said, 'Be seated. His Majesty calls the attention of the King's Table.'

Thana waited for the remaining seven Lords to sit, before he took his place, and immediately began the meeting. 'We have considered the death of Lord Mara. In his place, We will appoint Lord Nisus as High Lord of the Great King's Armies.'

A Ahmud Ki observed the reaction of the other Lords to Thana's unheralded news. Gerran, Eustice, and Kerry nodded with approval, extending congratulatory remarks to the dark figure succeeding Mara. Haephus motioned his hand before his face, and whispered what A Ahmud Ki took to be a blessing for Nisus' new office. The Drycraefter, Ardath, seemed unmoved, while Surdrok looked to A Ahmud Ki and raised a questioning eyebrow. Nisus' new title enhanced his role as the Great King's protector. A Ahmud Ki had considered Nisus a threat to his plans to gather power, but Thana's unexpected decision made Nisus even more powerful. He would have to be dealt with, and soon, before the issue of A Ahmud Ki's ascendance became too complicated. In his place, A Ahmud Ki would manoeuvre Surdrok, whom he owned because he promoted Surdrok's rise from Nisus' Royal Assassins to the rank of Lord of the elite Haardrishii.

'You've all heard the news,' said Nisus, standing to address them, for the first time, as High Lord. He had a cobra's presence, poised, ready to strike, but he spoke in a cool, deliberate voice, and he also had the necessary charisma of a leader, even a king, A Ahmud Ki reluctantly admitted, so he had to be stopped before he could acquire more power and status in Thana's court. 'One half of the Great Armies was destroyed on The Rim Shield by the Dragonlord's Army. The Dragonlord has made it clear he will attack the Kingdom, and soon. We must ready our defences,' the new High Lord argued. 'We can't hold the western reaches against a force as large as the one the survivors described. It would sweep our Armies aside. We need to utilize the resources we have, the natural barriers.' Nisus reached into his cloak and withdrew a rolled parchment, which he unravelled and laid on the table. The Lords eased forward to see. A Ahmud Ki recognised a map of the Kingdom. 'There are two ways the Dragonlord can enter the central region,' Nisus continued. 'West, through Central Gate, in the Andrakian Mountains. Or north, beyond the Abreotan Ranges, and down the Valley of Rivers. There are no other ways. The mountains form natural defences.' Nisus allowed the Lords to contemplate the limited possibilities the defence of the Kingdom presented.

'So, what is your proposal?' Ardath asked.

Nisus used his finger to diagram his strategy as he explained. 'Simple. We defend the narrow points. In these places, a small army can hold back a larger one for many weeks. We have our supplies at our backs in the whole region of the Plains of Ky. If we hold the Haagii in the Valley of Rivers until the winter rains, the natural barrier will be sealed with water. That leaves only Central Gate to defend thereafter.'

'And then what?' the white-haired Drycraefter asked.

Nisus glared at Ardath. 'The Haagii give up and go home,' he bluntly stated. Ardath shook his head in disbelief.

This is a rivalry worth fanning, A Ahmud Ki noted.

'What does Lord Ardath disapprove of?' Thana interjected.

Waeron Ardath shifted his serious gaze to the Great King. 'You have witnessed a mere demonstration of the might of this Dragonlord, as he swept away half your Kingdom's army in one single blow, and yet you sit there and believe a little resistance will send him back to his own lands like a chastened dog.'

'This is more than a little resistance,' Nisus retorted in a clipped voice.

Waeron Ardath stood and moved from the table to stare at a tapestry. 'Look around you, at the past,' he said quietly. 'See what the future brings.' He turned to the assembled lords, looking older and tired. 'There's a Dragonlord coming. Look at these pictures of the past, and see what he brings: armies of Haagii, and others, from the far northern lands, we've never dealt with in our lifetimes. And he brings the ancient creatures, creatures we've only heard described in bedtime tales by our grand dams when we were babes in arms. He brings the dragons.' Ardath faced Nisus, and asked pointedly, 'Have you ever seen a dragon? Have you seen its jaws, the fire it belches?' The Drycraefter turned to Gerran. 'Have you?' The young Lord shook his head. 'Pray that you don't,' he warned. He straightened to address the whole group. 'They're creatures of magic. No ordinary weapon can harm them. Their body scales are tougher than any armour. They fly, higher, and faster than any bird of prey. They're intelligent, but no man can reason with them. Only a Dragonlord can control them – he, and the tortured minions he sacrifices with dark magic to ride them. Dragons are brute power and evil. There is nothing you can imagine even remotely like them.' Ardath caught A Ahmud Ki's gaze. They stared at each other briefly, weighing each other up. Ardath broke contact and fixed his gaze on Nisus. 'If your plan was merely to stop a Haagii army, it would very likely succeed, but how is the new High Lord of War going to stop a dragon when it comes?'

Everyone turned to Nisus for an answer and, as they did, Waeron Ardath swept his white robes around his body, and left by the double doors, his halo of white hair shining as it caught daylight from a window in the Throne Room. Nisus sat in silent speculation. He had a workable plan, and he knew it would work. But dragons? Damn Ardath!

'I can stop the dragons.' A Ahmud Ki's statement startled everyone, and they turned to the Royal Advisor. The Great King's mouth gaped.

'How?' Nisus asked.

'Simple,' the Advisor replied.

'How?' Thana begged. 'Tell Us how you can stop the dragons.'

A Ahmud Ki shook his silver locks and pressed his palms

together beneath his dark, cropped beard. 'There's an Orb of Radiance, an Elvenaar artefact the Aelendyell keep hidden.'

Excited by his Royal Advisor's revelation, Thana stood at the end of the table, his pudgy stomach pressing against the table as he leaned forward. He didn't know what this orb his Advisor mentioned was, but it had to be the answer to his nightmare. It had to be. 'This Orb.' said Thana hopefully. 'What does it do?'

A Ahmud Ki cleared his throat, before proceeding. 'Dragons are magical creatures. Our absent friend informed you of that fact. The Orb is a magical device, created to repel most magical creatures.'

'Dragons?' Nisus asked.

A Ahmud Ki stroked his cheek. 'That depends on the practitioner. I'd have to have it, before I could answer that question.'

Thana paced away from his chair, agitated. 'Do you know where it is?' he asked, without looking back at his Advisor.

'I know where one would be,' A Ahmud Ki replied.

Thana turned sharply. 'Where?'

'In the Aelendyell forests.'

The Great King rubbed his fat palms together, nervously, grinding sweat between them. He glanced at Rheims. 'Where are those Aelendyell representatives?'

'They return in three days, Your Highness,' Rheims answered. 'My Liege promised them an answer to the riddle of Lord Laeowyth's disappearance.'

'Did We?' the Great King hesitantly asked, decidedly uncomfortable at the mention of Laeowyth's name. He turned to the assembled Lords. 'Do any of you know where Lord Laeowyth went?'

They shook their heads. Laeowyth's disappearance surprised everyone, but they'd forgotten the incident, in the excitement and confusion of the ensuing organization and march against the Haagii before the battle of The Rim Shield. The Aelendyell Lord was the official Aelendyell representative at the Great King's court, and his presence and participation in human political matters maintained a stable alliance between the two races. His mysterious disappearance, prior the outbreak of hostilities with the Haagii, unsettled the alliance considerably. Subsequent Aelendyell ambassadors, from the forest-dwelling descendants of the Elvenaar, unsuccessfully petitioned Thana for a resolution to the mystery, and the Great King's inability to explain Laeowyth's whereabouts precipitated a rapid deterioration in relationships, to the point where the Aelendyell Council of Elders, or Ieldran, were reluctant to name a successor to Lord Laeowyth until the Lord's fate was known.

A Ahmud Ki suppressed a smile at the unfolding circumstances. He was pleased to have effectively estranged the humans and Aelendyell. Accident provided him an unexpected opportunity to begin his acts of vengeance against the Aelendyell, when he inadvertently ported into Thana's Kingdom. They denied him free access to their magic, the secrets of the First and Second Ki, and drove him from his Aelendyell birthplace because he was a misfit, a bastard half-caste. When he stumbled into Lord Laeowyth, in the corridor of Thana's palace, all his stored hatred for his Aelendyell heritage surfaced. They tried to bend him to their rules and limitations, when he wanted no limitations to his quest, only answers. They scolded him for learning because they were all jealous of his natural aptitude for acquiring magic. The foolish Elder who tried to stop him leaving, on his last night in his village, paid for his error, but A Ahmud Ki, or Terin as he was then known to the Aelendyell, was forced to flee his home, flee westward into the land of the Ranu Ka Shehaala where he earned his new name, A Ahmud Ki: the Seeker of Power in the Ranu tongue. Since that time, he pursued his driving desire to learn and acquire each Ki of magic, the sources and skills of arcane knowledge, but burning deep within he harboured a personal oath, a promise to be revenged upon the Aelendyell who first denied him what he knew was inevitable for him to have: access to the Five Ki of magic. He wondered where the foolish Laeowyth travelled after he pushed him into the portal. Not that his fate mattered. The Aelendyell Lord was only the first to feel A Ahmud Ki's wrath.

'Instruct the Aelendyell that We will speak with them this afternoon at Our pleasure,' Thana directed to Rheims.

The Chancellor swallowed. 'My Lord,' he cautiously began, 'the Aelendyell will – that is – they will come as they have appointed.'

The Great King roared, 'They will come as We order!'

Bewildered, Rheims gave a desperate look of appeal to Lord Kerry. Kerry shifted uncomfortably in his seat, coughed politely, and asked, 'Begging My Liege's pardon, if I may speak?'

Thana glanced at Rheims, then back to Kerry. 'We listen.'

Kerry fiddled with his right thumb. Confronting Thana was never palatable. 'With all respect to the Office of Great King,' Kerry began, 'but Your Highness is forgetting important matters. You cannot direct the Aelendyell. According to the Laws of Abreotan, they are a free people, subject to themselves and their individual Councils of Elders.' Thana was turning red with anger, and Kerry's voice wavered as he rushed to finish his point. 'What the Chancellor was trying to suggest, My Lord, is that it would be more politic to ask the Aelendyell to attend -' Kerry faltered, and he averted his gaze.

A Ahmud Ki watched the fat king's face become more bloated with frustration as he listened to Lord Kerry's diplomatic reasoning, and he was amused by it. Thana's anger peaked. He slammed his chubby right palm against the table and asked emphatically, 'Am I or am I not the Great King?' He fixed his eyes on Rheims.

'You are the Royal Inheritor, the High Lord and Eternal Majesty of the Kingdom of Thana, My Liege,' Rheims obediently recited.

Thana turned to Kerry, who didn't look up. 'Hear that?' he cried triumphantly. 'Did you all hear that?' Mumbles of assent rose from the Lords, except A Ahmud Ki. He chuckled silently at the Great King's pathetic tantrum, until he realised the Great King was staring at him. He engaged Thana's gaze. 'What do you find funny!' Thana roared.

A Ahmud Ki smiled. Time to make another gambit in the game, he decided. 'Your Lords pander to your Great Majesty because it's their duty,' he amiably explained, 'but, behind your back, they call you weak, effeminate, a puppet ruler who cannot control them.'

Gasps, and cries of outrage interrupted the Royal Advisor's inflammatory remark. 'Silence!' Thana bellowed. The Lords reluctantly acquiesced in the wake of A Ahmud Ki's accusation. Thana watched them from maddened eyes, saw their anger, and interpreted it as resentment of him, instead of exasperation provoked by A Ahmud Ki's statement. A Ahmud Ki maintained his calm demeanour, clinically calculating the delivery of his next words. 'Go on, Royal Advisor,' ordered Thana.

'It's natural for your Lords to aspire to greater power, My Lord. You mustn't chastise them for it. A strong king needs strong lords. But you must show your people who rules your Kingdom. You must be resolute. Determined,' A Ahmud Ki took a deliberate breath before continuing, watching Thana's face to gauge the effect of his message. 'You can't let the Aelendyell dictate to you. You are the Great King. Your Kingdom, Your People are in terrible peril from the Dragonlord. Selfish Aelendyell claims to independence no longer apply. You are at war. In times of war, there can only be one ruler.'

Thana was staring past A Ahmud Ki, at the tapestries. Aian Abreotan wielded his sword. One king. Master of all lands. Saviour of all people. A Ahmud Ki was satisfied. Words, delivered at the right moment, wrought strong magic. He glanced at the other Lords, who were staring at him with hatred, indignation, shock. Nisus wore a visage of death, his dark eyes narrowed and menacing. A Ahmud Ki knew the risk he took in alienating the Lords of the King's Table, but the political repercussions were insignificant. Thana's response was all that mattered. Manipulating the Great King was enjoyable, though tiresomely easy.

Thana's voice broke over his thoughts. 'Instruct the Aelendyell to meet Us this afternoon in Our Throne Room. If they take offence, tell them they are under Our martial law and must obey, or be thrown into the castle dungeons.'

'But, My Lord -' Kerry protested.

Thana cut him short. 'Don't you dare interrupt Us when We are speaking!' he snapped. 'Sit down, or lose your title!' Kerry sat like a whipped dog. 'The Royal Advisor is right. You will obey Us, without question,' The Great King asserted. He tried to compose his short, fat figure into a more regal, imposing stance, by gathering his black and green robes around his ample self, and repositioning his griffin crown, stumbling as it threatened to slide off. A Ahmud Ki stifled a desire to laugh. 'High Lord Nisus,' Thana continued, 'Commence your plans for the defence of Our Kingdom. Instruct Us in Our Private Chambers what you require.'

Nisus nodded. 'I serve Your Majesty,' he said, with feigned subservience. Thana smiled faintly, acknowledging Nisus' obedient answer. A Ahmud Ki observed Thana was enjoying the flattery, but especially he noted Nisus' expediency in appearing to willingly serve the Great King. The new High Lord was going to be a very worthy opponent in the political game to control Thana.

'We instruct Lord Kerry to inform all peoples, and neighbouring lands, that We have declared a state of martial law throughout Our Kingdom!' Thana declared. 'All racial freedoms are revoked. All peoples within the boundaries of Our Kingdom are herewith under Our direct and absolute rule. See that it is done.'

'Yes, Royal Highness,' Kerry quietly replied.

'We also order Lord Eustice to declare all monies are at the call of the Royal Treasury. Trade of goods deemed essential for the defence of the Kingdom with foreign states will cease, as of now. We immediately appropriate all goods and monies currently available within the Kingdom.' Thana turned to A Ahmud Ki. 'Royal Advisor, We instruct you to sit with Us in audience with the Aelendyell, this afternoon. We will value your advice.' Thana addressed the assembled

41

Lords. 'We dismiss the King's Table,' he said, with a flourish, and whispered to Rheims. The Chancellor nodded to Nisus, who rose to join him, and they followed Thana through the golden door, at the head end of the table, into the Great King's private chambers.

A Ahmud Ki remained in his seat while the other Lords withdrew in animated conversation. Kerry and Haephus threw him dark looks as they left, but A Ahmud Ki responded by smiling, pleased he'd so simply, but effectively, put them out of favour with the Great King. But he was far from happy. Thana instructed him to meet face to face with the Aelendyell representatives. For years, he had awaited an opportunity to begin his revenge against the people who drove him from his home, yet he loathed the prospect of seeing them standing, immune to his presence, in the Great King's Throne Room. And he had a darker fear. What if one of the Aelendyell ambassadors knew him for what he really was – a murderer and thief? Would they dare expose his past to get the human king's support for Aelendyell justice?

Five

Chancellor Rheims trotted to the foot of the fifteen silver steps leading to the golden throne of the Great King. 'Your Highness,' he said, bowing his head, 'The Aelendyell emissaries are waiting.'

Thana gazed down from his royal throne with all the majesty he could command. Resplendent in his royal green, black, purple and scarlet robes, his griffin crown tilted awkwardly on his balding pate, sceptre firmly grasped, Thana was about to assert his authority in matters pertaining to his Kingdom. Hadn't that been his Royal Advisor's advice? He glanced at the Royal Advisor, from the corner of his eye. He cut an imposing figure, dressed in black and silver robes, his close-cut dark beard and flowing silver hair complementing his clothing. Together, they were an impressive pair. The Advisor was certainly better to be seen with than that scrawny excuse for a Chancellor, Rheims, who was opening the huge doors into the Throne Room to lead the Aelendyell through. Perhaps it is time to replace Rheims, Thana considered.

The Aelendyell followed the Chancellor into the Throne Room. There were six, in forest greens, their cloaks draped across their shoulders. They were as slight of build as the insect Rheims, but proportionately shorter, and they had the handsome features peculiar to Aelendyell – high cheekbones, almond-shaped green or blue eyes – and hair colouring, ranging from pale blond through to dark silver, marking them as direct descendants of the Elvenaar.

A Ahmud Ki studied the party. The front pair were clearly Elders. He observed maturity in their features, and they carried staffs inscribed with runes of lore. They would do the speaking. What magic do they possess, he wondered? The other Aelendyell were younger: three female, one male. Two at the rear shouldered Aelendyell bows, the wood detailed

43

with intricate runes and carving, and they wore short swords in their woven belts. They were clearly Weapon Bearers. The remaining pair, between the Elders and the Weapon Bearers, were more likely Lore Bearers. Both were female. He peered closer. None were familiar. Years had passed since he ran from the forests, so no one was likely to recognise him. It was highly unlikely these Aelendyell knew much of his home village. In his few months of research in the Great King's library, he discovered there were many Aelendyell communities besides the one he left, though human information was scant. He intuitively determined where his village might be, from studying maps of the Kingdom and relating the drawings to what he could recall of his flight after killing Elder Laeocwyddyn.

Rheims bowed before Thana's throne. 'Your Majesty, the Aelendyell emissaries,' he announced, with formality.

Thana waved Rheims aside with a lazy motion of his hand and shifted his weight to gaze down at the Aelendyell Elders. 'We have reason to believe you wish to speak with Us,' he said, in a tired, bored voice.

The Aelendyell Elder on the left approached the base of the throne, and said, 'It was you who ordered us before you.'

Thana heard the Elder's annoyance. 'That is Our wish,' he answered stiffly. 'We see you are wise enough to obey it.'

'May I remind the Great King we are Aelendyell,' the Aelendyell speaker said, resolutely, 'and, as such, we are not compelled to obey your orders. We come out of respect for your position, and to receive the promised answers to our requests.'

Good, noted A Ahmud Ki, the Aelendyell are going to be stubborn. He relaxed. He counted on Aelendyell pride to make the meeting uncomfortable, and if Thana was as clumsy as always in handling a confrontation, all would go well for A Ahmud Ki's plans.

'We have been advised that your independence from Our rule, whilst useful for you until recent times, is no longer practical, now that the Dragonlord threatens Our security,' Thana succinctly informed the ambassadors. 'You are to return to your villages and inform your people they are hereafter compelled to obey Our Royal laws.'

A Ahmud Ki watched disbelief spread cross the Aelendyell faces. The Elder, with the group, whispered to his companion at the foot of the steps, stepped forward, and asked, 'Who gave you this foolish advice?'

Thana looked to A Ahmud Ki. 'I did,' said the Advisor in a cold voice.

The Aelendyell ambassadors hadn't taken much notice of A Ahmud Ki's presence, but when he spoke their eyes were drawn to him, and he savoured their attention, knowing they were coming to terms with the Aelendyell heritage in his features: his long, braided silver hair and grey eyes. 'By what authority do you dare suggest Aelendyell should obey the whims of a human king?' asked the Aelendyell.

A Ahmud Ki stared at the Elder who challenged him, and slowly descended the throne steps. 'I am the Great King's appointed Royal Advisor. That's the authority I'm given. It is with that authority I explained to His Royal Highness the insecurity he faces trying to defend a Kingdom against a Dragonlord, when he cannot trust the support of those who rule themselves within in his fortress.' He saw anger sparkle in the Elder's eyes as he drew to one step above him.

'Who are you?' the Elder demanded.

'A Ahmud Ki,' A Ahmud Ki announced to his audience. 'And you?'

The Aelendyell squinted. The stranger's name didn't fit his appearance. Nothing made sense. He had Aelendyell traces around his eyes, and he wore a traditional braid in his silver-tinted hair, but his tall, athletic body had human definition, and he had dark facial hair, which was alien to the Aelendyell. He was neither human, nor Aelendyell, and yet both in one. His name was foreign. The aura of Thana's new Advisor sparkled with magical energy, threatening energy, dangerous energy. 'I am Elder Rhynothlae,' the Aelendyell answered. His instinctive fear urged him to recoil from this half-Aelendyell being before something wrong, something evil happened.

'Then listen closely to the instructions of your King, Rhynothlae,' A Ahmud Ki warned, as he levelled his gaze on the Elder. 'The Aelendyell are no longer a free people.' He turned his back on the Aelendyell and returned to his original position on Thana's right. He was tempted to impress the Aelendyell with a spell, but he reminded himself that real power sat in the hands of those who held more than they showed. Let the Aelendyell guess at his true being.

'We will take your message to the Council of Elders. It is they, not us, who will decide on your order,' said the Elder beside Rhynothlae.

'What decision?' asked Thana, mockingly. 'There is already a decision made. Your Council will obey Us.'

'As you wish,' the Elder replied impassively.

'Is that all Your Majesty requires of us?' Rhynothlae asked.

Thana looked to A Ahmud Ki. The Advisor nodded. The Great King took a breath, coughed nervously, and said, 'There is one other matter.' The Aelendyell waited patiently for Thana to explain. 'We require the Orb of Radiance.'

The Elders exchanged startled glances. Rhynothlae stared accusingly at A Ahmud Ki. 'We know of no such artefact,' his companion Elder calmly responded.

Thana hadn't anticipated denial. Again, he looked to A Ahmud Ki for support. The Royal Advisor smiled, ignoring Rhynothlae's warning glare. 'Are you certain you've never heard of this Orb?' he asked.

Rhynothlae was puzzled by the Advisor's question, phrased as if the stranger was uncertain of the Orb's existence. Was he protecting his Aelendyell heritage after all? 'There is no such artefact in the Aelendyell forests,' the second Elder repeated.

A Ahmud Ki nonchalantly shrugged his shoulders and turned away. 'There's no such artefact,' he informed Thana. The Great King shifted uneasily, rolling his paunch under his robes, feeling betrayed by his Advisor's unexpectedly meek capitulation on the issue of the Orb.

'If there is nothing further?' Rhynothlae asked. Thana

waved his hand to indicate he'd finished his business. 'There is the matter of Elder Laeowyth,' ventured the Aelendyell with greater determination.

'We have no further news,' Thana flatly replied.

'Your Highness will recall there have been several deputations to you, in the past months, requesting that you investigate the unusual circumstances surrounding Elder Laeowyth's disappearance,' Rhynothlae persisted.

Thana appeared bored with the Aelendyell. He turned his face away, and disdainfully picked his fingernails.

'Have there been investigations made?' asked the Elder.

Thana spun, stung by the Aelendyell's cynicism. 'Are you questioning Our authority?'

'You have no news at all?' the Elder asked.

'No. None,' Thana answered. 'There is none to gather. Your Elder simply disappeared. We had no warning of his leaving Our company. We cannot be held accountable for the irresponsible vagaries of your representatives. If you want your Elder Laeowyth, find the nuisance yourselves. We consider the matter closed.' Thana was fuming. How dare these people question his rule? The Royal Advisor was all too accurate. The haughty Aelendyell laughed at him, behind his back. No more. He was Great King Thana, Eternal Ruler. No petty Aelendyell Elder had the right to accuse him of anything! 'Anything else you wish to pester Us with?' he asked.

Tired of the Great King's irate mood, Rhynothlae nodded to his companion, as he responded. 'No, Your Highness. Only this. The Council of Elders asked us to inform you that, until Elder Laeowyth's disappearance is accounted for, there will be no Aelendyell representation in your court.'

Infuriated, Thana heaved his heavy paunch off his throne and bellowed, 'Go back to your forests and tell your Council they are under Our authority! Tell them that! Tell them their Great King denies them representation at the King's Table until this war is over! Tell them they will obey! Now get out! Out!'

Rheims scrambled for the double doors, and the Royal

Guards swung them open to allow the Aelendyell party to leave. As the Elders strode through, Rheims politely bowed, trying to maintain decorum, but the Aelendyell did not acknowledge him. In the wake of their pride, they were leaving an arrogant fool who dared to claim he was their king, and they desired nothing less than to be rid of the human ignorance.

Thana collapsed onto his throne, wheezing and puffing from his outburst. Rheims scampered up the throne steps, carrying a silver water jug, and he filled a goblet. The Great King took it, gulped a mouthful, and promptly spat it over Rheims' robes. 'Idiot!' he shouted. 'Bring me something worth drinking! Wine!' He petulantly hurled the goblet down the steps. Rheims scuttled after it, and went to fetch wine, glad to be out of the circle of Thana's wrath. The Great King rolled to face his Royal Advisor, and A Ahmud Ki saw the traces of fear in the corners of Thana's eyes as the frustrated regent spoke. 'No Orb. What now? How do We stop the dragons?'

A Ahmud Ki laughed. 'There's an Orb,' he chuckled. 'They were lying.'

'How do you know?'

'Wouldn't you, if you were them?'

Thana leaned back, to catch his breath, and reflect on his Advisor's reasoning. We'd lie, he thought. If We hated Us enough, We'd lie. 'But how do We get the Orb?' he muttered.

A Ahmud Ki leaned closer to the Great King's ear, a conspiratorial glint creeping into his eyes. The action made Thana nervous because it reminded him of his first encounter when A Ahmud Ki teleported to his side, confounding the Royal Guards and showing Thana that, if he wanted to, he could easily harm the Great King. 'We take it,' the Advisor whispered, mischievously.

Surdrok followed Pak through the tower's black wall with repugnance at passing through what appeared solid. He

48

shivered, as he considered the circular room.

'My Master's Visiting Room,' Pak explained politely. 'He'll attend in a moment. I've been instructed to wait outside.' Pak returned to the wall, repeated his procedure with an amber crystal that Surdrok observed for entering the tower, stepped through the wall, and was gone.

His assassin training sensitive to danger, Surdrok surveyed the room. It filled the base of the tower, but there were only eight low stools and a marble table at the centre. Apart from red cushions against the walls, it was bare, white, and not welcoming. Still, he preferred it to the over furnished monstrosities the other Lords owned. Their chambers in the palace were lavishly decorated with ornate tapestries, carved wooden furniture, and sculptured marble and ivory objects scattered everywhere, to accentuate their status. Not that he'd been invited to eat or drink with them. Except for Nisus, who was his Lord when he served as a Royal Assassin, they shunned him, but even Nisus regarded him as a lower being, and not an equal to invite for a meal.

Only this Lord, the Royal Advisor, gave him respect. He learned from castle sources that the Royal Advisor was instrumental in his rise to leadership over the Haardrishii, because he asked Nisus for the most ruthless, best-trained man in the Royal Assassins. For an unknown reason, the Advisor, or whatever he really was, chose to favour him. He figured he was being called to make a payback for the promotion.

He shrugged. He fully accepted his debt to the Royal Advisor. Favours required favours. All assassins understood the code binding men to other men. If that basic precept was ignored, there would be chaos and mistrust in every deal. What the Royal Advisor wanted now, he would deliver freely, if it was within his power. Since he was an assassin, before he was made a Lord, he expected the Advisor's favour would be associated with his former trade. That was logical. Not that it would matter. There was a debt involved. Simple, he thought, as he studied the room. I owe – I repay.

Movement to his left brought Surdrok sharply around.

49

The Royal Advisor, inexplicably, appeared in the chamber. Although there were stairs leading to the next level, they were behind Surdrok, and the Advisor certainly hadn't descended them. Surdrok hated magic. Users were unpredictable. 'I have need of your services,' A Ahmud Ki said casually.

Surdrok nodded, watching the Royal Advisor approach, and replied, 'I wondered when you would call my dues.' Surdrok studied the Advisor's handsome face, and his charismatic Aelendyell qualities. He hated handsome men. He inherited a ruffian's visage. As a child, other children said his mother must have been a Haagii for him to be so ugly, and they teased him incessantly. He learned to fight early. Being smaller than his antagonists taught him to work intelligently, secretively, so he was a natural assassin by the time he worked through Haardrishii training to be selected by the Royal Lord of Assassins, Lord Penther, Nisus' predecessor. When the score was even with this Royal Advisor, he could go back to his natural distaste of the man's appearance. For now, he had a debt to repay.

'Good,' A Ahmud Ki said, stroking his chin. 'We understand each other.' He stopped in front of Surdrok, establishing physical authority by forcing him to tilt his neck to look up, into A Ahmud Ki's eyes. 'I'll be brief. I want you to select your hungriest Haardrishii, a man with fire in his belly, a man who hates, like you and I can hate. He must be totally trustworthy. He must also be expendable.'

Surdrok's eyes narrowed. What was the catch? What was the cost to him to repay the debt?

'There's no catch,' said A Ahmud Ki, with a grin. 'And yes, I can read your mind as quickly as you think.' Surdrok physically recoiled, his eyes wide with shock. 'Send him to the Inn of Dragons tomorrow evening,' A Ahmud Ki continued. 'He must ask for the Shadow's Voice. That's all he needs to know. You have no questions, do you?' Surdrok had a thousand questions buzzing through his mind to ask the enigma standing before him, but the Advisor's tone warned him he was to ask no questions. He shook his head slowly.

'Good,' A Ahmud Ki concluded. He motioned with his hands, and rose rapidly to, and through, the ceiling, leaving Surdrok staring open-mouthed at what he'd seen and heard. Pak re-appeared to lead him out.

Six

Liam strode purposefully toward the yellow light of the Inn of Dragons. He saw the dark figures, lurking in the alcoves and doorways near the Inn, obscured by night – knew them to be thieves – and recognised the danger they represented.

Thieves had a penchant for attacking Haardrishii. They isolated them, subdued them, removed their black armour, and enjoyed publicly humiliating their victims. There was rarely malice intended in the attacks. The thieves only wanted to remind the Haardrishii that the city streets, by night, belonged to the thieves. Haardrishii were symbols of the Great King's laws that were designed to protect the wealthy, and foolhardy, who braved the city streets after dark. An individual attack on a Haardrishii was almost always bravado on the thief's, proving his guile and mettle to his fellows. Thieves who achieved a single-handed victory gained considerable status with other thieves.

Liam knew the tales. Very few Haardrishii fell prey to the thieves' ruses, but Haardrishii never walked alone at night. Walking there, now, opened him to unnecessary danger, but he felt safe from the thieves because of his mission. Lord Surdrok selected him to meet the Shadow's Voice at the Inn of Dragons. He was to ask for the Shadow's Voice, and he was to obey whatever instructions he was given. Obedience wasn't questionable. Haardrishii obeyed. If Lord Surdrok ordered a Haardrishii to die, the Haardrishii would die. Courage, loyalty, honour, and obedience: the four pillars of strength for all Haardrishii. No Haardrishii doubted them. If he did, he was no longer Haardrishii.

Liam was proud of his rank. He came to the Great City of Thana, seeking a new purpose, one befitting a true warrior: one to replace the path he had followed in The Vale. The Guardian Master in The Vale was Haardrishii once, but he failed Liam, left him to be dragged into slavery and war, altered his principles to suit the time, and damaged the purity of The Way's vision. So Liam came to the Great City to find the principles for living as a warrior in its purest form, in the ranks of the Haardrishii.

Hungry, homeless, his visions shattered, Liam threw himself passionately into becoming Haardrishii, adapting his Guardian skills to the shining black armour and weapons of the Great King's warrior elite, learning to use spear and sword, and to ride the arrogant black war steeds the Haardrishii rode with silent pride. Pushed by anger and disillusionment, he strove to be the best, the fiercest, the most proficient warrior in the Haardrishii ranks. He knew that's why Lord Surdrok chose him for this mission, and that's why he sauntered toward the Inn's doors, quietly confident no one would dare interfere with him. He was wary of the watchers though, and understood that tacit permission protected his progress, nothing more. Another night, he would be fair game.

The Inn wasn't crowded when he entered, but there was a thick mist of smoke, and a rowdy gambling game at a table near the ember-red hearth to his right. Three figures near the doorway slipped outside as he entered, and several faces turned to watch him. Haardrishii were the civil keepers of the Great King's law, and no one with a guilty conscience felt comfortable at night if Haardrishii suddenly appeared. Even the noise at the gambling table declined, although the participants feigned disinterest in Liam. He ignored the covert attention and approached the bar, which extended the length of the room, where a young girl was polishing mugs in a trough of warm water. 'Girl,' he said curtly. She flicked back her tousled dark hair and flashed bright green eyes at him, but dismay filled her features when she saw the stern face and Haardrishii armour. She dropped the mug, letting it smash on the floor, and scampered through a partially open door behind the bar. Two men leaning against the bar laughed briefly, before looking away to avoid the Haardrishii's stare. Irritated by the unexpected scene, Liam turned to the room, searching for another worker, or the proprietor.

'Can I 'elp you?' inquired a rough voice from behind. Liam contained his surprise and slowly turned to the source: a pudgy faced, middle-aged man, with cheeks and a nose ruddy from drink. 'I be th' owner of this establishment, lad. Detton Tomas by name. C'n I be of service to a Great King's soldier?' the innkeeper asked respectfully.

Liam leaned forward and whispered, 'I'm here to meet the Shadow's Voice.'

Detton Tomas grinned, and replied, 'Aye, lad. I figured that was it. Then you'd best come through t' back.' He pointed to a gap in the bar, and led Liam through the same door the girl had left by, into a dull room, lit by one flickering lantern. As Liam entered, Detton warned quietly, 'Mind your step, lad.' but before Liam could reply the light was extinguished, and he collapsed under a crush of bodies.

He had no idea where he was. Blindfolded, they carried him through corridors, up and down, twisting so many times he was totally disoriented. His captors eventually dropped him roughly on damp earth and he heard their boots clunk away. Had he fallen prey to a thievish attack? Had he spoken to the wrong person in the Inn? He wriggled his wrists, trying to free himself from the bonds chafing into his skin, but struggling was useless. Is this an elaborate test by Lord Surdrok, he wondered? The silence refused to answer.

Footsteps approached. Someone paused beside him. He sensed a presence kneeling, and a hand pressed against his forehead. Frightened? Liam jerked. The voice spoke in his head, not through his ears. Relax, warrior. I hear your thoughts as you can hear me.

'Who are you?' Liam demanded.

Your destiny, Liam. In me resides all that you are about to become.

Liam's mind raced. What is going on? Who is intruding in my mind? What is this destiny?

Relax, said the mind speak. You will learn it all, in good

54

time. You must trust only me. I am your god, and you are to be my disciple. You are the chosen one. Your coming has been prophesied many times, and now it is time for you to rise from the darkness of your past to begin your journey on the path of the future.

'Who are you?' Liam repeated desperately. Fear gnawed at his guts. He'd never felt such fear.

I am your god. Call me Berak N'eth. I call you Ethtroo Ka Nyaret – He Who Bears The Mark Of The Moon. You are the prophecy come to be. You are the future, the voice pronounced clearly and precisely. Liam felt the words sink deep inside his consciousness, as if he had no choice but to accept everything he heard. He couldn't resist the patterning forming in his memory. He was the prophecy. Come to be. The future. Ethtroo Ka Nyaret. What was happening? Berak N'eth. His god? What madness had he stumbled into? Who is Berak N'eth? Your god, the voice repeated. Blinding pain burst across his head, and he screamed. His back arched in agony as searing heat burned into the skin stretched tight on his forehead, and pain, unbelievable torment, wracked his body, until unconsciousness released him from the fire burning the flesh on his brow.

The giant of Tressel Deep stood in the castle gardens, staring up at the black finger pointing to the sky that was the Royal Advisor's tower. He'd seen the edifice from a distance, many times, when the Great King's Armies were training for war against the Haagii, and from within the castle grounds, when his companions and he assembled to ride in the Great King's procession, the day the Armies marched north, but he'd never studied it from close up. There were no seams, joins, or cracks in the building's ebony surface, and no openings for doors or windows. The tower was eerie, and he felt the same disaffection for the tower as he felt facing the hordes and dragons of the Dragonlord on The Rim Shield.

The Royal Advisor asked to meet him here, with Andra's sword. Claarn knew why. The Royal Advisor's pet

Apprentice came to demand the sword, but he refused to relinquish it. It was too fine a weapon to give to someone who wasn't a warrior. Besides, he reasoned, there was obviously a purpose behind the Royal Advisor's request. Something about the sword made it worth possessing. When Andra collapsed in the desert dust, dying from dehydration and exposure, too weak to struggle on, he passed the sword to Claarn, bequeathing it from warrior to warrior. The sword bonded the past with the present. For that reason, especially, he couldn't easily part with it for all the orders and demands of Great Kings and Royal Advisors. He knew it was an extraordinary weapon, because he'd seen the young Guardian cleave Haagii armour like cheese in the heart of battle, and not one drop of blood stained its bright blade. Claarn drew the sword from its scabbard and held the blade to catch the sun's rays. Beautifully crafted, honed to sharpness rare in any weapon he had owned or seen, it felt light, balanced and comfortable. He toyed with it, thrusting and sweeping at imaginary Haagii beneath the cool, green fern fronds that reached out from the garden's depths. 'I take it that you're Claarn the giant?'

Claarn saw a familiar figure, in dark grey robes, silver hair braided at the sides. The dog at Claarn's side growled. He put aside the sword. 'I am Claarn.'

Each man assessed the worth of the other. A Ahmud Ki was quick to notice the self-assured manner of the tall warrior, whose mane of red hair sprouted like fire in the sunlight. His physical size and undoubted fighting prowess were sound reasons for the warrior's confidence. The black dog at the warrior's side was an interesting addition. War dogs were rare in the Royal army. Claarn eyed the Advisor with disdain. Magic wasn't one of his favoured interests, and the Royal Advisor apparently held considerable potency in that art. Respect seemed appropriate, but not friendship. A Ahmud Ki moved to the edge of the path, and pulled a leaf from a fern. 'Should I be concerned about your dog?'

'He's young, and he won't harm anyone who doesn't intend on harming him,' Claarn replied. He lowered a hand to pat the black dog's head.

'You know why I sent for you?'

'You want the sword,' Claarn bluntly replied.

'It's not mine to have,' said A Ahmud Ki. 'But it's not yours either.'

Claarn cocked his head to the right. Had he heard correctly? He lifted the sword upright before his face. 'I hold it. The warrior who owned it gave the sword to me. You could say it is mine,' he reminded the Advisor.

A Ahmud Ki stroked his chin, and shook his head. He dropped the leaf and moved to the centre of the white gravel path. The dog growled again, and A Ahmud Ki considered using a spell to quieten it, but that would reduce his chances of getting the sword from the red-haired warrior, without resorting to avoidable means. 'There are great events in motion, my friend,' he said. 'Dark and strange changes take place, even as we speak. Do you understand what's happening?'

Claarn watched the Royal Advisor closely. He understood a game was afoot, but where was it leading? 'There's a war on,' he replied. 'I've heard talk that what we met on The Rim Shield was a Dragonlord. I take it that makes him a worthy enemy.'

Claarn's understatement provoked an ironic smile from A Ahmud Ki. 'Worthy is a condescending word. He'd take you, warrior, and rip out your heart while you were even beginning to think of drawing your sword from its sheath.'

'Perhaps,' said Claarn with a shrug of his massive shoulders. 'The last time we met though, he ran away.'

A Ahmud Ki smiled, remembering the simplistic warrior desires and ethics driving the giant's perception of the Dragonlord. The man's brash confidence stemmed from a naive belief in his personal principles: laughable, but true. 'There's so much you don't know. Have you heard of the prophecy pertaining to this time?' A Ahmud Ki asked.

Claarn shook his head. 'Prophecies are like tales we share around our hearths, tales to make sense of things after they happened.'

A Ahmud Ki took two steps toward his tower. 'It's written that, when the Dragonlord returns, one bearing the mark of the moon will rise to oppose him.'

'A tale,' Claarn stated blandly.

'No,' corrected A Ahmud Ki. 'No tale. See for yourself.' The wizard pointed to the archway that led into the gardens from the Great King's palace. Standing there was a Haardrishii warrior.

'A Haardrishii: I've seen them before,' Claarn remarked, with a wry smile.

A Ahmud Ki beckoned to the black armoured warrior and the Haardrishii approached. 'Take off your helmet,' he ordered.

Claarn watched the Haardrishii remove his black helmet, and when the man's ponytail dropped into view he immediately thought of Andra. He wore a ponytail, clasped with a silver circlet, as a badge to show he held the rank of Guardian in his home village. This Haardrishii must have come from The Vale. Then he saw the circular scar, surrounded by mystical symbols and runes, emblazoned on the man's forehead, a prophetic banner daring him to deny its existence.

'Behold!' announced A Ahmud Ki. 'The prophecy. One who carries the mark of the moon.

Claarn let his reason take hold of the vision. A moon-shaped scar unmistakably marked the warrior, just as A Ahmud Ki described, so it was possible the prophecy was genuine. Possibly, the giant considered, but it could be nothing more than a trick, and, although he couldn't decipher the cause, he was plagued by a memory that teased and eluded his mental grasp, even as he tried to make sense of what the Advisor was presenting to him. Despite the logic, a warrior bearing the prophetic mark, or one likened to it, stood before him. 'So, the prophecy appears to be true,' Claarn admitted, warily. 'What's that to do with the sword?' Even as he asked the question, he knew the answer. The sword was magical, a tool for the Advisor's saviour to use against the Dragonlord.

'It's only right,' A Ahmud Ki confirmed, 'that the one who bears the mark should also bear the finest weapon. How else can he defeat his foe?'

Claarn knew there were arguments to offer. He had no faith in prophetic visions, even though one apparently stood before him now. Besides, a nagging doubt still teased his memory, an indecipherable meaning he couldn't yet catch. Worse still, was he standing in the path of inevitable destiny by refusing to relinquish Andra's sword to A Ahmud Ki's protégé? Or was he being asked to satisfy another of the Advisor's whims in his bid to acquire greater power and status in Thana's court? He recognised exactly to where the Royal Advisor had brought him with this meeting. If he didn't quietly accept the direction of the prophecy, and hand over the sword, as A Ahmud Ki wanted, he suspected the Advisor would have no qualms about taking the sword by less favourable methods.

Under the circumstances, the sensible choice was to give up the sword. He turned the blade over and gazed at its craftsmanship. Andra's great-grandfather shaped the weapon. He remembered the young Guardian telling him the tale, beneath the starless night on Dragon Breath Plains. His friend's soul resided within. He inverted the weapon, pointing the carved hilt toward the Haardrishii warrior. Liam took the sword.

'A most wise decision,' A Ahmud Ki said, with a smile Claarn decided was as cold as ice on winter water. 'You'll look back to this moment and know how important a role you played in fulfilling the oldest prophecy of Abreotan's time. When the Dragonlord falls, you can claim a minor part in that fall.' The Advisor gestured to Liam, who withdrew from the gardens by the way he came, and walked wordless toward his tower, passing through the wall, leaving Claarn alone with his dog.

The giant remained, pursuing the elusive thought running through his memory that prompted his indecision to hand over the sword. The Guardian ponytail leapt in and out of his mind. The Haardrishii's face was familiar. Perhaps he was one of the Guardians who accompanied Andra and him on their journey through the Valley of Rivers. Perhaps – but that wasn't the issue he sought to solve. Andra's face faded.

Then it moved into sharper focus. The ponytail. No – something else – something he noticed, but hadn't considered deeply. He remembered – the young Guardian's cheek. He saw it now and understood what plagued him: a mark on Andra's cheek, a scar, shaped like a crescent moon.

"Friendship is neither giving, nor taking. It is acceptance."

"The forest and life: all else is illusion."

"Warriors in conflict share greater passion
than lovers in the act of love,
for while those lovers believe in life and death,
the warriors become life and death.
No greater understanding is there between people
than that which blood warriors share."

from A Collection of Aelendyell Sayings,
compiled by Drycraefter Enius Ardath

Seven

Unbearable pain, tightening his nerve ends, from far away, like ice reflecting dawn light on the mountains above The Vale. But he couldn't turn from the pain biting into him. He was burning, tumbling through a pit of fiery flesh.

He stood on a vast grey desert, grey dust stretching every direction: limitless. At the furthest edges, bright light gleamed: sharp, cutting light. He tried to move his feet, but they were caught. He looked down at the grey dust, filtering over his ankles like soft, caressing fingers, relentlessly rising. He struggled against its pull, but the dust kept rising. The sky shone bright blue, sunless. No sun. No sun. The sky was spinning. The sky was spinning.

The pain eased, and arms pulled at him. A hand gripped his shoulders. Firm fingers pried into his muscles. A face appeared – a familiar, strong face – the Guardian Master. Artega the Guardian Master of The Vale handed him a staff. He pointed left. They were on a high ledge, a precipice above The Vale's green beauty, which stretched out like a tapestry. The village – his home – was at the centre. But something was wrong, terribly wrong. People were running. Flames erupted in the wooden buildings, engulfing them in seconds. The Guardian Master tugged at his arm and pointed right. Shaggy, dusty figures dropped from a cave onto the ledge, and closed in, spears lifted. Leather armour rustled as they crouched and stared at him. Haagii: the enemy. Hatred creased their leathery faces. They rushed at him. He tried to lift his staff, but in its place found a heavy, battle-scarred sword he couldn't wield. The Guardian Master was laughing. He could hear laughter, see the spear points, and feel pain.

Dry unbearable, searing pain filled his throat, choking him. Dust was filling his mouth, and his lungs, like a rasping serpent. Water: he needed water, desperately.

He was aware of her, moving beyond his senses, the faint shadow of a passing cloud drifting silently across a sunlit hillside in mid-spring. At the edge of awareness, she was there. He wanted to tell her he was here, waiting, trying to fight through the pain and confusing visions, but he was on the other side of a wall of stone, and he could find no way through.

The shining black Haardrishii helmet accused him. The man climbed off his horse and strode toward him through a swirling cloud of grey dust. His legs were buried deep, and he tried to warn the approaching warrior about the dust, but cold wind silenced his voice. When the Haardrishii halted, he removed his helmet, and a mane of fiery hair flowed around the man's shoulders. Claarn stared at him, questioning, appealing to him. 'What do you want from me?' he struggled to ask, but nothing except a rain of grey dust issued from his lips. Behind the warrior of Tressel Deep, a dark winged shape grew, sweeping in with increasing speed from the circling sky. He tried to cry out, but the grey dust choked him, and pulled him down, drowning him. At the last, a huge ball of flame erupted around Claarn's form, melting the black armour. But somehow Claarn kept staring at him, with cruel accusing eyes.

She brought soothing coolness - water. She brought relief. Without her, he knew he'd die. Beyond the wall, he felt her, and she touched him – beyond the wall.

'You've failed your duty,' said the Guardian Master, dark

eyes flashing.

'The pigs. Queenie's slaughtered!' whined old Flintok.

'Coward!' yelled Claarn. 'Stay! Don't run!'

'Are you a friend?' asked Derik shrugging his shoulders.

They all stared at him, accusing him: his mother, Anedra, Alain, and Murdok.

'Pay them no attention,' laughed Tim Gaelus. 'Come my friend, let's away!'

Strong hands held him. 'No!' he screamed. 'No! We're doomed! We'll die. There's too many of them! Too many! And the creatures! The creatures in the skies! Too many! I can't stay! I mustn't!' They crowded in, trying to hold him down. Behind rose a towering wave of Haagii warriors threatening to break over them all. 'Let me go! Let me go!' he screamed at the wall.

Soft, musical, alien voices whispered at the edge of his dreaming. He cautiously opened his eyes to vivid green – leaves, boughs. The light hurt, despite the leafy filter, and he blinked. A girl's face slipped into view, and her beauty startled him: bright green almond eyes and a small face framed by long golden braids. She whispered in a lilting language, like the song of a forest bird, and disappeared before he could answer. By the time he rolled onto his side, he was alone in the strange room of boughs and leaves. He eased into a reclining position on the rush mattress bedding. The space was small, but airy, a room fashioned from the forest. Another bed stood by an entrance to the chamber, and pottery containers sat by his bed. Voices approached. He felt incredibly weak, and he shook as he struggled to support his weight on his elbow to greet the owners of the voices, but his body betrayed him, and he fell back, exhausted beyond measure, into unconsciousness.

He was aware of another face, male this time, exceedingly handsome, with fine-boned features, and the same green almond eyes as the girl. The man was examining him, and his features made him automatically think of Tim Gaelus, the mysterious friend he made, in the camp of the Great King's Armies, before they marched north to fight the Haagii. Tim hadn't marched. He disappeared the night after he guided Andra through the Great City.

'Can you hear me?' the man asked.

He nodded expectantly, but the young man's face withdrew, and he heard a brief exchange in the lilting alien voices between the man and the girl. Though he wanted to turn to see them, his body wouldn't obey his curiosity. It craved endless sleep.

Several faces peered at him when he opened his eyes again. They were like the other faces – male, green eyes, high cheek bones, long grey locks flowing loosely to their shoulders. They were nodding wisely, whispering. 'Who are you?' he forced from his lips, and his voice's fragility startled him – a bare rush of air.

All but one face withdrew: an old face. Age lines, thin but manifold, traced the man's serious features. 'I am Elder Tirenythlae,' the stranger answered. 'Who are you?'

The question sent him searching through his memories, as if he hadn't spoken his own name in a long time. Finally, he whispered, 'Andra,' but even as he heard his harsh whisper he thought it was sad his name seemed to have lost importance.

Days ebbed and flowed. He moved rapidly from wakefulness to sleep, but he could feel his body working, and pulsing energy quickening with each awakening. He knew he wasn't dying, but being reborn on his bed of rushes in a room of leaves.

The girl and her male friend were his constant companions, bringing food and drink, bathing him, tending to his needs as he healed. He tried conversing with the girl, but she merely smiled sweetly and shook her head, indicating his words held no meaning for her. Sometimes she laughed, and spoke to him in her lilting song-voice, but it was clear she didn't understand him anymore than he understood her. All he knew was her name: Mirithanyll. Her male companion told him that early in their conversations.

'And I'm Terawythanyll – Terath to everyone I know,' and he grinned, as he introduced himself. 'Here. Eat these,' he added, and held out a woven bowl of berries and nuts, which Andra gratefully accepted. 'You are improving steadily, Andra.'

Andra swallowed a berry and studied his provider. He'd asked questions between bouts of unconsciousness since he first woke, but now he wanted answers. He sat up, weakly, and crossed his legs. 'Terath,' he said, putting aside the bowl, 'I feel awake at last. Where am I? Where have I been?'

Terath shook his long grey locks. 'I can answer only part of your questions, Andra. The rest of the answers lie with the Elders, and those who brought you here -'

Andra held his hand up to interrupt Terath's speech. 'How long ago was I brought here?' he asked.

'A monaymbgong,' Terath replied. 'Sorry - in your worold-buend speech, you would say a month.'

Andra's confusion increased. 'What do you mean my worold-buend speech?' he asked, stumbling over the strange words.

'Your speech. What we speak now,' answered Terath.

'But aren't you human? Like me?'

Wonder filled Terath's face. 'I am Aelendyell, Andra. You are in an Aelendyell tun, or village, as you would say. Aelendyell are a different race from your people. We are descendants of the Alfyn and the Elvenaar. The land your people call their Kingdom was once ours. Time brought change. Now we keep to the thickest forests, where your people do not, and cannot, come.'

Andra heard Terath's explanation and remembered lost scenes from a dark building in the Great King's City, where almond-eyed waifs reached toward him from the shadows with bone-thin hands. He remembered how his city guide, Tim Gaelus, shook his head sadly, and told him the forest-dwelling Aelendyell had all perished. 'But I thought the Aelendyell were – were gone?'

'No,' replied Terath. 'Only from the world of men. In fact, you're the first worold-buend to set foot in our village for two generations. The forests are guarded. We allow no human within.' Before Andra could pursue the reasons why the Aelendyell deliberately avoided interaction with the people of Thana's Kingdom, Terath excused himself and left Andra to his meal.

Mirithanyll fussed around him, while he ate, and took away his bowl when he finished. He increasingly found her presence distracting, her beauty alluring, compelling. She always wore soft green, flowing garments that floated about her body, and her eyes were constantly laughing and mischievous, as she stole sideways glances at him. Her sensual lips charmed and teased him when she spoke in her musical voice. As his body's energy increased daily, so too did his infatuation for the Aelendyell maiden, who filled his waking moments with her constancy and smiling beauty – radiance unlike any he'd seen in a woman.

'Are you exercising?' asked the Aelendyell Elder, as he entered Andra's chamber, mid-morning. He approached the bed, where the young human was polishing his belt with sweet-smelling resin Terath provided.

'Daily,' Andra smiled in reply. 'Terath won't let me rest.'

'Good. Then it is time to walk with me,' said Elder Tirenythlae. He extended his hand to help Andra rise, and led him to the exit. When they passed through the arch, leading from the chamber, Andra saw they were walking on a broad tree limb, twenty spans from the ground. Overcome by an unwelcome rush of vertigo, he reeled back, but Elder Tirenythlae quickly grabbed his arm. 'Are you well?'

'Yes,' Andra gasped, as he steadied. 'I was just surprised by – well, by this.'

'Of course, I should have thought. You are not familiar with Aelendyell dwellings. So.' Tirenythlae spread his arms grandly. 'I welcome you to Wudufaesten Tun.'

Andra relaxed, as his balance returned, and he gazed at the fascinating scene. His eyes adjusted to the intense glow of forest greens, and he identified a multitude of tree houses camouflaged in the hearts of the huge elmoak trees, surrounding the one in which he stood. On the forest floor, moving across a luxuriant carpet of dried leaves, Aelendyell men, women and children were actively pursuing chores and games. He drew a deep breath, and savoured the fresh, rich odours of living nature. 'How many people live in this village?' he asked, as he studied three Aelendyell females fashioning arrows.

'Between two and three hundred, counting the childlings, of course. I cannot say for certain. Elder Kerrowynn does the numbering. He would know,' Tirenythlae explained. Andra continued to survey the tun, until Tirenythlae gently drew him to a rope ladder.

At ground level, Andra paused to catch his breath again. Even though he was lowered on the rope ladder, the exertion of walking and standing was his first in a long time, and his weakened muscles were reluctant, but his blood sang excitedly in his veins, and the air in his lungs was invigorating. 'Are you well?' Tirenythlae asked a second time, concerned for his guest's health.

Andra grinned in response to his guide's question, and said cheerfully, 'Very well. It feels good to be walking again. Anything's better than lying in bed.'

'Good,' Tirenythlae nodded. 'Then come this way.' The Aelendyell led Andra along the village's main thoroughfare between the gnarled roots of the giant elmoaks. As he followed, Andra became acutely aware of his physical difference to the Aelendyell. Not only was he a head taller than the tallest, but they were lighter-framed, even the ones who were muscled and dressed in warrior garb, and they all had almond-shaped eyes, set above sharp, high cheekbones, giving them uncommonly handsome features. They seemed equally as aware of him, as he passed with his escort, and the Aelendyell on the thoroughfare stopped to stare. He heard their lilting voices discussing him, though their words escaped his understanding.

'Ignore that,' said Tirenythlae, nonchalantly. 'They have been curious to see you since you were brought here. Most Aelendyell have never seen one of your kind. Their interest is not meant to be offensive.'

Andra spotted three childlings peeping at him, from behind a massive elmoak trunk. They were smiling, inquisitive, bright-eyed, nothing at all like their long-lost city cousins; the abandoned waifs Tim Gaelus pointed out in the warehouse.

At the end of the village, Tirenythlae directed Andra to a path that wound into the forest. 'This is the path to Hustingbeam – our meeting tree, if you like,' the Aelendyell Elder explained. 'Your questions will be answered at Hustingbeam.'

Tirenythlae led him into a large clearing, dominated by an ancient tree at its centre, older than the giants crowding the clearing's edge. Its branches swept majestically outward, and up, smothered in rich dark green foliage, and its grey trunk was worn smooth by time, so that even in the shadow of its broad canopy the trunk appeared to shine with mystical light. Beneath the sweeping boughs, ensconced on the great tree's gnarled, twisted roots jutting from the trunk, like the deformed, muscular legs of an ancient giant, sat eight more Aelendyell, all like Tirenythlae in appearance, dressed in long flowing green robes, intricate braids worked into their grey locks. As Tirenythlae and Andra approached, they rose and bowed, and one came forward to be introduced. 'Chanter Pyraneth,' explained Tirenythlae, 'the most respected Aelendyell in Wudufaesten Tun.' Andra bowed to the Elder, and the Aelendyell chattered a greeting in his native tongue. 'Chanter Pyraneth is officially welcoming you,' Tirenythlae informed Andra. 'He asks if you feel strong enough to sit with the Elders today?'

'I want to know answers to the questions plaguing me,'

Andra replied.

'Then I'll tell him you are willing to sit.'

'Just let me sit,' said Andra, fatigue seeping through his being, overcoming his sense of discretion before his hosts.

'Why must I live on the fringe of the village?' asked Andra angrily, as he studied the tree-hut Tirenythlae led him to, after the long and wearying session with the Elders. 'I feel like an outcast.'

Tirenythlae looked sternly at the young human warrior. 'You are an outcast, Andra. You are not Aelendyell. You have never lived in the forests. The Elders agree that, for the moment, it is best for you to abide outside the village. Perhaps it is best not only for Aelendyell, but for yourself as well.'

'What's that mean?' Andra asked, suspecting the Aelendyell had decided he was a danger to their home.

'Whatever you want it to mean,' the Elder replied, 'so long as it is good.' Andra looked askew at the Elder, unable to construe his cryptic answer. 'You will be well provided for,' continued the Elder. 'Both Retnayal and Mirithanyll will bring you food, water, whatever needs you desire. Your return to health is our prime concern. When that is achieved, we will decide further what is to be done with you.'

'Am I to remain outside the village?'

'For now,' Tirenythlae confirmed. He looked up, and smiled as he added, 'Aelendyell are curious at the best of times. There will be more dwellers from Wudufaesten out here to stare at you, than you will want. But if we keep you here, at least we Elders can justify our actions to keep our people away, for now.'

When the Elder left, Andra took stock of his temporary home. It was a cruder imitation of the tree homes in Wudufaesten, hastily built and lower to the ground, with a wooden ladder in place of a rope vine, presumably, Andra decided, to compensate for the less agile human who was to occupy it.

He clambered up the ladder, annoyed to be isolated. When he peered over the platform edge, to the base of his tree, to watch Tirenythlae leave, he saw two more Aelendyell figures melt into the undergrowth. Though he knew where they entered the bushes, once they were within they were invisible to his eyes. Guards? Was he really their prisoner, after all? How truthful were the Aelendyell being? He settled into his rudimentary home and squatted on the floor.

So much time had fled. So much time was lost. Tirenythlae said he lay in a fever for three weeks, and a deep healing sleep for another, before he'd regained consciousness. A month? What was the Aelendyell word for it? Monaymbel - something? He couldn't remember Terath's language, but four weeks, and more, had apparently passed since the horror of the battle at The Rim Shield. The Elders revealed that Aelendyell scouts discovered his body at the edge of Dragon Breath Plains. They found the others first – Claarn, Marella presumably – lost, dying of thirst, stumbling blindly out of the desert, and took them to the nearest human settlement, a tiny village nestled in the low hills, at the foot of the Abreotan Ranges. But not Andra. The Aelendyell only found him by chance when they decided to retrace the steps of the others to see where they'd come from. For all intents and purposes, he perished from thirst, but the Aelendyell who chanced upon his body were curious to discover an Aelendyell talisman around his neck, and when one studied it he felt a faint pulse stirring. They brought him to Wudufaesten Tun, the first place they entered, as they were returning to their tun deeper in the forest, and begged the Elders to take him, because they feared he would never survive the longer journey to their home.

Andra carefully fingered the soft leather thong holding the talisman Tim Gaelus gave him on the night the pair absconded from camp and sneaked into the Great City in the back of a furrier's wagon. Tim told him it was an important key that would open doors for him. Andra thought Tim meant doors in the city. He never imagined it might open other doors, doors not necessarily made of wood or stone or iron; doors into other worlds. It saved his life. He clasped the talisman in his palm and closed his eyes.

Alain, his friend from The Vale, was dead. The Great Armies lost the battle against the Haagii. Derik O'Dale, the tall, golden-haired Longbowman, was dead. And Stephen. Murdok. All his companions. Ten thousand warriors swept aside like flies. And Artega – the black pup he carried after the children in Ky gave him to Andra – the pup he named after his mentor in The Vale, Artega the Guardian Master – poor little Artega, lost in the confusion and slaughter on The Rim Shield. And Alain. Dead. All dead.

Overcome by a storm of grief, Andra tucked his head into his body, rolled onto his side, and curled up, clutching his knees. From deep within his soul, great wells of sadness burst into long painful sobs for the first time since he'd returned to the waking land of the living, and the young warrior wept for the loss of innocence. Outside his makeshift shelter, the darkening forest listened silently to the surging sorrow of his outpouring heart.

Eight

Bright birds flitted through the lower branches, reds, blues, and yellows flashing against the darker green leaves. Andra sank into the river's cool water and watched the birds chase each other into the trees on the opposite bank. The water, like silk, awakened his sensuality.

The forest was beautiful, peaceful, and he felt refreshed, reborn, renewed, and happy. The Rim Shield horror and darkness was a terrible dream he'd escaped for paradise. Though the dream haunted his nights, tearing away the fabric of security Wudufaesten wrapped around him, in the mornings, he could forget it, forget the nightmare, forget the pain he carried. The river cleansed him.

He rolled onto his back and tried floating. He was no swimmer. The Vale afforded no opportunity for learning to swim, and there was little need for the skill, although Erik, Alain and he had dipped into the stream running along the southern edge of The Vale after warm training days. Laughing at his clumsiness in the water, he struggled to his feet, and glanced down at his chest. Shape. Good. He tensed his right bicep. Better. The muscle was improving. Freyar's exercises were having effect. Strength was slowly returning. Muscle, wasted from lying near death, was recovering definition.

He lifted his left hand from the river to study a white scar along its back; a healed wound from the last encounter on The Rim Shield. The sight sent a shiver through his spine, and he thrust the offending hand deep into the waters. He carried the nightmare everywhere. He dipped his head into the water.

'Andra!'

He heard her voice, as he broke the surface. Where was she?

'Andra!' she repeated.

He turned to the far bank and saw Mirithanyll poised to dive. She arched through the air and entered the river with a faint splash. She didn't surface. He became concerned. She was nowhere to be seen. As he went to clamber out of the water to call for help, her smiling face bobbed into view, an arm-span from him. She scooped a handful of water and playfully flicked it at him. 'You had me worried,' he scolded.

Mirith's smiled broadened, and her bright laughter echoed across the river. With two strokes, she drew closer, but her presence caused Andra to backpedal. She was naked in the crystal water, and his nakedness would be as evident to her. His retreat caused her to look hurtfully at him with her green eyes.

'Mirith, I have no clothes on,' he tried to explain. His embarrassment puzzled the Aelendyell girl. He tried to walk on the pebbly bottom, but slipped, and as he struggled to regain his footing Mirith's arms enfolded him, as she helped him to stand. Her softness pressed against his side. 'I'm alright. I've got my footing,' he blurted, desperately trying to disentangle.

She laughed, said something in her own tongue, and her eyes sparkled. The glittering drops of moisture beaded in her blonde locks gave her hair a jewelled texture. Like the forest, she was beautiful, but her beauty and her presence unsettled him.

'Mirith wants to know why you're so coy about your body.' The intrusion of a third voice startled Andra. Terath sat on the near bank, in his green leggings, with a bow slung across his left shoulder. A faint grin graced the young warrior's lips. 'Well?' he asked, one eyebrow cocked.

Andra glanced at Mirith, who had found her feet in the shallower water, and was looking up at him with her smiling eyes. 'Tell your sister that I'm – well, I'm not used to swimming naked with beautiful women,' he replied. He expected a lively comment from Terath, but all he got was a question.

'Why?'

Surprised by Terath's serious demeanour, Andra was

compelled to describe his feelings. 'It's not a custom of my people. It's considered indecent,' he explained.

Terath nodded. 'I know humans have difficulty with nudity. I learned that much on my short forages into the world of people. But why?' he repeated. 'Are you all ashamed of your bodies?'

'Yes – no. I don't know. It's just something -' Andra left the sentence incomplete. He couldn't think why. If all human women were as beautiful as Mirith, and men as handsome as Terath, perhaps people wouldn't be so concerned with clothing. 'I think it's time to come out,' he mumbled self-consciously.

Terath crossed to a small shrub, lifted Andra's clothes, and waited for him to clamber out of the river. Mirith followed, and offered to help Andra dress when they reached her brother, but Terath said something to her, which only made her giggle cheekily. She shook out her hair, grinned, and dived back into the river, and swam for the other bank. 'What did you say to her?' Andra asked, as he slid on his leggings.

'I explained your dilemma,' said Terath with a grin. 'She's going to dress on the other side, so as not to embarrass you further.' Andra watched her slip out of the river. She stood on the opposite bank, waved, and disappeared into the forest. The vision filled him with a deep longing, a physical craving, but it also evoked a memory of another beauty – a sylph-like lady standing before an ancient tree, deep in a forest hall. The vision was familiar, a part of Andra's past, but he couldn't remember where he'd seen her, or when. 'What are your thoughts?' Terath asked.

Andra shook his head. 'Another memory,' he replied.

'Still of the battle?'

'No, something else - someone else.' Unconsciously, he rubbed his wrist along a faint line in his skin. Terath awaited Andra's explanation, but the young dark-haired warrior finished dressing silently.

When they returned, along the path toward Andra's tree home, two Aelendyell Weapon Bearers emerged from the forest to join them. Terath cheerily greeted them, and fell to chatting in their Aelendyell tongue, every so often explaining comments to Andra to keep him involved in their conversation. 'Kersin says the forest is restless. There's something brewing.'

'What do you mean?' asked Andra.

'He's been beamcraefting – communing with the trees, if you like. He says the trees are whispering messages of caution to each other.'

Andra couldn't disguise his astonishment at Terath's revelation. 'Kersin talks to trees?'

'In a manner. Actually, he listens,' Terath explained. 'It's an ancient Elvenaar skill. Most of us have a touch of it in us from birth, but only a few, like Kersin, practise it enough to become conversant. One day, he'll become adept at the skill and qualify for status as a Tun Elder.'

Aelendyell skills and magic fascinated Andra. Terath and Mirith took magic for granted, as a natural part of their forest life. Their magic reminded Andra of the bald Apprentice he saw thwart a warrior's drunken aggression with illusion in the Great City tavern. His was violent magic – magic designed to allow the practitioner to assert authority over his victim – but these Aelendyell loved gentle magic, magic for pleasure and fun. Mirith showed him a simple light spell. Terath demonstrated how childlings played hide and seek with small objects, by casting hide spells on the objects, and challenging their playmates to find them. He only half-heard Terath's voice interrupt his thoughts. 'Sorry. I was thinking,' Andra apologized.

Terath smiled. 'Now that's a dangerous sign,' he said. 'You're clearly getting a lot better. I said Freyar says you're a good pupil. You're gaining strength and endurance very quickly.'

Andra glanced at the second Aelendyell accompanying Terath. Freyar nodded. 'Freyar's a clever man,' Andra replied, humbly acknowledging the Aelendyell to whom he referred. 'He taught me exercises to restore my body. I feel good, much fitter. The past four weeks have been enjoyable.

I thought I was a prisoner when I saw these two on guard below my tree home, but your Elders are wise, and Freyar and Kersin are good companions. I still can't talk freely with them, but we communicate as we need.'

'Then all is well,' said Terath.

Andra stopped him, gripping his shoulders. 'I want to learn your language,' he said. Terath's face became serious. 'What?' asked Andra, surprised by his friend's reaction.

'You cannot. It is forbidden,' Terath announced.

'Why?'

'It is an ancient law. We dare not disobey it. Elder Tirenythlae warned us not to teach you anything. No human is permitted to learn our language.'

'But I already know some of your words,' Andra argued. 'Beam - that's tree, isn't it? Wudu - forest. Witan – know, or something like that. You call me a worold-buend – human? I'm already learning your tongue.'

Terath grinned. 'Words. It's all incidental. Elder Tirenythlae said that's a small price to pay while you're with us. The little you learn that way isn't a concern to us, but we are forbidden to teach you Aelendyell.' Terath's turning head informed Andra the subject was ended, and the three Aelendyell fell into rapid conversation, closing him out of their private worlds.

Despite their care and friendliness, Andra knew distrust lurked beneath their happy exteriors, because the Aelendyell guarded their culture from him. It pained him to be forced to remain apart, to be an alien. He was hardly a danger. They saved his life and nursed him to health, so he owed them anything they demanded, not the least being sincere and total trust. A Guardian respected honesty and sincerity, above all values. He had to prove that to them. He wanted their trust.

Mirith was waiting at the foot of his tree home when they arrived, and she smiled when she saw him. Her warm greeting forced him to look away, and as he did he caught Terath staring, but the Aelendyell quickly turned when shouting reached their ears, and asked, 'What's that noise?'

A green figure emerged from the trees, yelling, 'Aelendyell! Wea-gesith! Torn-genithla! Scyldan Wudufaesten!' as he sprinted past, into the forest.

Kersin and Freyar bolted in the direction of the village. Terath hesitated, hurriedly instructing Mirith, and he directed his attention to a confused Andra. 'Stay here. Mirith will keep you company. I'll return soon.' He ran after his companions.

'What's happening, Mirith?' Andra asked, as he stared after Terath's retreating figure. His pulse raced. Trouble – he sensed it – but what? Where? Mirith shook her head. She didn't appear to understand, but her demeanour changed. Her smile evaporated, and her face was solemn, thoughtful. Something other than a sweet Aelendyell girl stood before him, and she seemed more substantial, solid, threatening.

Distant shouts reached their ears. Several Aelendyell sprinted past, carrying bows, wearing swords, and shining chain armour glittered under their green cloaks. They plunged into the forest, in the direction Terath had taken. Andra could no longer wait. He clambered up the ladder, into his tree home, and re-emerged with a short staff he fashioned from a tree limb, two days earlier.

As he reached ground level, Mirith barred his way, and shook her head, emphasizing something in her lilting voice that Andra understood as meaning he had to stay. 'No, Mirith,' he firmly replied. 'I have to go. They may need help.' She stayed in his path. 'Mirith!' he asserted in half-warning. He held her stare to show he was determined to find the source of the disturbance threatening Wudufaesten, before he stepped past, and ran into the forest. She turned to follow.

He hadn't run in a long time, and he quickly tired and dropped to a brisk walk, breathing heavily. He had to start running again. His illness had cost him too much. When this day was over, he'd begin running like the Guardian Master and Murdok trained him to run. The path was difficult to follow, but as he reached the riverbank shouting rose, out of his sight, on the far side, and further downstream. There was no path along the bank, so he turned to Mirith for guidance. She looked at him with quiet eyes and shrugged, and her non-cooperation angered him. 'Mirith, please!' he pleaded. 'I'm a Guardian. I'm trained to protect. I've got to get there.' She smiled at his helplessness, apparently pleased that he couldn't pursue the issue further. She headed back along the path toward his tree home.

Her refusal to help left him no choice. He hunted for signs, or tracks, that would lead him to Terath and the other Aelendyell. A few paces from the river, he found bent fronds and the faint trace of a footprint heading into the forest in the direction he sought, and he charged in recklessly. Fighting through the thicker undergrowth exhausted was exhausting, but he broke through and stepped onto a wider path, and Mirith emerged behind him. Cries rose ahead, out of his vision. He stepped forward, but Mirith grabbed his arm. Thinking she was still trying to keep him from getting involved in Aelendyell affairs, he tried to pull free, but she held on and made a determined effort to drag him into the bushes.

The shouting grew, and Andra spied approaching figures through the trees. He recognised them – Haagii, their hulking bodies strapped in rough and ill-kept leather armour. He felt compelled to burst out and attack his sworn enemy, but Mirith held him tightly, shaking her head. He struggled with his intense desire, tried to fight it down, but seeing the Haagii closing the distance in a jog trot cut into his pride, and fired his need for vengeance. He remembered Claarn on The Rim Shield, with Alain, Stephen, and Senok. They were pointing to him, and to a sea of Haagii washing down the sides of a mountain.

Mirith shook Andra to direct his attention to a point, several spans from where they were secreted, and whispered, 'Glyph.' Though he couldn't understand the meaning, he stopped struggling and watched. The leading Haagii appeared to hit an invisible wall, the air danced with green crackling energy, and their bodies jerked and kicked, suspended in mid-air by an enveloping force. The five trailing

Haagii stumbled to a halt, their ugly leather faces terror-stricken by their fellows' fate. The crackle and hissing eased, and the two victims slumped to the path, charred, dead.

Mirith released Andra's arm. Seizing the opportunity, he leapt onto the path, his staff whirling in challenge. His sudden appearance broke the resolve of the shocked Haagii clustered behind their leaders' carcasses, and they turned to flee, but bowstrings thrummed from the forest margin, and four fell, arrows ripping through their tattered armour. The surviving warrior bolted in Andra's direction, and, when he spotted the young warrior barring his escape, he yelled and charged. Andra held his ground to the last moment, exactly as Artega his Guardian Master taught him, and as the Haagii sword swept through a lethal arc he ducked and sidestepped, whacking the staff sharply across his attacker's shins. Howling, the Haagii warrior crashed forward and Andra brought the heel of the staff down onto the Haagii's exposed neck. There was a snapping sound, the Haagii kicked twice and was still.

Nine

'The Elders have called us to meeting. You must attend,' Terath informed Andra, who peered down at the Aelendyell standing at the base of his tree home.

'Where?'

'Hustingbeam,' Terath replied. 'Hurry, I'll take you. The whole Tun is gathering.'

Andra grabbed his staff and scampered down the ladder to join Terath. Kersin and Freyar emerged from the trees. 'Is this about this morning?' Andra asked.

'Yes,' said Terath. 'The Waelwulf have never pushed so far into Wynwuduholt. Not in living memory.'

'But there were only seven.'

'They were forty strong, before they reached the path where you saw them,' Terath corrected. Andra reflected on Terath's information as he followed at a brisk pace. Forty Haagii: thirty-three slain before he saw them. The Aelendyell fiercely protected their forests.

Terath led them through Wudufaesten, and stragglers joined as the group headed onto the path to Hustingbeam. When they entered the clearing of the ancient tree, they found the entire Aelendyell tun gathering, young and old. The Elders sat beneath Hustingbeam, and Chanter Pyraneth and Elder Tirenythlae were talking with their colleagues.

As the last people straggled in, the Chanter stood, spread his hands wide, as if he intended to embrace everyone in the clearing, and silence immediately descended. Pyraneth whispered, and Andra felt a familiar sensation ripple across the heads of the Aelendyell and surround him, reminding him of another figure, one in silver robes with the same silvery locks as the Aelendyell Chanter, standing beside the Great King before the assembled Great Armies on the Plains of Ky. He realised the Great King's Royal Advisor had to be an Aelendyell too. Pyraneth's voice carried to his ears, without effort or strain. Lilting words washed gently through him, and though the meaning was a mystery, the import was clear. He heard words he understood – names of the village and the forest, and the name that Terath used for the Haagii – Waelwulf. Sadness, not hate, and an unusual quality of weariness tinged Pyraneth's voice. After Pyraneth, each Elder spoke briefly, and then the crowd dispersed, heading quietly along the path to their homes.

Andra turned to leave, but Terath stopped him, saying, 'The Elders wish to speak with you.'

They waited, until the last Aelendyell left, and Andra noticed that no one stared at him. They hardly even acknowledged his presence. Only a couple of childlings looked directly at him, with grinning faces and bright inquisitive eyes. Elder Tirenythlae waved for them to approach, and Andra, Terath, Kersin and Freyar strode across the empty clearing toward the Elders. As they walked, Andra was surprised to see that the grass in the clearing was unaffected by the presence of the Aelendyell crowd.

'We welcome you, Andra,' said Tirenythlae. 'I speak for Chanter Pyraneth, and all the Elders, in saying this.' Each Elder nodded to Andra, and Pyraneth came forward. The Chanter spoke, pausing for Tirenythlae to translate. 'Pyraneth wants you to know that he heard of your exploit, this morning, against the Waelwulf, and he extends his gratitude on behalf of all Wudufaesten,' Tirenythlae explained pleasantly. Andra witnessed a smile extending across the old Aelendyell's features, before he continued. 'He says he is pleased to see you are regaining your health. You are a formidable young warrior and your people must be proud of you. So, it is time you returned to your world.'

Astonished by Pyraneth's suggestion, Andra blurted 'Why?' and stared at the Chanter for an answer, forgetting his customary manners.

The Chanter's smile subsided, as Tirenythlae repeated Andra's exclamation, and when the Elder finished Pyraneth looked Andra directly in the eye, spoke slowly, and turned to sit. Tirenythlae explained. 'The Chanter says he is sorry to rush you away, but he does not want you to become involved in Aelendyell affairs. Wudufaesten is no longer a haven for you. You must go.'

'But –' Andra began.

Tirenythlae cut in abruptly, as Terath grabbed Andra's arm. 'The Wita have spoken worold-buend. You cannot question their words.'

Andra appealed to Terath for support, but the young Aelendyell shook his head, and urged Andra to leave with him, saying, 'There's no more to be said.'

'We will accompany you to the edge of Wynwuduholt, and onto the road that leads to a worold-buend village. After that, my friend, you're on your own,' Terath explained. 'Elder Tirenythlae ordered us to return quickly.'

Andra looked at him, at Freyar and Kersin, and lastly Mirith. 'I still feel like I'm being pushed out of here without a full explanation. What was said at Hustingbeam?' he asked.

'Perhaps some day I'll tell you,' Terath replied. 'For now, it's an Aelendyell matter, and not yours. We must leave at once, if we're to get you to the edge of the world by sunset.' Andra accepted a small woven sack of provisions from Mirith, and he savoured her beauty as she smiled. Wudufaesten would live forever in his memories of Mirith. He picked up his staff, and the small party headed toward the river path.

The Aelendyell moved swiftly through the forest, and Andra had difficulty maintaining their pace. They crossed the river, by following a complex, concealed route along tree boughs that stretched over, and interlinked, above the water. He couldn't match the agility of the slimmer, lighter Aelendyell, so he crawled across the natural bridge system, causing his friends to grin good-naturedly.

'It's best you're not staying, worold-buend. You'd struggle to go anywhere in Wudufaesten anyway,' Terath teased.

Across the river, they followed hidden, twisting pathways

for a long time, which left Andra so confused he doubted they were following paths at all. But Terath led them through green barriers with deliberate precision, leaving Andra to ponder how anyone not Aelendyell could ever penetrate the forests to threaten its people. Compared to this, the Valley of Rivers was a wide highway.

At one point, Kersin pushed past the others to join Terath, and he whispered a brief message. Terath indicated they should stop. 'What is it?' Andra asked. Terath raised a finger to his lips, ordering everyone to keep silent. Kersin moved into the undergrowth, where he rested his forehead against an old, stunted elmoak, remaining motionless as the party waited. When he returned, he was visibly agitated as he spoke to Terath. Terath shook his head, but Kersin persisted, until Terath reluctantly nodded. Then Kersin spoke to Mirith and Freyar, and they nodded. 'At least tell me, Terath,' Andra pleaded.

'We have to change our route. Kersin will lead.'

'But why?'

'We will see,' was all Terath said.

The party followed Kersin through a winding maze of trees. Every few paces, he paused to listen, before pressing on, until he stopped and asked Terath to check ahead. They waited, but when Terath did not return Mirith indicated they could venture forward.

Fifty paces on, they found Terath crouching on the path, signalling danger. Everyone dropped to their knees and edged forward to join him. Andra sniffed the air and smelled smoke. He peered through the leafy cover and saw why Terath had stopped.

Smoke curled through a bush to mingle with a billowing, slate-coloured cloud forming in the canopy. A yellow tongue of flame licked the bush's leaves, and they curled and died. More flame tongues erupted around the bush. Behind it, shadows moved, carrying torches, bending and touching them to the plants, and turning them into writhing pyres.

'Cwelere! Ecgbana!' snarled Kersin. He jumped to his feet and let loose an arrow. 'Forthferan!' he screamed, as a dark figure toppled.

Freyar stood and shot another, and Andra marvelled at the speed with which the Aelendyell nocked shafts and let them fly accurately to their marks. Several figures fell, before the survivors ran into the forest.

Mirith ran to the fire and began an Aelendyell litany, extinguishing the fires in the closest bushes, to Andra's amazement. But a thicker pall of smoke appeared in the trees to her left, heralding a larger fire, and flames danced across tree branches, like mischievous, ravenous red-gold creatures, defying the Aelendyell woman's magic. Shadows emerged from the smoke and foliage, carrying torches, and they pushed a captive Aelendyell before them. Bows hummed beside Andra, and three arrows arched lethally toward the Haagii. Screams of surprise and anger filled the air. Another trio of missiles found their marks. Incensed by the attack, the remaining Haagii charged the tiny Aelendyell party.

Andra met one warrior with the full point of his staff, sidestepped, and tripped a second. He struck a third warrior a cracking blow to the skull. More surrounded him, but he weaved and whirled the staff with his Guardian skill, keeping them at bay. Stunned and bruised, his attackers circled, unwilling to be the first to risk another blow from the human's staff. Out of the side of his eye, he saw Freyar's sword sparkle and fell another victim. Where was Mirith? The circling Haagii taunted him, laughed, keeping his attention ahead, but he knew instinctively what was coming. Without turning from his antagonists, he thrust his staff backwards with all his strength, felt it hit a solid object, heard a groan, and a spear clattered at his feet. With a full-throated cry, he went on the offensive, keeping control and focusing his energy through the staff, as wild confusion whirled around him. He was tiring rapidly. His strength waned. He stumbled, and a Haagii sword nicked his left arm, stinging him into renewed action. He dodged left and caught the Haagii warrior a sharp blow across the bridge of the nose.

The enemy lost heart and retreated. Andra checked if any

Haagii were behind him, but motionless figures lay on the ground. The Aelendyell dropped their swords, and resumed their bow-work, picking off Haagii stragglers as they disappeared through an ash-grey wall of swirling smoke, while Mirith feverishly worked her fingers as she chanted her arcane words – until she staggered and collapsed. Terath and Andra ran to her. She mumbled to Terath, as he cradled her head in his arms, and burst into tears. 'What did she say?' Andra asked.

'She says it's too late. The fire's too big for her to control. The trees cry with pain. They die.'

The fire roared toward them. Andra pressed Terath on the shoulder and ran to the limp form of the Aelendyell captive left by the Haagii. Tongues of flame licked the closest undergrowth. As he stooped to check the Aelendyell, he saw blood running from a cut on the young warrior's forehead, and his right arm was bent at an unnatural angle, but he was breathing. He scooped the Aelendyell into his arms, and staggered to his friends. Freyar pushed forward to relieve him of his burden.

'We can't stay here,' said Terath. 'Wudufaesten must be warned. Only the Elders can stop this.' They helped Mirith to her feet, and without a backward glance plunged into the forest. A short distance in, Kersin and Freyar disappeared. 'They'll travel faster than we can,' explained Terath. 'They'll warn Wudufaesten and our people will be prepared.'

Andra knew he was slowing the Aelendyell, because he was a clumsy human. 'Terath,' he said, pausing on the path. 'Take Mirith and go on.'

The Aelendyell stopped and clasped Andra's arms. 'An Aelendyell never leaves a hondgesella. Today we are brothers in arms.' Without waiting for Andra to answer, Terath led them into the forest, followed by Mirith who was regaining her strength. Andra needed no explanation. He understood he was accepted as he followed the Aelendyell toward their home.

They reached Wudufaesten in quick time, their return more direct than the paths they followed out, but the time for deceit was past as expediency ruled Terath's return. The trio met a large body of Aelendyell warriors at the outskirts of the tun, and an Elder was organizing them into groups. Behind the warriors, younglings, and Aelendyell men and women, were busily passing water vessels along a chain of hands, from the river, to the centre of the village, and into storage tanks above the tree homes.

'The water is a last reserve,' explained Terath. 'If fire ever reaches Wudufaesten Tun, the Elders will use all their powers to create artificial rain above the tree homes and thus quench flames threatening our homes. We pray that's unnecessary.' He mingled with the Aelendyell warriors, talking, organizing the defence of the tun, and exchanging information, while Mirith ventured toward the village centre, leaving Andra to watch the ordered Aelendyell activity. Every person in the tun was preparing for the anticipated Haagii attack. Every Aelendyell, even the smallest childling, seemed to know his or her function in the impending defence of the village, and they were going about their tasks quickly and calmly, as if they'd always expected to face such a threat one day.

As Andra watched the Aelendyell, he became aware of someone beside him, and turned to find Tirenythlae solemnly shaking his head. 'I'm sorry,' the Aelendyell Elder quietly apologized. 'We had hoped you could have left before all this.'

'The Haagii are my enemies too,' replied Andra. 'They cut down my friends on The Rim Shield.'

'Then perhaps you are here because it is meant to be so. We can no longer choose. The Ealdfeond direct our paths now.'

'It is The Way,' Andra answered.

The Elder looked deeply into Andra's brown eyes, as if seeking something hidden within their liquid pools, but then he blinked and smiled, and replied, 'Yes. It is, as you put it, the way of things.'

Andra watched the Elder walked away. His words reminded him of the Guardian Master, of Stephen, and the teachings of his people in The Vale. Even in the Aelendyell forests, it seemed he was part of The Way. He'd almost forgotten its philosophy in the past months, but the Elder's observations told him The Way had not forgotten him. Wasn't that one of its mysteries to which the Guardian Master often referred?

Terath returned, his brow knitted with worry. 'The news is bad,' the Aelendyell warrior said. 'Others bring word that fires are spreading throughout Wynwuduholt. The Waelwulf search for our people. They bring war to us.'

'What will you do?' asked Andra.

Terath stared into the forest. 'Fight,' he said.

They waited silently for the Haagii to appear on the riverbank. One by one, spear-toting leather-clad figures emerged from the trees. Crouching in his camouflaged hide, Andra estimated there were seventy to eighty Haagii. A shrill bird call echoed from the far bank, and the air filled with a flurry of arrows that fell among the hapless Haagii. Startled warriors tumbled headlong into the water, clutching at the deadly shafts, and cries of anguish rose as the survivors scrambled, over the outstretched bodies of their dead and dying companions, into the safety of the forest. A second whistle brought Andra and seventy Aelendyell warriors to their feet, and they charged from their hiding places to ambush the retreating Haagii. In a matter of moments, the last Haagii was dead.

Terath wiped his blade on a dead Haagii's tunic and swaggered toward Andra, a grim smile etched across his handsome features, making the Aelendyell look demonic. 'The Waelwulf come in numbers, but they are no match for us,' he said, as he surveyed the corpses littered along the riverbank.

'No,' Andra agreed. He glanced at other Aelendyell helping their few wounded comrades back through the forest toward Wudufaesten, and the dozen dead who fell in the fighting. 'No. The Haagii are beaten this time,' he said, as he rubbed a smear of Haagii blood from his cheek and looked up.

Above the canopy of trees, hung an ominous black cloud, a tell-tale sign the distant Haagii fires were sweeping toward Wudufaesten. He wondered how long a war the Aelendyell were facing. In that instant, he thought he heard a familiar keening, high and distant, like he had heard on the fateful night in the grey dust of Dragon Breath Plains, below The Rim Shield. It sent a cold shiver down his spine.

Ten

'I can only tell you what I saw on The Rim Shield. There were Haagii warriors by tens of thousands, like a dark sea across the valley, there were so many. And there were beasts in the air, breathing fire from their jaws. Believe me. I saw them,' Andra insisted.

Chanter Pyraneth lifted his face, and asked a question, which Tirenythlae translated for Andra. 'Were these creatures like giant flying lizards?'

Andra nodded. 'Yes. Brutish lizards with teeth like swords.'

'Draca!' Pyraneth hissed. Whispers ran between the Elders as Pyraneth scratched his head and walked several paces from Hustingbeam's trunk.

'What are draca?' Andra asked.

'They served the Ealdfeond against the Elvenaar,' Tirenythlae explained. 'We thought such creatures perished long ago. Your news is -' The Aelendyell Elder paused, as thoughts traced lines across his handsome face, and Andra wondered what the Aelendyell was reluctant to discuss. Tirenythlae looked to his fellows, cleared his throat and continued. 'Your news is great in import. The Elders will meet to discuss this matter. We thank you for sharing with us, Andra. Leave us.'

Dismissed without further explanation, Andra returned to the edge of Hustingbeam clearing, where Terath and Mirith were waiting patiently. 'What did the Elders say?' Terath asked, as they started toward the village.

'Not much,' Andra replied, 'but they're obviously concerned by what I told them about the creatures - draca I think was their word.'

'Draca?' responded Terath. 'What are draca?'

Mirith gasped.

Her reaction surprised Terath. 'Mirith? What is it?' he

asked.

She pointed along the path. Terath and Andra saw a Haagii warrior eyeing them.

'Wudufaesten!' yelled Terath in alarm. He drew his sword and charged, and with one swift stroke his enemy fell.

The trio raced into the tun to find the people of Wudufaesten embroiled in conflict – Haagii and Aelendyell locked in mortal combat. As the invaders poured in, they dropped and threw blazing torches to set trees alight, but the torches were swiftly extinguished by defenders before the fire could take firm hold. Swords rang. Battle cries filled the village. Knots of warriors wavered back and forth, dancing each other's deadly song. Above the turmoil, perched on tree home platforms, Aelendyell archers wrought havoc whenever they could take clear shots at the Haagii, who were using sheer weight of numbers to push into the heart of Wudufaesten.

Andra and Terath plunged into the battle. In the ensuing confusion, Andra lost sight of Mirith, and when he saw her again she was with a group at the base of a tree home, separated from Andra by a knot of struggling warriors. Haagii descended upon Mirith's group, so Andra tried to fight through to her assistance, but by the time he reached her the Haagii were piled at her feet, dead, terror inscribed on their death masks. Stunned, he stared at Mirith, trying to comprehend the contradiction in the girl who brought him back from death with her care, but could mysteriously deal out violent death to the Haagii.

The tide of battle slowly turned in the Aelendyell's favour, as the dwindling Haagii force withdrew to the southern end of Wudufaesten. Surrounded by Aelendyell warriors, a continuous rain of arrows from the treetop archers rapidly decimated their numbers. Handfuls of Haagii charged at their foes to escape the fatal arrow shafts, only to die on Aelendyell blades, and their bodies piled higher.

A rush of air, followed by an explosion in the canopy of a tree home, shocked everyone. Burning archers leaped to their deaths from their blazing boughs. Warriors beside

Andra turned their faces to the sky, and as Andra looked up a black shape rolled through the air, wings extended, before banking above the treetops. Inspired by the dragon strike, the Haagii rallied and attacked the Aelendyell with renewed vigour.

Andra disengaged himself from the onslaught, and headed for Mirith, but, as he reached her, above the din of fighting he heard the cry of his nightmare from The Rim Shield – the cry he feared. He pulled Mirith to shelter between the roots of the elmoak where she'd been standing and forced her to cover her head with her arms. They heard the rush of air, and another tree home burst into flame. Aelendyell screams filled the air. 'Draca!' he yelled. 'The Elders must be told!' Mirith stared at him with bewildered eyes, so he pointed at the burning tree. 'Draca!' he urgently repeated, 'Tell Elder Tirenythlae!'

She nodded, got to her feet, and clambered into the adjacent space between the tree roots to speak to another Aelendyell crouched there. The Aelendyell sprinted along the main path, through the village, toward Hustingbeam, while Mirith returned to Andra. She spoke, but he couldn't comprehend her meaning, and before he could ask her to repeat her words another fiery roar sent them sprawling for cover.

Despite their renewed assault, the Haagii were losing the initiative, but they were exacting a bloody toll, while overhead Wudufaesten was burning as fire ate into the heart of the elmoak tree homes with each pass of the black-winged dragon. Aelendyell archers gathered atop a larger tree at the tun's northern end, planning to meet the dragon's firestorm with arrow rain on its next pass. Andra couldn't see the creature through the smoke and tree canopy, only guess at its approach from the direction the archers faced, but he recognised the futility of the Aelendyell plan.

As he watched them preparing, Andra recalled the seething dark ocean on The Rim Shield, at the centre of which Derik O'Dale had stood tall, his blond hair shining gold, longbow poised while a huge black dragon hovered above him, belching sulphurous flame. He saw the heroic image and knew the Aelendyell and Derik were brothers: hondgesella.

The black beast flashed out of a column of smoke, fire streaming from its jaws, and another tree exploded. As the creature banked, the archers loosed a thick volley. Even Aelendyell accuracy couldn't judge the speed of the dragon, and most arrows failed to find their mark, but what appalled Andra was when the few shafts that hit the target bounced harmlessly off the creature's hide, as it disappeared into another roiling cloud of white smoke.

Elder Tirenythlae emerged at the far end of the tun and took in the devastation. Beautiful Wudufaesten was littered with carnage. Ancient tree homes were aflame. Aelendyell warriors were dead and dying. The Waelwulf had ravaged his world. The Elder's hands shook as he weaved a complex pattern with his fingers.

The dragon's cry echoed ominously through the village. The archers turned to face west, and drew their bowstrings tight, waiting. For what, Andra asked himself silently? Their arrows can't harm the dragon. Why even try? A ball of flame erupted around the archers, before they realised the dragon was on them, and the dragon swept through and was gone. The archers' platform disintegrated, engulfed by fire, and archers tumbled earthward like discarded torches.

Andra flinched, not at the devastation wrought by the dragon, but because a strange sensation passed through his body – not a shiver, not pain, just a feeling, as if hands reached in and through him. The air grew still, calm, cooler. Sounds became muted. Whispering voices emanated from the elmoak roots. Tirenythlae never wavered throughout the dragon's attack, and, as he ceased spell weaving, white mist formed in the tree canopy. Tiny drops of moisture rested on Andra's skin. Rain. The mist expanded across Wudufaesten, until the entire tun was caught in rain, tumbling from the mist. Raging fires sputtered and struggled, drowning. The last Haagii collapsed, face down in mud, on the main path.

Exhausted and bloodied Aelendyell warriors slumped beneath their scarred tree homes and soaked up the soothing moisture Tirenythlae conjured from the water storage. Andra anticipated the dragon's return, but the sky above the white mist was empty. Calm settled on Wudufaesten. The Aelendyell had won.

Out of the rain, Terath staggered toward Andra, and the Guardian saw his Aelendyell friend was cut across the cheek, and his right arm was soaked with blood. 'Terath!' cried Mirith, and she ran to his aid. Andra helped her to ease him onto an elmoak root, where they inspected his injuries. His cheek was sore and open, and would need serious attention, but his arm was more fortunate – a flesh wound that bled profusely but wasn't deep.

'We defeated the Waelwulf,' Terath murmured to Andra. He sighed and relaxed. 'Wudufaesten is safe.' He made an aside to Mirith, in Aelendyell, and his comment brought a smile to her face. She waved to a childling, emerging from her hiding place in the branches of her tree home, and sent her on an errand, while she tended Terath's wounds.

'You saw the draca?' Andra asked.

Terath nodded. 'I understand the terror in your dreams now,' he said quietly. 'I've heard ancient songs, about war between the Elvenaar and the Draca, as a childling, but I never knew half of what a draca was. If it wasn't Wudufaesten we were fighting for, I would run rather than face such a terrible foe.' Andra thought of the archers who perished atop the tree at the far end of Wudufaesten and doubted Terath. The Aelendyell were courageous.

The childling returned with a small emerald bag, which she promptly passed to Mirith, before scampering away. Mirith fished inside the bag and withdrew smaller drawstring pouches. She opened one, dipped in her hand, and withdrew a handful of bright blue powder. She applied to Terath's cut cheek, pressing the powder into his wound and holding her hand over the cut, while she recited a healing chant.

Andra could imagine his friend's discomfort. 'What is that?' he asked, referring to the blue powder.

'Healing powder,' Terath replied. 'It goes onto a wound before a balm, unless a poultice is necessary. Then we use the poultice first, to draw infection from the wound, as we did for you when you were brought here.'

'Doesn't that hurt?'

Terath grimaced. 'It does. But Weapon Bearers are taught not to show pain.'

Andra watched, fascinated, while Mirith worked her healing art. She was an individual of mysteries and talents that surpassed even her incomparable beauty. If he could learn to communicate with her, he would tell her how much she inspired him. So much he wanted to talk to her, listen to her, and learn what she was really like. He was intensely infatuated with her.

Over her shoulder, he saw Aelendyell men and women busy tending to those who'd been wounded, or finding the slain and moving their bodies to the side of the main path. He thought of Gavin, the young Guardian the Haagii slew in The Vale, of the Great King's soldiers who died on the march north, of his friends cut down along the top and base of The Rim Shield. Death stalked everywhere and everyone, in this world, and the Haagii carried it like plague.

Terath's hand on his shoulder broke his reverie. 'Come with me to the Elders,' the Aelendyell said, checking his bandaging was secure. 'We must find out what they intend to do.'

Freyar and three Aelendyell warriors met them at the junction to Hustingbeam. Freyar spoke to Terath, and Terath inexplicably broke into a run. Andra ran behind, wondering what trouble caused his friend to sprint ahead. They passed other Aelendyell heading toward Hustingbeam, but when they reached the clearing Terath stopped.

The Elders were seated in a ring around Hustingbeam, equidistant, motionless, facing outward, their eyes fixed upward. At the feet of each was a scroll, opened, face down on the earth. Andra couldn't see the Chanter. He went to move forward, but Terath prevented him, warning, 'You mustn't approach them. They're working a mighty spell to protect Wudufaesten from the Waelwulf and the draca. If you interfere, you will break the spell and the draca will return. While they stay there, we are safe.'

'Where's Pyraneth?' Andra asked, unable to find the Chanter. Terath pointed to the top of Hustingbeam. Chanter Pyraneth, in robes of shining silver, surrounded by an aura of light, sat cross-legged, rotating slowly, suspended an arm span above the crown of the ancient elmoak. The vision astonished Andra. He'd seen Aelendyell magic working in the tun's defence, but even that display hadn't prepared him for the magnitude of what he was witnessing. He gaped at the Chanter's slowly rotating figure, surrounded by a small crowd of Aelendyell who were coming and going, until Terath gently pulled on his arm and drew him away.

On the path to the village, they met Elder Tirenythlae, the only Elder not joined in the protection spell ring. 'You have seen?' he said to Andra as they met.

'Yes,' the young Guardian solemnly replied.

'The draca cannot harm Wudufaesten so long as the spell ring is unbroken and the Chanter's focus is clear,' Tirenythlae explained. 'My colleagues are weaving an ancient Elvenaar glyph. Its power is greater than any one of us can wield alone, so the ring is formed to channel our energies through Hustingbeam to the Chanter. He makes a great sacrifice for us all.'

'How long will they hold the circle?' Andra asked.

Tirenythlae stared into the middle-distance, and said resolutely, 'As long as the Ealdfeond threaten Wynwuduholt.'

Together, Andra, Terath and Tirenythlae entered Wudufaesten. The rain had ceased. Wet ashes smoked. The Aelendyell were cleaning the battlefield and they piled the Haagii dead in the centre of the main path. 'So what becomes of the Haagii?' Andra asked.

'They burn,' Terath replied.

Andra turned and asked, 'But I thought Aelendyell despised fire?'

'We do,' Terath said, sombrely, 'which is why the Haagii

will burn.'

Near Terath's tree home, Andra spied Mirith sitting on a tree root, playing hide with five Aelendyell childlings. He paused to watch, enjoying the bright giggles the magic game generated, turned to Tirenythlae, and said, 'I want to stay until this is over. I owe Wudufaesten my life.'

The Aelendyell Elder raised his eyebrows, and irony crept into his voice as he responded. 'You have no choice worold-buend. You cannot leave. The spell that keeps the Ealdfeond and his followers out, keeps us in. No one will leave Wudufaesten for a long time.'

Eleven

Perched on a tree root, Andra watched the childling's fingers tease his eyes around the white pebble. In a trifling, the pebble vanished. Andra reached to where the pebble had been – nothing but earth. Bright laughter greeted his astonishment. He searched wider, but the pebble remained elusive, while the childling giggled with glee as the clumsy worold-buend fumbled between small rooty growths. Disgusted, Andra shrugged his shoulders. 'I give up,' he said. 'Where is it?' The childling giggled, tossed her long blond hair back from her exuberant face, and touched a spot three fingers' width from the point where she first placed the pebble. The pebble flickered into view, and she laughed again. Andra grabbed the startled childling, and turned her upside down, to the amusement of her friends. She squealed excitedly at the new game, and squirmed out of his grasp, when he put her down. 'You're too cheeky, Harmor!' Andra growled, in mock anger. The Aelendyell childling scampered away, green eyes sparkling as she chortled impulsively.

'Are you teasing childlings again?'

Andra turned. Terath and Mirith were laughing. 'Am I teasing them?' he asked, grinning. 'Ask me who's doing the teasing?'

'They enjoy your company,' Terath noted.

'Yes. I thought they'd get over the novelty.'

'They have,' Terath replied. His voice took a serious tone. 'They accept you in their games, and that's a genuine privilege among Aelendyell childlings.'

'What do you mean?'

'Childlings,' Terath nonchalantly explained, 'are raw Aelendyell – lots of talent, lots of curiosity, lots of confidence. They're arrogant and unpredictable, in as many ways as they're cute and lovable. They don't accept discipline, unless it's from people of recognised authority, or sometimes an adult whom they decide to adopt.'

'What about their parents?' asked Andra.

'Parents?' said Terath, bemused by Andra's question. 'Oh, of course, you mean mother and father. I've seen it in worold-buend villages. Aelendyell aren't like humans who jealously divide into family groups. Wudufaesten is one whole family. A childling belongs to all and none. Adults are responsible for every childling in the tun. If a childling is good or bad, the adult nearest is duty bound to respond. It's always been so for our people.'

Andra glanced at the childlings who seemed to have adopted him without question. 'I only wish I had the magic to play their games at their level,' he said, as he leaned to his left to catch Harmor creeping up behind him. His move sent the girl tumbling between the elmoak roots for cover, amid the excited laughter of her companions.

Mirith laughed and commented in Aelendyell. Terath started to explain, 'Mirith says she –' but Andra cut in.

'She said something like, "There are things he still can do better than the childlings." Right?'

Terath stared at him for several moments, before asking, 'Well, yes. But – I mean, how -?'

Terath's puzzled countenance made Andra all the merrier. He pointed at the childlings, who had forgotten the adults and were engrossed in another game. 'Blame them. They're the ones helping me.' Terath's gaze shifted to the childlings, and Andra saw anger fleet across his friend's face. 'Don't be angry, Terath,' he pleaded in the childlings' defence. 'How else can we understand how to play the games if we can't communicate?'

'But the Chanter said we weren't to teach you the tongue. It's forbidden,' Terath insisted.

'You've kept your word,' Andra offered in appeasement. 'No one's taught me. Call it an exchange. They talk. I listen. Some things aren't difficult to work out. I hardly know enough of your language to say more than hullo, goodbye, and a few conversational titbits, and occasional curses, which the childlings use when they're angry.'

'You understood Mirith,' Terath argued.

'Understood, perhaps, but I couldn't formulate a reply. I don't know your words well enough.' Andra stood from kneeling. 'Besides, how accurate was I?'

Terath glared, before breaking into a smile, laughing, and saying, 'Close. Mirith said you were smarter than the childlings. I think it was a compliment.'

'Lift your aim slightly above your target. You're right-handed. Aim slightly right – thumb and ring finger on the shaft flight. Concentrate. See where your shaft will go. Let the shaft follow your thought.' Andra pulled his bowstring taut, as instructed, felt its tension in his wrist and bicep, balanced, released. The shaft warbled through the air and thudded into the fallen log, a hand span wide of its mark.

'Better than yesterday!' yelled Terath.

Andra let the bow hang despondently. 'Better,' he muttered, 'but still poor.' Freyar nocked an arrow and loosed it. It hit the centre mark on the log.

Seeing Andra's disappointment, Terath tried to hearten his friend. 'Freyar is Aelendyell. He was born with a bow in his hands. Don't compare yourself with him, until you've shot as many shafts as he.'

Andra looked at Terath, who was nocking his own arrow, and the Aelendyell winked. Andra grinned. 'You're right,' he admitted. He lifted his bow and prepared another shaft.

Stately elmoaks spread a protective ceiling across the forest floor, allowing sufficient light through to encourage lively fern and bracken between the richly leaved bushes. Quiet crystal streams trickled gently over silky pebbles, heading for the deep green river. Birds, honeyeaters predominantly, flitted through the branches, singing and squabbling, industrious in their search for nectar, and rainbow butterflies fluttered erratic paths from bush to fern. No breezes disturbed the forest floor. It was tranquil, utterly different from the Valley of Rivers, or Dragon Forest.

Dragon Forest haunted Andra. He remembered stumbling out of the forest, having missed the Great Armies march by several days. Something happened in that forest. Marvin the Longbowman plunged headlong into a tree, chasing a maiden's image, and was swallowed by a glowing pool of blue light. Artega, his black pup, went missing, so he ran back to find him. He instinctively touched his wrist and sensed the amber band melded there, invisible to the eye, yet sensible to his touch. The Aelendyell talked about their tree homes – beambyht – but there was another kind of tree home he knew – somewhere in Ethelreddor. Ethelreddor? The forest was Dragon Forest, but someone called it Ethelreddor. Who? He watched small tadpoles struggling against the run of a stream as he sat on the bank, on a moss rock, and wrestled with his evasive memory. Little black, half-shaped things – not fish, not frog – caught between two lives. He felt like them. He was half-formed, a warrior defeated on The Rim Shield, a living dead, a stranger trapped in a strange world. And there was a current moving against him, a current he couldn't identify or understand. All he knew, like the tadpoles, was that he had somewhere to go, and it was against the current.

He felt her presence as he had in his dreams. She was waiting, watching, outside his vision and touch, but he knew she was there. He'd known for a long time. He just didn't know what to do about it. He knew Aelendyell weren't shy about their bodies. Childlings often played naked, and adults bathed in the river, oblivious to each other's sexuality. If she was just passing, even if she dived in to join him, as she did the first time he bathed, he would be less self-conscious. But she did neither. She was somewhere there, on the bank, every time he bathed, watching him.

He loved running: the rush of wind across his face, blood

pulsing through his veins, the sting of air in his lungs. He dodged and weaved between the trees, leaves brushing his cheek, branches trying to slow his speed. Behind him, his pursuers' movements grew fainter. He was losing them. With a final burst of speed, he broke onto the main path into Wudufaesten, and span to face them.

Freyar appeared first, then Brefan and Terath. Three more Aelendyell stumbled from the forest, breathing hard. 'You are fast, worold-buend, even by Aelendyell standards,' Freyar gasped between breaths.

Even though Andra only caught snatches of the statement in Aelendyell, he understood Freyar's compliment and nodded with a smile. 'Tell Freyar it was my training, my skill,' he told Terath.

Terath translated Andra's explanation for Freyar, who replied, leaving Terath to relay his comment to Andra. 'He says you must teach the Aelendyell how to run like you.'

Andra knew Freyar was paying him a high compliment, because during his stay in Wudufaesten he learned Aelendyell arrogance seldom acknowledged that others could hold skills greater than their own. He was tempted to taunt Freyar in fun, but he held back when he saw genuine respect glowing in the Aelendyell's eyes. Instead, he said to Terath, 'Thank Freyar for his kindness, and tell him that I'd take pleasure sharing my skill with the Aelendyell.'

When they recovered their wind, the Aelendyell walked into Wudufaesten to go about their daily duties, while Andra remained at the edge of the tun. He strode back into the forest, and a short distance along the path, at its edge, he found the old tree stump for which he was searching, its blackened roots upturned, legacy of the Haagii attacks.

He flexed his muscle and ran his right hand over his left arm, feeling the definition he was rebuilding in his body. Every day, he was getting stronger, fitter, more powerful, becoming the Guardian and soldier he was before The Rim Shield massacre, and he felt good. He took a firm grip on two root ends, braced against the earth, and heaved, straining against the stump, willing his muscles to overcome its weight. The stump impassively resisted. He released his tension and breathed. Then he lunged forward with renewed vigour, pushing, lifting. The stump shuddered, groaned, and he felt it move, but he couldn't maintain his effort. He grunted and eased off. Breath gathered, he attacked the stump again.

Someone was waiting in his tree home. He felt it even before he climbed inside. Dusk shadows hid the far corner and the presence was there. His warrior instinct made him crouch and cautiously creep forward. Sweet forest breath filled his senses. 'Who's there?' No one answered, but something rustled. He saw a figure and lunged. 'Caught!' he cried triumphantly, as he grappled with flesh, but his joy turned to alarm when he found the flesh soft, compliant, and he heard a squeal of dismay and pain. He released his quarry, overpowered by the fragrance. The intruder sat up. 'Mirith!' he gasped. He screwed up his eyes to make out detail, and saw she wore a necklace and a belt, woven from fresh forest flowers, and nothing else. Astonished, he shifted uneasily away. She whispered Aelendyell words to coax him back, and he needed no translation to guess her intentions. 'Mirith. No,' he hissed. 'We can't.' She reached for him, her braided hair hanging over her breasts, her exquisite, fine frame silhouetted against the outside light. He breathed in the enveloping flowery fragrance and wanted desperately to sink into her. She was beautiful, desirable, sensual – but, when her fingers touched his arms, he checked his desire and grabbed her wrists. 'No, Mirith,' he said firmly, shaking his head. 'This can't happen. It's not right.' She stared into his eyes with hurtful appeal, and he weakened again. She wanted him. That's why she watched him bathe, and followed him. She was the presence. She was there from the beginning, when he sensed her at the far edge of his consciousness, while he was recovering from his wounds. She was everything about his Aelendyell experience. How could he refuse her? What right did he have to refuse her?

His body was willingly responding to her touch. What passions could she bring from him? 'No!' he yelled angrily. He pushed to his feet, strode to the edge of his tree home, and clambered down the ladder, without looking back. When he reached the ground, he let out an almighty groan of despair, and ran into the forest.

The dreams persisted. They reared out of the darkness, leaping over the passing weeks, searching through Wynwuduholt, plunging through the Elder's protection spell to invade his sleep with the same clarity and intensity, night after night. He woke in a cold sweat, sometimes crying out, sometimes lashing out in the dark at imaginary creatures. The Haagii poured over The Rim Shield, drowning his friends in a river of black blood. Dragons swept through the dark skies, their maws aflame. Alain called to him. Artega howled, and struggled through a sea of bodies. And always, always, the Haagii gathered in a circle around him, sneering, laughing.

Andra stood at the edge of Hustingbeam clearing, in the darkness of night, studying the glow shrouding the tree and the circle of Elders, and the Chanter rotating above it. He saw terrible beauty in their spell power. 'I must go.'

'I have been awaiting this request,' said Elder Tirenythlae, 'but the protecting glyph cannot be broken yet. The Ealdfeond remain.'

Andra saw the Aelendyell staring at his brothers, trapped in the circle of their own making. Did he regret not being there? 'Is there no way out? Am I trapped here?' he asked.

Tirenythlae remained transfixed a moment longer, before he answered, 'No. There is a way. Chanter Pyraneth foresaw you would need to leave. He left a key for you, in my keeping.'

'Thank you,' Andra sighed.

'But,' the Elder continued, 'there is great danger

involved. The key might enable you to pass through the protecting spell. Our messengers use it in times of great necessity. But, you see, no worold-buend has ever used an Aelendyell spell. If the key doesn't shield you from the protecting spell - '

'I understand,' Andra replied quickly, 'but I'll take the risk. I can't remain in Wudufaesten. I need to return to my own people, to The Vale, where I belong.'

Tirenythlae nodded. 'Pyraneth said you would choose to go. Come. I will arrange your leaving, if that is your wish.'

'That is my wish,' said Andra.

Twelve

The party paused five paces from a shimmering ripple in the texture of the air. Beyond the glyph, Andra saw the wanton devastation wrought by the Haagii, the forest scarred by dark patches of scorched earth and blackened trunks and stumps of burnt elmoaks, and the surviving greenery stained with browns and oranges of dead and dying leaves. The Haagii destroyed the forest's beauty with deliberate hatred, and, but for the protecting glyph, the same fate awaited Wudufaesten.

'This is where you can pass,' Terath announced, and he pointed to a rune scribed on the earth. 'The Watchers report there are no Haagii camps near here. The closest is to the south. A hundred Haagii corpses lie at the edge of the spell ring, but we don't know what lies beyond that fringe. Before the Haagii did this, it was a day's steady walk from here to the edge of Wynwuduholt. Are you sure you want to go?' Terath asked.

Andra turned to him. 'Yes. I no longer have a choice.'

Terath nodded. 'I understand.' He reached inside his tunic and withdrew a silver chain with a tiny amber pendant, which he placed around Andra's neck. 'Elder Tirenythlae said you were to wear this. It has a spell of Elvenaar origin. When you pass through, the pendant will vanish.' He paused to look Andra directly in the eyes. 'You know there's a danger?'

'Yes. Tirenythlae told me.'

A hand touched Andra's shoulder, and he turned to Freyar who stood beside him, holding a bow and quiver. He spoke in Aelendyell, which Terath translated for Andra. 'Freyar wants you to take his bow, as a gift. He says you need more than a wooden staff, once you go beyond the protecting spell.'

Andra knew an Aelendyell didn't part lightly with his bow. He also knew he couldn't refuse Freyar's offer, without offending him. He accepted the gift with a grateful smile, and said, in halting Aelendyell, the best he could manage, 'Thank you. You are hondgesella, Freyar.' Freyar's eyes widened with wonder, and the others gasped as they realised he used their language, albeit roughly. Then Freyar laughed, and clasped Andra tightly in friendship. The bond was sealed in parting. Andra bade farewell to those who accompanied him to the edge of Wudufaesten, before turned to Terath. 'I can't thank you for my life,' he said quietly, 'only owe it to you, and Mirith. I won't forget.'

'You carry our trust, Andra of The Vale,' Terath replied. 'No worold-buend has been to Wudufaesten in my living memory. Remember that also, my friend.'

'I understand,' Andra confirmed. 'Say goodbye to Mirith. I didn't –'

'I'll tell her,' Terath cut in. 'She knows you are going. She asked me to give you something, just before you step through.'

Terath walked with Andra to the point where the Elder's spell divided Wudufaesten from the world beyond. He handed Andra a small food bag and a waterskin. 'Elder Tirenythlae said you must clasp the amber gem between your index fingers and concentrate on a point you intend to reach beyond the point you leave,' he carefully explained. 'If you lose concentration, even for a moment, the spell will break.' He held out a small, embroidered pouch. 'Mirith's gift.'

Andra took the pouch. It was light, but when he opened it he saw blue powder within. 'What is it?' he asked, perplexed.

'Healing powder,' Terath replied, 'like the powder Mirith used on my wounds, after the battle in Wudufaesten, only much stronger. It's rare. Mirith and Nathenyell, alone, know its secrets in Wudufaesten. You rub the powder into an open wound and the wound will heal. The healing process is slow, and you'll slip into a deep sleep, but it will work. Your wounds were healed with it. Mirith has never given any away.'

Andra held the pouch softly. 'Tell Mirith – tell her – I am greatly honoured,' he murmured.

Terath placed a hand on Andra's shoulder and spoke in a low voice so the others couldn't hear him. 'Mirith is my byrd-frithmage. There is no real translation for that in your tongue. The closest worold-buend word is 'sister', but she is more than that to me, and I to her. We're very close, closer than I can explain. She tells me all her secrets, Andra. I know why you must leave – all your reasons, my friend.' He forced Andra to meet his gaze. 'I know Mirith's heart is with you.'

Andra shuffled uneasily as Terath made his revelation. 'Terath, I –' he stammered, but Terath interrupted before he could begin to explain his feelings.

'There's no time,' he said, stepping back. 'Go. Work the spell. May you journey with Elvenaar guidance and fulfil an Elvenaar ellen-weorc!'

Andra watched Terath retreat to his Aelendyell companions. He wanted to explain, wanted to return to Wudufaesten, wanted to see Mirith, but knew he could not. His path led elsewhere.

He swallowed hard and faced the shimmering field. He grasped the amber pendant between his index fingers, as Terath instructed. It was cold. He had to concentrate on a point of destination. He chose a shattered elm-oak trunk, twenty paces away, concentrated, and advanced. The air crackled with wild energy, as he entered the glyph's field of magic, and it tugged at his clothing, wrenched his hair. With each step, greater violence swirled round him, until he feared he was going to be blown off his feet and torn apart by the raging winds. Heat erupted. He forced fear from his mind and concentrated on the tree trunk. It drifted closer, closer, as he pushed against the pressure of the protecting spell created by the Elders and the Chanter of Wudufaesten.

The winds abruptly ceased, replaced by a cooling breeze on his face. Three more steps. He reached the burnt trunk. He'd passed through. He eased the pressure on his index fingers, realising the amber gem had dissolved, as

109

Tirenythlae promised.

When he turned toward Wudufaesten, where the rich green forest fringe ran in a curve, and right to its edge there were signs of burning, Terath, Freyar and their companions waved. Then the Aelendyell melted into the forest, as if they were never there. He was outside, alone, and if Terath was accurate, a day's walk from the nearest human habitation. He shouldered Freyar's bow, checked he had everything, and began his trek through the twisted wasteland.

Haagii tracks crisscrossed the charcoal ash, but Andra avoided them, risking leaving an individual trail for the curious to follow in his determination to get out of the devastated forest.

At midday, he crept down a creek bank and washed the caked layer of ash from his face. He nibbled bright violet wild-berries from the food-pack Terath provided and rested under the cover of a partly charred bush at the bank's edge.

As he rested, he heard guttural grunts, close by. He crouched and listened. The Haagii were arguing, as they approached and passed. He hoped they wouldn't notice his tracks, in the ashes, leading like a beacon to where he was hiding. The Haagii stopped a couple of paces from the bush and broke into boisterous argument again. Andra hazarded a peek and counted five enemy warriors. He wanted to reach for his staff, but it was strapped to his back, and movement might attract his foes. The argument abruptly ceased. One Haagii turned and appeared to stare straight at the young Guardian. Andra tensed, ready for discovery, but another grunt distracted the Haagii's gaze, and he returned his attention to his fellows, oblivious to Andra's presence.

The Haagii moved on, but Andra stayed in the bush for a long time before he chanced creeping out. The Haagii tracks disappeared into the forest. Satisfied he was safe, he clambered down the bank, waded the shallow creek, climbed the other side, and continued east.

Later in the afternoon, as shadows of the burnt elm-oak trunks cast skeletal shadow fingers across the wasteland, he skirted three Haagii encampments, the last a large one on an island, in a fork of streams. Though tempted to estimate numbers to see what the camps contained, he pressed on, avoiding risk of capture, knowing he had to reach a human settlement before darkness. From there he could plan a journey home, however far he was from it.

He reached the perimeter of Wynwuduholt at dusk. Beyond the forest was a vista of low hills and valleys, studded with copses and single trees, and a dark smudge of mountains rose in the distance. He remembered Terath's instructions, before he stepped onto a road that ran north/south, bordering the forest. The Aelendyell said nothing about a road, only that Andra should head due east once he was beyond the edge of Wynwuduholt. He wondered if the Aelendyell had forgotten this detail? Or perhaps I've emerged at the wrong point? Following the road seems the obvious choice because it will lead to villages and towns, but how far will I need to travel from this point before I find one? Terath told him to head east. Trusting his friend's advice, Andra cut across the road, into the hills.

The rising moon is a blessing and a curse, he mused, as he moved up and down hill and valley, searching for village lights. The moon lit his way with its silvery wash across the landscape, making travel easy, but he zigzagged from cover to cover because its light could easily betray him to wandering enemy patrols. He wasn't certain the Haagii had ventured beyond the forest, or would be patrolling in the dark, but he wasn't prepared to take unnecessary risks to find out.

As much as he searched, there were no village lights, and no village. The breeze freshened. Clouds scudded across the face of the moon, darkening the sky and land. Terath inexplicably misinformed him. No. He knew his Aelendyell friend would never do that. It was more likely that he'd lost his way backtracking in Wynwuduholt to avoid Haagii. The road was his only option.

He began a frustrating, fruitless search for the narrow ribbon he crossed at dusk, and in the end, cold and tired, he stumbled upon a deserted hovel at the crest of a hill. The door was torn off, and no one dwelt within, so he made a rough bed, ate, drank a little, and drifted into restless sleep.

Morning sunlight slanted through a gap in the wooden wall onto his face. Andra rubbed his eyes, and sat up, shaking out his black hair. He ran his fingers through his locks and measured them by feel. His hair had grown, since he spent time in the forest, but he no longer wore a Guardian ponytail. He felt he had to earn the right to wear it again. The massacre on The Rim Shield robbed him of his badge of honour as a Guardian among his people in The Vale. He had to return home, and begin again, because the old Andra died in the dust of Dragon Breath Plains during the retreat. Wudufaesten was his rebirth. He was alive again, refreshed, but no longer a worthy Guardian, not until he journeyed home. He picked up his staff and bow, and walked out of the deserted, musty hovel, into the crisp morning air.

Patches of white mist huddled from the sun's probing light in the valleys. To the west, Wynwuduholt stretched north and south as far as he could see, and smoke columns rose at points along the forest's edge. He turned south – and then he saw it, at the foot of the hill on which he stood – a village. A rough track led from the hut. Terath had been right with his directions. Andra simply missed it in the darkness.

Excited, he ran down the hillside, glad to be returning to his human world, but, as he drew closer, his exhilaration evaporated like the disappearing morning mist. The few remaining buildings were blackened and scorched by fire, and at the centre, by a partially destroyed well, lay a pile of cremated corpses, grotesque limbs jutting out. The rancid stench of death hung in the air.

He searched the ruins, finding nothing useful, only mutilated corpses that hadn't been dragged to the communal pyre. In one storehouse, untouched by fire, he found the body of a woman huddled over her three dead children, her arm curled around them in a futile gesture to protect her babies from the axes of the merciless Haagii. The smallest child's cold, sightless eyes stared in horror at the shattered doorway. The grisly discovery flooded Andra with anger, and he rushed outside, and yelled his impotence at the sky, until his throat hurt, and he collapsed and sobbed for all his dead friends.

Later, he climbed the hill to survey the land. The mountains east looked like the Andrakian Mountains, but he wasn't certain. The Aelendyell knew little of Thana's Kingdom, and nothing of the Great City. Elder Tirenythlae gave him scant information, to help him find his way home, explaining that, apart from the village to the east, the Aelendyell had heard of a worold-buend town to the south, but no Aelendyell from Wudufaesten had ever been there. Andra had to make his own choice. The road had solidity.

Haagii ruled the road. Andra spotted the enemy patrols before they saw him and slipped into the low hills to follow the road from a distance, travelling south, along the ridges to keep it in view. Throughout the day, he came across detritus left by the invaders – bones, discarded rubbish, old campfires – and five times he spotted Haagii warriors wandering the road. Fortunately, the weather was cool and breezy, making rapid travel easy for him, but he found three villages like the first – burned, the inhabitants slaughtered – and he began to wonder if all his world had perished, and he was the last remaining one.

Lost in a fog of despondency, he stumbled blindly over a crest, and blundered into a Haagii foraging party. Their undivided attention on something resembling a hessian bag, and their stunned surprise at his sudden appearance, saved him from death, and by the time they drew their swords he had sprinted to a rocky outcrop. Discovering fresher game, the three Haagii discarded their object of interest and advanced. Andra unhitched Freyar's bow from his shoulder, nocked an arrow, drew aim and fired. The shaft buried into the central Haagii's shoulder, and he crumpled, howling with pain. His companions hesitated. Andra seized his opportunity and charged, staff whirling, smashing the nearest Haagii's sword from his grasp. As the Haagii recoiled, Andra brought the staff up under his chin, knocking him senseless. The third Haagii panicked, seeing Andra turn to attack him, and ran, leaving his wounded companion to Andra's mercy.

Andra watched the fleeing Haagii bolt down the hillside before crossing to the wounded one. Contorted with pain, the Haagii's flat, leathery visage looked uglier than ever. The black eyes flicked open. Seeing his tormentor, the enraged Haagii spat, and Andra dodged a vicious kick before he brought his staff swiftly down across the Haagii's temple, killing him.

Andra examined the object that had amused the Haagii. The rags squirmed when he touched them, and he jumped back in alarm, staff ready. The rags wriggled again. A voice squealed, 'Let me go, you rats! When my dad gets you, he'll kill all of you!' Andra cautiously poked the rag pile with his staff, which prompted another shrill outburst. 'Leave me alone! I hate you, hate you, hate you!' the rags screamed.

Andra rolled the pile over, and tousled brown hair and a girl's dirty face appeared. She spat. 'Nice to meet you,' he said, wiping the spittle from his face.

The girl's eyes were bright, uncommonly bright blue. 'Who are you?' she demanded suspiciously.

'I'm Andra. You?'

'Milly,' she coldly replied. 'That's what my dad calls me. My real name's Millander, but I like Milly.' She looked past Andra and asked, warily, 'Where are they?'

'Who?'

'The Hagmen.'

'They're gone,' said Andra. 'I chased them away. Where's your dad?'

Milly shook her head and looked downcast. 'I don't know.'

Andra helped the girl out of the rags, that turned out to be a crude bag, and loosened her arm and ankle bonds. He guessed her age at twelve, or thereabouts, but in her present condition her age was difficult to judge. She was dirty, bruised, her smock shredded, and she had a long, weeping cut across her back. 'Does that hurt?' he asked.

She rocked her head. 'Uhuh. A lot. The Hagman cut me with his sword when I tried to run away.'

'Turn around.'

'Why?'

'I want to look at the cut.'

Milly turned reluctantly. 'You're not going to hurt me?' she guardedly asked.

'No,' he replied, as he studied the wound. It was long, deep, and turning septic. He untied and opened Mirith's pouch. 'Hold still. I'm going to put some healing powder on the cut.'

'Will it hurt?'

'No.' Andra sprinkled blue powder into the cut. 'Lean forward.' The girl obeyed, and he filled the wound with Mirith's magical dust.

'It tingles!' she said, shrugging. 'But it doesn't hurt as much now.' She turned to him and smiled. 'Thank you. I feel sleepy,' she mumbled. 'I'm going to sit down.' She slumped to the ground. A moment later she was fast asleep.

Andra closed the pouch and hooked it on his belt. He knew they couldn't stay there. The Haagii who escaped would return with others. He collected his gear and stooped to lift the sleeping child into his arms. She was light to carry.

Only once did he have to seek cover, to avoid a roving Haagii band, during the late afternoon. Toward evening, he found a resting place, in a clump of trees, on a hillside overlooking the road. It was a good vantage point from which to keep watch. He placed his sleeping burden on the earth and made her as comfortable as he could. The hillside protected them from the stiffening breeze. He would like to have lit a fire to warm them, but that would be death, so as sleep enclosed him he cuddled the child to protect her from the cold air. For the first night, in a long time, he slept without dreaming.

Thirteen

For two days and nights, Andra carried Milly's unconscious form, as he headed southward, shadowing the road from the neighbouring hills.

The first day, he backtracked several times to dodge Haagii squads, and he discovered two more human villages, buildings burned, and the inhabitants slaughtered like the first, but he avoided entering them. Late that evening, he saw much of Wynwuduholt ablaze, the fires making the dark sky above the forest glow crimson and gold, as the invisible pall of smoke blanketed the stars. The Haagii were actively spreading their fiery destruction, and the size of one fire told Andra an Aelendyell tun had been less fortunate than Wudufaesten. Warrior for warrior, he knew the Haagii could never match the Aelendyell for courage or skill, but they poured out of the desert of Dragon Breath Plains like a vast, interminable tide of death, intent on overwhelming even the strongest resistance through sheer weight of numbers.

The second day, signs of Haagii movement on the road lessened considerably, and by mid-afternoon he'd travelled some time without finding any sign of Haagii disturbance. Wynwuduholt curved westward, toward a barely visible cliff in the distance, but the road continued south, across a flat plain, toward another dark patch of forest. His burden was tiring him, and his food supply was nearly exhausted. He considered veering west, into the forest margin to gather berries and nuts, but decided against the risk of Wynwuduholt. Besides, he reminded himself, he travelled most of the day without happening upon a village, so one would be close.

From the last crest, before the hills sank into a wide plain, he spied a town astride crossroads. The road he shadowed cut through the town and continued south. Another road spanned east/west from the eastern mountains, through the town, and along the southern Wynwuduholt margin. Dotted at varying distances around the town were huts and sheds, and Andra passed three such establishments on his way toward the town.

He stopped at the first hut, but found no inhabitants. The place was bare and deserted, a discovery that filled him with foreboding, but there were no signs of burning, or death, normally present after the Haagii passed. The second and third buildings yielded nothing either. The people were gone – but to where? And why?

He cautiously approached the town, assessing and noting possible cover the outlying buildings might offer. If the enemy were already in the town, he needed a quick escape plan. Evening was closing in, which was to his advantage, but the flat plain was treeless, and there was nowhere close to elude pursuers. He could never outrun them carrying the sleeping child.

Nearer to the town, he became aware of a dark shape: a wall. He'd never seen a wall encircling a Kingdom town, but perhaps these people knew the Haagii were within two days of their town and they had fortified to resist attacks. He hoped his assumption would bear fruit.

He followed the perimeter of the wooden palisade to a gate entrance on its eastern side. Dark figures moved along a parapet, and a voice challenged him from a crude tower above the gate. 'Who goes there?'

Apart from Milly's brief exchange, it was the first human voice he'd heard for months. 'My name is Andra,' he replied.

'What's your purpose?' the voice asked taciturnly.

'I have a child needing attention.'

'Where have you come from?'

'North.'

Stony silence greeted his answer. Wondering impatiently what was taking the tower guard so long to respond, he called, 'Can I bring in the child?'

He heard furious whispers above, followed by another pause. Wood scraped against wood, and the gate eased open, barely enough for him to squeeze through with Milly.

He was greeted with a hedge of spear points and mistrustful faces. 'Put the child down!' a man ordered.

'She's sleeping,' Andra answered amiably. The last thing he wanted, under the circumstances, was to aggravate his hosts.

'Put her down!' the voice repeated with greater emphasis. Andra shrugged, and obliged by gently lowering Milly to the ground. As he straightened, hands wrenched the staff and bow from his back, but he relaxed, concentrating on remaining calm, despite his unwelcome treatment. A spear poked him menacingly in his chest. 'Now, where do you come from?' a harsh voice inquired.

Andra recalled the nervous response he received for his previous answer to the same question. 'The Vale,' he answered.

'Where's that?'

'North of the Great City.'

The men exchanged more whispers, and Andra noticed their spear points lower. 'What brings you here, so far from the Great City?' a man queried.

'I serve in the Great King's Armies.'

The spear points pulled away, but his answer was greeted with objectionable disbelief. 'A mercenary!' a voice interjected. 'No wonder he carries light weapons and no armour.'

The interrogator stepped from the shadows, a heavily bearded man, with a face bloated from indulgent drinking and eating, and squinting eyes. 'Under normal circumstances, I'd see you run out of the town on the end of a pike,' he scowled, 'but these aren't ordinary times no more. We need every arm we can get, and a seasoned arm most of all. Follow me.'

'What about the girl?' Andra asked, glancing at Milly's sleeping form.

'She'll be properly cared for,' the man curtly replied. 'For now, you come with me.'

Andra followed his host's stout frame. The few people in doorways, along the street, watched him warily as he passed, and he felt distrust permeating the town. The bearded man turned left into an inn doorway and knocked. From within, a voice ordered 'Enter,' and Andra's escort stepped aside to usher him in.

The smoky room stank of stale beer. Several faces turned to scrutinize him. 'This way,' said his escort, leading him to a round table, where five men were smoking long, thin pipes.

A tall, broad-shouldered man stood to greet him. 'Who have you got here?' the tall man asked.

'This one was at the gates just now, carrying a little girl. He claims he's come from the Great City,' the guide explained.

The tall man studied Andra, taking in every detail, before he said, 'Sit,' to Andra, and added, 'I'll see to this, Franklin,' dismissing the stout man. Andra pulled a rickety seat to the table, and sat, but the smoke cloud generated by the men's pipes at the table made him cough violently. 'Get him an ale!' the tall man shouted. A mug of foaming brew was set beside Andra's arm, and he took a pull at the ale, enjoying the cool wet sensation in his throat. 'Thirsty?' the tall man asked.

Andra nodded. 'Yes. My water ran out.'

'What's your name?'

'Andra.'

The tall man pointed through the blue haze. 'I'm Carrol. This is Dirk, Ferret, Mark, Len the Greaser.' Each man acknowledged Andra as he was introduced. Three had the rustic look of farmers, but Ferret's beady eyes suggested an honest day's work was not in his normal line of business. His face reflected a darker form of cockiness Andra associated with his lost friend, Tim Gaelus. 'So, who's the little girl?' Carrol asked.

Andra knew, from his experience with Franklin the gatekeeper, that his answers had to be carefully worded. 'I found her unconscious. Do you have a healer in the town?'

Carrol nodded. 'Sister Emiris will see to her.' He leaned across the table and asked, 'Why do you come to Spurl?'

Andra weighed up the possible reaction of this stranger

119

to the truth. If he knew for certain where he was, he could mask the truth with greater art, but lying didn't come easy to a Guardian. Still, he had a vow to keep to Terath and the Aelendyell, not to reveal where he had been, which he would never forsake, especially to strangers. 'Curiosity,' he said. 'I haven't seen much of the Kingdom, beyond my home and the Great City.' He watched Carrol's face for a sign of mistrust, but the man remained solid and serious, as if awaiting further explanation.

Andra chose to add nothing more, so the tall man leaned back and grinned. 'You carry weapons. You dress light and travel light. Only a hunter or mercenary would do this in these times. How many Haagii did you see?'

Andra relaxed. He could honestly answer Carrol's questions about the Haagii. 'A few, but there's a host in the hills and forest north of here.'

Carrol nodded again. 'That much we know. The palisade around the town was built last week. We've got people from the villages, north of here, who escaped the Haagii raids, but not many. The Haagii burned and slaughtered wherever they went. So much for the Great King's promises!' He spat to the side of the table to express his disgust with Thana.

Dirk's voice, deep but cracked, cut in. 'Some say the Great King's Armies were massacred, and we've naught to protect us from them followers of the Dark Lord but ourselves. What've you heard?'

Andra saw the labour of seasons in the farmer's furrowed lines. 'It could be true,' he said warily, 'but the Great King has other armies.'

'If he has,' said Mark, with an edge of bitterness, 'he's keeping them around the Great City, and letting us who live this far west do as we may well please!'

There is much resentment in this town, thought Andra. The Great King has abandoned his people. 'How far west are you?' he asked.

Carrol looked at him curiously. 'I thought you said you'd travelled from the Great City.'

'I have,' Andra corrected, trying to cover his error. 'But I didn't travel direct. I hunted a bit. This is all new territory for me.'

Carrol carefully considered Andra's reply, before answering his question. 'Seven days by the Great King's roads. Four and a half days, or so, across the countryside.'

'And where's the next town?'

'Port,' said Dirk. 'Two days south. It's a city these days.'

The conversation turned to preparations in the town for impending Haagii attacks. 'Of course, you'll stay to help defend the town,' Carrol directed to Andra.

'No,' he said quietly. 'I must return to The Vale. There's great peril facing my people, and as a Guardian I have no other choice but to be there.' He was aware of the men staring with disapproval.

'As you choose,' said Carrol with a disappointed grunt. 'But we can't give you more than a day's provision if you leave. We've more need of it here – women and children to feed if the Haagii attack.' He paused to let his message weigh on Andra's conscience. 'Your business at this table is ended. See Sister Emiris if you want a place to sleep tonight. She'll find space in her stables.'

'Where do I find her?' Andra asked.

'In the convent, beyond Rata Lane. Ask anyone on night patrol. They'll direct you. Leave us to our preparations.' Carrol turned his attention to the others, dismissing Andra from their company.

Outside the inn, Andra was glad to breathe fresh air again, but the darkness was depressing. They expected him to stay and help defend the town, but he knew that, when the Haagii came the palisade, the mercenaries and farmers wouldn't stop them, no matter how desperate the defenders were. If two Wheels of the Great King's Armies, ten thousand trained warriors, were swept aside by the Haagii on The Rim Shield, what hope did a mere town of untrained and frightened people have before a numerous and relentless enemy? He fought his guilt. The Vale called him. He had to return home.

By asking, he found his way to the small stone gateway

of the convent, where a woman in a dark cloak and cap met him. She wanted to know his purpose, and when he explained, she let him enter. 'I am Sister Carita,' she said politely. 'Welcome to our holy home.' The woman lifted a candle to light the way across the tiny courtyard, and by its light Andra glimpsed the woman's face. She wasn't very old, he judged, but she was mature. Her cap drooped to mask her dark hair, and he saw a pretty face trying not to look pretty. 'The child sleeps still. What happened to her?' the woman asked as they walked.

'Haagii attacked her village,' Andra explained. 'I think her parents were killed, but I'm not sure. I found her enslaved by a group of Haagii.'

'Then you have done a great kindness by her, and she will forever be in your debt. Veras, bless the name,' Carita replied. She led Andra through two doors, along a corridor, and into a small candle-lit room. A woman, wearing the same dark green garments and bending over Milly's sleeping form, turned and smiled as they entered. A lock of greying hair escaped the confines of her cap. 'Sister Emiris,' said Carita softly. 'This man brought the child into the town.'

Sister Emiris straightened and made a circular sign in the air before Andra. 'Veras keep you,' she said. 'I am Sister Emiris.'

'Andra,' he replied. 'How is she?'

'Resting,' she informed him, 'but she's strong.'

The sleeping girl's rags had been removed, and she'd been washed and dressed in a clean white nightgown. The tired, angry child he rescued in the hills had the innocent beauty of all sleeping children. 'Thank you,' he said to Emiris, who smiled again.

'We thank you,' she replied. 'But now we must let her sleep.' Sister Emiris shuffled them out of the room and closed the door. 'Have you eaten?' she asked. He shook his head. 'Then eat with us,' she offered. 'We would welcome your company.'

Emiris and Carita led him along three corridors, but as they passed one partially open door, he glanced in and saw several women and children sharing food, or bedding down for the night. 'Who are they?' he asked as they continued.

'Poor farming folk who lost husbands and brothers to the Great King's Armies,' Carita answered. 'They are part of our family now.'

He swallowed, wondering which men he marched north with belonged here in his place. Did the people know their husbands, sons, fathers were slaughtered by the Haagii and dragons?

'What troubles you?'

Sister Emiris' question startled him out of his contemplation. 'Just unpleasant thoughts.' He observed her dark eyes trying to read his face.

She turned to a door and opened it. 'Please,' she gestured. He entered an austere small room furnished with a table and five chairs. Women wearing the same garb as his hostess occupied three spaces. A modest fare of fruit, salad, bread and water was spread on the table. 'Sit there,' Emiris indicated. 'I will fetch another chair.' She left by one of three doors in the room and returned with a wooden chair.

All five women bowed their heads, and made a circular sign on their chests, as Emiris sat. One recited a prayer of thanksgiving. 'Veras bless the food which we now take to renew the energy we use in your holy work. We offer our thanks for the path you have shown us, the love you shine upon us, and the humility you teach us every day. Always be it so. Veras, bless the name.'

When the prayer ended, Emiris turned to Andra. 'Our guest at supper is Andra.' She turned to the others. 'He brought the little girl out of the bonds of the Dark Ones.' The sisters faced him, smiled and made the circular gesture. Emiris said to Andra, 'They offer you a blessing.' She lifted bread towards him.

The meal was passed wordlessly. Andra respected their silence, and ate quietly, and not until water was poured in each goblet did Emiris speak to him again. 'The girl carried a terrible wound on her back. Am I right in saying it is only freshly healed?'

123

'It is,' he replied.

'How?'

He couldn't explain to her that he used Aelendyell healing powder. Terath and Mirith warned him to keep their Aelendyell existence secret. 'Something I was given a long time ago by an old friend in The Vale. I used it on the girl's wound.'

'It healed wondrously,' observed Emiris. 'Is there more?'

'Unfortunately, no. There was barely enough for the girl.' He lied again. Twice in one day. That he lied to this gentle-natured woman, who seemed full of caring and kindness, made him feel sick in the pit of his stomach, but he had no choice because of his binding oath to Terath.

After the meal, Sister Emiris took Andra to a small chamber and, when she opened the door, he saw a bed, and on it his bow and staff, and gear the gatekeepers had taken from him. 'You can sleep here,' she said. 'I will wake you early so you can journey on.'

Her unexpected offer perplexed him. 'How did you know I was leaving? I could be staying to help defend your town.'

'I know you are not,' she said.

'How?'

'You are drawn to your home, Andra. You must go there. Your path, though, is fraught with danger, every step of the way, and you will not complete your journey home until you master a great challenge and become something more than you are now.'

Sister Emiris' revelation stunned him. 'I don't understand what you mean, Sister,' he confessed. 'How do you know these things? What challenge do I face?'

'How do I know?' Emiris asked. 'Veras has given me the blessing of a vision. I've seen what will or might be. If you stay in Spurl, you'll die like everyone else. That is not your destiny, so you must leave in the morning. I ask only one favour. Take the child with you. She is part of your destiny, though Veras has not revealed how.'

'I can't take the child,' he argued. 'She's still ill. I'll be travelling fast, and across the countryside -'

'Take the child,' Emiris insisted. 'There is no other way. In the morning, she will be well again. And I will see that you get horses.'

'I can't ride.'

'The child will teach you,' replied Emiris. 'But enough. You also need sleep. Goodnight,' she said perfunctorily. She made a circular sign, and headed for her chamber, leaving Andra staring after her receding form, swimming in a pool of confusion.

Fourteen

Pre-dawn light filtered through a ceiling of grey clouds as Andra stretched and slipped the bow over his shoulder. 'Aren't they pretty?' Milly said, stroking the nose of a bay horse.

Andra studied the chestnut mount being led toward him and felt decidedly uncomfortable. 'Yes. They're beautiful creatures,' he agreed, trying to mask his anxiety. He remembered the Haardrishii war horses entering The Vale, their riders carrying Great King Thana's order to conscript all Kingdom warriors into his Great Armies for the war against the Haagii. They were great black steeds of muscle, their hides covered with segments of shiny ebony armour. The horses before him were small in comparison to the magnificent warhorses, but he respected Milly's enthusiasm for the creatures. She'd woken from her long healing sleep, as if nothing had happened, her eyes bright and happy.

'This one's called Yarela, and yours is Chester. They like me,' she chattered, as she snuggled against the bay's neck.

Sister Carita handed Andra a rein, and said, 'Chester is a friendly horse. He knows what a rider expects and does all the work for you. In fact, if you talk to him, he will understand. The reins just help steer direction, sometimes. There is not much else to know. Oh, except if you ask him to run, he will run like the wind.' Andra noticed the horse's ears prick forward as Carita uttered the word 'run'. The woman laughed. 'See? Do not use that word unless it is needed.' Milly had clambered aboard Yarela and was walking him around the small stable enclosure, at the back of the convent. She crooned into the horse's ear at every opportunity. 'Milly loves horses,' said Sister Carita, with a fond smile. 'Sister Emiris says her father was a farrier. He put shoes on horses.'

'How does Sister Emiris know that?' he asked.

'She has a talent, blessed by Veras,' Carita replied. 'Sister Emiris somehow can look at a person, and know where they've been and where they are going next.'

Andra could not grasp Carita's explanation any more than when Emiris revealed her vision to him the previous night. The women were full of personal riddles and mysteries. 'Do you have a talent?' he asked.

Carita smiled. 'In a way. I can tell whether a person I meet has good or bad within them. It doesn't matter if they try to mask it. I see their true being. You are a good man, and Milly a good child at heart, though a girl of mischief too.'

A door in the main building creaked open, and Sister Emiris emerged, carrying two bags. 'These are provisions for you and Milly, enough for ten days,' she said, as she approached.

Andra gratefully accepted her offering. 'I should stay.'

Sister Emiris shook her head. 'You know you cannot. One more warrior in this town will make no difference when the Haagii come.'

'And they will come, won't they?' he asked.

'Yes,' said Emiris firmly. 'They will come.'

'Then why don't you get the people to leave? Why don't you and the sisters get out before the Haagii come?'

'The men in this town believe they can turn the Haagii away,' Emiris said, shaking her head sadly. 'They will not leave. The women and children won't leave their men. And we can't leave because there will be many who will need comforting at the end, and because I've seen the vision for us. There is no other place to run. Soon the Haagii will spread everywhere, and the Dark Ones will strive to dominate all people. The Sisters of Veras have no role to play beyond Spurl and our convent. Veras has shown me that we must stay here.'

Andra desperately wanted to tell Emiris that her visions were nonsense, that she could change them, that no one can see what will really happen in the future, but he was stopped by the certain gaze on Emiris' face, a resignation no argument would alter. 'I can only thank you for your

127

kindness and help,' he said. 'I wish there was more -' but he left his sentence unsaid.

'You must go before daylight reaches over the mountains,' Emiris said calmly. 'The watch sleep at the eastern gate. Go with Veras' blessing.'

Andra struggled onto his horse, took a final look at the small and silent sisters in the semi-light, wheeled unsteadily, and followed Milly out of the stable yard. The street was empty, except for four stray dogs that lifted inquisitive noses to watch them pass. Sister Emiris was right when they reached the eastern gate. Both guards were sleeping. Andra dismounted, and quietly lifted the locking beam, before he ushered Milly and the horses through the gates and followed. Outside, he called, 'Watch ho!' remounted, and the pair headed due east.

'Why did you shout?' Milly asked, as they rode away from Spurl.

'I couldn't let them leave the gate unlocked, could I?' he replied.

'How did you make me better?' she asked.

'It's a secret. One day I'll tell you.'

'Are you a magician?'

He laughed. 'No Milly, I'm no magician.'

'Oh.' The tone of decided disappointment told him he'd diminished in her estimation.

Sunrays spread a mantle across the distant mountains, and snowy peaks glittered, as the morning sun struggled to peer over. Andra tried adjusting to the horse's rhythm, but he felt like he was constantly slipping from the saddle.

By contrast, Milly relaxed and chatted about features of the countryside. She drew his attention, when Spurl threatened to slip from sight behind them, and later pointed out a line of trees bordering a meandering river, which cut their path. They passed abandoned farms and a tiny hamlet, vacated for the assumed safety of Spurl. The plain dissolved into gentle hills, and the motion up and down slopes only made Andra feel more precarious atop his horse.

At midday, they halted on a crest, overlooking a sweeping bend in the river, and from their elevated position Andra studied the sparkling waters, wondering how they were going to cross. He searched the riverbank for a bridge or potential ford, until he spied a dark shape beneath willows on the near bank: a barge. 'There's a man on that punt,' said Milly cheerfully. 'He might take us over.'

'He might,' said Andra, 'but we'd better be careful. And, if he wants money, we'll have to find another way.'

'Money's not a problem,' Milly replied, as she kicked her horse forward. 'I've got some.'

Andra followed her down the hillside, clinging to the mane of his mount. She had money? How? The child surprised him. Aware there might be danger at the punt, he tried to catch her, but it was all he could manage merely to stay in his saddle, and by the time he reached the riverbank she was talking to a man aboard his punt. 'Milly!' Andra scolded, as he reined in Chester.

Milly ignored his chastising glare. 'The man says he'll take us across for a gold piece.' She reached inside the red tunic Sister Emiris had given her and withdrew a small leather pouch, which she opened. A gold coin glittered between her fingertips before she tossed it to the ferryman.

'Where did you get that?' Andra asked, unable to hide his astonishment.

'Sister Carita said you'd need some money to get to the Great City. She and Sister Emiris gave it to me to hold.' She replaced the pouch in her tunic and urged Yarela onto the punt.

Andra greeted the ferryman, as he boarded, a stout man, broad-shouldered from his trade, but noticed the man's eyes were fixed on something else. 'We've company as it seems,' he said. Andra turned in his saddle to look back up the hill Milly and he descended. On the crest, were armed warriors and, by their stature, he recognised them as Haagii. 'I don't like their looks, lad,' the ferryman remarked. 'Can you pole a punt?'

'I can learn,' Andra replied.

The ferryman handed him a second pole, and they set to pushing the punt into the river. Seeing their quarry making an escape, the Haagii broke into a run down the hillside. The punt seemed to move slowly, the Haagii quickly, and they barely poled a quarter of the distance out into the river when the first Haagii reached the riverbank. 'Push harder, lad!' the ferryman yelled, as a spear thudded into an upright post on the ferry's deck. Four more spears fell close to their target, but the distance steadily increased and they were soon out of range, well into the middle of the river, where the long poles barely touched the bottom. The ferry floated with the current, before the ferryman ordered Andra to pole again. 'Now, lad!' he called. 'We've done with drifting. The bottom's within reach. Push!'

Within moments, they reached the bank, and Milly disembarked the horses. The ferryman took the pole from Andra and held out his hand in an open offer of appreciation. 'You'll be needing somewhere to feed your horses and grab a bite to eat. With them mongrels on yon shore, I'll not be plying my trade today, so I'll be going to me home over yon hill, and I'd be pleased if you and the little golden lady would join me.'

Andra took a long look at the Haagii warriors across the river and wondered if they were a loose hunting band, or part of the larger Haagii army descending on Spurl. If he stayed -? 'Are we eating with Bear?' pleaded Milly, pulling at his sleeve.

Andra caught the ferryman's eye. 'Is that your name? Bear?'

'As everyone has been prone to call me, nigh on most me life,' the ferryman replied, with a wink. 'Seems to be to do with me size, I guess.'

Andra smiled, and rubbed Milly's hair playfully. 'Yes, Milly, we'll eat with him.'

The ferryman's hut was a short walk from the river, nested beneath an overhang in the side of a small hill. From the front, Andra estimated the hut to have two rooms.

'There is my home,' Bear said proudly. 'It'll be good to have guests,' he added. He ambled forward and opened the front door, while Milly showed Andra how to hobble the horses. 'Be at your cooking, Hanna!' he called. 'We've guests to feed.'

A woman shouted within, 'Then bring them in, you great clot! I've scones aplenty.'

Andra was surprised by the hut's interior layout, when he entered. A door led left into a second room, as he guessed, but directly ahead, in the rear wall, another door opened into the hill, and into more rooms dug out of the ground. The hut's tiny outward appearance belied its true dimensions.

Bear guided Milly and Andra through the left door, where they met Hanna, a short woman of ample proportions. Andra likened her stature to the Shaddites in the Great King's camp, outside the Great City, before the northward march. Roly-poly cheeks bunched into a broad smile. 'You're welcome to sit and eat at Hanna's table,' she said, and grinned warmheartedly. 'Such a handsome young warrior and beautiful little girl. These are sore times to be travelling the King's Lands.' She bent to her hearth, lifted a heated tray of scones from the embers, and placed it on the rough wooden table in the room's centre. 'Don't be shy about eating. Bear eats like his animal namesake, don't you my Bear?'

The ferryman took a playful swipe at his wife, which she ducked as she moved away from the table. 'That woman will feel the back of my hand one such day for her cheek!' Bear scowled, with a wink at Milly, who laughed.

Andra enjoyed the warm camaraderie between husband and wife, as they bossed each other, and made grim mock threats throughout the meal, and didn't doubt Hanna could match her husband blow for blow, if it ever did come to blows between them. Not that such a thing would ever eventuate, he decided. Bear and Hanna were comfortable in each other's presence.

After they ate, Bear insisted on showing Andra his home. He led him through the doorway into the hillside, and revealed a house of six rooms, four excavated from the hill. 'Who needs to be making good money to buy timber or stone for a house, if he has a good shovel for digging, and a place to dig?' Bear boasted, as he showed Andra his private ale room. 'Do you like a drop of the amber fluid?' the ferryman asked hopefully, as he toyed with the tap on a small vat.

'I haven't drunk much of it,' replied Andra. 'All I know is it makes my head go fuzzy and warm if I drink too much.'

Bear laughed heartily and clapped him on the shoulder. 'Then share a drop with me.'

As Bear drew him into the room, a frightened scream ripped through the small house. Andra sprinted to the front rooms, with Bear in pursuit, and found Milly crouched against the front door, a spear point thrust through the wood. Someone was heaving against it. 'They've come!' cried Milly. 'They killed the horses!'

Andra reached for the bow he leaned against the wall in the entrance room and nocked an arrow. A silhouette appeared at the window, to the left of the door, he loosed his shaft, and the target yelped with pain and toppled away. Bear lumbered across to join Andra, wielding a huge double-bladed axe. 'They'll not get through my door without paying a heavy price for entrance!' he bellowed, and wrenched the door open, snapping the spear shaft in the motion. A dozen Haagii warriors charged, waving swords, hell-bent on blood. Andra hitched his bow and raised his staff, catching the first Haagii under the chin, while Bear's axe cleaved the helmet of a second who tried to leap over his fallen friend. Two more blows from the defenders saw two more Haagii fall, and the remainder retreated, aware they could only rush the door in pairs, a strategy favouring the defenders.

As they hesitated, Andra saw the Haagii look above the doorway. Bear gripped Andra's shoulder. 'Look,' he urged. Wisps of smoke were creeping through the thatching. 'They think to burn us out. No matter,' said Bear, as if he expected that strategy. He turned to Hanna, who was holding a large skewer, and said, 'Lead the child through the out tunnel, woman. Take the fork toward yon mountains. Be as quick as you've a mind to.'

Hanna immediately took Milly's hand. 'Come, young missy,' she said, and grinned. 'We've a trip to take that'll ruin their day's pillaging,' and she led the girl into the hillside.

'My guess is they'll rush one more time,' said Bear to Andra. 'There'll be fire above us, soon enough, but they'll want at least one more chance for blood.'

'Let's encourage them,' said Andra, unhitching his bow. His first shot dropped the foremost Haagii, and the others yelled and pointed at the hut, until more warriors joined them. Reinforced, they rushed the door again. Staff and axe took their toll, and five more Haagii died before they withdrew, but the roof was fast becoming a raging inferno, and heat and smoke filled the room.

'The roof will fall very soon!' Bear shouted above the crackling flames, and as he spoke burning pieces tumbled into the room. 'We leave now!' he yelled.

Andra followed Bear's broad frame into the rear-most room, where Bear stopped, facing the solid wall. He pressed against a chunk of rock jutting from the earth, and a section swung open, revealing a dark tunnel angling into the ground. Bear ushered Andra in, pulled the rock-face shut again, and darkness closed around them.

Fifteen

When they reached Hanna and Milly in the tunnel, Bear led the way. Andra floundered against walls, and bumped his head on the ceiling, until all sense of direction was knocked from him, yet Bear led them unerringly onward, and Hanna trailed, offering encouragement, comforting Milly, who was unsure of the embracing darkness. The mystical awareness Bear and Hanna had for tunnels and darkness fascinated Andra, as greatly as the Aelendyell ability to find trails through impenetrable forest. He gritted his teeth, and blindly followed his invisible host through the earth, but after a while his thighs ached from stooping, and his back screamed with pain.

Memories of Murdok's trainings seeped into his thoughts, as he forced himself to keep moving. Trainer Murdok's methods had been brutal, but Andra and his companion Guardians from The Vale endured the incessant punishment and extended their fitness and strength.

He was aware Milly had quietened considerably, and she didn't answer when he whispered her name. Instead, Hanna's crackly voice responded, 'The little lass is fine. Be on with you. There's a way to go as yet.' So, they pressed on, until Andra was sure he was going to collapse from exhaustion. When Bear's voice floated to him, out of the eerie darkness, telling him to rest because they'd reached the out hole, Andra audibly sighed and sank against the tunnel wall.

'I'll be checking for company, before we use the out hole. It's cleverly disguised, but these are fearsome times. You wait here, a bit, till I get back,' Bear instructed. Feet shuffled away, in the darkness.

'Hanna?' Andra whispered.

'Here I be,' the stout woman replied.

'Where's Milly?'

'Asleep.'

'Already?'

'She's been asleep for quite some while, I think,' said Hanna quietly.

Her answer astonished Andra. If Milly was asleep, then Hanna carried her the entire distance without rest or complaint. To do that, she would have to possess phenomenal stamina, he realised, and he silently chided himself for his weakness while he massaged his throbbing muscles.

'There's nothing to be seen. We go out.' Bear's proximity startled the young warrior, but when he heard the big man moving away he scrambled to his feet, put his hands against the wall, and followed the line of the tunnel, until fresh air caressed his cheek.

Night blanketed the world and stars glittered in the cold sky, but there was no moon. Andra stretched, relieved to be out of the cramping tunnel, but without moonlight he could only see a dark smudge rising to touch the sky behind them. 'Where are we?' he whispered.

'Is the child still asleep?' Bear asked Hanna, before answering Andra's question.

'She sleeps,' Hanna replied.

'We've come up a half day's walk from the town of Axxon, at the mouth of Central Gate,' Bear explained. 'From the hilltop behind us, you'll see yon lights of the town.'

'Why did you build this tunnel?' Andra asked.

Bear's laugh came in a deep, rolling rumble. 'I built no such thing,' he chuckled. 'Hanna's folk built it. Shaddites. Well, Shaddite rebels, eh my fine woman?'

'You'll be respectful about my kin, Bear, or this'll be a fair place for you to get a thrashing,' Hanna warned. 'If they'd never built it, you'd be a fine supper for them northern devils by now.'

'Peace woman!' he growled. 'Take no notice of her, lad. I sure as well don't.'

'You're pressing, husband Bear,' she threatened.

'Shush. I'm telling the lad about the tunnel,' Bear said

meekly, and prodded Andra to climb the hill. 'Keep watch, woman. We'll take in the view.' He talked casually as they walked. 'Hanna's folk weren't too well off, digging tin and metal and silver from the mountains, for the Great Kings. They worked long days and nights, in low tunnels, for little gain. Most cleared out a long time ago, and headed back to their ancestral homes in the Dwarven Range, somewhere beyond the Lake of Tears, but a few thought it more likely for them to get some of their treasures and work back from the Great Kings, so they took to highway banditry, robbing caravans and travellers and the like, and especially taking after any of the Great King's shipments to the west.

At first, they surprised everybody, and no one got hurt, but then the Great King started sending soldiers to protect the shipments, and then he sent soldiers to catch the outlaws. A few got caught, and it got awful tough for the rest to take goods and get away. The soldiers knew the tracks into the mountains, most of them anyway, and they ambushed the rebel Shaddites every time they could. Wasn't long before there was but a few of them left. So, Hanna's great-uncle got to thinking, and he figured the soldiers wouldn't expect an honest man to be robbing by night, nor a Shaddite to head across the plains, if he was chased. He set up the ferry business back at the river, and he and his partners dug this great long tunnel to here as their way of moving about unseen. It proved right. He made good honest living out of the ferry, and a real good living out of the Great King's highway.'

Andra was fascinated by the tale, and when Bear appeared to finish he pursued his curiosity. 'What happened to Hanna's great-uncle?'

'Ha!' Bear laughed. 'Fortune's as fickle a thing as Great Kings. The Great King got so mad about old Fergal's doings he sent a squad of his best black riders, them Haardrishii, out to catch the rebel. And they did. Seems they outfoxed the old Shaddite, and caught him red-handed, holding up a merchant carrying the Great King's gold in a wagon. They hung him on the spot, then drew and quartered him as an example to others. His partners got away, though, and are probably still hiding somewhere back in their ancestors' homes. But them Haardrishii never found out his secret tunnel. When I married Hanna, she told me all about it. Seems it was a family legend. So, we came out here to find out if it was true – and you've seen the proof.'

'Is it useful for you?' Andra asked, trying to frame his question delicately, in case the ferryman took offence at suggestion he was a robber, but the only response he got from Bear was a disgruntled grump.

'I've been along it but four times, and this was the fourth. My great-great grandmother might have been a Shaddite, but I've less love for dark tunnels in the ground than I figure you have, lad. And I'm a touch too lazy to go robbing people of what's not mine in the first place. I pole a ferry. That's the best of my trade. I do what I know,' Bear finished, as they crested the hill. Away to the south, a tiny maze of flickering lights danced on the flat plains, beneath the dark wall of the Andrakian Mountains. They stared at the lights in silence for a time, knowing what each saw, understanding what the vision meant. 'By Uthgor, God of War, they spread like fire,' said Bear with solemn anger.

As he watched, Andra saw tiny balls of flame, sudden specks of light, silently exploding above the dark earth where Axxon burned, and shivered, remembering The Rim Shield. This far already. How fares the Great City?

Bear sensed Andra's fear and placed his big hand on the warrior's shoulder. 'Let's back to the women,' he said. 'We'll take another way.'

In darkness, the climb was terrifying enough, but now Bear had Andra clinging to the sharp edges of the cliff, his face pressed against a cold, unforgiving rock, barely moving more than a half-step at a time. So often he swore he'd missed his footing, felt as if he was going to fall, only to have Bear's large, invisible hand steady him, followed by Hanna's calming voice, reassuring him that he was making good progress. Like Tim Gaelus, these two could see in the dark, could see what Andra could not, and his life was held entirely in their trust as they climbed.

When morning's first grey light filtered down, and the world took shape out of the formless night, Andra's fears multiplied because he could see what he had to be afraid of. Perched on a winding ledge, above a precipice plunging a thousand spans to sharp, hungry rocks below, Bear inched forward, pressed against the cliff, and behind him Hanna eased her rotund frame along the ledge, Milly firmly strapped to her back. If he was close to panic, what would the girl do when she woke to this absurd view? 'Don't look down, lad,' Hanna warned. 'Better you don't know some things.'

'Keep coming,' urged Bear. 'We're nearly there. After this, the way's easy. We'll rest around the corner.' Bear led them to a broad ledge, protected by a jutting pinnacle of rock, which formed a natural amphitheatre. A small tunnel opened at the back of the ledge. The respite was welcome. 'The next section is just tunnel that rises higher into the mountains. This is one of the oldest roads the earliest Shaddites travelled, before they were forced to work for the Great Kings,' said Bear, as he helped Hanna off the thin ledge. Milly squirmed and yawned.

'The girl's awake,' said Hanna, matter-of-factly, and continued, 'Legend has it this road is Dwarven. They were smaller and more agile than our people, so it's likely to be true. My kin rarely went this way because it became too difficult for most folk.' Andra winced at the use of the term 'road' to describe the way they climbed into the mountains. They'd wound through abrupt foothills, beneath the Andrakians, and entered a tiny cave, through which he crawled on hands and knees, before emerging on the 'road' that began as a path and ended on the treacherous ledge from which they alighted. No one in their right mind would travel this way.

'Where are we?' Milly asked, and she yawned. 'Where are the horses? Where's Yarela?'

Before Andra could move to the girl, Hanna was bent over her, giving her a warm cuddle. 'We've come a long way from home, my girl. We couldn't bring the horses here,' she explained.

'The Hagmen killed them,' Milly said with finality. Tears welled in her eyes.

'They did, girl. That they did,' said Hanna gently, and she held Milly against her, while the girl cried.

The tunnel frustrated Andra, and he relied completely on Bear's guidance again. 'I don't like this silly old tunnel,' Milly said, her voice betraying her annoyance. 'I hate dark places.'

'Just a little further,' Hanna whispered from behind. 'Keep your hand on Andra's back just a bit further.'

Bear stopped. 'I think there's an old way station here somewhere,' he said. 'Run your fingers along the wall, about an arm span or so up from the floor. Tell me if you find an old chain link embedded in stone.' Andra thought Bear's instruction absurd. He couldn't see a thing, and he wondered how he could help under the circumstances. 'Keep feeling,' Bear urged. 'It's about here someplace.'

Andra sighed and shrugged. He bent down and gauged an arm's span height on the wall, and began to run his fingers along it, until he touched something cold, smooth, oval-shaped. His fingers traced its size. 'I think I've found it,' he gasped.

Bear shuffled back and his hand pushed Andra's aside. 'You surely have, lad. You've a good touch in them hands.' Bear grunted as if straining. 'Tight,' he said. 'Probably rusted. Been a long time since it's been opened, I should think.' Andra heard a clunk in the darkness, and something slid on stone. A musty odour reached his nose. 'There's four steps down, lad,' Bear said. 'My hand will guide you. Hanna, help the little lass.' Andra was led down into a space. He couldn't judge its size, but at least he could stretch his arms.

'Where are we?' Milly asked.

'A way station,' Hanna replied. 'The Dwarven built these

along the tunnel to give travellers a place to stay or rest. It's good because they're close to each end, which means travellers could rest in safety before going out into the open world. My grandfather told me about these places.'

'Under here,' Bear cut in, 'are tunnel highways that drop deeper into the mountains. The Dwarven built them in the Days Before when they were the only people in The Land. They mined great riches here. Legend has it there are halls and palaces, somewhere in these mountains, where the Dwarven Kings held court. Some say treasures lay locked in massive vaults, where the Dragonlords couldn't get to them, and are there still. Shaddites in the past tried to find them, but never did.'

'That's why they are legends, husband,' Hanna quipped.

'Hush woman,' Bear snorted with mock contempt.

When Andra heard Bear fossicking, he asked, 'What are you looking for?' before considering the absurdity of his question in total darkness.

'What I can find,' Bear answered casually. His answer was followed by a sharp scraping, and Andra glimpsed sparks. More furious scraping followed, until Bear held aloft a burning torch. 'Still works,' he announced with satisfaction. 'I wondered if there'd be any left. Seems we've stumbled on a lesser-used station.'

Spreading light opened the space, but Andra was disappointed, because the room was smaller than he imagined, barely big enough for a dozen standing adults. Milly squinted up at him, and he noticed Hanna bent over a metal-bound chest placed against the wall. The chamber was tiny, but the mirror sheen of the walls, ceiling and floor was remarkable. The stonework was flawless, the seams meeting perfectly to form a squared pattern. 'There's not much left,' said Hanna, as she closed the chest and straightened.

'What's this?' asked Milly unexpectedly. All three turned to see the girl toying with a metal ring in the wall by the door through which they entered. The ring was hard to distinguish, even in the light, being mottled like the stone wall in which it was embedded. Andra wondered how Milly even discovered the camouflaged metal ring.

'Best not touch, young girl,' said Bear in a level tone. 'These aren't our things.'

Andra detected the underlying warning in Bear's tone, and quickly added, 'Listen to Bear. We don't –' but Milly was pulling the ring outwards. Grinding stone on stone filled the room, as the centre portion of the rear wall sank to become a dark doorway. 'Milly!' Andra chided in exasperation.

'Now that's something,' Bear mumbled. He lifted the torch and peered into the opening. His yellow torchlight revealed a steep and narrow stairway, leading down, into the heart of the mountain. The steps were smooth and short, clearly made for someone of much smaller stature than a human. 'Well –' breathed Bear, caught for words. 'Hanna. Be looking here.' Hanna and Milly pushed through, forcing Andra to the back. He heard Hanna suck in her breath as she looked down. 'What do you make of it?' Bear asked.

'I shouldn't want to guess,' she replied, with an unusually soft quality to her voice, 'but I've heard the tales.'

'Is this one of your legends?' asked Milly.

Hanna shook her head gently in disbelief. 'I've heard the tales,' was all she could repeat. 'I've heard the tales.'

'But why didn't we look?' Milly asked for the third time.

'It wouldn't be fit for us to go where it's not ours to go. Legends are best left legends. Who knows where that stairway leads to?' Hanna patiently explained. 'And there's no time. We've got to get you and yon lad to the Great City.'

'But why?'

'Milly!' growled Andra, vexed by her insistent curiosity.

'I just want to know why,' the girl persisted. 'Sister Emiris sent me with you. She gave me the gold pieces to give you when you needed them. But no one's told me why I need to go to the Great City.'

Andra squatted before the girl, looked deep into her bright blue eyes, and for a moment felt as if he might be drawn into their liquid depths and forever lost, such was the intensity of their colour and clarity. 'Milly,' he said slowly. 'There's a big war going on, bigger than anything. The Haagii – the Hagmen – are hurting lots of things and lots of people. Sister Emiris sent you with me so they wouldn't hurt you anymore. There are lots of people in the Great City. And I must find my home too. You have to come so you won't get hurt.'

'My Dad will wonder where I am,' Milly whimpered. 'I want my Dad. I want to go home. Why didn't you take me back to my home after you found me?'

Andra saw pain in the girl's eyes. Since he rescued her from the Haagii, in the hills beside Wynwuduholt, she'd had no time to comprehend the extremity of her losses, because Mirith's healing balm made her sleep while Andra carried her to Spurl. She'd left Sister Emiris' convent unusually happy and well, riding a horse, and enjoying the unexpected adventure. Hanna carried the girl's exhausted body through the long tunnel, and up the mountainside the previous night, and her brief rainstorm of sorrow for the slaughtered horses was only her first blind realisation of how threatened and maimed her little world was. Andra was certain her father was slain by the marauding Haagii. He'd seen the carnage in the villages, and there was no evidence of villagers escaping the ruthless attacks. He stared up at Hanna, searching for support. The short, heavy woman's face was lined with concern, the wrinkles on her face accentuated by the limited light from her husband's torch, but she stared back sadly, and shook her head. He swallowed, accepting it was his task to tell the child the truth. He put both hands gently on Milly's shoulders. 'Milly,' he said, mustering all the tenderness he could, 'your father's dead.'

Sixteen

They travelled the ancient Dwarven road, through the heart of the mountain, emerging in the early morning on a path winding down the eastern face of the Andrakian Mountains. A bright sun rose above the Ureykyeu to greet them, and lit the Plains of Ky with yellow rays, lending colour to the dying autumn grasses. Andra felt he was making a homecoming seeing the Plains he marched across with the Great Armies, and he breathed the fresh morning air.

Bear held out a hand, as they stood on the uppermost point of the path. 'Your city lies ahead,' he said, 'but Hanna and I will not go beyond this point. The Haagii may have broken through the Central Gate, but I don't believe that could be so. The Great King would send his Haardrishii to hold it, at all costs. If the Haagii have broken through, then there's not much future for anyone to be had on the plains anyway. Hanna and I will head back along the old road, and find a place to remain, until it's safe enough for us to go home and see what we can save from the ashes.'

Andra clasped the ferryman's hand and warmly shook it. 'Thank you for your help, Bear. You take care of Hanna.' He winked at the short stout woman.

'It will be me what's looking after this lummox,' Hanna snorted, and she grinned as she hugged Milly to her bosom. 'And you take care of this young man, my girl, or Hanna'll be after your britches.' Milly smiled weakly, her first since learning of her parents' deaths, and to Andra it looked as if she would never release the woman. 'There, there, girl,' Hanna gently chided. 'You've a way to go yet. Hanna'll keep you in her heart.' Reluctantly, Milly let go of Hanna and went to Andra's side, and as she leaned against him he put his hand on her shoulder.

'Uthgor protect you, and guide your staff, my friend!' called Bear, as heartily as he could in farewell, though the big ferryman's voice betrayed his sadness at parting.

'And you!' Andra replied. He waved to the retreating figures of the ferryman and his half-Shaddite wife, as they descended into the Dwarven tunnel entrance cleverly hidden in the natural cleft of the mountain rock.

Andra and Milly followed the winding downward path, for a while, before Andra halted on a ledge, which opened a panoramic view of the land to the east. He couldn't see the Great City, nestled beyond the low hills to the south, and the town of Ky was a full day's walk away, but to the north his eyes were attracted to a single finger of rock projecting from the plains, between the Andrakian Mountains and a spur of the range he knew bordered the Valley of Rivers. 'Have you seen that place before?' he asked Milly, as he stared at the geological aberration. She shook her head.

By mid-morning, they reached the foothills, where Andra suggested they find water and rest. He searched and discovered a brook leaping down a tumbling bed of polished rocks, its waters glittering with reflected sunlight. Heartened by the brook's beauty, he retrieved water, and the pair refreshed as they rested.

Milly kept to herself. The bubbling smile and happy face she'd worn out of Spurl was replaced with melancholy, and she seemed permanently lost in gazes at the air immediately before her. Andra tried to make conversation, but she only nodded, or shook her head, in answer to direct questions, and ignored him when he made general observations about their journey or the surrounding land. The girl's mood worried the young warrior. He had that mood, in Wudufaesten, when he dwelled on the slaughter of his friends on The Rim Shield. He wanted to lift her out of her sorrow, but he knew she needed time to reflect, time to adjust to her tragedy. She is a child, after all, he reminded himself, watching her stare into the pool. Time, as much as any care, will heal her heartbreak.

At midday, they stumbled onto the King's Way, the road running west, from the Great City through Central Gate in the Andrakian Mountains, and before long a small, slow procession of wagons headed toward them from the southeast. Andra pointed out the approaching vehicles to Milly, and she gazed with abject disinterest at the growing specks on the open road. He heard rhythmic hoof beats to his right, and two riders crested a rise on the road, west of them, sweeping by in a thunder of dust toward the wagons. He recognised the black armour, and black Haardrishii mounts. They reined in, when they reached the lead wagon, and a brief conversation between riders and the driver ended with the Haardrishii spurring their horses southward again, leaving the wagons to resume their journey.

Shortly after, Andra heard the steady clip-clop of hooves from the west, and another horse appeared over the crest, but this one moved slowly, pulling a wagon. 'Come on, Milly,' he said, lifting the girl. 'We'll ride to the Great City.'

As the wagon drew alongside, he hailed the driver, a thickset man with a long, thick grey beard. 'Can you spare space for two, my friend?'

Without slackening his pace, the driver yelled, 'If you can get aboard, you can ride! I can't stop. Great King's orders!'

Andra jogged after the ambling wagon and tossed Milly aboard, before he swung into the cart, and clambered over the angular, sheet-draped cargo to join Milly and the driver at the front. 'How far do you go?' he asked, as he settled onto the plank seat.

The portly driver kept his eyes fixed ahead, as he muttered, 'To the Great City with this lot.'

'What do you carry?'

'Corpses,' the man replied.

Andra eased back to study the rocking cargo he climbed over, and saw a hand, in a black gauntlet, drooping from beneath a sheet. 'How far to Ky?' he asked, endeavouring to direct Milly's attention to matters other than the back of the wagon.

The driver tugged at his beard with his right hand, and replied, 'We should be there well before dark.'

'Have you lodging there?'

The driver grunted ironically. 'At the Great King's

pleasure, my boy, which means I'll be sleeping in the back of my wagon along with my passengers, if I can't find a barn.'

The line of wagons heading toward them closed, drew abreast, and the drivers waved grimly as they passed. The wagons carried siege and war machinery, catapults and ballista, and following the last was a thin line of soldiers, carrying pikes and spears. Many seemed mere boys to Andra, their expressionless faces and dull eyes locked on the back of the soldier marching ahead. No chatter, no laughter, no free-flowing banter, like there was when he marched west with the West Wheel of the Great King's Armies. 'More lambs to the slaughter,' the driver grumbled. 'Children to fight a Great King's war.'

Andra watched the last soldiers straggle past, all adolescents, barely strong enough to lift the spears and swords, looking sadly foolish in their ill-fitting metal breastplates. 'How goes the war?' he asked tentatively.

The driver looked askance. 'Where've you been not to know?' he inquired.

Realising his error, Andra tried to cover his question by asking, 'I meant what recent reports have you had, since coming from Central Gate?'

The driver turned toward the road to answer. 'Axxon is ash. It's burned for three days and nights. There are dragons, though we are forbidden to speak of them. The Haardrishii hold Central Gate at a terrible killing. The Great King's Armies are nothing since those who marched north disappeared. One army holds a line in the Valley of Rivers. The Kingdom is in ruins.' He paused, as if considering a problem, turned to Andra and bluntly asked, 'Where've you come from?'

Better to tell part of the truth, thought Andra. 'West,' he replied. 'From Spurl.'

'When? There's nothing but Haagii west of the Central Gate.'

'We came through the mountains,' Andra casually informed him. 'The Haagii couldn't find us there.' The driver looked long and hard at Andra again, and he knew the man didn't accept his explanation, but he seemed reluctant to

146

challenge his story. Andra changed the topic by asking, 'What's the finger of rock that sticks straight up out of the earth to the north of here?' remembering his earlier view from the mountain ledge.

'You'd be talking about Dragon Tooth,' said the driver.

'What's it for?'

'No one really knows. There's all sorts of tales and legends about it, I suppose. I heard it's the remaining tower of an ancient castle built by giants. Some say it's hollow and full of gold. But no one's found a way into it, so it's just talk. I've never been near it, and I'm not interested in it.'

The driver's abrupt conclusion told Andra conversation was at a close. He sat back, and chatted to Milly, pointing out old farms and tiny hamlets they passed as they travelled toward Ky, but the girl remained unwilling to be drawn from her despondency. Eventually, he let the child dwell in her solitude, and observed the passing countryside alone, wondering how much longer it would be before the Haagii overran the plains and places humans possessed. They were at the gateway. Where was the army holding the enemy at bay in the Valley of Rivers? Did The Vale perish? No. He knew Guardian Master Artega would never let that happen. He had to get home.

The driver's prediction about lodgings in Ky was accurate. There were no inns, no barns, and no places willing to let them stay for free, but Andra didn't fancy sleeping the night in a wagon loaded with bodies. Milly reminded him she carried gold pieces from Sister Emiris, which meant they could afford lodging in the inn, but Andra warned her to keep them aside, telling her they'd more likely need them in the Great City. He eventually convinced her to rest beneath a tree, beside a small thatched cottage, a short distance from where the driver tethered his horse and parked his wagon, and despite the ground being hard and cold, sleep came rapidly.

By afternoon, the following day, the wagon entered the

outskirts of the Great City, and Andra noticed changes, the major alteration a half-constructed stone wall sweeping from the castle plateau to the southern tip of the town, before disappearing east. Buildings had been demolished to make way for the wall, and those beyond its perimeter were either empty, or partially dismantled, or burnt. A gateway with no gate greeted them, and two unkempt soldiers, their chain-mail vests in serious need of a polish, stepped out to bar the wagon's progress. 'Who travels the Great King's Way?' a gangly soldier croaked, as the wagon rumbled toward him.

The driver reined in and spat on the ground. 'Give up on your foolish games, Ned,' he said, with a friendly sneer, 'or I'll have to get down and whip your hide.'

Soldier Ned grinned a toothless grin and stood aside. 'Just doing my duty, Hubert,' he responded amiably. 'That's the Great King's law.'

'A pox on the Great King! And a pox on both of you as well!' growled Hubert defiantly. He snapped his reins, leaving the soldiers laughing as the wagon passed through the gateway.

The city road was empty. It meandered toward the city centre, crossing streets and alleys, before joining two larger roads, at a y-junction, beneath the towering cliffs of the castle plateau. People milled in the streets there, and wagons and merchants moved steadily north and south. No one was travelling west.

Hubert reined in, and said, 'I've got to deliver my cargo to the castle, my friends, so I'll be leaving you here. I don't know what your business is, and I've little care to know, but you'll find taverns and shops, and the market square, south of here. If you want advice, and I'll give it for free, the best place to get lodgings is the Abreotan Tavern, southern end of the King's Way. Mort Havelock, and his wife Jessy, owns it. If you tell 'em Hubert sent you, they'll take good care of you.'

Milly and Andra watched Hubert steer his death wagon through the trickle of traffic, before Andra took the girl by the shoulder and headed south along the broad street. He was aware of shadowy men loitering in doorways, and he was quick to observe that very few young men travelled the street. Older merchants, boys, girls, some women, were going about their errands, but there were no young men. They passed several shops, but when they reached a large building proclaiming itself as the Inn of Dragons, recognition flooded through Andra because it was the inn Tim Gaelus brought him to on the night they absconded from the Great Armies' camp. Predictably, two men lounged in the entrance.

What was the proprietor's name? Tom? Thomas? He couldn't recall the name. 'Wait here, Milly,' he said, and headed for the entrance, thinking if he went inside he might remember the proprietor's name. Neither figure in the doorway moved to let him pass. 'I'd like to go inside,' he said quietly, but neither moved. Sensing their intention to make trouble, something he was anxious to avoid with Milly present, he said, 'I'll come back later,' and stepped back into the street.

A stiletto dagger glinted in one man's hand. 'Where do you think you're going?' he asked with quiet arrogance.

Andra concentrated on the weapon, and said carefully, 'I've got no concern with you, friend. I only wanted to see the tavern owner.'

'Well I've got concern with you,' said the man with the dagger. 'I like your bow.'

Andra saw the direction the confrontation was heading. Merchants and people passed behind him, ignoring anything they might inadvertently see in the inn's entranceway, in case they were dragged into a nasty scene. 'Thank you, it's a good bow,' he answered, trying to play down his assailant's animosity.

'Then perhaps you'd like to give it to me. As a gift, one might say,' said the thief with a wicked sneer.

'Andra. Who are you talking to?' Milly called from the middle of the street.

Her plaintive voice nearly distracted him, but Andra kept

his eye on the dagger. 'I have to go, gentlemen,' he said politely. 'Excuse me.' As he turned, he saw the flash from the man's dagger, but he anticipated the attack, and swung his arm to ward off the thrust, spinning his assailant into the street with his momentum. 'There's a lot of witnesses,' he said. 'I'd let well enough alone.'

He measured his opponent. The man was lithe, light of foot, well balanced. Out of the corner of his eye, he noticed the second man hadn't moved from his leaning position. The first thief straightened, as if to walk away, and lunged, the dagger glancing Andra's ribs as he dodged. Milly screamed. The thief nimbly turned to attack again, but Andra kicked upward with his right foot, catching his opponent a swift blow to the chin. Stunned, the thief couldn't avoid Andra's clenched fist. The blow knocked the thief backward, and he crashed through the inn door.

Andra glared at the second man, wondering why he remained impassive. His face was masked, hidden by shadow, and a closely drawn hood, but he started laughing heartily. His companion emerged from the inn, with a bloodied nose, tossed a small purse of coins to him and sat on the doorstep. The second thief emerged from the shadow, and sauntered toward Andra, spinning the purse on his fingers. He threw back his hood, unveiling handsome, smiling features. 'So, it's true the dead can rise again,' said Tim Gaelus. 'You still fight like a wild man, Andra of The Vale. Well met, my friend.'

"Only in remembering past sorrows can future joys be assured."

an Aelendyell saying

> "Hatred of kind -
> insidious, most vicious.
> gnaws at compassion,
> rots reason with cankerous sores,
> until all that remains, of a man,
> is a husk,
> a hardened shell,
> empty of all qualities human."

excerpt from Passion and Power, a poem by Drycraefter Waeron Ardath.

Seventeen

'Pak!'

Pak started from his reading. Master Ki was calling from the upper levels, his voice communicated through the tower walls. 'Yes, Master?'

'Spells of Charming and Binding: have it ready for me.' A Ahmud Ki instructed.

'Yes, Master, at once.' Pak rose from his stool, and rifled through the scrolls, books, folders gathered on the table. He remembered the text to which Master Ki referred because the Master earlier indicated keen interest in it. At first, he couldn't find it, but a frantic search uncovered the text just as he became aware of his master's presence.

'Where is it?' asked the Advisor.

'Here, Master,' Pak replied, bowing his head and holding the book toward A Ahmud Ki.

A Ahmud Ki took the thin text and spotted the dishevelled pile of literature on the table. 'Messy creature, aren't you?'

Pak bowed lower. 'I apologize, Master. I will tidy it up immediately.'

'Good. I want the texts organized, according to information. See it's done,' said A Ahmud Ki firmly.

'Your will, Master.'

A Ahmud Ki incanted a spell and rose through the levels of the tower to the Spell Chamber. He dispelled the darkness in the chamber with a light sphere and sat on a worn wooden stool at his oak desk, carefully opening the frayed book to avoid tearing its yellowed pages from the decayed binding. He turned the pages, one by one, searching ancient scripts, and reading rapaciously, as he always did, absorbing minute detail. Finally, he concentrated on one passage, and read it, again and again, memorising it, until he had it word perfect. Then he closed the book and levitated to the uppermost room of the tower; his Meditation Chamber.

Soft amber light bathed the entire room, emanating from four crystal pyramids gyrating slowly at each compass point, halfway up the walls of the circular space. At the room's centre, where A Ahmud Ki stood, a circular mat covered most of the Meditation Chamber's floor, and on it was a red robe.

A Ahmud Ki removed his silver and black robes, and pulled on the red robe, shivering at its cold silken touch. There was an amber pendant, where the robe had lain, in the shape of a woman, although the outline and features were deliberately blurred: Fareeka. He placed the pendant around his neck. Here, he was Ithosen, Holy One of the Ranu Ka Shehaala, and he unshackled the memories of ten years in the Empire of Leiksha Ithrandyr Shehaal, while he bathed in the amber glow.

He spent a long time in silence, allowing the spell text to mingle and flow with Aelendyell and Ithosen ideas, weaving their fabric into a new form, one peculiar to his being, one he could create at will. He worked all magic into new forms, running them through the vast store of the Four Ki he had acquired. But behind the forming and shaping, he always felt a more powerful presence, something greater, someone with ultimate energy beyond his wildest imagining guiding the shaping process: Berak N'eth, the Ranu Supreme Being who enabled him to learn the Third Ki. Beneath all else, Berak N'eth moved like a strong, deep current, sweeping A Ahmud Ki's expanding knowledge along a cosmic river of magical consciousness that he hoped to comprehend in all its majesty and power. In the amber glow, A Ahmud Ki rocked, drifting in the ebb and flow of learning.

Pak slipped through the wall, collected the amber crystal key, and climbed the marble stairs to the Visiting Room where A Ahmud Ki waited. 'Is this suitable, Master?' he asked, holding a heavy platinum chain.

A Ahmud Ki took the chain and inspected it. 'Perfect.

Where did you find it?'

Pak lowered his eyes nervously, before answering. 'In Thana's Personal Chambers, Master,' he confessed. 'There were no other chains like it in the castle, and no merchant in the Great City professed to having one either.' Pak waited for A Ahmud Ki's reaction, fearing perhaps his theft may have overstepped the limits of his freedom to take risks. The Royal Advisor started laughing. Pak sneaked a glance at his master's face.

'Look at me,' A Ahmud Ki laughed. Pak obeyed. 'You've done very well. How did you get this?'

Pak's confidence surged, hearing his master's pleased tone. 'I used the old secret passage that we – I mean you – found in the castle library. It was easy, Master.'

'Have you ever been a thief, Pak?'

'No, Master!' he vigorously denied, but he regretted his outburst and bowed his head submissively. 'I apologize, Master.'

'Accepted,' A Ahmud Ki said, still grinning at his servant's cunning. 'In fact, I think it's time you learned thieving skills, Pak. You spend too much time reading. You should develop other skills.'

Pak kept his face turned down from his master. He tried not to think. The Master can read thought. But how do you avoid thinking? He'd read a text with a spell for preventing others reading thoughts, but he didn't want to risk learning it, in case, by using it, he inadvertently infuriated Master Ki. He desperately wanted to learn magic, to be strong and powerful like the Master, but he seemed unable to learn even simple spells. Had Master Ki suspected he was trying to learn? 'As my Master wishes,' he replied, trying to mask his feelings. He distrusted thieves, hated them. His only brother died in a tavern brawl, backstabbed by a thief. If he'd been a warrior, he would've sworn an oath of revenge against his brother's murderer – but he was no warrior.

A Ahmud Ki sensed the servant's discomfort. Pak was reading too much, lately and he was entertaining ideas of learning magic. That privilege was reserved for carefully selected Apprentices, and Pak lacked the intellectual qualities to learn magic. Besides, he needed a servant whose mind was focussed on serving. If he allowed Pak to learn magic, the servant would understand the master and his motivation, and the strength of the master's power over the servant would dissolve. 'Good. I'll arrange for your training to begin. But now, I have a more pressing matter. Fetch Liam to the tower.'

Pak bowed, and scampered down the stairs, while A Ahmud Ki ascended to the Spell Chamber, to work his new spell into the platinum chain.

Thana sat uneasily on his throne. He'd ordered extra green silk cushions to increase his comfort, but cushions did little to support the discomfort inside his heart. His Kingdom was in turmoil. Runners returned from the edge of Dragon Breath Plains with daily reports that a massive Haagii army was crossing the desert and assembling along the foothills of the Abreotan Ranges. Emissaries to Targa and Andros returned with the disappointing news that those peoples were too involved with preparing to defend their lands against the Dragonlord's onslaught to lend the Great King assistance. The Aelendyell cut diplomatic ties with the Kingdom over the Laeowyth incident, and no reply had been received from the Ranu Ka Shehaala because the emissary hadn't returned. High Lord Nisus was frantically redeploying troops north into the Valley of Rivers, and west to Central Gate to defend the Plains of Ky, and Surdrok's Haardrishii were reluctantly marching toward Axxon to bolster the defence forces there. The Dragonlord was coming to avenge his ancestor's justice, and Thana was going to die.

The Great King sighed, shifted his corpulent body, and turned despondently toward Rheims. 'Tell him We are ready to hear his news,' he sighed again, sending Rheims scuttling to fetch the Royal Advisor, but he remained intent on his thoughts, wringing the gilt edge of his royal green smock anxiously between his fingers.

The Royal Advisor sent word he'd solved the riddle of the prophecies concerning the Dragonlord's return. Thana knew only part of the ancient prophecies. He did know he wasn't destined to defeat the Dragonlord. Abreotan's sword was long lost in the mysteries of time, and he, Thana, thirty-seventh descendant of that Great King, was no warrior.

Rheims returned, with A Ahmud Ki in silver robes beside him, and they were accompanied by a figure in black Haardrishii armour. Why does the Advisor require a Haardrishii escort, Thana wondered? The Chancellor and Royal Advisor stopped at the base of the throne dais. Rheims bowed, and moved to his usual station, while A Ahmud Ki looked up at Thana and smiled. 'We hear you have an end to Our woes, Royal Advisor,' Thana wheezed, catching his breath as he shifted his cumbersome weight in the throne.

'Your Majesty is familiar with the ancient prophecies of Abreotan's seers?' the Advisor surreptitiously asked.

Impertinent as always, thought Thana as he considered the question. Perhaps We've let him overstep the mark once too often. He remembered Nisus talking with strong disaffection for the Royal Advisor in his Private Chambers, as the High Lord of the Great King's Armies outlined his strategies for defending the Kingdom. Who is the Great King here? 'Of course,' he snorted. 'Dare you presume Our knowledge is inadequate on such matters?'

A Ahmud Ki didn't appreciate the Great King's attempt at authority, but he smiled with greater friendliness, as he replied, 'Not at all, Your Majesty.' He indicated for the Haardrishii to stand beside him.

Thana was intrigued by the warrior's sword, deliberately visible, swinging from his belt, because it wasn't a traditional blackened Haardrishii weapon. The warrior also wore a heavy platinum neck chain, an adornment alien to any Haardrishii, and Thana thought the chain looked very familiar, like one that he remembered lay among his great-grandfather's old trophies in the Royal treasury.

'You recall that several prophets speak of a saviour who will rise to oppose the Dragonlord when he returns again,' A

Ahmud Ki stated.

Thana nodded knowingly, as he searched his memory for any fragment of reading such a prophecy. Perhaps he read that. He wasn't certain. Reading history was boring. His childhood tutors schooled him in all the history of his ancestors, each successive king and the occasional queens who held power in the Kingdom after Abreotan, but he ignored most of their tedious instruction, fascinated only by tales of dragons and heroes, interested more in luxury and fine living than in learning. Perhaps he heard it. The Royal Advisor need only assume he had. 'Repeat it to Us so We can determine how well the Royal Advisor knows what he talks of,' he said offhandedly.

This fool is fast becoming a pointless irritation, thought A Ahmud Ki. His ineptitude is only exceeded by his ignorance. 'It is written that, at the time of the Second Coming, one who bears the mark of the moon will rise to oppose and defeat the Dragonlord.'

'Ah, yes,' said Thana. 'We remember that well.' He glanced to the left of his throne, down toward Rheims, for confirmation of the prophecy. The spindly Chancellor was nodding his sparse grey hair in agreement. So it was true. 'What is your point, Advisor?'

If he continues this condescending manner, A Ahmud Ki considered, it might by simpler to kill this idiot king now and take over the Kingdom by force. That would almost be preferable to enduring the man's gross ego. But such action lacks the subtle pleasure of manipulating people, he reminded himself, and that pleasure is one of the greatest satisfactions of holding power - helping others unwittingly destroy themselves. 'I've found the warrior,' he announced, and turned to the Haardrishii. The warrior removed his helmet. Thana stared at the patterns and scars etched across the man's forehead. At the centre was a circle – a full moon. Thana's flaccid jaw dropped in astonishment. 'Behold!' A Ahmud Ki shouted, his voice resonating through the Throne Room. 'The Saviour is come! He who will oppose the Dragonlord stands before you!' On cue, Liam drew his sword and held it high above his head. A circle of light appeared at its tip, and grew, radiating outward, until it touched every corner of the room and every person standing within. I like that effect, A Ahmud Ki thought with an inner smile. That should impress the Huge King.

Thana was riveted to the vision. It was true. The prophecy was true. The Kingdom would be saved. He would be saved. He wouldn't have to face the Dragonlord. His ancestor had foreseen it and was protecting him across time. He was saved, not doomed. Overwhelmed with joy, he burst into hysterical laughter, his death sentence reprieved by his Royal Advisor.

A Ahmud Ki watched the Great King's transformation with delight. The idiot believed he had what he wanted. He waited, until Thana's fit subsided, before adding the last information. 'If Your Majesty will permit me to speak once more?' he asked with unusual deference.

Thana's creased face wobbled assent, tears glistening in the slits of his eyes.

A Ahmud Ki drew a breath and continued. 'The Dragonlord comes. We must be prepared. I see Nisus is carrying out his plans, so I will fulfil my promise. The Orb of Radiance will be brought to the Great City. No dragon will touch the heart of Great King Thana's Kingdom.'

Thana couldn't speak for emotional joy when he heard A Ahmud Ki's pronouncement. He waved his hand, dismissing the Royal Advisor and the Saviour, collapsed from his throne and wept into his hands.

As Liam and A Ahmud Ki reached the double doors, A Ahmud Ki took a backward glance at the pathetic vision of the Great King sobbing at the foot of his throne, and he smiled. One more step forward, he contemplated. The fat fool is sealing his own fate without understanding where his real danger lies. That is real political power.

Eighteen

Liam stood in his stirrups to survey the forest from the summit. The forest swept south, from beyond the Abreotan River to the western edge of the Andrakian Mountains, a green wall defying human touch, populated by Aelendyell who refused the Great King's orders and were going their selfish ways. Somewhere, in the heart of the forest, was a treasure, desperately needed by the Royal Advisor, to protect the Kingdom from the Dragonlord's host. He was Ethtroo Ka Nyaret: the warrior of prophecy. The God of Power, Berak N'eth told him so, and he would bring the Orb of Radiance to the Great King. Liam wheeled his steed and galloped down the slope toward the waiting party.

'Well?' the Royal Advisor asked, as Liam reined in.

'The forest is half a day's ride,' Liam replied.

A Ahmud Ki turned to the others and pointed southwest. 'We'll camp at the foot of that mountain, near the edge of Elvenaar Forest.' He prodded his horse into a canter and led them toward the indicated destination. Beneath a rock overhang, near the summit of a hill, five hundred paces from the forest verge, they set about making camp.

A Ahmud Ki dismounted and observed his company. Liam was necessary. Surdrok was correct to select him for the role of the Saviour. He was intelligent and able, strong, of few words: a fine Haardrishii under other circumstances. He was obedient, especially because he wore the platinum chain A Ahmud Ki fashioned for him. He ordered Liam to never remove the chain, even when bathing. Locked under A Ahmud Ki's will by the spell wrought into the chain, Liam was eternally the Advisor's servant, to be manipulated whenever necessary; a useful tool. It was essential he carried the Orb to Thana, to put beyond doubt his claim to the Saviour.

A Ahmud Ki borrowed four of Thana's Royal Guards to bolster the party's fighting prowess. Trained to unquestionably obey orders, they enjoyed the additional honour of being selected to serve their Great King on a secret mission. Two guards tended to the horses, while the remaining pair accompanied A Ahmud Ki into the forest.

Then there were the three Orrin provided – members of The Hand of the Thieves Guild: assassins. A Ahmud Ki noticed how they looked decidedly uncomfortable riding in the open air, but the success of the escapade in the forest depended on their skills, more than any others. A Ahmud Ki discerned traces of Aelendyell heritage in the shape of their eyes, and their finer features, although he gathered that fact was virtually unacknowledged by them.

A party of seven was too large to sneak into the forest, but A Ahmud Ki knew they wouldn't go undetected for long, even if one entered alone. He needed protection, skill, intelligence. Pitfalls and traps awaited them, especially in Heolstorcofa. Seven will be hard pressed, he considered, but the Aelendyell won't account for my presence, and that will be their downfall.

He climbed partway up the hill to survey the blanket of forest. Lush greens rippled in the late afternoon breeze and light washing over the leaves. He hadn't stepped into a forest since his escape from his home, and a part of his soul yearned to leap out, plunge in, and run wildly between the trees, soaking up the fragrances and visions of his childling memories. But teasing and fighting, ostracism from his community, bitterness, and hatred haunted those same memories. He was half-caste, not a true Aelendyell, rejected as a bastard and scorned by his peers. And he was ecg-bana, a slayer of his people. He used the magic he stole from the Chanter's Well of his village to kill an Elder who foolishly tried to stop him. They tried to deny him what he was destined to have – the Ki: the power of all magic. He hated their ignorance as much as he hated their arrogance, but he had more magic than any Aelendyell Elder ever dreamed of possessing, and his sworn vengeance was ripening. He would take the Orb of Radiance from Heolstorcofa to show the Aelendyell someone greater than their Elders was among

161

their people.

He looked northwest. Was that dark smudge on the horizon his old home, Wynwuduholt? One day he'd wreak vengeance there. For now, he'd begin with the oldest enclave of Aelendyell culture: Elvenaar Forest. '

'Master Ki?' A Ahmud Ki turned to Liam, who was bowing politely as he spoke. 'We await your instructions.'

The years hadn't dulled his knowledge of Aelendyell ways. The path through the pre-dawn forest was invisible to human eyes, but A Ahmud Ki spotted subtle twists in fern fronds, bent leaves, faint bare earthen patches marking the Aelendyell pathway, and led the party between the trunks and roots of moss-encrusted elmoaks. From a distance, in the green cloaks and boots the assassins provided for disguise, they might pass as an Aelendyell party, and A Ahmud Ki remained bareheaded, his silver Aelendyell locks shining with dewy dampness, proclaiming his heritage to casual observers to enhance the party's appearance. The rest hid their human features beneath hoods. Liam wrapped his cloak over his Haardrishii armour, giving him an unusually bulky body for an Aelendyell. The Great King's Royal Guards were the least comfortable in the semi-darkness, confused and awed by the Royal Advisor's ability to make a way through the forest out of nothing. The taller man, Kurtis, kept scraping his shins against unseen obstacles, and his muffled curses amused the assassins.

A Ahmud Ki paused frequently when the first rays of morning light filtered through the trees. A multitude of birds began their morning chorus, high in the branches, and insects flitted like spots of living light in and out of thick pockets of mist drifting through the trees, but A Ahmud Ki ignored them, intent on his purpose. Whenever he paused, he flicked through pages of the Aelendyell Lore Book inscribed in his memory, recalling passages describing the site of the ancient burial chambers of Heolstorcofa, before he pressed on.

He led the party to the edge of a small clearing, abutting a creek, and told them, 'You are too noisy. Remove your boots.' Kurtis was going to complain, but, Luke, the shorter Guard, was obeying the instruction, so he followed suit. 'There's always a Watch set by Aelendyell,' A Ahmud Ki briskly explained. 'Usually the Watch doesn't extend more than a short walk from the village or tun, but these times of war will have changed that. We need to go as -'

'There!' Liam whispered sharply. A Ahmud Ki turned from the guards and stared across creek where Liam pointed: trees and undergrowth. He watched, but saw no movement, and heard no sound, except the babbling water at his feet. 'I saw three of them,' said Liam calmly. 'They were following before we stopped.'

A Ahmud Ki gave him a stern look. 'Share your observations with me in future,' he tersely ordered.

An assassin joined A Ahmud Ki, his dark eyes peering up at the tall Advisor. 'Shall I slip to the other side and see what I can ferret out?' he asked eagerly.

A Ahmud Ki shook his head. 'Not yet.' Disappointed, the assassin returned to his fellows.

For most of the morning, the Aelendyell shadowed the party. A Ahmud Ki wondered if their disguise had failed, but he doubted it. If the Aelendyell suspected they were more than just a mobile band of fellow forest dwellers, they would have been stopped by now. They crossed two wider trails, roads by Aelendyell standards, that A Ahmud Ki knew led to a nearby tun, probably the home of the Aelendyell who followed them. He intended to avoid as much contact with the Aelendyell as possible, on their inward journey, especially their habitations. Aelendyell were creatures of curious habit, and the party's disguise would dissolve if they were confronted.

By midday, their followers withdrew, and Liam took care to inform the Royal Advisor. 'There'll be others,' A Ahmud Ki warned quietly. 'They've extended their Watchers well beyond normal boundaries.' They didn't stop to eat. A Ahmud Ki showed Liam berries and fruits they could pick quickly, and the warrior quietly instructed the others to eat on the move, as they pushed deeper into Elvenaar Forest. Later in the afternoon, another Aelendyell pair stalked the group, briefly, before melting into the forest. A Ahmud Ki guessed they accepted the party was Aelendyell and saw no threat. That made him smile.

Liam had never ventured into ancient forest. The Valley of Rivers was the oldest he'd entered, where the space between trees, allowing myriad pebbly streams to course toward Rainbow Lake, was vast compared to the narrow paths twisting between the trunks and roots of the massive elmoaks in this place. Awe and dread filled his heart. The ancient Kingdom tales he heard in the Haardrishii hall, in the Great King's castle, didn't do justice to the old forests' true magnificence. Someone told him the Aelendyell were descendants of an older race, the Elvenaar, who ruled the whole Kingdom when it was forest from border to border. He focussed on A Ahmud Ki's back, and imagined him as an Elvenaar wizard leading them through his home, and he saw a shadow of the ancient past walking before him in the fading forest light.

Certain they'd successfully skirted Aelendyell villages throughout the day, A Ahmud Ki allowed the assassins to sneak to a stream to collect water for everyone, before he led the party on a circuitous route to a rise, topped by a rocky outcrop. He said they could rest a while, to eat and sleep, if necessary, to restore their energies.

Liam crossed to the southern side of the granite blocks and stared into the forest. 'Clever choice for a break,' said Kurtis, who stood beside him. The descending darkness obscured the Royal Guardsman's features. 'Very easy to defend. The wall makes it a veritable castle.'

'Except, in the dark, you won't even hear an Aelendyell coming, let alone see one,' said Liam, in an even voice, and he continued to stare into the darkening forest, ignoring Kurtis' presence.

'True,' Kurtis replied. Disgruntled by the Haardrishii's cold shoulder, he walked back to where his companion was settling to sleep. He'd tried to start a friendly conversation with the warrior who bore the ornate sword and was touted as the Saviour, but he hadn't expected much civility from a Haardrishii. He hadn't received it, either. They never change, he decided, as he sat beside Luke, and fossicked in his pack for a bite to eat.

Liam heard Kurtis leave and was glad to be left alone. Why did the Advisor bother to bring them, he wondered? The waking night forest whispered. Leaves rustled, and huge boughs stretched and groaned, as the cooling night air enveloped them. Faint scratchings betrayed the forest animals, foraging, or retreating to sleep. It had been a long time since he took a night watch over The Vale. He remembered bright daylight fading into soft evening purples and mauves, and the drifting mantle of night sky, sparkling with stars. Village sounds, and the scents of dew-damp plants, flickered through his memory. He was dimly aware of his nearby companions, but he refused to let them intrude on his reverie. He wanted to escape to The Vale, walk into the village of his people, and hold the sword aloft to show them what he was becoming. Had the Guardian Master known this? Had he foreseen the prophecy, and deliberately let him go for that reason?

The Guardian Master knew. The voice inside his head – a familiar voice: Berak N'eth. How? How did he know? He knew. I willed him to know. Your coming from The Vale was always intended to be. That is why you are here. You are the Saviour.

Liam touched his forehead. His fingertips brushed the edges of the arcane scars acquired in Berak N'eth's presence, the night that he was sent to find the Shadow's Voice. The Guardian Master let the Haardrishii take him, and Andra, and Stephen and Alain, because he knew the prophecy. He'd hated the Guardian Master foolishly. When they met again, he would embrace his old master, thank him, and apologise for doubting him. Liam dropped his hand to the sword hilt and felt the pattern worked on it. He was chosen for destiny, for greatness. He was Ethtroo Ka Nyaret – the Saviour.

A Ahmud Ki relaxed his concentration from Liam's mind. The warrior was primed, again, to believe in his immortality. Good. That was an essential ingredient for a strong prophetic fulfilment. The pleasing factor was that, every time he needed to add confidence to the warrior's understanding of his prophetic duty, Liam provided him with the levers. Whoever this Guardian Master had been, A Ahmud Ki agreed he'd done Liam and A Ahmud Ki a favour in letting the warrior be taken from The Vale. Between the sword he gathered from the dead soldier, and the body of this Haardrishii standing alone in the darkness, The Vale had helped him to create a convincing prophecy. He would thank this Guardian Master appropriately, one day. For now, there was brief rest, and an Orb to steal.

Nineteen

'There is no margin for error. When the Watchers fall, you must reach the water's edge, use the sword's spell to form the bridge, and cross to the island. The passage is dangerous. When the spell is invoked, follow directly behind me. One wrong step and the waters of Gnornung will swallow you forever. Understand?' A Ahmud Ki waited for assent from the party. He turned his grey eyes on Liam. 'You know the spell words?'

'Yes,' the dark-haired warrior answered.

'If you get them wrong, we perish,' A Ahmud Ki reminded him. Liam saw the warning in the Advisor's stare and knew he carried their lives in the sword's power. He clutched the hilt, as if it was his promise. A Ahmud Ki glanced at the three assassins, who nodded, and silently slipped into the greenery, vanishing like the Aelendyell they were stalking, before he turned and strolled out of the bracken where they were hiding, and headed for two Aelendyell warriors on the lake shore.

Liam gazed at the crystal deep-blue lake, fed by streams and rivers running from the surrounding mountains, that spread through the forest heart. A Ahmud Ki called it Gnornung – an Aelendyell name meaning the waters of sorrow. The forest crept to the edges, and dipped into the water, but nothing disturbed its mirror surface, not even a breath of wind. Liam felt unusually sad, even as he gazed on its loveliness, as if its depths held secrets to life he could never begin to know. He was aware of stifled movement, at the periphery of his vision, as A Ahmud Ki approached his quarry. The Aelendyell warriors looked up and called out what Liam presumed was a form of greeting in their lilting tongue, to which the Advisor replied as he raised one hand. The Aelendyell threw their arms out, like rag dolls, and dropped to the ground. The assassins leapt from the bushes and retrieved their daggers from their victims' necks. 'Come on,' Liam said, as he pulled on Kurtis' arm, and the three warriors sprinted to join their companions.

'Let it be done,' A Ahmud Ki ordered.

Liam lifted the sword, point upward, and faced a small green island bulging out of the lake waters a hundred paces away. 'Erka Metsub Poran!' he recited.

A Ahmud Ki stepped onto the water. His boots sank a finger's width, but the water buoyed the Advisor. 'It worked. Quickly,' he beckoned, and he led Liam and the party, single file, onto the surface of the perfectly still water.

Liam focussed on the blade of the sword, and A Ahmud Ki's back, willing the spell to hold. Behind him, came Kurtis, awestruck, because his feet seemed to find solidity below the lake's surface. The Saviour had created a magical path. The others shared his overwhelming sentiment, the assassins bewildered by their progress on water.

A Ahmud Ki knew otherwise. He led the party toward Heolstorcofa, grateful he'd remembered the finer details about the magical Elvenaar bridge that invisibly spanned from shore to island. He'd added a nice touch, he thought, making the others believe Liam's sword had conjured a spell to enable them to walk on water. None would doubt the Saviour's power.

The green hump of island grew, as they approached, and A Ahmud Ki's passion welled. The Lore Book told many tales of this ancient Elvenaar burial mound: the most sacred of sacred places revered by the Aelendyell, the remaining physical link between their ancestors and their future outside the teachings of the Lore Book, lying at the heart of the oldest of forests. Heolstorcofa held the mortal remains of the last Elvenaar sorceresses and princes. Once in a lifetime, an Aelendyell expected to make pilgrimage to Heolstorcofa, to stand on the island's green verge and dream. Dreams of greatness could be dreamed, dreams of magic without limits, of beauty without sorrow, of world without end. Here Aelendyell could hear Elvenaar souls stir in Gnornung's royal blue depths, whispering, urging them to touch their beginnings, in the first moments of time when the land was one whole forest and none but the Elvenaar knew its secrets. Powerful magic oozed from the lake.

For several moments, A Ahmud Ki bathed in its wash, wanted to succumb to its touch, wanted to throw away his hatred, his vengeance, rescind his desire to steal from the tomb of his half-ancestors, but he focussed against the pull of his heart and concentrated on getting off the waters of Gnornung before the sorrows of time dragged him into their depths. Another step, and his feet rested on the island's crisp grass.

The others followed him onto the island and gazed at the calm water, reaching to the surrounding forest nestled beneath the mountains east and west, drinking in the beauty of the place. A Ahmud Ki ignored the scenery and searched for an entrance to the Elvenaar tomb, but he only found earth and grass. Frustrated, he ordered the others to search. The others in the party stooped, the assassins on all fours, scouring the tiny island, but they found no sign of an entrance. 'There's nothing here,' Liam said.

'Wrong island,' an assassin murmured under his breath.

'Get back!' A Ahmud Ki snapped. 'Go to the edge of the island.' The party withdrew to the shore. As soon as they moved away, A Ahmud Ki whispered an ancient litany, weaving his hands and fingers through complex patterns, focussing his full attention on the island's centre. The others watched in amazement as the air above the grass shimmered, and a crystalline image appeared, growing solid, until they gazed upon a broad-trunked emerald tree sprouting from the heart of the island.

'By Teka! It's beautiful!' cried Kurtis who couldn't contain his wonder.

A Ahmud Ki dropped his hands and motioned to the others to join him before the crystal tree. 'Things are not always as they seem to be,' he said with a smug smile, because he remembered the allusions to the sacred gateway in the Lore Book. To an assassin, he said, 'Step through.'

The assassin hesitated, unsure of the wisdom in stepping

into a tree trunk, until he shrugged with resignation and stepped in. 'Where's he gone?' Liam asked.

A Ahmud Ki turned to his protégé. 'It's an ornate stairwell hidden by magic. He's gone down to make sure it's safe to enter.'

Liam was decidedly uncomfortable in the presence of so much potent magic. He fingered the pommel of his sword and reminded himself that he held a great deal of power. He created the magical bridge across the lake. What other feats of magic could the sword perform?

The assassin reappeared. 'There's a stairwell leading into the island,' he said excitedly. 'It's dark at the top, but there's light from some sort of door or wall at the bottom. You can see through it. There are coffins everywhere.'

'Heolstorcofa,' A Ahmud Ki murmured. 'We go in,' he said. 'There's not a lot of time before the Aelendyell guards are discovered on the shore, so we move quickly. Don't touch anything, without my express permission. Understand?' He glared at them, emphasizing his instruction. They nodded obediently. 'Stop at the glyph, at the bottom of the stairs,' he warned as he stepped into the emerald tree.

Liam passed through the crystal illusion, into the dark stairwell, but he was aware of faint blue light further below. Cautiously, he descended, testing each step out of habit, even though the assassin had already been down. The light grew stronger, but even when they reached the bottom of the stairs its blue incandescence remained soft to the eyes. Liam waited beside A Ahmud Ki, and stared into the depths of a spacious, low-ceilinged chamber, beyond the light filling the doorway. The silhouettes of burial biers were scattered randomly through the vast chamber, the resting places of the last of the fabled Elvenaar. The further he followed the Royal Advisor, the more he didn't understand. Lost worlds, ancient legends, tales he'd heard whispered by his father and the Guardians, and Haardrishii, were coming to life before his eyes, and, strangest of all, he bore the mark of the moon, the sign of the one who was destined to bring these things together again, against the Dragonlord. He. Liam. Someone touched his shoulder. A Ahmud Ki.

'Before you is a glyph. Do you know what that is?' the Advisor asked. Liam shook his head. 'It's a barrier,' A Ahmud Ki explained, 'like a solid door of magic. And it needs stronger magic to unlock it.' He gestured to an assassin, who drew a stiletto blade from beneath his cloak: a long, thin murderous dagger made expressly for quick, efficient assassinations. 'Watch,' A Ahmud Ki ordered.

The assassin weighed the weapon on his fingertips and flicked it at the glyph. As it hit the magic wall, a brilliant burst of crackling energy exploded before their eyes, and the dagger dropped, smoking and warped, to the foot of the stairs.

'That,' said A Ahmud Ki flatly, 'is a glyph.'

Startled by the display of raw energy, Liam asked, 'How do we get through that?'

'You must use the sword,' A Ahmud Ki replied. He stepped forward to study the glyph as closely as he dared, knowing that the trick was to make sure he wasn't seen breaking the glyph. The others had to believe Liam used the sword's magic. He turned to the party, and said, 'There'll be a blinding flash when the sword destroys the spell. I advise you to turn your faces away.' The assassins and Royal Guards immediately did as instructed. A Ahmud Ki moved behind Liam, and told him to approach the glyph, sword point extended, and walk through. 'The sword will protect you,' he whispered. 'It will drain the energy from the glyph. Believe in Berak N'eth. Say Eknor Morgawyll. The words will break the spell.' He grinned. The words meant nothing. He made them up, like he created the others Liam chanted to conjure the magical bridge; that already existed beneath the lake. Gullible. He watched Liam draw his sword and lower the point toward the glyph. This would be risky. His timing with his spell to break the glyph had to coincide with Liam reaching it. A fraction too early, and Liam might suspect. A fraction too late, he'd have to find another Saviour. Silently, he weaved his magic, unseen by those whose faces were

171

turned away.

Liam moved toward the glyph, with the sword extended, praying to Berak N'eth the Advisor's judgment was correct about the sword's power. As the tip threatened to pierce the glyph, he was engulfed in a bright flash of light. He baulked, shutting his eyes to shield out the light, but he felt no pain so he pushed through. When he opened his eyes, he stood intact within the Elvenaar tomb, surrounded by an alien history. A Ahmud Ki and the others were entering, no longer held back by the glyph. The sword had triumphed. It held the very power the Advisor said it held, because he was the Saviour, and Berak N'eth protected him.

'Touch nothing in here,' A Ahmud Ki reminded them.

The assassins had already spotted the platinum and gold and silver, adorning corpses laid out on the tops of their biers. A life's fortune tempted them and they assessed the risk of taking, despite the Royal Advisor's orders, but they also knew they'd pledged an oath of obedience to the Shadow's Voice in accepting to travel with the Royal Advisor, and were subject to the loss of one hand upon return to the city if they broke their pledge. Reluctantly, they remained stationary, awaiting instructions, while A Ahmud Ki surveyed the chamber.

Spying four small archways, leading into stairwells at varying points, A Ahmud Ki indicated each exit and directed members of the party to investigate, leaving himself and Liam remaining in the chamber. The Royal Guards were first to return, Kurtis leading. 'What did you find?' A Ahmud Ki asked.

'Nothing,' Kurtis reported. 'We can't see. It's too dark. There's a terrible stench down there, like something's rotten.'

A moment later, an assassin emerged from an archway, and sidled toward them. 'Nothing but an empty room with a weird pattern cut into a marble floor, and lots of crystal giving off light in the ceiling.'

A Ahmud Ki's curiosity sparkled. Had the assassin found an Elvenaar prayer room? That place would store vast magic reservoirs, magic he never even read in the Lore Book, whole portions of the Second Ki that were obscure, or hidden from his understanding. He instinctively turned toward the archway, tempted by his desire to acquire magic, the passion coupled with his need for revenge through so many years. 'Advisor!' Someone tugged his sleeve. Who dared? He turned to the assassin. 'I think I found it!' the assassin said excitedly.

'Found what?' A Ahmud Ki demanded, irritated his interest in the crystal prayer room had been so rudely interrupted.

'The Orb!' the assassin announced.

A Ahmud Ki blinked. The Orb of Radiance: their purpose for being there. He focussed. 'Where?' The assassin led A Ahmud Ki, Liam and the others toward an archway, and they entered, descending a narrow stairway that dropped sharply into the earth in a tight spiral. Darkness swallowed them, and Liam fumbled blindly.

'There's no point. We'll kill ourselves in this darkness,' grumbled Kurtis from behind. 'Why didn't we bring torches?'

'Use the sword,' A Ahmud Ki said, out of the black void below Liam.

How? wondered Liam. I don't know how.

Focus. Concentrate on light coming from the tip of the blade, said a voice in his head.

Liam concentrated. He heard A Ahmud Ki whisper in the darkness, as a small sphere of light formed on the point of the sword, radiating softly to illuminate the steps and walls. 'By all that's wonderful, that sword is a miracle!' Kurtis blurted.

At the bottom of the stairwell, the group paused. They were gazing into another space, a small room, cluttered with pedestals, and each pedestal was bathed in a stream of amber light emanating from a source high above. At the room's centre, mounted on an obsidian block, sat a sphere the size of a large melon, glowing amber like the other artefacts on the neighbouring pedestals. 'Is that it, Lord Advisor?' asked the assassin who stumbled upon the room.

A Ahmud Ki continued to stare, as if he hadn't heard the assassin's question, until he nodded slightly, and confirmed, 'That is the Orb of Radiance.'

With caution and reverence, the party followed him into the chamber, inspecting the objects displayed on the pedestals. Liam saw rings, and rods, and a helmet, all bathed in the amber rays from the ceiling. He glanced up and saw, rotating high above, a crystal, a million jagged points jutting from its multi-faceted surface, emanating amber rays directed precisely at the pedestals. One solid, central beam focused on the Orb.

A Ahmud Ki was drawn inexorably toward the Orb. He saw the others staring up at the crystal and knew they misunderstood the source of light in the room. It didn't come from the crystal. It merely received and reflected the beam transmitted by the Orb. The Orb was the source. The Orb was the most potent magical vessel the Elvenaar created. The Lore Book described it in detail – how it could channel magical energy from a multitude of sources into one, how it could perform a spell by multiplying its potency a thousand times, how it could repel and attract magic. It was believed to have come from the Genesis Stone, the gift that fell from the stars during the Time of Making. Its limitation was that it could perform only one function at any given time. In Heolstorcofa, it served as a ward to protect the ancient Elvenaar artefacts from theft. It acted as a glyph.

A frantic scream shattered the silence. A Ahmud Ki span to see an assassin shuddering in severe agony, his right hand caught in a ray of amber light above a silver dagger on a pedestal. Face twisted in pain, trapped like a fly pinned to wood, he writhed violently, unable to withdraw his hand, which was blistering, burning black in the beam. In desperation, he plunged his other arm into the beam to pull the right hand free, and shrieked as it suffered the same fate. His fellows rushed to his aid.

'Stop!' A Ahmud Ki ordered. 'Too late. You can't help him. He's already dead.'

The victim's eyes rolled up, the whites shining

grotesquely in the amber glow, and his body twitched and jerked as the deadly magic ripped through his veins. An instant later, it was over, the acrid stench of burning flesh stinging the nostrils of those in the room. Kurtis turned away, fighting a compulsion to vomit.

'I warned you all not to meddle. Now you see why.'

Startled by A Ahmud Ki's passionless words, Liam wondered what cold reason drove the Royal Advisor. It couldn't be love for anyone. He was cruel, calculating.

'This is our quest,' said A Ahmud Ki, facing the Orb. 'Removing the Orb is my task. When the light alters to white, you must gather the artefacts from the pedestals. Waste no time. Leave nothing. Liam will lead you all back to the burial chamber. I will bring out the Orb.' He turned to the Orb and flexed his shoulders and arms.

Gazing into the amber radiance, he cast his mind through the Lore Book, visualising the ancient Aelendyell script, reading the secrets and lore of the culture he detested. The Orb was the product of complex sorcery, cloth woven from the fabric of time and space by the gods. Disentangling it from the spell binding it to its present function, was a worthy challenge, he decided, but not one to rival his ambition to break down the legerdemain which held the ancient Dragonlords in thrall after their defeat by Aian Abreotan. That was a true challenge. This was pleasant practice. When he recalled all he needed, he focussed and steadily recited the first fragment of spells, moving his hands in the patterns required to complement his words.

Slowly, the amber hue faded from the light and brightened into bluish white. A Ahmud Ki couldn't shift his attention from the Orb to see if the others were obeying his instructions to remove the artefacts as the magical fabric oscillated through a precarious balance between stability and instability. A flicker of concentration could be fatal if the balance moved the wrong way. So he let sound, at the edge of his senses, tell him they'd gathered everything and were vacating the room to ascend the stairs. Sweat trickled down his brow, but he didn't dare acknowledge it. Instead, he moved his hands cautiously through a new pattern, and let his spirit feel the texture of the fabric surrounding him subtly change. He drew a slow breath, murmured the spell words essential to the next phase, and eased the Orb from its base, caressing it, calling it into his power, under his mastery.

What seemed an eternity passed for Liam and the others, waiting in the burial chamber's dull glow. Liam concentrated on the sword's light spell, willing the light to increase in intensity, but it remained impassive, and he assumed that the spell was limited in brightness. Kurtis and Luke were whispering, their conversation too low for his ears, but he figured they were examining the items they carried from the room. The remaining assassins moved through the chamber, looking hungrily at the treasured items they couldn't touch, fascinated by the unreachable wealth atop the Elvenaar corpses, their habitual curiosity tempered but not stilled by their companion's grizzly death.

Liam looked back at the stairwell entrance where the Royal Advisor remained. The Orb was precious. He'd heard the city's safety depended on its return. They made easy travel through the forest to this place, but that was before they slew any Aelendyell, or profaned and pilfered their burial chambers. What would they meet on the homeward journey? Death? No. He was the Saviour. He was chosen to defeat the Dragonlord. He wasn't destined to die in the forest. That wasn't the prophecy. It wasn't The Way. No. They would get home with the Orb.

A Ahmud Ki emerged, bathed in a green glow flowing from the Orb. The Advisor was smiling, as he approached, and he drew the others around. 'We have what we came for,' he said, with a nonchalant nod. 'Time to leave.'

Twenty

'Go into the forest and wait for me. Stay alert.' A Ahmud Ki's instruction prompted the group to withdraw into the green foliage. He waited until he couldn't hear their footfalls, before he gazed across the blue waters of Gnornung toward the island, where the crystal emerald tree glittered. He lifted the Orb, with both hands, above his head. 'What I cannot have for now, none shall ever have,' he pronounced. Slowly, deliberately, he recited Elvenaar words of the Second Ki. The Orb's radiance changed from green to amber, as his voice drifted across the lake, and its glow intensified. Exhilarated by the surge of power, he increased the speed and pitch of his incantation, until a bolt of raw energy shot from the Orb, across the lake, and exploded the tree, shattering its crystalline structure and sealing the entrance to Heolstorcofa. Sparkling emerald shards tumbled through the air and dropped noiselessly into Gnornung's deep waters, and as they struck the lake's surface the Orb radiated an amber beam that dissolved the invisible bridge, cutting access to the island. A death-cold breeze swept across the lake, radiating from A Ahmud Ki, churning the lake's surface from deep royal blue to storm grey, breaking the magic that had held the place intact for centuries, obliterating the link between Aelendyell future and Elvenaar past. Sighs and lamentations rose from the waters, voices crying, calling piteously, until silence swept outwards in the wake of the breeze and smothered the sound like a choking blanket, leaving A Ahmud Ki staring at a dark, listless lake, trapped within its forest walls.

He had struck his first vengeful blow, a blow that would show all Aelendyell how powerful he had become, a blow that would warn them not to cross his path or try to prevent him from reaching further, deeper into the realms of magic that he was destined to possess. He lowered the Orb and waited until the amber glow reverted to soft green, before he turned his back on Gnornung and entered the forest to find the others.

Luke looked surprised as he turned to Kurtis, as if he wanted to say something important, but his lips refused to move. Then he toppled forward, shattering the shaft of the Aelendyell arrow buried in his chest, as he struck the earth. The assassins dived into the undergrowth at the edge of the path, while Liam crouched, sword drawn, eyes and ears searching the surrounding forest for a sign of their invisible assailants. Fear rose in his throat. There was nothing worse than an unseen foe. Kurtis ignored the danger as he kneeled beside Luke's body, stunned by the death of his companion. Only A Ahmad Ki appeared unmoved. He remained motionless, exposed and vulnerable, waiting.

Silent moments passed. Liam felt the forest was threatening to close in. A voice spoke to his right. Three Aelendyell figures stood in the forest, partially camouflaged by their green and brown attire. Two had bows trained on A Ahmud Ki. The central figure was unarmed, and looked very much like the Royal Advisor, except the Aelendyell was shorter and beardless. The Aelendyell spoke to A Ahmud Ki, and Liam listened to the interchange, but the alien language eluded his comprehension, although the Aelendyell's anger was unmistakable. In contrast, A Ahmud Ki was quiet, determined, in control.

Kurtis rose and the Royal Guardsman's hand clutched the hilt of his sword. A Ahmud Ki noticed his movement and whispered sharply, out of the corner of his mouth, 'Remain still.' Kurtis didn't release his grip on his sword, but he halted, watching and listening.

Liam glanced at the underbrush where the assassins had disappeared. They were experts at their trade, he marvelled, before returning his attention to the Aelendyell. The central Aelendyell was agitated. He pointed at Liam and Kurtis and waved his finger viciously as he spoke. Liam saw figures emerge from the bushes beside the Aelendyell before he fully understood what was happening. The Aelendyell fell without a struggle, their throats cut, and the speaker cried with shock and threw up his hands, too late to avoid the same fate. The assassins moved with ruthless efficiency.

'Bring their bows!' A Ahmud Ki ordered. He turned to Liam and Kurtis, and indicated Luke. 'Bring him too. We can't leave clues.'

They moved as rapidly as they could, along the narrow path, until A Ahmud Ki led them into secluded shelter provided by a thick bank of blackberries, where he let them pause for breath. 'He stays here,' he said, pointing to the body. 'Just make sure he's covered well.' Liam helped Kurtis secrete Luke's corpse deeper in the blackberry briar, dragging foliage to conceal it. Kurtis' unrequited anger seethed. The assassins kept lookout for sign of pursuit.

When they were finished, A Ahmud Ki called them together. 'Lay out the artefacts you carried from Heolstorcofa.' Liam and Kurtis placed the rings and dagger before A Ahmud Ki, who glared at the assassins. 'All of them.' The assassins shrugged and unloaded the items to which A Ahmud Ki alluded. He gathered them and placed them in a bag he carried inside his cloak. 'These are items of magic. None of you have the understanding to wield such things. Remember that. I am the one to whom they rightfully belong. There's no point to believe otherwise.'

'What now?' Kurtis' abrupt question was in everyone's mind. Liam wanted to know how the Royal Advisor intended to get them out of the forest.

A Ahmud Ki examined a ring, and answered casually, 'We leave as we entered.'

'But the Aelendyell will be searching for us,' Liam argued.

'The Aelendyell will be searching for humans,' corrected A Ahmud Ki. 'We'll resume our disguise, and we'll pretend we're searching for the intruders as well. That way we can justify cutting through the forest, rather than keeping to paths. We'll take our time. There's no point running. We can't outrun the Aelendyell communication system, and we'd give ourselves away too easily by running. If we're stopped or spotted, no Aelendyell must escape. Is that clear?'

'What about those back there?' asked Kurtis. 'Surely the Aelendyell know where we're headed if they found us?'

A Ahmud Ki shook his head. 'They didn't even know about Heolstorcofa. They stopped us as intruders.'

Understanding registered on Kurtis' face. 'You mean they killed Luke just to stop us?'

A Ahmud Ki had a lever. He could breed Kurtis' hatred for Aelendyell and utilize it in the city before the Great King. 'Aelendyell slay any human on sight, if he should wander into their forests. For us, that's not an issue. Our fates are already sealed because we've slain Aelendyell. They'll show no mercy. Neither can we.'

'By Teka, I'll avenge Luke's death,' growled Kurtis, spitting to emphasize his contempt. 'I'll kill every Aelendyell who dares set foot in the city. They'll die by their own rules.'

A Ahmud Ki let the poison work. He'd lied. The Aelendyell they killed knew they ravaged Heolstorcofa. The Elder intended to take them to his Council for trial, by force if necessary. That was the basis of his exchange with A Ahmud Ki. The others weren't to know. Their escape from the forest depended on the intensity of their hatred. Liam was under his control through the chain. He could depend on the assassins by their nature. Kurtis had to be manipulated.

After leaving the blackberry hideaway, A Ahmud Ki led them along obscure paths, and cut through forest tracts to avoid contact with Aelendyell. They passed within visual contact of two Aelendyell groups moving slowly through the forest, but they seemed content to believe they were another search party looking for the human intruders who desecrated Heolstorcofa.

Shadows lengthened as the afternoon faded into early dusk, but A Ahmud Ki kept them moving at a brisk pace. Liam hadn't recognised a single familiar feature in the forest landscape, so he assumed the Advisor was leading them out a different way. Fortune favoured them thus far, but they were a day and night away from their horses and the open hills below the Andrakian Mountains, and in the heart of Aelendyell territory.

The sudden appearance of an Aelendyell bowman, barring their path, brought them to an abrupt halt. Liam heard movement in the trees and knew other Aelendyell were there. The bowman spoke in his native tongue and drew his bowstring tighter. He looked to A Ahmud Ki. The Advisor drew in his breath and the dark forest exploded in brilliant light. Liam drew his sword and dodged left. Bowstrings thrummed. One arrow thudded into a tree trunk beside his right arm. Close. He could see, despite the light, as if he was in a tunnel within it. An Aelendyell leapt through the light-wall, sword out, but Liam cut him down before he regained his balance. A second arrow whistled harmlessly past. Kurtis was locked in combat with another Aelendyell. A Ahmud Ki was shouting. 'Follow!' Liam checked if Kurtis heard. The Royal Guard parried a thrust from the Aelendyell, lunged and killed the warrior, and turned toward A Ahmud Ki.

The light evaporated as rapidly as it appeared, and they plunged into a mad scramble through the early evening, desperately following the Advisor, bobbing and weaving to avoid being struck by outstretched limbs and branches. Liam heard the sounds of pursuit, faint but closing, and knew they could never outrun the Aelendyell in the forest. They broke cover and sprinted across a clearing toward a central clump of trees, and as they gained the trees the pursuing Aelendyell entered the clearing, in full view. Liam quickly counted fifteen shadows, but the failing light made counting difficult. The assassins loaded the Aelendyell bows they'd stolen, targeted the charging figures, and fired. Two Aelendyell fell before the warriors were upon them again.

Swords clashed. Liam swung and cleaved his opponent's skull with uncanny ease. He cut down a second Aelendyell. A third leaped at him, and he drove the sword through the warrior's gut, impaling the victim, staring into the dying Aelendyell's horrified eyes before they glazed over. He slid the sword from the body, and went to wipe the blade on the warrior's jerkin, but the blade was clean, shining, untainted by the blood. Before he could consider what he'd seen, another attacker pressed him, his sword smacking against his Haardrishii armour. He turned, ducked, and rolled, springing to his feet. The Aelendyell flicked his sword in his hand, and thrust forward, but Liam brought his sword down, smashing the weapon from the Aelendyell's hand, and cut upwards, slashing the warrior's face. The Aelendyell tumbled backwards, and lay at A Ahmud Ki's feet. The Advisor smiled approval. Three Aelendyell broke from the melee and retreated into the forest to raise the alarm.

A Ahmud Ki led the group into the night, forcing them to move quickly to put distance between themselves and their hunters. Because Kurtis and Liam couldn't see in the gloom, the assassins took charge of guiding the warriors. Liam was certain they changed direction, though he couldn't explain how he knew. They struggled through a multitude of creeks, and changed direction again, moving with greater surety along the bank of a larger stream. The moon occasionally broke through the canopy, illuminating their world with eerie silver light, but when it disappeared Liam and Kurtis stumbled in the darkness. Twice Kurtis missed his step and fell into the stream, which the assassins found funny as they retrieved the Royal Guard, leaving Liam to wonder at the character of men who could find amusement even when death pursued them. A Ahmud Ki stopped them once, to wait in the darkness until five Aelendyell passed, oblivious to their presence, and he did not let them move on until he was certain the Aelendyell were long gone.

The ground rose sharply and was rocky underfoot. They were climbing, and Liam had to search for secure footholds. When the next patch of moonlight broke through, he saw they were above the forest canopy, scaling a steep slope below a cliff face. They'd reached the mountains. A Ahmud Ki led them onto a curved ledge that extended slightly from the cliff, and Liam presumed it gave an unimpeded view of the forest and ground below in daylight, providing a suitable point of defence if the Aelendyell came. 'We rest here,' the Advisor announced, and an assassin took watch.

The Aelendyell were there. Liam sensed them gathering in the darkness below. The assassin on second watch had warned the party of their arrival. Liam knew they were trapped by a people intent on revenge, backs against a wall of rock. He hugged the sword to his chest and wondered why its blade stayed so pure.

A Ahmud Ki slipped two rings from Heolstorcofa onto his left hand and picked up the Orb of Radiance. His audience was gathering in the forest below, coming to see a performance he was preparing for them. He would surprise them with his power, leave his mark, and ensure the Aelendyell remembered A Ahmud Ki.

Kurtis was cold and hungry. He hadn't eaten for a whole day. Why the Advisor led them to this ledge he couldn't fathom. It was a death trap. Sooner or later, enough Aelendyell would arrive to drive them down from here, and their fate would be sealed.

The assassins sat, sharpening their daggers. They laid the arrow shafts along the lip of the ledge so they could reach for them when the battle started. Everything they did was methodical, relaxed, as if facing death was common routine.

A rock rattled below. The Aelendyell were climbing the slope. A Ahmud Ki stood, spread his arms wide, shouting magical words at the sky, and for the second time that night light burst over the forest. This time, a huge sphere floated above the trees, shedding its brightness on the climbing warriors. The assassins launched shafts at the blinded Aelendyell, forcing them to retreat down the slope, until the last one melted into the trees. The eerie sphere burned overhead. 'What now?' Kurtis asked.

'We wait again,' A Ahmud Ki calmly replied. 'They'll send the Elders to talk, now they know they're not dealing with ordinary people.' As he finished, he let the sphere of light fade, until darkness and moonlight remained. He whispered

183

to the assassins, 'Time to prepare. Take three arrows with you.' The assassins obeyed and scaled the cliff silently.

An Aelendyell voice spoke from the night.

'What do they want?' Kurtis asked.

'They want to speak with us,' A Ahmud Ki explained. He answered the voice, in Aelendyell, 'Tell your Elders to come forward. I will listen.'

'With whom do they speak?' asked the voice.

'Tell them they speak with one who bears power beyond their understanding,' A Ahmud Ki replied, smiling with self-congratulatory confidence.

'No name?'

'A Ahmud Ki.'

A glowing light danced in the forest, and A Ahmud Ki watched five Elders emerge to stand at the base of the slope, their faces upturned to him. 'Why does an Aelendyell wrong and shame his people?' an Elder called.

'What? No greeting?' A Ahmud Ki chided. 'I thought at least a little respect to be shown to a superior.'

'An ecgbana gets no respect,' the Elder replied.

'Ecgbana is an Aelendyell word for murderer,' A Ahmud Ki pointed out, 'but I'm not Aelendyell. Your people disgust me!'

Liam heard the vicious hate cutting through A Ahmud Ki's words and fear clutched his heart with ice.

'Why so much hatred?' an Elder asked.

'Why so much stupidity and weakness?' A Ahmud Ki retorted.

Another Elder came forward, his silver hair and green robes flowing like liquid. 'You have the Orb of Radiance. It is not yours. It must be returned to its rightful place.'

A Ahmud Ki laughed. 'It's in its rightful place.' He held the Orb before his gloating face, its green glow visible to the Aelendyell. And then he felt an unusual pressure in his left arm and saw the arrow shaft before he felt its stinging bite. Pain and rage exploded through him. He tightened his grip on the Orb, as he tottered at the brink of the cliff for an agonizing moment, braced himself and screamed spell words at the forest, projecting all his furious energy through the Orb. The Orb flashed into red light, and a mass of fiery darts shot outwards, burning neat holes through the Elders, before crashing into the trees behind them. A wall of flame erupted along the forest edge.

Terrified by A Ahmud Ki's vengeful display, Liam was unaware of the rope dangling beside him until Kurtis drew him to it. 'We're going up,' the guard informed him, as he put a rope end in Liam's hand. 'The assassins. Above.'

'What about the Advisor?' Liam asked awkwardly.

Hearing the question, A Ahmud Ki replied, 'Go up. When I've finished here, I'll join you all in the hills, further north. Don't wait. We don't have time.'

Liam tied the rope firmly to his waist, as did Kurtis with his rope, and they made the scrambling climb up the cliff face, and out of Elvenaar Forest, pulled over the lip by the assassins. Liam paused to watch the flames raging uncontrolled into the forest, before he followed the others north, along the ridges of the Andrakian foothills.

Twenty One

'The war goes on,' said Tim with a sardonic smirk. 'Each day the Great King's Haardrishii scour the streets for victims to press-gang into the Great King's service. They get younger by the day, and harder to find.'

'So, how've you avoided the Haardrishii?' Andra asked, remembering Tim's overnight disappearance from the camp of the Great King's Armies before they marched north.

'They don't take thieves,' replied Tim with a wink, as he turned to see what Milly was doing. She was playing 'Grab' with a younger boy in the corner of the room. Their target was a copper coin atop an overturned wooden pail, and the object of the game was simple – grab the coin faster than an opponent. As the young men watched, the children shared a tacit word of go and hands flashed at the pail. Milly held up the coin. 'She's good,' observed Tim with admiration. 'She'll make a great little thief.'

'I don't think the Sisters of Veras would want her to learn how to steal,' said Andra.

'What better occupation?' Tim countered. 'Even in the middle of a war, there's a living to be made from it.'

Andra was determined to get an answer. He knew Tim too well from past acquaintance to let the matter drop. 'So how come the Haardrishii won't touch thieves?'

'They know better. If a thief disappears, so will a Haardrishii. They've got enough problems maintaining their army, without losing men in their own backyard.'

'Is that all? A threat?'

Tim leaned forward, as if he was about to divulge a secret, because his light green eyes sparkled with mischief. 'Not entirely, though that's the main gist. My personal bet is that the Shadow's Voice has an arrangement with High Lord Nisus. You see, the High Lord's also responsible for the Great King's assassins, and assassins, whether they be from The

Hand or the Great King's castle, can't operate in the city without the Guild's blessing. I'd say there's a little political bargaining taking place.' He sat back to watch Milly at her game, leaving Andra to ponder the implications.

'Don't you feel any compulsion to defend the Kingdom?' Andra inquired, after a moment's reflection.

Tim raised his eyebrows, as if he didn't understand Andra's question. 'I'm no soldier. Five moments in the frontline of battle, and Tim Gaelus would either take to his heels or be dead. There's no honour running from battle, but there's no point dying either. I let soldiers do that. That's their job.'

'But what about the Dragonlord? Surely you can't just wait here for him?'

Tim sauntered to the hearth, picked up a poker, and stoked the embers, red and gold sparks rising through the flue. 'There's an army defending the northern reaches of the Valley of Rivers. Another army and the Haardrishii hold Central Gate. The Great King's new champion has brought the Orb of Radiance to protect the Great City from the dragons. And even though I don't believe all the talk being spread by others that this new Saviour, blessed by the Great King's Royal Advisor, will slay the Dragonlord, I'm certain the Dragonlord has met his match. If he hasn't, and he does sweep aside the armies and the magic ranged against him, what hope do I have in trying to fight him? Better to keep out of his way, isn't it?' He gave the fire a final prod, to emphasize his point, and went to give Milly instruction in the art of pickpocketing.

Tim's logic annoyed Andra. They had to fight the Dragonlord. Eventually, the endless battle at Central Gate would drain the Kingdom of defenders, and then the Haagii would pour through and claim the Plains of Ky, even without the aid of dragons. He'd seen the multitude on The Rim Shield; a vast, dark tide, threatening to engulf the Kingdom. The Haagii had to be defeated at Central Gate. Yet part of Tim's reasoning fitted the Guardian Master's philosophy. Don't blindly oppose a greater force. Bend and flow with its

187

energy. Find a way to use its strength against it. The Way – but was there a way against the Dragonlord's hordes?

The door opened and a woman entered, and even in rough woollen clothes Andra was drawn to her raven hair and enticing profile, as she moved to where Tim and the children were engaged in sleight-of-hand. She left with the children in tow, Milly waving cheerfully to Andra as she slipped out the door.

Tim sat beside his friend. 'Nerille will see they get a wash and a bed. She said she'll put Milly in her room.'

Andra gazed at the closed door, wondering where Nerille fitted into Tim's underworld. The last time he was with Tim, the women he met worked for a jovial, if obese, red-haired woman named Patti. He'd shared a night with a woman in Patti's brothel for the first time, and he could never forget the sensual touch of her body. She was beautiful; not in the pure way Mirith was beautiful, but beautiful to touch, to hold, and to be part of in the act of loving.

'Andra?' a voice murmured at the edge of his thoughts. He blinked and saw Tim smirking at him. 'Pleasant thoughts?'

'Yes,' Andra answered. 'Very pleasant.'

Tim stood and went to a small cask perched on a shelf, selected two pottery mugs from beside the cask, opened the cock, and filled both mugs with syrupy liquid. He crossed to the hearth and placed the mugs at the edge of the foremost coals where they would quickly warm. As he squatted to his task, he talked, his back to Andra. 'You haven't really told me the whole story of your rescue, my friend. How long were you in the forests with the Aelendyell?'

His question was direct. Andra had improvised a tale he'd already shared with Tim, a tale in which his rescue from Dragon Breath Plains occurred through sheer good fortune, when an old shepherd, searching for straying sheep, happened upon him. Terath asked him not to reveal Wudufaesten Tun to Andra's people, so he was under oath not to tell Tim, but he knew Tim hadn't believed his story from the outset. 'Why the Aelendyell forests?' Andra asked, attempting to draw him.

Tim rocked on his heels, watching the mead mull by the fire. 'You carry an Aelendyell bow. I read the runes carved in it. The Weapon Bearer to whom the bow belongs is Freyar.'

'I found it,' Andra said quietly.

Tim laughed, and carefully turned one mug. 'Aelendyell don't lose their bows, Andra. They'll die before they'll part with them. The runes in Freyar's bow tell his tun's history. That's sacred information that Aelendyell fanatically guard. You were given the bow. Either that, or you killed him to get it.'

Tim's calculated accusation stung Andra, who glared at the thief crouched before the hearth, and stated flatly, 'I killed no Aelendyell,' but his stern denial only brought a warm smile to Tim's face. In the glow, Andra saw how remarkably like the Aelendyell Tim really was. He shared their fine profile, the large oval eyes and handsome beauty that marked all Aelendyell, although it was blurred in his features; heavier, less refined. Quartercast: that was the term Tim used to describe himself the night they sneaked into the Great City to introduce Andra to city life. Tim could see in the dark, the one major legacy his ancestors passed on to him.

With care, Tim retrieved the mugs and carried them to the table, and slid one toward Andra. 'There's another thing,' he said, continuing the conversation, as if Andra had already confessed. 'I found this.' He reached inside his tunic and withdrew the pouch of healing powder that was Mirith's parting gift.

Andra's eyes widened, disbelieving the pouch's sudden appearance on the table, while his hands instinctively touched his belt and found the pouch missing.

'It's Aelendyell healing powder,' said Tim. 'Very rare. In fact, I don't think any people in the Guild have even seen it.' Andra took the bag from the table and slid it into his trousers, but Tim grinned mischievously, raised his mug preparing to drink, and gibed, 'I've seen good thieves lift prizes from there too, my friend.'

Tim's humour was pervasive, and Andra couldn't help but smile as he lifted his mug to sip at the warm liquid. Its aromatic warmth bathed his cheeks, and the spicy odours sparked a vision of Mirith, in long flowing robes, before a backdrop of elmoaks in Wudufaesten Tun. Relaxation spread through his weary body. What harm could telling Tim really do? He was part Aelendyell. If Terath knew Tim, he'd approve, Andra reasoned, as he gazed at the thief across the rim of his mug. 'There's one more thing,' said Tim, lowering his mug. 'You know the truth about the talisman.'

Andra shifted his left hand from the mug and fingered the thong at his neck. Of course Tim would know. He'd given him the talisman in the first instance. It was an Aelendyell item. 'I was told what it really is. It saved my life at least twice.'

'Then it's a greater gift than I intended,' Tim said, with unusual solemnity. 'Here, in the Great City, the Guild accepts it as one of the signs of recognition between certain members. There are others that you'll learn. Don't wear it openly. Don't display it to anyone outside the Maze. And be choosy, even in the Maze. Very few bear such a talisman, though every Guild member will recognise it. I'll teach you another sign to use when I get permission from the Guild to admit you.'

'What about Milly?' Andra asked, remembering his charge from Sister Emiris.

Tim leaned back on his chair. 'The girl's identity is easy. She can be a street novice. If she shows promise of beauty, Patti will take her under her wing. You're the real problem at this stage.'

'How am I a problem?'

'You're a warrior. If you're caught on the street, they'll march you off to war again. I've got to convince the Guild you're an assassin. Teka give me help,' he laughed, and raised his mead in salute to his open-mouthed companion.

Too many unanswered questions: too many riddles. Andra

tossed and turned, sleeplessly, on his rough bedding, and sat upright in the semi-darkness. A solitary candle flickered by the doorway of his bare room, and beyond the doorway were the rasping snores of thieves. The Guild's members might work silently, but they slept as noisily as a tavern brawl. He clambered from his upper bunk and dropped as quietly as he could to the floor.

The stone underfoot was cold, as he crept to the doorway and peered into the adjoining room's dark interior, where sounds of sleep echoed against the ceiling. Even a clumsy thief could sneak in here and cut everyone's throats, he mused. So much for thiefly vigilance.

Tim had read the runes on Freyar's bow and recognised Aelendyell healing powder. He knew the talisman's double function. He was a thief, an assassin, and a member of The Hand, as he called it. He was a city-dweller. Yet his understanding of the forest dwelling Aelendyell couldn't be learned in the city. He was a paradox, a fascinating riddle Andra felt compelled to unravel. He was tempted to risk feeling his way to the door into the corridor from the next room, but there was every possibility he'd disturb a sleeper, and then be escorted back to his bed. If only he could sleep. They weren't keeping him locked up, below the Inn of Dragons, but he wasn't free to come or go either. Tim asked him to be patient while the Guild decided his fate, but Tim was sure they would approve his entry into The Hand. At worst, he'd have to meet the head assassin, the person referred to by members as Death's First Hand, but Tim said that was very unlikely. He promised he had a good tale to spin to keep Andra's identity hidden. He sighed and crept back to his bunk.

Outside the door, Tim removed Andra's blindfold. Andra blinked and rubbed his eyes to adjust to the lantern light. 'Is this it?' he asked.

'This is it,' Tim cheerily replied. 'There's nothing to worry about. Death's First Hand only wants to see who you are. I think my story interested the Guild.'

'Do I knock?'

'That's generally the sign of good manners.'

Andra adjusted his jerkin and knocked on the wooden door. Tim certainly spun a tale. As Andra was led blindly along a twisting maze of tunnels, Tim outlined what he told the Guild. He recounted the night of their illegal excursion into the city, when in the Inn to gain a table Tim told a group of men that Andra was a Royal Assassin. Later, the men ambushed Andra, apparently exacting revenge for the assassination of one man's brother at the hand of the Great King's Royal Assassins. Fortunately, Tim saved Andra's life, but Tim told the Guild the night's killing was Andra's work. So, Death's First Hand summoned him, presumably to exact the truth. Beyond the door, a feminine voice invited him to enter. Andra glanced questioningly at Tim, who shrugged and grinned. He turned the handle.

The room he entered had a low ceiling, but it was spacious. It was also well lit by at least twelve lanterns on the right and left walls, and Andra easily picked the detail of furniture spread before him. Two chairs were arranged before a table in the room's centre, and a desk hewn from very dark wood occupied the far left corner. A shelf over the desk was filled with rolled parchments. A door led from the far right corner, and the right wall was adorned with narrow tapestry strips hung between lanterns. The floor wasn't earth or stone, but polished wooden planking, making Andra's footsteps echo as he stepped forward. The only missing detail was the owner of the voice who invited him in.

'Behind you.'

Andra turned toward the woman's voice, and simultaneously saw the door he entered closing, with Tim disappearing beyond the door. He felt exposed and alone. Death's First Hand studied Andra from where she stood, holding him with her silence while she assessed his worth. She pointed to the chairs at the central table.

He was struck by her cold elegance, as she crossed the

room to join him at the chairs; her skin pale, her lips so red. Her sumptuous black hair, falling to her waist, heightened the contrast by framing the pallor of her face. A dark cloak, clasped at the neck with a gold dagger brooch, hid her feminine contour, but she was tall, and Andra perceived fluidity in her motion that implied feline fitness and agility. When she sat opposite, her ice blue eyes, large and liquid, were deep pools, threatening to draw him into their depths and, oddly, he immediately thought of Milly. She also had the same ice-blue eyes. He had expected a man, but now he understood why this woman was Death's First Hand. In her beauty, he glimpsed the awful magnificence of death; death not as victim but as perpetrator, as a change not an end, as a statement of something binding, permanent, personal, and infinite.

Twenty Two

'The point, Tim, is she didn't believe a word of your story. She knows I'm not an assassin. She seemed more interested in the scar on my cheek than anything else,' Andra explained, and self-consciously stroked his cheek.

Tim leaned on the back legs of his chair. 'Death's First Hand obviously believes in the prophecy. Your scar caught my attention when I first met you.'

'What prophecy?' asked Andra, irritation rising in his voice.

'The one the Great King's Royal Advisor recently resurrected.'

Andra waited for Tim to continue, but as usual the thief gave little away. 'Tim, I haven't been back more than a week. What prophecy?'

Tim coughed to clear his throat, before replying, 'There's an old belief that the Dragonlord will be beaten by a warrior who has a moon on his face. Like yours.' As he finished, he stood and walked toward the door.

'You think that's me?' Memories, vague ones, tugged at him. He'd heard someone else mention his connection with a prophecy. Hadn't Tim said something about it before?

Tim shook his head. 'No,' he said, but added, 'well, I did briefly, when I first met you, but I was wrong. The Royal Advisor found the warrior. He's the Saviour I mentioned before, the Great King's champion. On his forehead, there's a circular moon and Elvenaar runes. He's the one spoken of in the prophecy. Your scar's an interesting coincidence, but a lot less obvious.' As he finished, though, Tim continued to stare at Andra's cheek. 'The other coincidence,' the thief said, after pausing, 'is that this warrior almost certainly came from the same place you came from. He wears a ponytail, like you and your companions wore when the Haardrishii first brought you to the camp.'

Andra's eyes widened. 'You mean he's from The Vale?'

'Maybe,' replied Tim. 'But it's only a coincidence.'

'What makes you say that?'

'The warrior is Haardrishii, Andra.'

'Where can I see him?'

Tim heard the anticipation in Andra's words, and shook his head, as he said, 'It's unlikely you can. But I do know the Great King intends to hold a parade along the King's Way, in two days, to celebrate the arrival of the Orb, which this warrior brought from the Aelendyell forests. I'd say it's certain the Saviour will be on show as well.'

'Then we'll be there too,' said Andra.

Milly rubbed the pebble's smooth surface between her fingertips. Aaron pointed at the block of wood to the left in the corridor. The challenge was set. She carefully judged the distance and hurled the pebble. The block tumbled. 'Amazing!' whistled Jen, who was watching the demonstration of throwing accuracy. Aaron bowed his head despondently.

'Oh, come on, Aaron,' Milly coerced, pulling at his arm. 'Lucky shot, that's all.'

Aaron shrugged his bony shoulders. 'Sure,' he mumbled. 'Except you've hit it nearly every time. And me, just twice.'

Milly hugged the dark-haired boy who'd become her friend in the short time since her arrival in the Great City. 'It's not fair, really,' she tried to explain. 'I used to throw stones all the time with my father. He used a sling to catch pigeons and rabbits. I couldn't use his sling very well, so I threw stones instead. It's only practice.'

'Take heed, lad,' said Jen, as she ruffled Aaron's hair. 'The girl's good at this, but she doesn't brag.'

'She's good at everything,' muttered Aaron. 'She runs faster than me and steals quicker at 'Grab'. She can even read and write.'

Jen gave Milly a look of surprise at Aaron's last revelation. 'Can you now, my girl?' Milly nodded. 'Does Patti know this?' Jen inquired, eyebrows raised.

Milly shook her head. 'No. I only told Aaron. My father used to say reading and writing are powerful weapons and shouldn't be waved in people's faces.'

The philosophical message made Jen smile, and she shook her short brown hair as she put a hand on each child's shoulder. 'Aaron, you've got a very talented friend. You're lucky. Don't feel belittled. You could learn a great deal from this friendship. And Milly should teach you. But I think we better see Patti first.'

'Nice bow,' said Roy, menacingly, as he lifted from the end of the bunk. His two companions leaned against the bed frame. 'I'd like a bow like this,' he continued, running his broad, freckly hand across the runes. Andra sat up on his bunk, woken by the entry of the three thieves, and watched Roy, waiting for him to put the bow back and move on, or make conversation. 'Should I take it?' Roy directed to his companions.

'Does yas likes it, Roy?' grunted the man, with a short bushy moustache and goatee.

'Yeah, Munce, I do like it.'

'Then takes it, Roy. I's'll lets ya.'

Andra understood what was happening. He swung his legs over the edge of the bunk, and landed on the floor between Roy, Munce, and the third man. 'What's your problem?' asked Roy diffidently.

Andra rested on the balls of his feet, trying to maintain a calm demeanour. 'Just curious to see what you were doing. I hadn't expected visitors.'

'We ain't visitin',' the third member spitefully replied. A bitter face, thin nosed and scarred across the mouth by an old dagger or sword slash, peered from under thin matted hair.

'Nah. Roy's jus' foun's 'is bow,' added Munce.

'Nice bow, isn't it?' said Roy, holding it up in the low flickering light.

Andra smiled. 'Beautiful,' he agreed amiably, but he carefully measured his opponents. 'Nice game, but I need my sleep. Time to put the bow back.'

The third thief scowled, flicked a thin dagger into his hand, lifted it dangerously close to Andra's eyes and hissed, 'I don't think you unnerstan'. It's Roy's bow. You'd best crawl back into your bunk and go beddy byes, while we're still in a good mood, eh?'

'We don'ts likes thieves,' added Munce. 'Especially them that tries to steal Roy's bow.'

The dagger point touched the end of Andra's nose. 'Sorry,' Andra apologized. 'I didn't realise it was Roy's bow. My mistake.'

'Make sure it's ya only mistake,' hissed the dagger wielding thief, 'or I'll cheerfully slit ya throat.' He prodded Andra's chest with the point. 'Now get in ya bed.'

Andra turned on the pretense of climbing back into his bunk, but watched for movement heralding an attempt to stab him in the back. 'Come on, lads, let's go,' chuckled Roy, as Andra climbed onto the bunk, and the three thieves headed for the doorway.

'What about the arrows?' Andra called after them. As they turned, he launched from the bunk, heaving into the thin nosed man with his muscled weight, flattening him against the doorframe. His attack caught Roy and Munce off guard, and he was on his feet before they recovered or drew their daggers. They regarded their winded companion, writhing on the floor for want of air. Andra held out his hand, and said, 'I believe you've got something of mine.' Munce slipped his dagger from its sheath, but Andra's foot lashed out and up, sending Munce's weapon flashing from his hand to embed in a roof beam. The thief yelped with pain and shock, and dropped to his knees, holding his injured wrist. 'I'm very tired,' said Andra looking at Roy.

The thief ran his fingers across the hilt of his dagger, assessed his companions, and unhitched Freyar's bow from his shoulder. 'I must've made a mistake,' he said, watching Andra. 'This is obviously your bow. My mistake.' Roy gingerly handed Andra the bow.

Footsteps approached from the adjoining room, and lantern light spread as Tim Gaelus appeared in the doorway. Munce was still on his knees, whimpering. The third man was tottering to his feet, looking pallid, in obvious pain. 'Sorry, Andra. If I'd known you had visitors I'd have knocked,' he said laconically, winking at Roy.

'It's alright,' replied Andra. 'They're just leaving.'

Roy took Andra's advice and helped Munce to his feet. As the three made to leave, Tim grabbed Roy's arm and whispered in his ear. Roy threw Andra a startled glance, and left with his sore companions.

When the departing footsteps faded, Tim turned to Andra and asked, 'Are you alright?'

Andra nodded. 'They wanted the bow. I didn't realise thieves would steal from their own in the Maze.'

'It's not uncommon, especially for older thieves to take from the less experienced. Roy probably figured you were only a visitor, and therefore fair game,' Tim explained, 'but I think it serves a good warning. We'd best store that bow in a safer place. It's too tempting for some of my colleagues.'

'Where?'

'There are places I know. Best if I take it now.'

Andra passed the bow to Tim. 'And what did you tell Roy as he left?' he asked. Tim grinned wickedly. 'Don't tell me,' said Andra with a resigned sigh. 'I'm an assassin. Right?'

'Of course,' said Tim. 'What else?'

It was raining. Grey clouds closed out the sunlight. The King's Way ran with water, the earthen road fast becoming slush underfoot, and the few people, gathering to watch the proposed celebratory parade of Great King Thana, huddled in doorways or peered from half-shuttered windows. Andra stood at one window of the Inn of Dragons, with Tim, and several thieves whose names he hadn't yet remembered. In front of him, Aaron and Milly pressed against the window frame. Milly was excited because she'd heard there was a

198

Great King and she was eager to see him. 'Will he come, Andra?' she asked hopefully.

'I doubt it,' said a thief over Andra's shoulder. 'His Royal Highness wouldn't like to get mud on his horses' hooves now, would he?'

'Are they beautiful horses, Andra?' Milly continued, ignoring the thief's cynicism.

Andra rubbed her tousled hair. 'His horses are the finest in the Kingdom.'

'What are their names?'

Incredulity filled Andra's face at her question. 'He has hundreds of horses -' he began, but Tim cut over his voice.

'- And he knows each one by name. There's a broad chested white one called Prince, and another bearing the title of Lord Leto, and a bay who leads the others in the stables, who is called Destrac. Each horse has its place and its purpose.'

Milly smiled, her eyes sparkling with joy. Over Tim's shoulder, Andra caught two of Tim's companions stifling sniggers. 'Which one will he ride today?' Milly asked.

'Who knows?' said Tim, his eyes wide with imagined wonder. 'Each horse has a turn to bear the Great King. Perhaps none.'

'Why none?'

'Even horses need a rest from royal duties. Watch, and we'll see which ones come today.'

The girl smiled and leaned out the window to look along the King's Way as far as she could. Andra grinned, and shook his head in admiration of Tim, at which the thief pulled a horrendous face, much to his companions' amusement. 'You need a good woman, Tim Gaelus,' said one man. 'It's time you raised your own kids after that performance.'

'No woman could keep him standing still long enough to make him a father,' scoffed a second.

'She'd be better lying him down,' chipped in Detton Tomas, the innkeeper at the bar, and the group chuckled at their mirth.

They waited a long time, until a lanky youth with straggly

dark hair appeared at the Inn's entrance, and spoke to a thief, before he jogged away in the rain. Andra watched him crisscross the King's Way delivering messages to other figures. A moment later, his message was relayed from the door. 'The royal parade is descending the Castle Road.'

'So the rain hasn't scared off the Great King,' grunted a man at the back.

'The Royal Advisor probably stopped it raining directly over his head,' said another.

'It wouldn't surprise me,' a third concluded.

'Can he do that?' asked Milly.

'Do what?' replied Andra.

'Make it stop raining?'

'No.'

Trumpets blared, and the head of the parade appeared: four Haardrishii horsemen, black armour glistening with rain, their war steeds champing at their bits, ears flattened, steam rising from their nostrils. Andra felt Milly draw in her breath at the sight of the magnificently groomed horses, clad with black plate armour like their riders, their tails plaited and bobbed. 'Look at the horses!' she cried. 'Aren't they just perfect!' Andra placed both hands on her shoulders, and he could feel her trembling with excitement as the Haardrishii trotted past, the horses' hooves flicking up mud. The girl loved horses. How much it must have hurt her to see the pair they rode from Spurl slaughtered by the Haagii.

Behind the Haardrishii came six priests in pairs on grey horses. Andra recognised the orange and red robes of the Priests of Teka, but the last time he saw the priests they were walking, swinging incense to cleanse the way for the Great King. A team of oxen appeared, flanked by six mounted Haardrishii, drawing a large caged cart, a cart that reminded Andra of the wagons used to transport Claarn and the warriors of Tressel Deep when they were brought to serve in the Great King's Armies. A dark mass huddled behind the bars, and jeering reached his ears as the cart passed groups further up the road. As the cart drew level with the Inn of Dragons, he saw why the crowd jeered. The dark mass became a jumble of thick, dirty arms, legs, torn clothing, long matted hair, sullen eyes staring into space; a load of living dead, Haagii war prisoners. Curses and mutterings erupted around him, and hatred boiled within his heart, but behind the leathery masks Andra recognised the fear, the desolation, and the hopelessness that the caged Haagii felt. For a moment, he peered into the dark eyes of one of the passing prisoners, saw their emptiness, and pitied his enemy.

Two blond warriors, superb in physique, with large sheepskin cloaks protecting them from the rain and cold, rode white chargers, the horses as impressive as the riders. Andra remembered that these were the Great King's personal guards, and looked past them for the Great King, but he wasn't to be seen. Instead, the warriors were followed by a solitary figure on horseback, wearing the customary armour of the Haardrishii, but he was helmetless, and his long black hair, pulled back into a ponytail, bobbed in rhythm to the horse's motion.

'That's the Saviour,' Tim muttered in Andra's ear. 'He has the prophetic markings. Look, as he comes closer.'

Andra needed no prompting to examine the rider's features. Already teasing familiarity drew his eyes, and, despite the strange armour and the circumstances, he knew the rider, recognised a lost friend, and felt the pull of The Vale. The rider was Liam.

As Liam reached the Inn, Andra saw other changes in his Guardian friend, who he thought returned to The Vale after escaping the Haardrishii in the Valley of Rivers. Liam's severe hairstyle exposed his scarred forehead, the prophetic markings Tim described, although Andra couldn't discern the detail. Around the warrior's neck was a heavy metal chain, and a silver pendant sat against his chest, shaped like a woman, but the form was obscure, indefinite. There was one more thing. Hanging from Liam's belt was a fine crafted sword, resting in relief against the horse's ebony coat, the sword Andra's father, Malcolm, presented to him when he left The Vale for the war: the sword of Cedwyn.

'Where are you going?' cried a startled Tim, as Andra forced a passage through the press of bodies and skipped to the inn's door. Andra didn't answer. He pushed through the crowd in the doorway and sprinted after Liam's receding form. 'Come on!' yelled Tim to the others. 'They'll kill him before they'll let him talk to the Saviour.' Thieves bolted after him.

'Liam! Liam!' Andra called, as he reached the warrior's horse, but Liam did not look down. 'Liam! It's me! Andra!' He grabbed the horse's saddle strap, and screamed, 'Liam!' Liam's gaze remained fixed ahead, oblivious to Andra's presence. Hooves pounded the mud. Andra turned to see two Haardrishii bearing down, lances pointed at his chest. He rolled under the belly of Liam's horse to avoid their charge, and clutched his companion's mailed gauntlet as he bounced to his feet on the other side of the horse. 'Me, Liam! Andra! The Vale! Home! Remember?' Liam remained unmoved, but the Haardrishii wheeled, hooves churning the King's Way. Andra realised there was no point continuing to try to divert Liam's attention, and prepared to duck beneath his horse one more time, but the Haardrishii anticipated his manoeuvre and reined in their mounts. The street crowd pressed in to watch the new source of excitement.

In a flurry, both Haardrishii were surrounded by thieves, pulling them unceremoniously from their horses into the mud beneath packs of bodies. Tim appeared out of the whirling confusion to grab Andra. 'By Teka, you bring nothing but trouble!' the thief growled, and dragged him through the crowd, and down a side-alley. At the back of an outbuilding, near the inn, Tim heaved against a water barrel and lifted it, revealing a vertical tunnel. 'In, Andra! Your life depends on it,' he ordered. Wordless, Andra dropped to the tunnel floor two spans below.

Twenty Three

'As I feared,' said Tim, bending his head to enter the small alcove where Andra waited. He closed the hatch door and squatted. 'The Great King wasn't very happy to hear that one of our people attacked his Saviour. The Guild has been ordered to find you.'

'But I didn't attack Liam!' Andra protested. 'I only tried to speak with him.'

'The order's been given.'

'Who gave the order?'

'The Shadow's Voice.'

'Who's that?'

Tim eased onto his backside. 'I don't know, Andra,' he said. 'To be honest, nobody in the Guild knows, except Guild Master Orrin. There have been changes of late, since Orrin started issuing orders on behalf of the Shadow's Voice. No one questions them, though some say it's Orrin trying to amplify his authority without taking full responsibility for it. I don't mind the changes. The Shadow's Voice favours assassins over other thieves. There have been jobs required, even while the war's going on.'

'So what happens now?' He stared at Tim in the dull torch light, trying to decide whether his thief friend would turn him in.

'I'll find a place to hide you,' Tim reassured him.

'Where?'

'In the Maze. Where else? There are so many tunnels and rooms under the Great City, it would take an army years to find anyone.'

'But the Shadow's Voice has asked the thieves to turn me in. Thieves are looking for me, not an army,' the young warrior insisted.

'There's plenty who'd happily turn you in to gain pocket money and favour, I grant you,' Tim agreed with a malicious wink, 'but there's also plenty who turn blind eyes to everything, even orders from the Shadow's Voice. I have one place you won't be found, and we'll disguise you, if necessary. In a week, the incident will be forgotten. The Great King hasn't got time to concern himself with trivial incidents. Chances are the Shadow's Voice is only issuing the order on the pretext of looking, knowing we'd never turn you in.'

'Then why hide at all?'

'Because,' began Tim, with a stern frown, 'some people don't understand subtle political manoeuvres, only orders.' Tim reached inside his tunic and withdrew a crusty breadstick and a waterskin, which he offered to Andra. 'Refreshments. You'd best remain here, until the excitement dies down. Then I'll take you somewhere more comfortable.'

Andra took a drink, but stowed the breadstick to his left against the wall to eat later. After he wet his throat, he resumed the conversation because myriad questions whirled in his mind. 'Why didn't Liam acknowledge me?'

Tim shook his head. 'Who knows? What wrong did you do to him before?'

'I didn't,' Andra denied. 'At least it wasn't my doing. We were all forced to come to the Great City to join the Great King's Armies. The Guardian Master said it was The Way, but Liam felt he'd been sacrificed without hope. He ran off in the Valley of Rivers. I thought he returned to The Vale.'

'Perhaps he's still bitter,' Tim suggested. 'Some people depend on a leader, or god, or belief to shape their lives, and when it's taken from them or shown to be false they loathe it.'

'It wasn't like that. He didn't even look down to see who was calling him. Even when I pulled his gauntlet, he seemed oblivious, as if he was somewhere else entirely.'

'Then perhaps it's just arrogance,' said Tim with a sweeping gesture of his right arm. 'He's the Saviour, the one anointed by a prophecy and destined to change history. Perhaps he sees himself as existing beyond this mortal world. Why look down at a common thief who calls him in the street?'

'If I was an assassin,' replied Andra in a distant voice, 'I could have killed him before the Haardrishii arrived.'

'Perhaps, but he's the Saviour. He's not destined to die at the hands of an assassin, according to the prophecies, so why should he fear anything?'

Andra sighed with exasperation. Tim had an answer for everything, but he wasn't convinced. Liam's fixed gaze disturbed him because it was unnatural. 'The rains came too early,' Andra murmured cryptically.

'What do you mean?'

'I was returning to The Vale when I came here. I want to go home, go back to being a Guardian. That's what I really want to do. I don't even know if my parents are still safe from the Haagii.'

'What's rain got to do with it?'

'The Valley of Rivers floods in winter. It's impassable then. When we came south with the Haardrishii to join the Great King's Armies, we only just beat the floodwaters. I'd hoped to return to The Vale before the rains came, but now I must wait.'

'Patience is an important skill. You'll have time to learn while you wait out the winter here. When the questions stop being asked about your whereabouts, you can pretend to be an assassin, like me. While you hide, I'll teach you the trade. By the time you can travel home, you'll have new skills. Interested?'

Andra saw Tim smile, but he kept a solemn expression, and replied, 'Teach me, Tim Gaelus. I'd be honoured.'

'It's clear,' Milly whispered, and beckoned for Andra to follow. He entered the narrow corridor and trailed her small frame. She ascended a short flight of steps, paused before a wooden door, and knocked – three raps, pause, two raps. A tiny hatch opened, and a feminine face peeped at Milly. Andra heard a key in a lock, and the door gaped open. 'Come on,' the girl urged, and disappeared inside. Andra obediently followed.

The room was warm, and the aromas that greeted Andra were sweet and enticing. Tim brought him here the first time they escaped to the Great City from the Armies' camp. The brothel owner was a short, plump woman with orange hair. He noticed a rug on the floor and remembered that it hid a trapdoor because that was how they entered last time. The woman who let them in, chatting with Milly, was attractive, her face framed by short brown hair. Milly obviously knew her, and Andra marvelled at how easily the orphan girl he rescued from the Haagii had acclimatized to the Maze. Tim said she was a natural thief. Andra was beginning to believe it.

'So you're Andra,' the woman said, straightening to look at him.

'Yes,' he replied.

'Milly's told me all about you,' she continued with a gentle smile. 'She says you're a brave warrior and very kind. She's quite proud of you.' At the last comment, Milly glared at the woman, and turned her back to hide her embarrassment, a reaction that only brought a sweeter smile from the woman as she moved closer to Andra. 'I'm Jen,' she said.

Andra battled shyness. Even dressed plainly as she was, in a long, loose smock that hid her bodily charm, Jen exuded a sexuality Andra associated with the women who lived here. He remembered Lisette's dark ringlets, her warm sensuous lips, and her guiding touch. Remembering the name of the woman in charge of the brothel, he asked, 'Where's Patti?' to direct his thoughts from sex.

'She's at a Guild meeting, but Tim told me what's required. I'll show you where you'll be safe, for the time being,' Jen explained, and took his hand to lead him through another door, into a familiar passage, lit by green light.

Tapestries hung along the walls, between the six doors to the girls' rooms, and as Jen led Andra and Milly, Andra studied the tapestries and saw the explicit embroidered erotica, detail he overlooked on his first visit. He glanced at

Milly, but she appeared disinterested in anything around her, and he rationalized she had been along the corridor in the past three or four days. At the corridor's end, Jen pressed on the wall, causing it to revolve and open into another space, and she led them through and closed the panel. They waited in darkness, until Jen lit a lantern on the wall.

The light spilled down four short steps to a room with furs strewn across the floor. A cold hearth sat in the left wall, with a charcoaled cauldron resting before it, and a large circular wooden tub occupied the room's centre. Two doors led from the far wall. 'We relax here, on occasion,' Jen informed Andra. 'Patti keeps this part hidden from anyone else in the Guild, and certainly from customers, so we girls can meet and bathe without ever worrying about intruders. The hearth's big enough to warm the whole room, and the bath can be filled with warm water. We often share a lukewarm bath. It's very relaxing,' she explained, with a smile Andra interpreted as coy. 'The rugs keep the room warm.'

Jen descended the steps and indicated Andra should follow her to the left door, which she opened. 'This is where you can stay.' The room was small, but bedding in the corner, and a jug and plate of fruit, made it inviting. Andra found a lantern on the wall, and Jen helped him to light it.

'What do you think?' Milly asked.

'Very comfortable,' said Andra. 'Better than sleeping in the thieves' quarters with Tim.'

'Can I sleep here too?' Andra's startled gasp caused Jen to break into laughter. 'What's so funny?' Milly grumbled.

'Nothing,' sputtered Jen, trying to suppress her giggle.

'Then, can I sleep here too?' the girl repeated, offended the adults were not sharing their thoughts with her.

Before Andra could reply, Jen broke in to say, 'No, Milly. Patti wants you to stay with me. You've got to learn your lessons and help me teach the other kids.'

'But I can still do that if I sleep here,' the girl argued.

Jen gave Andra a knowing smile. 'Yes, that's true, Milly, but Andra has a lot of things to do, and Tim will want him to learn as well, so you'd be left out and alone a lot.'

Milly looked despondently at Andra. 'Is that true?'

Andra nodded, feigning disappointment. 'Sorry, Milly, but Tim wants to teach me, and I'll probably be up late at night and up again really early in the morning. It's better if you sleep with Jen.'

Milly considered the adult reasoning. 'Okay,' she decided. 'I'll stay with Jen. But you promise to see me every day, Andra. And don't leave here without me,' she said with determination.

Andra put on a solemn expression and took Milly's hand. 'I promise with a Guardian's Oath.'

Sweat beaded on his palms. His hands were slipping, losing grip on the wall. He flexed, pushed harder against both surfaces. His back ached. 'That's very impressive,' said Tim, staring up at his protégé, pressed across the ceiling of the corridor, spanning from wall to wall between feet and hands. 'You can come down.' Andra released the tension in his body, and dropped to the floor, landing heavily on his feet. 'We'll need to work at that, though. You land like a wounded bull.' Andra hauled in a deep breath, and wiped perspiration from his forehead. When he reopened his eyes, he saw the needle point of a long, thin dagger barely a finger's breadth from his face. 'Seen one of these?' Tim asked.

'Once. Your friend attacked me with one outside the Inn of Dragons, if you remember.'

'It's yours,' said Tim, handing over the lethal tool. It was exceedingly light. The handle was barely wider than the blade and no guard separated the two. 'An assassin always carries one.' He reached inside his boot to withdraw a similar weapon. 'Inside the boot is common practice. Some carry them inside their sleeve. An associate of mine always clips his to the side of his short sword, but I think that's pointless.' He tumbled the dagger in his fingers with practised ease as he continued Andra's instruction. 'Stiletto daggers are for personal assassinations,' he explained. 'You must be very close to the victim. They can't be thrown. No balance. You need to press up against the target and slip the blade in neatly. Here.' He pointed to a gap between Andra's ribs. 'The heart. Anywhere else, except perhaps the temple or eyes, is worthless.' He slipped the stiletto into his boot and pulled out a broad bladed dagger, one with which Andra was familiar. 'Don't stab a target in the chest with one of these. Even the back's risky. Too many ribs. Too much wasted space. I've watched an apprentice assassin botch his job: twenty-three wounds with a dagger before the victim died. That's murder, not assassination.' Again, he played with his dagger, twirling it round his fingers. 'An assassin's tools are extensions of his being. You must feel the weapon, be the weapon.' He stopped his demonstration. 'There are two places worth a dagger strike,' he said grimly. 'The neck.' He mimed a throat being slit. 'And the groin.' He indicated the target point on himself. 'The victim bleeds to death very quickly. The work's clean and effective.' He flicked his dagger into the air and caught it, before sliding it inside its sheath. He pulled a length of fine wire from his belt and flexed it in the grip of both hands.

Andra listened, and watched with fascination and dread, as Tim detailed a variety of killing techniques, demonstrating his arsenal of simple but fatal weapons. He was witnessing a dark side of his friend he glimpsed when Tim slew one of three men who attacked Andra, the night they ventured into town. There were two Tims. One was cheerful; a practical, fun-loving thief, who enjoyed risks, tall tales, wine, women, and good companionship. The other was a silent, ruthlessly efficient, killing machine, capable of assassinating a specified victim with emotional detachment. How can two opposites make one being, Andra pondered? Which one is really my friend?

Twenty Four

Nisus watched the grey rain drifting across the Plains of Ky toward the castle plateau. Winter was setting in, and he was pleased. The Valley of Rivers would swell with angry streams and rivers, Rainbow Lake would flood, and snow would cap the mountain peaks and fill the higher valleys, closing access to the Plains of Ky from the north and northwest. Reports told him that snowdrifts were building in Central Gate, where remnants of his beleaguered South Wheel Army, and the Haardrishii, held the main force of Haagii at bay. The snow wouldn't stop the attacks, but it would diminish their ferocity, and give his desperate soldiers much needed breathing space, because the Kingdom's reserves were spent. He could draw most of the East Wheel Army away from the Valley of Rivers, if it was impassable for the winter and part of the following spring, and use them to reinforce Central Gate, but there were no men left on the Plains of Ky, except old merchants, peasant farmers, and rough youths. The Haardrishii press gangs rounded up everyone else: except the thieves.

Nisus turned from his turret window and moved to his table to study the maps. The thieves' immunity to forced service for the Great King irked him. Surdrok secretly refused to comply with his orders to have the Haardrishii seize every hale thief for the Armies, and while some enlisted voluntarily Nisus knew most of the thief population in the Great City had simply disappeared inside their secret tunnels, emerging now and then to conduct their illegal business. They were a protected species. Worse, it was common knowledge the thieves intended to remove a Haardrishii for every thief taken into captivity to serve the Great King, and although the Haardrishii weren't directly his concern Nisus couldn't afford to lose any of the Kingdom's most adept soldiers in a foolish game of revenge in his city. So the thieves were left alone, outside the Great King's jurisdiction, a wasted source of soldiers. As head of the Royal Assassins, Nisus even personally tried to convince the Guild to encourage thieves to enlist to bolster the defences at Central Gate, but the Guild's representative, Orrin, said the Shadow's Voice expressly forbade their involvement in the Great King's problems. The matter was closed. Nisus had asked to speak with whoever this 'Shadow's Voice' was, but Orrin said that wasn't possible, and withdrew from the meeting, leaving Nisus standing in an outbuilding, behind a soothsayer's shop, like a common petty seeker of aid.

What he feared most was the inevitable collapse of the defence plan he created. He was justified in putting all the Kingdom's energy into defending Central Gate, because the Haagii seemed obsessed with taking it, and reluctant to seek other ways into the Plains of Ky. The Andrakian Mountains were virtually impassable to anything but small, experienced parties, and the Haagii would have to risk marching through Elvenaar Forest, to the south, to go around the southern tip of the Andrakians – a military strategy that would pit them against the guerrilla tactics and magic of the Aelendyell, and cost the Haagii dearly in lives and time. Reports from Central Gate showed the Haagii army grew daily, despite the horrendous losses they suffered with each attack upon the Kingdom's defensive walls closing the main pass, so it was apparent they were determined to force passage through the gap, onto the plains, by sheer attrition. When the Haagii army first arrived, dragons burned Axxon, spreading terror through the ranks of the Kingdom soldiers, but the dragons mysteriously withdrew, and did not attack Central Gate as Nisus and everyone feared they would. It was as if the Haagii generals were wasting time – as if they, too, weren't overly concerned about the coming winter. Their daily battles were more like chess moves, gambits designed to test the defences, so that, when it came time to really break through, they would do it with ease, because they would know their enemy's strengths and weaknesses. That factor, the unknown reasoning driving the Haagii warfare, unsettled

Nisus, and made the game of playing High Lord of the Great King's Armies more than a challenge.

He flicked aside the map of the Central Gate and looked at the next one, detailing the Great City. The Great King valued his advice, and honoured him with two titles, making him the most powerful man in the Kingdom, after the Great King, but the Royal Advisor stole the limelight with his opportune discovery of the Saviour and the theft of the Orb of Radiance from the Aelendyell. Thana's favour was being redirected.

Nisus had no love for the Royal Advisor. Ever since his arrival from Targa, he'd sought power. It annoyed him that A Ahmud Ki was succeeding; steadily and deliberately reeling the Great King into his purpose. Thana's insecurity was a path to his favour, but while the two of them competed for his favour neither could hope to win the greater prize. The Royal Advisor was too critical a risk to ignore or upstage. He held too much close to his chest, and only revealed his cards when it was essential. Within his black tower, he was impregnable, and Nisus despised the Royal Advisor's magic. There was only one recourse to ensure that he, Nisus, would succeed the childless Great King, and that was to eliminate any threat to his claim. Being Lord of the Royal Assassins made the task easy. The Royal Advisor had overstayed his time in the castle. Resolved, Nisus bent to his maps and began planning his winter military operation with renewed enthusiasm.

Thana wheezed and coughed at the head of the King's Table. He hated the cold winter air because it made his chest ache and his breathing rasp. He'd heard Nisus' report on the state of affairs regarding the war. At least the Haagii were stopped by the new High Lord's strategies, but he'd sacrificed half the Kingdom to achieve that goal. 'When can We expect the Haagii to be driven back to their own lands?' Thana asked, peering at the High Lord.

Nisus hoped the Great King wouldn't ask that question.

He shifted his feet and cleared his throat. Better to be falsely confident than truthful, he decided. 'The Haagii won't find much to eat on the western plains, at least nowhere near enough to feed their army,' he stated. 'They've wantonly destroyed the produce and burned whatever forest they've been able to penetrate. Winter will eat at their stomachs. I predict they'll withdraw within a month. If they do persist until first spring, they'll be sorely weakened by hunger and illness, and disinclined to carry out a protracted battle for Central Gate. On the other hand, our soldiers will be refreshed and rested, and reinforced, and we'll take the battle to them, as we did last spring, and push them back.'

'Back to The Rim Shield again?' A Ahmud Ki asked, quietly reminding Nisus of the tragic military blunder the previous High Lord made in pursuing the enemy across the desert of Dragon Breath Plains, only to be hopelessly trapped at the foot of the escarpment separating the warring nations.

Nisus glared at the Royal Advisor. 'Back to Uz Erhaag,' he coolly replied. 'I'm not as limited as my predecessor.'

Thana brightened with Nisus' news. He had chosen well to appoint the man to High Lord of the Great King's Armies. 'We thank High Lord Nisus for his strategies. Because of him, We still rule Our Kingdom,' he said with smug approval. Then he focussed on A Ahmud Ki. 'We also give Our thanks to the Royal Advisor for finding the Saviour, and for setting the Orb upon his tower to keep away the dragons.'

Nisus interrupted. 'The Royal Advisor has indeed brought us all a blessing,' he said courteously, although A Ahmud Ki heard mocking undertones in Nisus' words. 'But I won't feel safe until this Saviour meets the Dragonlord and slays him. When can we expect this to happen?'

Political games. A Ahmud Ki smiled imperceptibly. Clever ploy. Force the same brash confidence from an opponent so the Great King can witness who's the bigger liar.

'Well?' Thana asked, eager to hear when the prophecy would be fulfilled. 'We await your answer.'

A Ahmud Ki rose and surveyed the collected Lords. 'I cannot foretell the fulfilling of a prophecy, Your Royal

Highness. Only a prophet can do that. For the prophecy to reach its conclusion, the Saviour must first meet the Dragonlord. It appears from High Lord Nisus' reports the Dragonlord is still in Uz Erhaag, still waiting on The Rim Shield.' Disappointment clouded Thana's pudgy face. 'But rest assured it will happen,' A Ahmud Ki added. 'Remember that the prophecy has already begun.' He sat, secretly cursing Nisus for trying to force his hand publicly at the King's Table, and he toyed with the idea of sending a probing thought into Nisus' mind, an act sure to unsettle the High Lord's confident demeanour, but he restrained himself. Never give much away. Better Nisus should feel confident. A Ahmud Ki had other plans afoot.

'There will be no prophecy fulfilled.' All eyes turned to Waeron Ardath. The white-haired Royal Drycraefter fixed his gaze on A Ahmud Ki.

Thana broke through the confusion. 'We would appreciate an explanation, Lord Ardath,' he demanded.

Waeron Ardath did not rise to reply. 'The Lord Advisor has presented a likely candidate to save the Kingdom. Who can argue? The warrior has all the markings the prophecies speak of – or at least markings that can be interpreted as the markings of prophecy. He even bears a sword that, so I've heard, can make spells. And he has brought the Orb, however illegally, from the Aelendyell, to ward dragons from the Great City. All these things are impressive. They point to greater things. The Lord Advisor says we can expect them,' Ardath paused. A Ahmud Ki waited for the Drycraefter to make his point. 'But there's a flaw in all this,' the Drycraefter continued. 'You see, all the elements of the prophecy are not yet brought together. Two parts are missing, and without them, the warrior Liam is no more than that: a warrior.'

A Ahmud Ki was perplexed but fascinated by Ardath's revelation. Either he was bluffing for an as yet unknown political gain, or else he knew something about the prophecy A Ahmud Ki did not. The former was very much out of character for Waeron Ardath. He was normally content to watch the others play political games while he remained aloof. The latter was unthinkable. A Ahmud Ki had searched through all the tomes and volumes referring to the prophecy in Abreotan's time. There was nothing he'd left out.

Ardath's interlude delighted Nisus. He leaned back and smiled, enjoying watching the two practitioners of magic tussle before the Great King. The Drycraefter's assistance in humiliating the Royal Advisor was totally unexpected, but warmly greeted, by the High Lord. Seeing A Ahmud Ki exposed as a charlatan was all he hoped for, from the outset, although he had personally been unable to find the fault. But Ardath had.

'If there are two elements missing, which are they?' Thana asked, looking decidedly worried. His fear of the Dragonlord had dissolved with Liam's appearance, but now it rushed back in, a black nightmare of horror threatening to subsume his being in sleepless nights and empty days.

Ardath hesitated before answering the Great King, and A Ahmud Ki understood the reason for the Drycraefter's reluctance, knowing that sharing his knowledge would allow his antagonist an opportunity to fabricate the missing details from the prophecy. Ardath was astute, a worthy intellectual opponent A Ahmud Ki respected, because, like A Ahmud Ki, he maintained a firm hold on what he knew, never bragging, never foolishly exposing personal strengths or weaknesses.

'The prophecy, as I have it recorded in the Ancient Lore,' Ardath carefully explained, 'says the Dragonlord will only be defeated by one bearing the mark of the moon who dies and is born again. He will also wield a two-edged sword.'

'Is this true?' asked Thana, staring at A Ahmud Ki in the hope the Royal Advisor would rebut Ardath's argument.

The Advisor dipped his head in mock respect for Thana's authority, and said, 'It's true.' He'd missed nothing though. What was Ardath's problem? 'I see no inconsistency in the prophecy,' he asserted, turning his grey eyes on the Drycraefter.

'Your warrior has not died and been born again,' said Ardath steadily.

'Is that all?' A Ahmud Ki laughed. 'What's death, Lord

215

Ardath? Is it when we cease to breathe, go cold, no longer warmed by the pulsing of our blood?' This was an easy problem to solve. 'Physical death is only this much. But there's also death of the spirit, of ideals, of philosophy. In the land of Ranu Ka Shehaala, the Ithosen talk of 'inyela' – death of the heart – when one no longer has a purpose to live. When I found the warrior, Liam, his heart was dead, his reason for living gone. Once a Guardian from The Vale, he'd been abandoned by his master, and he came to the Great City seeking another path, a new life, a chance to be born again. And so he has been, because the gods came to him, and marked him as the Saviour, the one bearing the mark of the moon.' A Ahmud Ki sat back, pleased with his impromptu explanation, and allowed himself a gloating glance toward Nisus to enjoy the frown creasing the High Lord's forehead.

'What has the Lord Drycraefter to say?' asked Thana, less unsettled having heard one part of the prophecy re-established with no effort.

Ardath shrugged. 'Interpretation of prophecies is not my province. I think the Royal Advisor admitted as much earlier as well. I see no reason to argue.'

He's capitulating too easily, thought A Ahmud Ki. There's something more he's holding back.

'What was the second element?' Thana persisted, eager to hear the Royal Advisor completely deny the Royal Drycraefter's skepticism.

Ardath's face became solemn. 'The sword,' he said firmly.

'What about the sword?' asked Thana.

'Common prophecies fail to name the sword, but it is named in the Ancient Lore. The one who opposes the Dragonlord must wield the sword of Abreotan. No other sword contains its legendary power.'

'But the Saviour has a magical sword,' insisted the Great King. 'He wears it. He used it to retrieve the Orb. Our own Royal Guards witnessed its magical powers.'

'It's not Abreotan's sword,' Ardath reiterated.

The statement brought silence to the King's Table, and

the Lords turned to A Ahmud Ki, awaiting his reply. Thana fidgeted nervously with the golden hem of his purple cloak.

A Ahmud Ki was assessing what he'd heard. Ardath was referencing a text he hadn't read, something called the Ancient Lore, which Ardath obviously had in his keeping, and therefore he retained information that A Ahmud Ki didn't have. It was pointless trying to probe Ardath's mind for details. The Drycraefter had previously demonstrated that he understood A Ahmud Ki's mind spells and could deflect them. If Ardath spoke true, and A Ahmud Ki had little doubt that he did, then he had a complication to overcome concerning his artificial incarnation of the prophetic figure destined to overthrow the Dragonlord. Much as he disliked gambling, unless he knew the outcome, he was obliged to play Ardath's game. He knew his bluff was being called. 'The Lord Drycraefter is correct,' he nonchalantly admitted. 'The sword the Saviour carries is not the sword of Abreotan.'

The Lords reacted with shakings of heads and gasps, while Nisus nodded knowingly, openly approving of Ardath's exposure of a fraud. Thana slumped in his chair, and muttered, 'Then We have no Saviour,' crestfallen by A Ahmud Ki's admission.

'On the contrary,' said the Royal Advisor. 'We have no sword.'

'But without the sword there is no prophecy,' Lord Gerran cut in.

'I don't see your logic,' A Ahmud Ki replied.

'You promised Us a Saviour from the Dragonlord and gave Us a false one!' Thana protested.

The Great King's simple-mindedness irritated A Ahmud Ki. He stood, pushing away his chair, and his tone was venomous as he responded to Thana's accusation. 'You have your Saviour. Already he's brought the Orb to keep the dragons at bay. And that task he's done without Abreotan's sword. Can you ignore what you have witnessed? A prophecy is an unpredictable thing. Now that the Haagii are quietened by winter's hand, and the dragon threat eliminated, the Saviour will find the sword of the prophecy

217

and fulfil what he has begun. If you doubt that, you're doomed, because you show neither courage nor hope when the reason for both stands before you! Liam will wield the Sword of Abreotan.'

A Ahmud Ki strode from the assembly, black and grey robes streaming in his wake, leaving Chancellor Rheims to scuttle after him to close the Throne Room doors. Outside, A Ahmud Ki paused to listen for the argument he was certain would erupt in his absence. Predictably, Nisus started it, and he was pleased his dramatic exit had the desired effect. But he also had a problem to solve: to find a sword lost in the mists of time.

"A wise king has no friends, only acquaintances, servants, and subjects. Friendship is a privilege based on trust, and a wise king who wishes to reign long in his Kingdom trusts no one."

extract from The Golden Burden, written anonymously in the reign of King Ermine, 18th descendant of King Aian Abreotan.

"Trust a friend with your life.
    Lose both in doing so."

Assassin's maxim.

Twenty Five

A Ahmud Ki pressed the panel behind the library wall, closing the passage. He was alone, but darkness wrapped around like a comforting friend, and he paused in the musty silence, savouring its peace. Waeron Ardath's revelation disturbed him. There were prophetic details absent from the texts Pak and he found in the Great King's library, details also missing from the fragments of prophetic vision stored in the Aelendyell Lore Book. Without Abreotan's sword, he couldn't complete the synthesis of the warrior, Liam, with the prophecy, and that left him exposed to his critics, particularly Nisus.

There were other minor irritations. Despite his orders to Orrin, the thieves hadn't uncovered the individual who attacked the Saviour during the parade. There were weaknesses in his network, weaknesses he couldn't accept. The incident didn't carry significance, he tried to convince himself, but doubt nagged at his conscience. Why would anyone dare attack the incarnation of a prophecy?

And there was Thana. The fat king's confidence had grown too much in Nisus' company. The High Lord's defence campaign was proving successful despite enormous odds, and Thana was beginning to believe his Kingdom's safety rested in Nisus' military acumen, even though they all knew the Dragonlord had only just begun his invasion without personally taking part or bringing his awesome power to bear. Ardath's outburst had sown further seeds of distrust in the Great King's mind toward the Royal Advisor. Should the Great King decide to exercise his authority, what could A Ahmud Ki expect? Thana had to be convinced that he, A Ahmud Ki, was the only true authority in the Kingdom.

There were answers. He knew there were answers. Some were buried deep in the earth beneath him. He would first seek there. Then he had to speak to Ardath, alone, and discover the information the Drycraefter withheld, and from what source he drew it. Ardath wasn't one to use bluffs. There had to be truth hidden, somewhere. He could deal with Nisus when the Dragonlord's hordes renewed their war effort and revealed the inadequacies of Nisus' plans. Thana would then be his to control. And so would be the Kingdom.

The passage ended at stairs that twisted and dropped sharply, between the hollow castle walls, into the plateau rock beneath them. A Ahmud Ki ignored the many small doorways as he descended, intent on following the main passageway to its end. The plateau was a veritable warren, a fortress excavated beneath a castle, large enough to hide an entire army. The complex of doors and tunnels reminded him of the Maze beneath the Great City. If the way down was disguised behind an anonymous door, any one of the multitudes of doors along the main passage, he might not find it for months.

He descended another flight of steps and emerged in a small chamber where a portcullis barred further progress. Beyond the portcullis was a large metal door, like the one he remembered blocked access to the cavern, where he arrived, when he teleported from the Inner Sanctum of Mareg's prison beneath Targa. The obstruction probably explained why the Guild thieves weren't using the tunnel complex beneath the castle, but he was certain the two mazes were linked at, or beyond, this point. He used a spell to pass through the solid barriers to emerge in a tunnel.

Again, he stood in a self-contained space because the tunnel ahead was blocked by a rock fall, a portion of which was excavated to enable someone to get through. The thieves had obviously explored this far, but no one could penetrate, or unlock, the metal door. Upon inspection, A Ahmud Ki found dents and scratches on its metal face, but no significant damage because it was an arm span thick. He clambered through the gap in the rock fall, and descended the sloping tunnel, until it entered a large cavern he recognised, even in darkness: the Deep Cave.

The last time he stumbled in here, he lit the entire

chamber with a brilliant light spell, sending bats into a frenzy and startling a group of thieves, but this time he decided to scan the jumbled stalactite and stalagmite formations with Aelendyell vision to detect heat shapes. Warm spots hung from the ceiling. Bats, but no one else. Good. He knew one exit from the Deep Cave led to the Guild's Maze, and a mass of boulders in the centre covered another exit: a shaft dropping into the heart of a Dragonlord's lair. He'd come from there. He'd return. But he spotted a dark smudge, in the far wall, that he hadn't seen last time in the confusion, an exit the destination of which he didn't know. That is worth checking first, he decided. As he prepared to leave the Deep Cave, A Ahmud Ki pulled the cowl of his cloak over his head to hide his conspicuous features, in case he should meet anyone from the Guild.

The tunnel became a narrow stairwell that angled up. The cool air dropped further in temperature, and A Ahmud Ki felt the stirrings of a faint breeze on his face, as he reached the top of the stairs. Traces of daylight touched the walls of a cavern, a step ahead, and a shallow lake spread before him, filling a cave that swept in a smooth circle toward its mouth in the base of the plateau. He was standing at the birthplace of Dragon River: a river that rose from natural springs, deep in the earth beneath the plateau, and flowed out of the cave, through the Great City, and across the Plains of Ky, to empty into the Lake of Peace. He admired the cave's beauty, and the silent water.

The only incongruity was a rope dangling a wooden pail from a shaft in the ceiling, from a well on the castle plateau. In times past, the plateau would have been an impregnable fortress, with its height above the surrounding plains, the maze of tunnels, and its natural water supply. He wondered if the ancient King Abreotan had deliberately built it so, and why his descendants had neglected the strength their forefather left them? When the Kingdom was his, he'd revive the real castle Abreotan had designed – the fortress in the plateau.

A Ahmud Ki descended into the Deep Cave, and made

certain no one had entered in his absence, before he crossed to the mad jumble of boulders at the centre.

He studied the problem. Passing through wasn't essentially difficult, but under the rocks was a vertical shaft, so, once through, he'd have to relax and concentrate on levitating to avoid a fatal fall. The real problem was determining exactly where the shaft began under the rock pile. If he misjudged the position of the shaft's entrance, he would pass into solid earth and be entombed forever. He considered taking the risk, but he chided himself for Aelendyell recklessness, and resolved to have Orrin's thieves clear away the boulders to make the task easier.

Disappointed not to explore the Dragonlord's tomb, he headed for the exit to the castle, but he had learned where the passage led, and satisfied his belief that it connected to the Maze. In future, it would be much easier for the Shadow's Voice to speak to Orrin, though the Deep Cave would need to become taboo territory for thieves. There were always answers to problems.

He glanced at the night sky as he paused on the pathway to his tower. Storm clouds obscured the stars, and a crescent moon raced between dark cloudbanks, as if desperate to hide from an unseen pursuer. The wind whistled across the castle parapets, but barely stirred the trees in the Royal Gardens. He liked storms. Full of wild, raw energy, they were like the untapped magic that drove the Dragonlords, the style of magic he wanted to drive him as fiercely as his passion to possess it. Against the night sky, his black tower was invisible, save for a faint silver glow emanating from the Orb of Radiance at its peak. The Elvenaar were wondrous magic wielders to create such a reservoir of vast energy, he begrudgingly admitted, and he emulated their powers in his mastery of the First and Second Ki, but he would be a Dragonlord too, and rise far beyond their legendary ability. He was chosen by destiny. Karrilyon told him so. Berak N'eth had blessed him. Lost in dreams of power, he headed through the garden's dark foliage, pulling his cloak tighter to keep out the cold air.

He was shocked by the sudden jerk against his throat. Fists pressed against his neck, pulling something thin and sharp tighter against his throat, and a bony knee drove fiercely into the middle of his back. He crashed onto the gravel path, pain sparking through his eyes, as an immense weight on his back pressed him into the ground and forced air from his lungs. He was choking, being choked. Blood red curtains closed across his eyes. He tried to flail at his attacker with his arms and legs, but heavy boots stomped on them, mercilessly pinning him to the ground. The garrotte cutting into his neck was crushing his windpipe with its increasing pressure. He couldn't cry out. He couldn't breathe. He couldn't move. He was being murdered.

At the edge of consciousness, he heard heavy breathing in his ears. Then a voice yelped, and the pressure on his arms and legs disappeared. Someone else cursed, and the weight on his back shifted to one side. He seized the opportunity to heave sideways, and felt his assailant fall back, but the wire around his throat snapped tight, sending pulsing agony ripping through his body. Arched crazily by the pull of the garrote, he blocked out the pain and incanted a single spell with fierce desperation, no sound coming from his blue lips, for lack of air, as he frantically weaved his hands. The assassin screamed, released his grip, and writhed in agony at the path's edge, his hands pressed against his temples.

A Ahmud Ki staggered to his feet, swaying crazily, gagging for air. The gardens swirled in a dark pool. Someone groaned to his right. He tried to focus, but the darkness roared in. The path was spinning away, the sky, the trees and he was falling, the darkness rising to swallow him.

Orrin paced nervously back and forth, waiting. The bats resettled on their roosts in the Deep Cave, once they accepted his lantern's intrusion, but its light threw eerie shadows across stalactite and stalagmite formations, making the Guild Master uneasy, even with six Guild members labouring at a pile of boulders. The Shadow's Voice called him here. He visited the Deep Cave many times to seek the elusive passages that all thieves knew led into the Great King's castle, but he never considered moving the boulders. Why shift them? he wondered. The castle is up on the plateau, not deeper underground. But the Shadow's Voice had a reason for moving the boulders and Orrin dared not disobey. There was a power afoot in the Guild the others could not comprehend, and he, Guild Master Orrin, the most powerful Guild Member, had become its tool. If the others knew their orders came from the Great King's Royal Advisor, Orrin would be a dead man. But what could they do to stop it? The men heaving the boulders grunted and swore. Orrin was Guild Master, and if he wanted the boulders shifted then that's what he got, but none of the thieves considered the job Guild work and did it under compulsion.

The labour was testing and long, but gradually the jumbled pile diminished, until only one enormous monolith remained. The combined efforts of the six thieves could not budge it. 'Begging Master Orrin's pardon,' a bearded member of the working party puffed, 'but this last boulder's not going anywhere.'

'Try harder,' was Orrin's abrupt reply. He didn't need the Shadow's Voice's disapproval for failing to be ready.

Another thief spat and swore. 'Maybe Master Orrin would give us a hand?' a third asked, sarcastically.

Orrin's anger was aroused, but he approached and put his shoulder against the rock. It still wouldn't move.

Tell them to stand back.

The intrusion of the voice in his head stunned Orrin. He straightened and peered into the recesses of the cavern, searching for the dark figure he expected to see.

Tell them to stand back, the voice repeated.

'Get back from the rock,' Orrin ordered. The thieves obeyed, if somewhat curious by his instruction, but as they shuffled back from the rock all six men buckled at their knees and collapsed. The hair on the nape of Orrin's neck bristled with fear. 'What in Teka -?'

Relax Orrin. They are asleep.

'Wh-where are you?' the Guild Master stammered.

To your left.

Orrin turned toward the far wall of the Deep Cave. A tall shadow moved toward him, took form in the light, and became the sinister shape of the Royal Advisor, although his head was obscured by a closely tied hood. His eyes appeared to shine in the lantern light.

You've done well, Orrin. My congratulations.

Orrin didn't relax, despite the unexpected compliment. He had no reason to trust the Royal Advisor. Fear ruled his obedience. 'We were just about to shift the last rock,' he said, attempting to cover his failure.

No need. It can remain. We'll call it a monument to your labour. I want it to stay there. Understand?

'Yes,' he replied obediently. He hated hearing the voice inside his head. It was weird. Wrong. Why couldn't the Royal Advisor talk like anyone else, especially if the other thieves were asleep? They were asleep weren't they?

I said they're asleep, Orrin.

Orrin physically winced. He couldn't even keep his own thoughts private.

No. You can't hide anything from me. Remember that.

The glittering grey eyes were staring straight at him, and the Guild Master felt less secure than ever. 'What is it you want?' braved Orrin, determined at least to show some strength.

Have you found the thief who attacked the Saviour?

'No. I had some leads but -'

It doesn't matter. The issue is closed. I have far more important matters for you to deal with. As of this moment, the Deep Cave is no longer part of the Maze. Any thief caught here is a dead man. Understood?

Orrin nodded. Why close off the Deep Cave, he wondered?

Don't question it, or you will be as dead as any thief caught here.

Orrin dismissed the thought.

Wise decision. Only you, as Guild Master, may enter the Deep Cave. From now on it is the sanctuary of the Shadow's Voice, and you will receive instruction from here. Understood?

'Yes,' Orrin replied.

I have a gift for you.

Orrin watched in fascination as A Ahmud Ki produced a platinum neck chain from his robes and held it before the lantern to let flecks of light sparkle on its links.

Wear this as a sign of your office and your standing with the Shadow's Voice.

He slipped the neck chain over Orrin's head, and as Orrin accepted the gift his fear of the wizard melted like ice before fire. He was protected by the Shadow's Voice. Who could touch him now?

There's one more task. I need four assassins. They must be the best you have.

When the interview was over, Orrin left the Deep Cave, intent on fulfilling his master's wishes, satisfied he'd done well. He left without his six Guildsmen. As far as he was concerned, he never took any with him. The Deep Cave was a forbidden zone to the Guild. No thief was to enter it ever again, except the Guild Master.

A Ahmud Ki watched Orrin's retreating form. With the chain in place, like Liam, he would serve well. The Advisor gingerly rubbed the stinging wound encircling his throat and swallowed painfully. Without a voice, he was grateful for the mind spells he learned as an Ithosen, and in Targa. There was much to do. He glanced at the bodies of the thieves sprawled on the cave floor. Messy, but at least they wouldn't talk about their work in the Deep Cave. Even Orrin had forgotten them. He stared at the monolith covering the trapdoor of the vertical shaft to the Dragonlord's tomb. Entering correctly would no longer be a problem, but he would have to wait. There were more immediate plans afoot, and they had to turn out right this time.

Twenty Six

There were rumours. The attendant Lords of the King's Table whispered the gossip with shakings of their heads and knowing nods: the Royal Advisor was dead, assassinated in the Royal Gardens by unidentified assailants. High Lord Nisus smiled at the news.

Great King Thana was distraught: an assassination within his own castle, one he hadn't ordered? 'How did you come by this news, Rheims?' Thana asked, his squinting eyes fixed on the Chancellor's thin visage.

Rheims glanced apprehensively around the assembly and held out a note on parchment. 'This letter, Your Highness. His servant, Pak, brought it to my chamber this morning. He was speechless when I questioned him further.'

'Have you seen the body?'

Rheims nodded. 'Yes, Royal Liege. He was lying at the edge of the path before the black tower. He had a deep cut across the face –' Rheims paused, squeamish at the memory. '- and a dagger stuck in his chest.'

Nisus listened to Rheims' description of A Ahmud Ki's wounds with disgust. The victim was dead, that was certain, but the Royal Assassins he picked for the task apparently did a poor job; messy and unprofessional. He would upbraid them for sloppy work.

'And where is the body now?' asked Thana, looking pale, and worried that one of his pillars of strength had been so easily torn away by death's hand.

'The servant, Pak, took it into the tower,' Rheims replied.

Nisus coughed. 'If I may interrupt this solemn news?' he said. 'It seems the Haagii are finding a new way to infiltrate our defences.'

'What makes you think it's the Haagii?' asked Lord Kerry.

'Who else?' Nisus replied lifting his eyebrows. 'Thieves?'

'Could be possible,' said Kerry.

Nisus shook his head. 'Even their work is more efficient than this murder, as Rheims described it. And they've nothing to gain by the Royal Advisor's death.'

'Who will gain by this murder?' asked Gerran.

They looked to Nisus for an answer and saw him staring at Waeron Ardath. The white-haired Drycraefter sat with an implacable face. 'No one,' said Nisus, his implicit accusation already silently suggested. 'Only the Haagii. After all, wasn't it the Royal Advisor who first alerted us to the return of the Dragonlord?'

'How could Haagii get into this castle, kill the Advisor, and not even be seen, let alone caught?' argued Lord Haephus, disbelief etched on his brow. 'That's an absurd explanation, Nisus.'

Nisus shrugged. 'Come up with a better alternative, Priest.'

'Any alternative will be much darker than the one Nisus offers,' said Ardath unemotionally. 'One at this table knows the truth. The rest must merely speculate the reasoning, although we know the answer, if we search deep enough.'

The Lords glanced uneasily at each other, and the Great King watched apprehensively, wondering whom he could no longer trust at the King's Table, apart from Nisus and Rheims.

A Ahmud Ki stared at his own corpse on the tower's marble floor. Beside it lay bodies of men he recognised as Royal Assassins, men who worked for Nisus. How close to death had he come? A silly price to pay for carelessness: Nisus reminded him of the thin line between mortality and immortality, taken him briefly across it, re-awoken a primal fear he'd almost forgotten. For his effort, Nisus would be rewarded accordingly.

A Ahmud Ki bent over his dead self, and silently weaved his hands, breaking down the illusion spell, until Pak's form reappeared, cold and distant. The only features to remain constant were the wounds on Pak's face and chest, fatal blows he received saving his master's life. If Pak hadn't chanced to step outside at the time A Ahmud Ki chose to return from his exploration of the secret passages in the castle, the Advisor could well have died a rather pointless death. Yet, he reasoned, there is no chance involved because I am part of a destiny greater than Nisus' brief vision of time. I cannot die at the hands of the Royal Assassins, if that is not meant to be, he decided. But he heeded the cautionary message the attack brought. There was no point being foolhardy.

Ardath didn't believe in ghosts, but one waited for him in the hallway. A Ahmud Ki bowed slightly, an unusual deference from the Royal Advisor, alive or dead, and indicated with a gesture he would like to enter Ardath's chambers. The Drycraefter had no choice but to acquiesce to the request.

Inside, Ardath used his burning taper to light three lanterns hanging from the centre of the ceiling, and their brightening glow opened the room to A Ahmud Ki's gaze. He had never seen such a cluttered assortment scattered across shelves, small tables and a desk. Boxes, opened and closed, odd devices made of wood, paper, and metal, circling spheres, scrolls, vials, pottery jars, mirrors and gems, and a host of items A Ahmud Ki couldn't aspire to name, were piled haphazardly on every level surface, and mobiles hung randomly from the beams supporting the ceiling. On a perch, near the buried desk, was an owl, blinking at the light, its great eyes shining like green discs. A wall was filled with a library of ancient volumes.

Ardath blew out the taper and scratched his head. 'I'm not sure whether I should be greeting you, or conjuring a spell to turn you away,' he said finally, turning to gaze at the half Aelendyell. 'I never trusted you alive, and even if you are dead I think I trust you even less.'

The Drycraefter's honest wit drew a smile from A Ahmud Ki. He looked at Ardath and tried to concentrate, but Ardath effortlessly turned aside his probing mind spell. 'We've talked about this before,' said Ardath calmly, as he noted A

Ahmud Ki's disappointment. 'I know the mind spell, and how to protect my thoughts from it, so you waste your time trying to draw secrets from me that way.'

A Ahmud Ki's impassioned gaze puzzled him, as he finished talking, until the Advisor opened the neck of his robes to expose the deep cut and bruising on his throat, and he forced a sharp hiss from between his teeth and shook his head.

Ardath's eyes widened. 'You mean the dead can't speak?'

A Ahmud Ki pointed to his head and made a pleading gesture for Ardath's cooperation. Reluctantly, Ardath agreed, and relaxed his defences against A Ahmud Ki's spell, but he was prepared to protect himself if the wizard tried subterfuge.

I'm hardly dead, Ardath, despite Nisus' henchmen. I don't die that easily.

Ardath smiled. At least he wasn't communicating beyond the grave, unlike Lord Haephus who claimed to do it frequently, though never publicly.

Haephus is an idiot, A Ahmud Ki projected.

'I don't know whether I really like someone listening to my thoughts,' replied Ardath with a frown.

I can't help that. The spell works that way.

'So whose body did Rheims see?'

My servant's. He was killed trying to save me. I used illusion, swapped identities for a while. Better Nisus thinks I am dead.

'Your attackers?'

Dead.

Ardath nodded, and moved toward his desk, winding between the fragments of his odd collection. 'Why are you here?' he asked.

I need answers.

'To the prophecy?'

Ardath had second-guessed him. Yes. The details I've missed. How do you know them?

Ardath paused. A Ahmud Ki felt the mental barrier rise,

cutting communication, while the Drycraefter considered his request. Ardath shifted items on his desktop, without any observable purpose, but when he stopped he looked up at A Ahmud Ki with a curious expression. 'If political games were more my forte, and they're not, I would have you concerned, wouldn't I?'

A Ahmud Ki suddenly felt uncomfortable in the Drycraefter's presence. But why fear someone less powerful? Perhaps. But you don't play political games, so the question is invalid.

Ardath laughed, and stroked his white beard thoughtfully, aware he was letting A Ahmud Ki inside again. 'I'm the Royal Drycraefter. You've never really worked out my function, have you?'

No. I admit not entirely so.

'Look around. What do you see here?'

A Ahmud Ki didn't look. Junk.

Ardath said amiably, 'Perhaps some of it is. A thousand years of junk. From my father. And his father, And his father. And his father. Right back from the time the first Drycraefter, Faro Ardath, served King Aian Abreotan in the Dragon Wars. See those books on the walls?'

This time A Ahmud Ki looked, understanding that the man he considered less than his equal was teaching him a lesson.

'They're continuous records of every event that's ever occurred in the Kingdom's history. From Abreotan to Thana. You'll even find your name in the last chronicle. I'm writing it. That's the Ancient Lore. Every successive Drycraefter must maintain the chronicles, detailing every word written, every word spoken of significance, every action taken.'

And the prophecy? A Ahmud Ki asked anxiously.

'In its full and original form,' Ardath replied. 'As delivered to Abreotan by the Aelendyell Oracle Hilanyelath.'

A Ahmud Ki's pulse quickened. At last he would read the full words and find the flaws in his planning.

'I know what you're thinking now,' said Ardath steadily, 'but there's no need to read it. I have no reason to keep the truth from you, whatever your motives.'

A Ahmud Ki glared at Ardath, but the latter had already pulled up his protective mental curtain.

'The prophecy goes, word for word, like this,' Ardath blithely continued. 'In time to come, the Dragonlords will return to plunder the Kingdom of men. There will be death and darkness, and the future will seem lost and forgotten. Out of the confusion will come a warrior, born again to be the new King, and he will bear, against the Dragonlords, Abreotan's Sword of Fire, as Abreotan himself has done, and he will destroy, forever, the last Dragonlords. But the Saviour's world will bear a bloodied loss, and a great change, even as he slays friend and foe alike in the final conflict.' Ardath breathed out, as he completed his recitation, seeming to drop from a minor trance. He focussed on A Ahmud Ki, and said, 'You see? Liam is not who you claim him to be. I understand your purpose. You, like me, doubt the substance of prophecy, because we are rational men who understand the science of magic. Perhaps I'm even more cynical, because I read and record the real world of people. Prophecies bear little real fruit, rare coincidences at best, in all the chronicles of the Ancient Lore, yet they are full of records of them. If you choose to create a prophecy, do so. There's no threat from me, even if I don't approve of the deception. All you need to know is that I know. We understand each other. Nothing more.'

A pained expression crossed A Ahmud Ki's face, so Ardath relented with his mind shield. *Why did you tell the others?*

'Why not? I value truth, above all things. If Liam was the prophetic saviour, you wouldn't have been concerned by the cynical statements of a tired old Drycraefter, would you?'

And where is Abreotan's famous sword?

Ardath's curiously sly grin returned, as he reached and stroked the head of his owl. The bird's moon disc eyes opened and closed in synchronization with his touch. 'Aian Abreotan's last wish was that his sword be hidden until the new Saviour arose. You see, he believed the words of the

234

prophecy. Magic was more strongly woven then.'

Where? A Ahmud Ki insisted.

'The Ancient Lore doesn't say.'

You're lying!

Ardath put up the barrier a final time. 'I never lie, Advisor. Learn that, and you'll understand a great deal more about me than your pride lets you presently see. There's no Drycraefter record of the sword's resting place in the chronicles. But a poem, written by a Lord Jarrod, details the legend of the sword. I came across it, many years back, in the Great King's library. Search there if you must.'

A Ahmud Ki nodded silently. He tried to convey his appreciation for Ardath's help, but the Drycraefter had shut off mental communication, and was preparing to sit at his desk to write. Dismissed abruptly, the Royal Advisor walked into the darkened corridor, closing the door in his wake. He had more answers. Ardath wasn't an enemy, but neither was he a friend.

Nisus swung down from his mount and straightened his black robes in the light spilling from an unshuttered window. His Haardrishii escort remained on their horses, as ordered, and three Royal Assassins secreted themselves in a doorway across the street, as an added precaution. His instructions were to enter the cottage alone, but he wanted secure protection in the streets of the Great City at night.

Orrin's message couldn't have arrived at a more opportune time. The capitulation of the thieves to serve in the Great King's Armies was inevitable, he reasoned, but he was pleasantly surprised to receive Orrin's offer to negotiate the conditions so soon after their previous and less successful meeting. The addition of the thieves to his military campaign would enhance his status with Thana, and his eventual ascension to the throne was virtually assured with the assassination of the meddlesome Royal Advisor.

He stamped his boots to drive the chilling cold from his feet, while he awaited the signal from the cottage where

Orrin proposed to meet. Mercifully, it wasn't raining, despite the passing storm two nights before. The only query he had about A Ahmud Ki's murder was the disappearance of the two assassins who conducted the attack. Rheims' said they hacked the Advisor to death, an unorthodox manner for trained assassins, so perhaps they were too ashamed to face the Lord of the Royal Assassins after having performed their task so incompetently. He didn't know the answer because no one had seen them since – and that was odd.

A horse snorted, interrupting his thought, and as he looked up he caught sight of a flickering candle in the darkened cottage window: Orrin's signal. Nisus nodded to the Haardrishii, before he crossed to the cottage, and entered, briefly silhouetted against a dull candle glow.

A thief, garbed in loose jerkin, cloak and leggings, dirty cream in colour, held the candle Nisus had seen. Nisus glanced about the room, and when he saw it was empty he was alert. 'Where's Orrin?' he demanded warily. The thief nodded and pointed to the floor. Nisus saw the outline of a trapdoor with a raised pull ring. 'Down there?' The thief nodded. Nisus didn't like the arrangement at all. It smelt too much like a trap. 'Orrin said he'd meet me here, inside the cottage, and this is where I'll meet him,' he said decisively. The thief seemed indifferent to his authority. 'Understand?' Nisus asked. The candle bearer nodded silently and banged his booted heel three times on the trapdoor. Nisus' hand slipped to the long-bladed dagger beneath his robe, and he edged toward the door as the trapdoor lifted. Orrin's battered face appeared. 'This isn't as planned,' said Nisus, agitation wavering in his voice.

'Does it matter?' asked Orrin. 'I've a fire down here. And wine. If we have to talk business, let's be civilized about it.' Nisus remained unmoved, weighing Orrin's intentions. 'Of course. I understand,' said Orrin placidly. 'Perhaps another time.'

He began to close the trapdoor, but Nisus said urgently, 'No. We talk now. I'm coming down. No tricks.'

'Thieves' honour,' grinned Orrin.

The space Nisus entered below the cottage was cosy and comfortable, if basic in furnishing. A table and two chairs sat to one side, and a fire burned brightly in one corner. Doors led left and right. Nisus stiffened when he saw two bodies slumped across a second table by the right door. 'You said alone,' he hissed, drawing his dagger from its sheath.

'We are,' replied Orrin with a smile. 'Those two are dead.'

Nisus screwed up his face with quizzical concern. 'Dead? Why are they here?' he asked. What is Orrin's game? he wondered.

'They're assassins. Or were,' Orrin explained. 'They messed up their job. You should know that assassins can't afford to make stupid mistakes.'

Nisus immediately thought of the two he used to kill A Ahmud Ki. That's why they didn't come back. They feared this kind of retribution. He stared at the corpses in the partial shadow and didn't notice Orrin move toward the left door until the Guild Master spoke again.

'Have a look at their faces, my Lord. I think you know them.'

Nisus threw Orrin an alarmed glance, and saw both doors open simultaneously, admitting two thieves in black. He recognised the trap into which he'd blundered, and knew the dead assassins were his assassins, the ones commissioned to kill A Ahmud Ki. But why were they here?

'The Royal Advisor sends his greetings, Lord Nisus,' Orrin added, closing the door, as he disappeared into the Maze.

Tim waited in a dark alcove. Poised above him, on the roof, a second assassin watched the narrow, poorly lit street for their targets. Tim caressed the short crossbow, designed to be held in one hand, and locked a metal dart into position. It was a cleverly machined tool, a trademark of The Hand assassins. Of all weapons, it was Tim's favourite because it was portable and silently efficient. Death's First Hand had selected Morris, Frith and him to fulfil a favour. She told them they were The Hand's best assassins, and this task

237

required only the highest skilled and trustworthy men. Her compliment was nice, but Tim saw beyond it and knew their targets were important; probably dangerous to the Guild. Killing in cold blood didn't motivate him, even though he was good at his trade, but he enjoyed the challenge of catching targets unaware, and completing his job with minimum fuss or pain.

An alley cat mewed above, Morris' signal the targets were approaching. Tim switched off his thoughts. The speed with which the targets arrived surprised him. There was no mistaking their dark dress, as described by Death's First Hand, but they moved as if fearing pursuit, and with the grace of experienced assassins. He squeezed the trigger of his crossbow. His target, the left figure, leapt backwards, as if pulled by an invisible wire, and collapsed. Morris' agreed right-hand target pitched face forward, kicked once, and was still. Both had metal darts buried in their heads. Their orders were, as always, to confirm a fatal hit, and leave immediately. There was no doubt both victims were dead. Morris had already melted into the shadows of the rooftops, but Tim lingered, plagued by irritating curiosity.

The street was silent and empty. Against instruction, Tim crept forward and kneeled beside the target Morris felled. The dead man wore assassin black, exactly like Tim, his head and face masked by black cloth. Tim grabbed an arm and rolled the victim over. Glazed eyes stared up, but there was uncanny familiarity about them. He ripped down the mask and found his answer; gazing into the face of Karl Emmer, a fellow member of The Hand. Tim's guts tightened. He glanced left and right, to make certain no one was watching, before he rose and slunk into the night.

Twenty Seven

Tim sat brooding at the edge of Andra's bed, staring blankly into the warm goblet of mead Milly brought in from Jen. He'd been mysteriously absent for four days, and now he was back - silent, and so much out of character Andra was worried. He touched Tim's bent shoulder, and said, 'Whatever burden you're carrying, it can't be too great to share with a friend.' Tim kept staring into the goblet, maintaining his distance, so Andra squatted beside the bed. 'Where have you been?' he asked.

The thief lifted his eyes, and in their crystal orbs Andra saw confusion and frustration, emotions he never associated with the Tim Gaelus he knew. 'You know the answer,' said Tim quietly.

Tim had taught Andra The Hand's Code of Silence. Assassins never discussed any feature of his or her tasks, or named targets. To do so was a death sentence, if word got back to Death's First Hand. 'You've had to kill someone you knew,' Andra said softly. His perceptive statement knitted Tim's eyebrows, and while Tim neither confirmed nor denied his words, the young Guardian had his answer.

He stood and crossed to the door. In the adjoining room, two of Patty's girls were giggling and bathing in the central tub, washing off the care of their night's work. Milly had gone to bed. He checked no one was likely to disturb them, closed the door, and returned to Tim. 'A Code of Silence exists now. You know I'll tell no one,' said Andra gently. 'Twice at least, I've owed you my life. That's a debt I can never repay. Unlock the pain to me, Tim. Please.'

Tim squinted up at Andra, as if judging the true worth of their friendship for the first time, and the faintest smile fleetingly crossed his lips before it disappeared. 'Speak a word of what I'm about to tell you, Andra of The Vale, and you are as dead as any man touched by The Hand. If you speak this to anyone else, I will already be dead.'

'My life is yours,' replied Andra.

Again, Tim smiled, as Andra made the Assassin's Oath he'd taught him in the passing days. When he began to speak, his voice was low, and the words came painfully. 'My last target was a friend,' Tim said, and glanced up at Andra, as if expecting a reply, but Andra had none to make. Instead, the Guardian waited for Tim to continue. Tim looked away. 'I've been trained to kill for The Hand, since I was no older than Milly. I hit my first target at fifteen, a merchant, who defaulted once too often with Guild money. Though I know my skills well, I've not killed a great many people in the profession. Death's First Hand tells me I'm her best assassin. I get only special hits. And they don't come often. Last time was over a year ago, before I even met you. An official of Great King Thana's court killed two street urchins for sport to amuse his friends. I had to hit him inside the castle, something The Hand never normally does. I enjoyed meting out justice. It was a not-too-subtle warning, to Thana's minions, not to treat poor people's lives lightly.' Tim returned his gaze to Andra. 'Four days ago, Death's First Hand called me and a friend to her chambers, and told us we had a very special hit to conduct, for no less than the Shadow's Voice. We weren't to ask questions. Apart from the source of the request, nothing seemed unusual. But after the hit, I broke the rules. I checked who we'd hit.' Tim paused for emphasis and clenched his left fist. 'We killed two fellow assassins, Andra. Do you understand? Two of our own men.'

Andra saw anger welling in Tim and wondered how he'd feel if the Guardian Master asked him to kill another Guardian. He knew he couldn't kill a fellow Guardian.

'I asked myself why, Andra. Why would Death's First Hand sanction a hit on two of her own people? Why did the Shadow's Voice order such a hit? Had they broken the Code? I've often wondered how anyone would be punished for that. Maybe that was the answer.'

'Perhaps that is the reason,' offered Andra.

'But I knew one of the dead men really well,' said Tim

emphatically. 'He was never likely to do anything against the rules. I considered him one of the best assassins in The Hand. Now he's dead.'

Tim broke off, and Andra gave his friend a moment to recollect his thoughts, before he asked the question he wanted to ask. 'Why have you been away for four days?'

Tim shook his head and wiped his lips with the back of his hand. 'To think. It was stupid of me to check the bodies. I thought I was being foolish. Death's First Hand had her reasons. And she'd have good reasons for the hit. I was being unnecessarily sentimental. That's not an assassin's way. But I heard a rumour in the streets that Thana's Royal Advisor was dead. Someone blamed his murder on The Hand. I was fascinated. I never considered The Hand would strike against Thana's most important officials. The repercussions for the Guild would be unprecedented. The Guild holds enormous power in the Great City, but Thana's a mad king capable of making business far less profitable than it already is. Something else wasn't right, either. If Death's First Hand ever worked against so important an official, I'd almost expect to be involved. I'm the only assassin who's been inside the castle to work.'

'Perhaps,' Andra mused, 'but then who else has been in? The Code of Silence must prevent you from knowing that.'

'We're thieves, Andra,' Tim confessed. 'We talk. Carefully. To friends. The Code of Silence means we don't talk unnecessarily. But word gets around.'

Tim stood to listen at the door. He eased it ajar and peeped out. When he was satisfied no one was present, he closed it again. 'I wanted answers,' he continued. 'Instead, I found more questions. Two days ago, Thana's High Lord turned up floating in Dragon River, caught in the reeds behind Methir's baking shop. The Haardrishii came and carted the corpse away, as quickly as possible, but by then it was common knowledge, throughout the city, that The Hand has assassinated him. That's two of Thana's officials dead, both apparently targets of The Hand. Worse, the High Lord is Lord Nisus.' Andra vaguely recalled the name but couldn't place it. 'He was Lord of the Royal Assassins, Andra.'

Andra recalled the vision of the black robed assassins in the Great King's parade before the Great Armies, although he couldn't remember seeing anyone leading them.

'Some even suggest he was Thana's likely successor, if the Great King died,' said Tim. 'He was the most important man in the Kingdom, after Thana himself. His murder virtually puts the Royal Assassins at war with The Hand. Imagine if a Royal Assassin killed Death's First Hand. There'd be total uproar.' Tim's voice had risen, and his manner became more agitated. Aware of his emotion, the thief took a deep breath, before he went on. 'No one in The Hand, no one I can trust to talk quietly and forget they talked, know anything about a hit on either the Royal Advisor, or Lord Nisus. In fact, a couple figured I'd been part of the hit on Nisus, because Morris and I were out on the night he was assassinated.'

'How do they know when he was killed?' asked Andra. 'You said he was only found two days ago.'

'Street thieves saw him head into the back streets with two Haardrishii and a couple of Royal Assassins. He never came back when they went to raise the alarm.' answered Tim. He took a longer draught of mead and sat on the edge of Andra's table. 'I realised the connection when I found out where Lord Nisus had gone. The assassins we killed that same night were heading away from the area where Nisus apparently arranged to meet someone. I know Karl Emmer and Ty hit Lord Nisus. Everything points to that. They were as good as anyone in The Hand. What I can't understand is why Death's First Hand would order the Lord's assassination, especially knowing what will happen, now, between both groups of assassins, or why the Shadow's Voice would then order the deaths of the assassins who made the hit. It doesn't make sense.' Tim stared into the bottom of his goblet. 'Then yesterday, I heard one more curious rumour. The Royal Advisor is alive. He was never attacked by The Hand.'

'That's one less problem then, isn't it? Proves the attack

on the Royal Advisor was only a rumour, probably mistaken for the attack on Nisus,' Andra suggested hopefully.

'I thought so too,' agreed Tim, 'but now I'm not so sure. You see, the rumours about the Royal Advisor's death were spread before Nisus was hit. Why would that happen? Somehow, there's a link in all this. But I just can't find where. I can't justify the killing of two highly skilled assassins. There's something decidedly wrong with it all.'

'But how can we find out what's happened?' Andra asked.

'I don't know,' replied Tim. 'I just don't know.'

A Ahmud Ki walked the broad corridor, toward the entrance to the Royal Gardens, preoccupied with pleasant thoughts and necessary problems. There was much to do. His audience with Thana had gone according to plan, once the Great King fully comprehended the circumstances and events of the past week. The reappearance of his apparently dead Royal Advisor left Thana speechless, and the doddering king nearly had apoplexy when A Ahmud Ki, whose corpse he witnessed spattered with blood a matter of days before, in the Royal Gardens, broke into his thoughts to communicate mind to mind. Caught totally off guard and flustered with the news of Nisus' assassination hard on the heels of A Ahmud Ki's own apparent death, Thana was primed to be influenced, and A Ahmud Ki seized his opportunity. He planted suggestions in the Great King's mind for a reshuffle of the King's Table to accommodate the loss of Nisus, and convinced Thana that he, A Ahmud Ki, should be appointed the new Lord of the Royal Assassins, because he, more than any other lord, knew how important the Great King's security really was, having come close himself to being assassinated. Thana couldn't argue. Chancellor Rheims nodded vigorously, when Thana sought his advice, stunned to see the dead standing uninjured before him in the Throne Room. So, he held the seal of the Royal Assassins, which, together with his hold on The Hand assassins through Orrin, gave him control of the two deadliest groups in the Kingdom.

His first task was to defuse potential rivalry between the assassin groups over Nisus' death, and, as leader of both, that was easy. He approached the heavy oak door, at the corridor's end, and walked through as an Apprentice opened it for him and respectfully bowed. Pale sunlight tried to light the Royal Gardens, but wintry clouds interfered, maliciously intent on keeping the world cold and miserable. Controlling the weather would be a potent magical ability, A Ahmud Ki considered. He'd tampered with minor spells that suggested there were greater ones hidden in another Ki, but weather control, on a large scale, eluded him. Perhaps the Dragonlords knew the answers.

Eight Apprentices sat cross-legged at the base of his tower, intent on memorising and practising their arts. He surveyed them surreptitiously, as he approached, and remembered he'd neglected their lessons in recent days, because of the unplanned chain of events. That was another task he had to complete. The only disappointment he felt was that there was a lack of real arcane talent among the Apprentices. Most struggled to conjure more than illusion spells, and then only weak ones. Only a couple, like Peret, had the innate wisdom to become the magic they were attempting to learn, and progress to more challenging levels, but none were ever likely to rise to the abilities of the Targan sorceresses, or Ithosen, or Aelendyell Lore Bearers. As humans, they were limited, even within their spirits.

The deputation of Apprentices he sent to Targa, more than four weeks before, hadn't returned. Thana's, and Nisus' requests for military help fell on deaf ears in Targa, but A Ahmud Ki expected a positive response because of the associations he'd struck with Lady Jasmin and the Targan Rebels who defied the Order, when he lived there. He'd lost his communication crystal when the Dragonlord attacked his mind through it, and he wanted it replaced. It was a rare commodity in Targa, but he only needed one piece to form as many as he needed. He just needed the first one.

Seralinna's face flashed into his thoughts. He'd loved no

one except her, and no one since. Her long auburn tresses shone in his memory of the Targan sunlight, and her free smile teased his memories. She befriended him and grew to love him, though she never comprehended what he was destined to become. Mareg tore her from him, in the Inner Sanctum, when the Dragonlord broke free and wantonly destroyed the chamber to demonstrate his awesome energy. A Ahmud Ki saw her die. It was his fault. He tampered with the Dragonlord's tomb.

He let Seralinna's vision fade into the dull light of the day when he saw the eight Apprentices abasing themselves before him, awaiting his passing. There is always power, he reminded himself. Already, he'd advanced his power another step in the Kingdom, as Lord of the Royal Assassins with Nisus' unfortunate demise, but he couldn't neglect his Apprentices.

He entered the black tower, and levitated to his library, where he called a light sphere into being, before going to the table where Pak always laid out texts for his master to read. For the first time, since the attempted assassination instigated by Nisus, A Ahmud Ki understood his loss. Pak was dead. The library was empty. He flicked open one book, Prophetic Words of Erino, and gazed at Pak's scribbled notes on parchment. The servant was dispensable. He'd known that from the outset. He'd even been concerned that Pak was beginning to learn too much about A Ahmud Ki's passion, becoming too ambitious for power, and understanding too much magic, to remain a worthwhile servant for long. But Pak had also been a companion in a land where he held no one as a friend, and his absence left a void, isolating A Ahmud Ki. Thana was an idiot. Liam and Orrin were tools. He didn't want friends. He didn't even need friends. But he did need a trustworthy servant.

He returned to the tower's lower level and stepped into the Royal Gardens. Immediately the Apprentices placed their faces to the earth, in the manner of the Ranu Ka Shehaala before superiors. It was a custom A Ahmud Ki demanded they obey. He studied their grey woollen backs, deciding.

You. Third from left.

The chosen Apprentice, hearing A Ahmud Ki's voice inside his head, cautiously raised his eyes to look at the Master. Beneath his shaven head, dark blue eyes sparkled.

Your name.

The Apprentice glanced left and right, before answering, 'Damon, Master.'

Follow. You have a new calling.

Astonished by the sudden change in his fortune, Damon looked one more time at his prostrate colleagues, who were oblivious to his unexpected honour, scrambled to his feet, and followed A Ahmud Ki to the blank face of the ebony tower.

The amber glow of the Ithosen Meditation Chamber bathed A Ahmud Ki's body, as he lay, spread-eagled, on the circular prayer mat. Above him, the four crystal pyramids spun in a tiny orbit, focussing the energy of their amber beams on his exposed throat, working their magical healing. Eyes closed, he concentrated on the Ithosen spell Karrilyon helped him to master, during his two-year apprenticeship in Yul Ithrandyr. He excised the wound the morning after the attack, but the internal damage caused by the assassin's garrote was healing far more slowly. He wanted his voice. Mind spell communication was exhausting over long periods, and a strong voice was a powerful tool of manipulation. It had to be mended.

Twenty Eight

High Lord Surdrok stood on the wall of Central Gate to survey the Haagii frontlines. The brittle winter sun glinted on cold iron and icy pools, amid the jumbled array of makeshift hide tents and siege machines, where Haagii warriors were trying to keep warm beside small campfires that sent up thin, twisting columns of blue smoke. Between the opposing armies, the gap was littered with Haagii dead. The Haagii made no attempt to retrieve their wounded after each onslaught. They left them to die, and let the corpses putrefy, charging over them, grinding them into the snow and muddy earth. Surdrok appreciated the still morning air because its freshness filled his lungs, but when the breezes picked up he, like the warriors under his supreme command, hoped they didn't blow from the Haagii lines, because the stench of rotting bodies was nauseating.

He wondered when the Haagii would attack today. They'd maintained their campaign throughout the early winter months, despite the cold, the rains, and the snowfall, and although the frequency of attacks diminished their ferocity didn't. Almost a third of Central Gate wall was demolished, or damaged and rebuilt, because of the Haagii's persistence, and the South Wheel had lost over half of its soldiers in defence of the wall's weaker sections.

Surdrok turned from the view and walked toward the stone steps leading to the valley floor, where the warriors of the South Wheel huddled inside their hides, keeping the morning cold out, leaving the campsite desolate and stark white from overnight snow. Only Haardrishii were on guard along the parapet, their black armour shining in contrast to the white slopes.

The Great King's messengers had brought news of Surdrok's appointment to the High Lord yesterday, news that dumbfounded him, because he had lost favour with

Thana, in recent weeks, while Nisus' standing increased, and the arguments continued about the Haardrishii's role in the war. Now Nisus was dead, and he had Nisus' title, an ironic twist of fate he quietly appreciated. He suspected the Royal Advisor had a hand in events, and that he now owed the Royal Advisor a new debt. He did not have the same desire to lead as Nisus had. Whereas Nisus dictated the Armies' and Kingdom's fortunes from the safety of the Great King's castle, Surdrok intended to remain at the battlefront where, with his own eyes, he could see the situation and make judgments. He was no general, no tactician like Nisus. He would fight on instinct and direct observation because it was the only way he knew how to fight.

He paused on the steps, aware of a rush of air above him, and glanced up. A boulder hurtled over the battlements and smashed into a small hide tent in the middle of the South Wheel's camp, crushing its occupants. The alarm spread, voices echoing from the slopes of the valley, and soldiers scrambled out of their tents, juggling armour and weapons, heading for the wall's safety, as three more boulders thudded into the encampment. The attack was coming.

Surdrok led a body of warriors onto the rampart, and from their vantage point they saw a sizeable Haagii company struggling through the slush, into the snow at the valley's mouth. Two Devis shouted orders, and a line of tall, blond archers prepared their bows for the approaching enemy. The Longbowmen pleased Surdrok because they went about their duty much like the Haardrishii, determined and single-minded, while so many of the new soldiers who clambered into position along the wall were less committed, poorly trained substitutes for the soldiers slain in the pre-winter onslaught.

One hundred and fifty paces from Central Gate wall, the Haagii met a fierce rain of arrows from the Longbowmen that cut many down and filled the air with cries of pain and death. Scanning the oncoming enemy, Surdrok spotted squads carrying ladders to scale the walls. Snow hindered their progress, and a second volley of arrows fell among the Haagii, killing and wounding many more. Yet, they came on. He admired their fanatical ignorance of their fellow's deaths and wondered if the Haagii were ever afraid of the massacre they marched into every day.

A ragged battle cry rose from the enemy, and the Haagii broke into a haphazard charge, their ranks degenerating into a screaming rabble. Another arrow storm cut a swathe, but the survivors reached the base of the wall. Very few ladders remained. Two were hoisted, and warriors began climbing. The defenders waited, until the first Haagii nearly reached the battlements, before pushing aside the ladders.

A larger Haagii group gathered beneath the gate tower, lugging a crude battering ram. With nothing to throw from the walls, the Kingdom warriors watched the Haagii leader exhort his soldiers into organization, to break down the gate. Surdrok passed a warning to the Haardrishii Devi on duty, and by the time the Haagii battering commenced Haardrishii warriors were assembled, waiting until the Haagii were on a backswing for the next ramming. The Devi ordered the gate open, and the Haardrishii charged into the Haagii ranks. Shocked, the Haagii warriors dropped the battering ram and fled, and the few who remained were embroiled in bitter combat with the ruthless Haardrishii defenders.

When the watchers on the wall saw the main Haagii force bulge toward the fighting at the gate, to aid the beleaguered and decimated battering company, a horn sounded above the noise of battle, and the Haardrishii, their strategy successful, retreated behind the safety of the wall, forcing the gate shut in their enemies' faces. A dozen more boulders thudded to earth beyond the wall, before the Haagii attackers disbanded and loped back to their lines, allowing the defenders to assess their losses, relieved the day's battle was brief.

Surdrok watched their retreat with a rare wry grin. Every day, the routine was followed. A Haagii force stormed Central Gate and was repulsed. Every time the Haagii losses were great, the defenders' losses minimal, but each attack and each day gnawed away at the South Wheel's reserves. Nisus never understood the Haagii's tactics. Surdrok did. If he was the Dragonlord, with unlimited resources of manpower, he'd fight the battle in the same way, inexorably wearing down the nerves of the defenders with vicious and bloody sorties, demonstrating the immensity of the power ranged against the Kingdom's forces by liberally sacrificing soldiers.

'Lord Surdrok.'

He turned to the voice that called from below the parapet, and saw a giant of a warrior, cloaked in heavy woollen garments, and sheepskin boots to protect his feet from the cold. He stood with three similarly dressed companions, two of whom were women, and a black war dog accompanied the little party.

'We've been beyond the mountain's edge,' said Claarn.

High Lord Surdrok beckoned for Claarn to ascend. He admired the warrior of Tressel Deep because he was a fighting man, a warrior in the true tradition of courage and honour, one eager to take the battle to the Haagii, so he appointed Claarn as second-in-command at Central Gate, after receiving his own appointment as High Lord, recognizing the warrior's leadership qualities as well as his weapon prowess. Above all, Claarn's loyalty was unquestionable.

Claarn bowed his shaggy head almost imperceptibly, as he drew up before Surdrok. He respected the shorter man's authority, as head of the Haardrishii, and newly-appointed High Lord of the Great King's armies, and he accepted that Surdrok honoured him with promotion, but warrior to warrior Claarn knew he was Surdrok's superior, and in Tressel Deep, the home from where he'd been dragged over a year ago, respect was earned, man or woman, by a warrior's ability.

'What have you found?' Surdrok asked.

'More puzzles than answers,' replied Claarn. 'All is not as it seems on the plain before us.'

The ambiguous answer irritated Surdrok. He was a plain thinker and speaker, and he expected the same in return. 'I don't want riddles, giant. Explain what you found,' he ordered.

Claarn took the liberty to squat against the battlement before he began to describe his excursion through a section of the mountains into the fringe of the Haagii lines. 'The mountain paths are barely passable. Marella nearly lost her life on the return. There's no danger of the Haagii sneaking around Central Gate in significant numbers. We did come across one small party, searching for a path in the lower foothills on the western ridges, but they lost interest.'

'You let them escape?'

'They mark the place where we met,' Claarn nonchalantly replied. He peered over the wall toward the Haagii lines and gestured with his broad right hand. 'The whole plain is a black sea of Haagii, as far as the eye can see. They arrive regularly from the north and the west, bearing their ragged tribal banners. Every group carries another standard as well; a pole with a black dragon carved on top. These poles are everywhere across the plains. They outnumber us manifold times.'

Surdrok expected that news. Even from their wall, the Kingdom warriors could see the Haagii numbers multiplying daily. He was waiting impatiently for Claarn's reason for concern. 'You said there were puzzles,' he prompted.

'There are,' said Claarn. 'Among the Haagii are others I don't know, warriors who wear no armour and ride horses. They seem to keep apart from the Haagii. And there are others who come dressed in green robes. Their heads are shaven like the Royal Advisor's Apprentices, but they wear swords. There are others, many others, like the ones we met on The Rim Shield, blond warriors with black armour like your Haardrishii, who move through the vast army like lords. Everyone steps aside for them, as though they're scared of them.' Claarn eased up to his full height, towering over Surdrok, making the High Lord feel somewhat insignificant on the wall of Central Gate. 'And,' he continued, staring

251

across the steep valley toward the plains, 'there are dragons.'

Surdrok listened with interest to Claarn's report, curious as to the origins of the new groups Claarn described, but the hair on the nape of his neck twitched at the mention of dragons. Like everyone, he assumed the dragons had flown north, after Axxon was obliterated, because no dragon attacked Central Gate. Why the Dragonlord held them off mystified Surdrok at first, until he came to terms with the attrition campaign being run through winter, but to know the dragons were still present, hidden out on the plains with the Haagii army, filled him with unaccustomed dread. 'Where?' the High Lord asked.

Claarn waved to indicate north. 'Nesting in the crags, beyond the forked rivers that run into Abreotan River.'

'But you never went that far north.'

'No need,' replied Claarn. 'We saw them circling and sweeping toward the mountains. They were landing to roost. Five of them. The same ugly brutes we saw on The Rim Shield.' Claarn dismissed himself from Surdrok, seeing the latter lost in meditation, and returned to his companions. Together they headed for their tents and well-earned sleep.

Surdrok stood on the wall for a long time, contemplating the possibilities and challenges that Claarn's news presented to him, as the new High Lord defending Central Gate. The East Wheel army was within two days of arrival to reinforce their position. The Royal Advisor's magical Orb protected the Great City from the dragons. Did its influence spread this far? How could the dragons be stopped if they came with the melting snows of spring? The role of High Lord seemed to grow out of proportion for Surdrok, and he shivered at the icy touch of a mid-morning breeze.

A Ahmud Ki traced the filigree lettering on the small book face. Beneath a dusty collection of texts, he'd found the object of his search; Lord Jarrod's poetic scribbles, written, according to the manuscript's foreword, thirteen years after

King Aian Abreotan's death. Ardath promised the secret location of Abreotan's sword was locked in there. He flicked through the pages, scanning poems for references to the sword, until, halfway through, he found 'The Legend of Abreotan's Sword' and feverishly read the stilted words.

"Said Argarven, the Dwarven King,

'Forge bright the blade in fire red

That gushes from the mountains' heart.

Dip deep the point in fire gold

That near the moonsprings doth start..."

He skipped the details of how the sword came into existence within the Dwarven forges, and how the Elvenaar secured its being with their blood and amber gems set in its hilt to aid the human king to defeat the Dragonlords.

'For in the heartstones set complete

The ring of protection, circle of courage,

Magical spells the darkness defeat ...'

The words whirled through his mind, absorbed at a glance.

'A flash of fiery flame erupted;

Abreotan, slayer of dragons,

And evil powers all corrupted,

Storms from the citadel Andrakis ...'

Page after page the epic poem followed the life of the legendary weapon, beyond the Dragon Wars to the aging king's autumn days.

'And in me Age his victory seeks,

Where neither dragon, nor Dragonlord,

Could bring pallor to my cheeks,

Nor my arm humble, nor my mighty sword...'

and A Ahmud Ki read on, until the final page of the saga unfolded the sword's secret resting place.

'Take this, my faithful companion,

My sword of fire, the biting tongue

That dragons it slew many a one.

Take it, so he, who after comes,

Can seek it anew, touch its essence.

Hide it 'neath the watery well

253

Of the sacred tower of Cennednyss.

There, bind it with potent spell,

And seal its fate with keepers ...'

A Ahmud Ki blinked and lifted his eyes from the poem. Cennednyss: an Aelendyell name, a corruption of an Elvenaar word, which translated to 'birthplace' in the human language.

He rose from his stool and crossed to the map collection Pak gathered before his death, selected a scroll that detailed the Kingdom, and returned to his desk. A cursory glance of the map proved fruitless: no Cennednyss. He searched thoroughly, without success. Perhaps the poem was legend after all, because no named place on the map corresponded with Cennednyss. He sat back in thought. Ardath would know.

He cast his eye across the curled parchments from the Great King's library. Then he understood. He went back to the map collection, and searched, until he found one bearing the title, 'The Kingdom of King Aian Abreotan as of the New Reign until His Death', pulled it from the rack, and unfurled it. Different places. Different names. The Great City was called Andrakis. Anedya was a larger trading centre called Battlehelm. Castles dotted the landscape: Waeterfaestenn, Mecenyss, Faestnyss. And Cennednyss. It was perched on a rocky island, on the western coast, beneath The Bitter Peaks, though they bore the Aelendyell name Faestengeat on the old map. The place existed after all, and, according to Lord Jarrod's poem, Abreotan's sword was there. He'd found no other references to the sword's fate. Cennednyss was his only certainty.

A Ahmud Ki rubbed his trimmed black beard. He had Liam, his synthetic creation of the Saviour, moon symbols and all. He had the Orb. He knew the whereabouts of the sword. The prophecy was nearly complete. There remained only one flaw, a factor even Ardath failed to mention at the King's Table, though to do so would be most impolitic of the Royal Drycraefter. The bearer of Abreotan's sword would become the Kingdom's new king – which posed a problem for the fat Great King currently squatting like a rancid toad on the Dragon Throne. However, his days were numbered, because A Ahmud Ki had already laid plans for an unfortunate accident to occur that would bring Liam to the throne when he returned with the sword.

Twenty Nine

Pouring rain turned the King's Way into a quagmire, the mud sucking at the Aelendyell boots and clinging to their sodden clothes. Those who watched the procession did so from the dry shelter of their buildings, barely able to recognise the visitors to the Great City beneath their drawn hoods and cloaks. Winter had come, with a vengeance greater than anything the Dragonlord could summon, as far as the people of Thana's Great City were concerned.

The dismal procession struggled over the stone bridge spanning the swirling waters of Dragon River, ignored by the guards huddled within their tiny posts, and began the wearisome climb up the winding Castle Road. Despite the conditions, the Aelendyell moved as one, intent on a single purpose, a grey body of resolution approaching its source of discontent.

Guards crouched beneath the castle battlements above the gates cursed when they heard faint voices. The gatekeeper looked out, and grumbled irreverently, until the foremost figure standing in the rain pulled back his sodden hood to reveal the braided locks of an Aelendyell Elder. The gatekeeper sent a guard in haste to the Royal Chambers, to fetch the Chancellor, and then he unlocked the entrance door to admit the Aelendyell, apologizing for his indecision and inappropriate language as he bowed. The Aelendyell ignored him.

Rheims was flustered. 'Tell me again!' he snapped at the guard who blundered into the Great King's library to find him. 'How many?'

'My Lord, thirty I guess. I didn't take time to count them, on account of Gatekeeper Garth's displeasure.'

'Thirty?' repeated Rheims. 'Why thirty? Why in this

weather?'

The guard shifted uneasily. He didn't like being privy to the Chancellor's bouts of talking to himself. There were rumours the old man was madder than the Great King.

'Well then, bring them to the Royal Dining Hall!' Rheims ordered. The guard saluted and turned to take his leave. 'Wait,' said Rheims, pulling absently at his ear. 'Go to the kitchen first and see that a warm meal is prepared for them. Tell the cooks it's Aelendyell food, you know, nuts and fruits. What they like.'

'Yes, my Lord,' replied the guard.

'And see that there's dry cloaks ready for them,' said Rheims. The guard nodded, caught between staying and going. 'And set an attendant boy to stoking the hearth in the Hall,' the Chancellor added, and paused, staring at the floor. The guard waited, anticipating further orders. The Chancellor glanced up and stared at him. 'Well? What are you waiting for?'

The guard saluted one more time, and left the library, glad to be free of the mad Chancellor. Even Gatekeeper Garth was bearable, in comparison.

Thana peeked at the assembled Aelendyell throng from his spy hole in the northern wall of the Royal Dining Hall, a device he used in pre-war days to study his attendant guests, and ambassadors from other lands, before deciding whether he really could be bothered to eat with them in a public venue like the Dining Hall. He'd never seen so many Aelendyell gathered in his palace, except on his coronation day, when it was customary for the peoples of other lands and races to send representatives to honour the new king. He was fifteen then. The world had changed. So had his relationship with the Aelendyell. They were disenfranchised in his Kingdom, subject to his martial law because they refused to aid him in the war against Mareg. Why had they decided to visit in the middle of the worst weather of winter?

'They want the Orb returned.'

Thana, caught peeping, turned guiltily to face the Royal Advisor beside Chancellor Rheims. 'We would appreciate more courtesy in delicate situations,' Thana pouted, in his defence. It irritated him immensely when the Royal Advisor seemed to read his thoughts. He hoisted his stomach, and waddled toward A Ahmud Ki, full of self-importance in his royal green and black robes. 'We expect them to ask Us about the Orb. What do you advise We should reply, Royal Advisor?'

A Ahmud Ki wondered what game Thana had in mind. 'I advise Your Highness to tell them the Orb is essential to the protection of the Kingdom. Without its presence here, the Dragonlord will tear the Kingdom apart in a matter of days.'

'And if they argue?' Thana asked.

A Ahmud Ki was tiring of Thana's stupidity. The Great King only wanted his ego flattered, to boost his fragile confidence when he had to face the Aelendyell. 'Remind them you are the Great King, all powerful ruler of the Kingdom, Abreotan's living descendant. You, alone, are the inheritor of the responsibility to keep the Dragonlord at bay, and the Aelendyell must obey your wishes accordingly. That should impress them.'

Thana detected mockery in A Ahmud Ki's final line, and paused, staring up into the Advisor's grey eyes, but he couldn't hold the gaze against so imposing a will, and broke away. Instead, he turned to Rheims and informed him, 'We will hold audience in a short time. Tell the Elders We wish them to be dry and comfortable first.' Rheims bowed and left the room.

A Ahmud Ki addressed Thana immediately after the Chancellor withdrew. 'I advise you to disarm the Weapon Bearers,' he warned, a comment that puzzled the Great King. 'Your Majesty has in possession an ancient artefact prized dearly by Aelendyell culture,' A Ahmud Ki explained slowly, determined to emphasize his point. 'Its potency is legendary. I doubt they'll want to leave here without it. Not willingly.'

Thana edged toward his spy hole, fidgeting nervously with his golden neck chains. 'You're not suggesting they would –' The Great King left his sentence unfinished and took a compulsive peek into the adjoining room. For the first time, he was vividly aware of the bows and swords the Aelendyell carried, or wore beneath their gear, exposed only as they accepted the dry cloaks Rheims provided for them. He saw the threat to his security. 'But what if they refuse?'

'It's wartime. Exercise your discretion,' advised A Ahmud Ki. 'If they're offended, let only the Elders enter the Throne Room to meet with you. But have guards watch the Weapon Bearers in here, from outside the room.'

Thana couldn't question the Royal Advisor's reasoning. Of all the people in his palace, only the Royal Advisor knew what to do in moments of crisis. He'd already contemplated retiring the bumbling Rheims. Perhaps now it was time. 'We thank you for your caution, Royal Advisor. We will arrange a reward for your astuteness very soon. We have great need of a new Chancellor.'

A Ahmud Ki gave an uncustomary bow before Thana. 'I would be honoured,' he said quietly, without looking up for the Great King's reaction, and he left Thana to contemplate the consequences of his decision.

Great King Thana perched precariously on the edge of his throne, his weight threatening to roll forward down the steps to the floor. He adjusted his crown, to look regal, and creased his pudgy face into an imperial frown of authority. Whatever purpose the Aelendyell brought before his court, his intention was to show them he ruled the Kingdom. The rain on the roof of the Throne Room sounded like a distant boulder rolling interminably along a hollow stone corridor, and it pleased Thana. Rain was always a blessing, interfering with affairs of state, and locking everyone indoors, and that meant he could loll in bed, without fear of unnecessary interruptions from ambassadors and visitors. These stupid Aelendyell deliberately plodded through abysmal weather to disturb his pleasurable peace in the middle of winter, and that irritated him.

A commotion in the corridor, beyond the Throne Room doors, drew his attention. The doors burst open, and Chancellor Rheims was bundled in, ahead of a dozen Aelendyell. The intrusion woke the Throne Room Royal Guards, whose startled response was to level their ceremonial lances at the intruders. Rheims saw the brewing conflict and scurried toward the foot of the Throne steps, gesticulating for Thana's attention to avert the impending crisis. Thana lurched off the throne to stand, legs apart, arms akimbo, staring angrily. 'We demand to know the reason for this unmannerly entrance into Our Throne Room!' he ordered tersely, but within he was full of fear at what might eventuate if the Aelendyell were hostile.

'Most Gracious Highness,' Rheims panted, dropping to his knees, 'the Aelendyell won't listen to reason. Their warriors refuse to relinquish their weapons, and the Elders come here to demand an explanation.'

Thana had hoped there wouldn't be confrontation. He didn't like the possibility of violence inside his palace, especially so close to his royal personage. He looked at the Aelendyell, who were surrounded by fifteen Guardsmen, and saw they were undaunted by the threat of sharp points at their throats, almost arrogantly confident they weren't in danger. A tall figure in silver and black moved from behind Thana to stand beside him on the dais. The Great King felt safer with the Royal Advisor there. He also noticed shadows moving in the wings of the Throne Room, and realised the Royal Assassins were taking positions to defend him. The Royal Advisor thought of everything. He surpassed Rheims in every way. Surer of his personal security and power, Thana composed himself, and announced, 'Close the doors. We'll address the Aelendyell, who've so rudely arrived, as it is Our pleasure to do so. Guards, return to your stations, and allow the Aelendyell to advance.'

The Aelendyell held their ground, until the Royal Guards fully withdrew, before they crossed the room to the foot of the steps below Thana. A Ahmud Ki inspected them carefully, counting their number, searching for discrepancies. Of the fifteen Aelendyell in attendance, only four were Elders. Another five had the appearance of Lore Bearers, four being female, but the remaining six were Weapon Bearers. Though they had no visible weapons, their bearing was unmistakably balanced and athletic, the stance of highly trained warriors. He assumed the Aelendyell were plotting a gambit to regain the Orb, a move that wouldn't be entirely diplomatic if their negotiation failed. 'Why do you choose to come to Us in such unpleasant weather?' asked Thana casually, as he eased his frame back onto the edge of the throne.

An Elder came forward, without formally bowing, and said abruptly, 'When a thief is known in an Aelendyell tun, it is customary to confront him and ask for the return of that which was stolen.'

His barb took the desired effect. Thana sat stiffly in his throne, both hands gripping the arm supports. A Ahmud Ki saw the familiar red anger flush the Great King's cheeks, as he wheezed, 'You dare call Us a thief?'

'You dared to steal the sacred Orb of Radiance from Heolstorcofa,' the Elder retorted. 'I cannot call you anything else, under the circumstances.'

Thana rose to his feet, and shouted, 'All that is in the Kingdom is Ours! We stole nothing. We took what is rightfully Ours, by royal privilege!'

A Ahmud Ki saw the tension tighten among the assembled Aelendyell, and Aelendyell hands slipped beneath cloaks to hidden weapons. He glanced toward the assassins at the edges of the Throne Room. 'Nothing in Elvenaar Forest is yours, human King!' cried the Aelendyell Elder vehemently. 'The Ieldran have met, and they choose to ignore your empty posturing. The stealing of the Orb will not be endured. Aelendyell died at the hands of your royal murderer!' The Elder thrust an accusing finger at A Ahmud Ki and the Advisor saw a face of pure hatred staring up at him.

A Ahmud Ki smiled in return, letting his lack of concern for the Aelendyell woes sink home to the Elder and his companions, silently baiting their aching desires for revenge. If the Aelendyell wanted to start a fight in the Throne Room, he would willingly accommodate them on the pretense of protecting Thana. He turned toward the Great King, and said, dispassionately, 'I think the Aelendyell have overstepped their welcome, Royal Thana. They insult your house and your name with their petty accusations and vengeful words.'

'Staelgiest!' screamed the Elder in his native tongue. 'Morthorwyrhta!'

A Ahmud Ki turned to witness the Elder's hands spinning a fierce arcane pattern to which he reacted immediately, whispering three Ithosen words he'd long ago worked into a powerful spell, and directed his energy toward the Aelendyell. The Elder stiffened with shock, his mouth fell open, his body convulsed, and he sagged to the floor, like a heavy bag of potatoes. The Aelendyell Weapon Bearers whipped out their swords, but Royal Guards and Royal Assassins, spears and daggers at the ready, surrounded them.

A Lore Bearer bent toward the body of the stricken Elder, and she leaned against his chest. She whispered to the remaining Elders, who were staring at A Ahmud Ki, locking gazes with the Advisor. 'What is it you have done to Elder Aswython?' one ventured.

A Ahmud Ki glanced at Thana, who crouched and sweated, as if preparing to run behind the shelter of his throne, before replying to the Aelendyell's question in the Aelendyell language. 'The Elder's mind is locked away for a time. It's an effective spell, one I could just as easily use on you all, if you persist with your foolish bravado.' He watched the Aelendyell reaction. They looked at each other, assessing the possibility of the Advisor's magical strength being greater than their own. 'Don't doubt it,' he added, with authority. 'I, alone, stopped more than your small party, at the edge of Elvenaar Forest, when I took the Orb. You are no match for me.'

'What are they saying?' Thana whispered, nervously relaxing his desire to run and hide.

'They're apologizing for their rudeness,' said A Ahmud Ki, with a wry grin, but he watched the Aelendyell Elders from the corner of his eye, in case they were willing to risk an attack.

'They don't look like they're apologizing to Us,' Thana said quietly, seeing the drawn swords and the Aelendyell encircled by the Great King's protectors.

'They are,' replied A Ahmud Ki calmly. He turned to the Aelendyell, with an ingenuous smile, and said, 'Great King Thana accepts your generous apology, and wishes you safe journey back to your homes.'

As he finished speaking, the Throne Room doors burst open, and two Royal Guards ran in. 'Your Highness!' one yelled, gasping for breath. Blood soaked through the shoulder of his jerkin, beneath his chain mail. 'The Aelendyell Weapon Bearers and an Elder from the Dining Hall have forced their way into the Royal Gardens!'

Thana stared at the Aelendyell at the foot of his throne. Treachery in his own castle: what was he to do? He turned to A Ahmud Ki for advice, but the Royal Advisor was gone.

The Apprentice at the door was unconscious, victim not of a blow but of a spell. A Ahmud Ki straightened from examining the body, and hurried into the gardens and teeming rain, to find a wall of Royal Guards, ten paces from his black tower, facing a line of Aelendyell Weapon Bearers at the tower's base, bows drawn, trained on the Guards. He pushed to the front, searching for the Elder who led the Aelendyell, but he wasn't to be seen. There was no possibility he could have passed through the tower's magical wall. The Aelendyell didn't possess that spell capability, and no Aelendyell Elder could understand or break down the glyph operating on the tower's structure. Frustrated, he glanced up, shielding his eyes against the stinging downpour, and found his answer. The Aelendyell Elder was levitating to the tower summit where the Orb was located to work its magical protection against dragons. A Ahmud Ki walked forward, but an

Aelendyell bowman warned him to stop. The Elder was nearly at the top of the tower, battling to concentrate on his levitation spell in the pouring rain. A Ahmud Ki gave the threatening bowman a cursory glance. An instant later, the astonished Aelendyell saw a falcon flash through the rain toward the tower's crest.

Saturated through the feathers, A Ahmud Ki reshaped at the top, and waited for the Aelendyell Elder to reach him. The rain pelted on his bare head and shoulders, drumming in his ears, blinding him to vision no further than the tower's edge. Out of the curtain of water, the Elder edged tentatively onto the tower's curved roof, struggling for a foothold, as he relinquished his spell, unaware of the Advisor's presence. Then he spied someone between him and his goal – the Orb of Radiance – and straightened, pulling his sodden grey locks away from his forehead in a futile bid to see more clearly. The rain was merciless. 'Go back!' A Ahmud Ki shouted above the roar of the rain. 'You cannot take the Orb! I forbid it!'

The Elder squinted and shook his head. 'The Orb is Aelendyell! It must be returned!' he cried.

'It stays!' yelled A Ahmud Ki. The Elder took a hesitant step forward, trying to find purchase on the slippery, ebony surface. 'No further, old one!' A Ahmud Ki shouted in warning. The Elder looked straight at him and raised his hands. A Ahmud Ki pointed one finger, and yelled, 'Legitu!' A thin bolt of crackling energy arched from his finger to the Elder's chest, and the Elder's body jerked backwards at the shocking touch, disappearing over the tower's edge.

A Ahmud Ki stared emptily into the grey wall of water for a moment, before he lowered his finger. He felt tired. His arm, the source of spell energy, ached. He shook it, to relieve the pain, and moved toward the edge without a backward glance at the glowing Orb. On the drenched earth below, the dead Elder lay spread-eagled before his anguished kin, his robes awash with mud and rain, and A Ahmud Ki felt a pang of pity for the old Aelendyell who gave his life in a futile attempt to return a sacred object to the Elvenaar burial chambers in Heolstorcofa. He knew the Elder, though the Elder hadn't recognised him. He had been the Chanter of Terin's village, when the young half-Aelendyell defied his Elders, and ran to the land of the Ranu Ka Shehaala, to be reborn as A Ahmud Ki. Fate had drawn them fleetingly together again. The old Aelendyell must have risen to join the ranks of the Ieldran: the Aelendyell Council of Elders. Now he was dead, and A Ahmud Ki had taken one more step on his path of revenge against the Aelendyell he hated, but this time it left him with unusual distaste in his heart.

Thirty

'It's been a long time,' said Jasmin, extending her hand, as she approached A Ahmud Ki in her quarters aboard the Targan ship. Sunlight splashed through narrow arched windows lining the vessel's side, and its glow enhanced Jasmin's charm.

'Too long,' A Ahmud Ki graciously replied. The Royal Advisor took her arm, as much to steady his balance from the unaccustomed rocking of the ship, as to be polite. 'Do you mind if we talk alone?' he asked, as he withdrew a chair for her at the small oak table in her room. Jasmin turned to her attendant, and dismissed him, then sat, and waited until A Ahmud Ki sat beside her. 'What's the news in Targa?' he asked.

She hesitated, taking in his appearance, before she answered. 'A lot has happened since you released Mareg from his bondage,' she began. 'The High Council has reformed and Lady Tarnyss' successor has been voted in by the Order.'

'Who?'

'Her sister.'

'Lady Corinna?'

'Yes,' replied Jasmin with a sigh. 'You know her?'

A Ahmud Ki grinned mischievously. 'I had the pleasure of making her acquaintance once,' he said. 'So, nothing has changed really.'

Jasmin's eyes brightened. 'There are changes,' she said. 'We Rebels have returned to our seats in the Order of Power. Lord Marcus sits on the High Council. President Corinna is stern, like Tarnyss was, but she's also willing to listen to reason, and that's why we agreed to return. We are united against the common enemy.'

'Which is why you come as ambassador,' A Ahmud Ki concluded.

Jasmin nodded, her single plait of brown hair bouncing against her slender neck. 'The High Council heard your Great King's requests for military aid against the Dragonlord and the Haagii. We took them before the Lord Keeper, but he refused aid, arguing that Targa needs every warrior for its own defence, if the Dragonlord comes.' She shifted her gaze to the nautical map of the Targan and Kingdom coastline. Outlined at its edges were sea dragons, warning of uncharted and treacherous waters. 'We know the extent of Mareg's power. No ordinary human army can stop a Dragonlord. The Order bands together all our sorceress and sorcerer Specialties, in the hope our combined magic will stave off Mareg.' Jasmin turned back to A Ahmud Ki. 'Your name is hated in Targa,' she whispered. 'When you came to me in my keep to learn my Specialty I'd already heard village witches speak of a prophetic arrival, but I doubted its truth. When you released Mareg, destroying Tarnyss, and the old High Council in the Inner Sanctum, the prophecy came into being, and I could no longer refuse to believe. The Age of Darkness is returning.'

A Ahmud Ki was fascinated to hear Jasmin talking with supernatural fear, because he remembered her as level-headed, a person resolved to establish political justice in her world, but the Jasmin beside him seemed insecure, uncertain in his presence. 'We make use of prophecies when it's necessary,' he said nonchalantly, and changed the topic. 'I sent a request to the High Council.'

'It has been heard,' Jasmin responded.

'And?'

'I bring one item with me. It's all we can spare,' she said apologetically. 'Only a few such items remain in Targa.'

A Ahmud Ki smiled, pleased to know he had access again to a communication crystal. 'Where is it?'

Jasmin reached inside her cloak and carefully uncovered a small amber crystal sphere, which she held up for the wizard's inspection.

He took the gift, stood carefully, and lifted it to the light. 'Beautiful,' he breathed, and dropped it, letting it shatter

267

against the table's edge. Jasmin shrieked with horror as she leapt from her chair. A Ahmud Ki carefully scooped a dozen fragments into the palms of his hands and placed them on the table. He selected one shard, cupped it in his hands, closed his eyes and incanted a making spell. A moment later, he held a new crystal sphere, identical to the one he destroyed. He passed it to Jasmin, who stared in awe at the product of the wizard's magic. 'Thank you, Lady Jasmin,' he said, as he stooped to collect another fragment. 'You brought me a communication crystal, so I'll send you back to the High Council with two crystals as a token of my appreciation for the Council's generosity.'

Damon adjusted his grey smock and the platinum chain Master Ki presented to him. He placed a tiny pyramidal crystal key at the wall's base, invoked the Ithosen spell that allowed entry and exit from the Master's Tower, stepped through, and ushered waiting Apprentices through the wall. One by one, the Apprentices moved to mats, organised in concentric rings, and sat, cross-legged, staring blankly at the platinum chains curled before their respective places. Damon instructed them to face outward from the circles' central point, which they all obediently did, waiting silently for Master Ki's arrival. Each Apprentice concentrated on his lessons: an Apprentice first learns patience; an Apprentice waits until he is spoken to; if an Apprentice must wait a lifetime for the Master to speak, 'Feran dja' – so be it.

Peret waited in the gathering, reciting the arcane lore for hypnotism in his mind, to keep boredom at bay. The Master promised to speak to him about the Dragonlord and The Rim Shield, but the meeting never eventuated, after he retrieved the sword for the Saviour. Peret was disappointed, but since the attempted assassination of Master Ki he understood the difficulty that the Master was under. It was not his right to question the Master's purpose. He gazed at the chain on the floor and silently repeated his mantra.

Death's First Hand secretly questioned Orrin's request after he left her. He wasted the lives of two of her best assassins on a contentious task – the murder of Nisus – and now he wanted three more assassins, without explanation. She wasn't accustomed to providing assassins for the Guild Master without being fully informed as to their missions, but, since the advent of the Shadow's Voice, Orrin was tight-lipped about his intentions. Three more assassins, without knowing what would become of them, was unacceptable, although she had no real choice in the matter but to grant his wish.

She smoothed back her dark hair and summoned her servant. A girl appeared in the doorway and bowed respectfully. 'Ask Tim Gaelus, Meryl Dwyer, and Denys to come to my chamber immediately,' said Death's First Hand, with a faint smile for the girl. The servant bowed again and slipped away on her errand.

'I said no.' Tim glanced at Andra for a response.

'Why?'

'I have a bad feeling about it. Death's First Hand wouldn't tell us the purpose of the task, or who the target was to be,' Tim explained. He shifted his eyes to Patti, who squatted at the table with a dress she was embroidering.

'How can you be sure, my Tim?' the chubby bordello mistress asked, looking up from her work. 'It's not unusual for the task to be kept secret before the night of the hit.'

Tim lifted a foot onto a chair and leaned forward. 'I felt it Patti. I heard it in her voice. She doesn't like it either.'

'What do you mean?' asked Andra.

Tim gesticulated, as he explained, emphasizing his passion. 'She called three of us together: me, Denys, and Meryl. I know Denys and Meryl are part Aelendyell, like me. They grew up with Patti, didn't they?' Patti nodded to confirm Tim's story. The assassin continued. 'Well, they're both very good at the trade, but not the best. Not like me, or

Morris. Now it makes sense to partner them, with me to take charge, to make sure they do the hit right, so I guess I was needed in that role. Then Death's First Hand said she had an important hit, sanctioned by the Shadow's Voice. I didn't like the sound of that. The last hit he ordered was on the High Lord, and Morris and I eliminated the assassins. I didn't want to argue, so I listened to what she had to say, but I'd already made my mind up the task wasn't for me. I could see what might happen. You know we can refuse a task. It's part of the Assassin's Code, in case the hit's a friend or relative, but it's rarely invoked, because of our sense of honour. I asked her who the target was, but she said she wasn't privy to that information. Master Orrin would tell us all we needed to know, when it was time. She seemed displeased, and I knew she was telling the truth about not knowing. That also made me uneasy. Then I realised why we three were chosen. We're all excellent with bows, easily the best archers in the Guild. I asked Death's First Hand if the target was another royal personage, like Nisus, but she shook her head, and repeated she didn't know. She seemed to understand my concern, because when the interview was over she asked me to remain behind, after Denys and Meryl left.'

'Did you?' asked Andra.

'Yes.'

'And what did you learn?' Patti inquired, putting her sewing to one side.

'Nothing. And a lot. She asked me why I was so full of questions. I said I normally expected more detail about a task, before I accepted it. I explained that the last time I worked I'd found the task distasteful. I hadn't expected to hit fellow assassins. I knew I took a risk in saying that to her, but her reaction was even stranger than I expected. She stared as if she was surprised to hear what I'd said. Then she asked me to repeat it, and explain what I meant. I told her about the events of that night, how Morris and I lay in ambush for our targets and ended up hitting the two who hit High Lord Nisus. She shook her head in disbelief and turned away from me. I don't think Death's First Hand knew the full details of the night's adventure either, until then. When she turned back, she looked angry, and I thought perhaps I'd overstepped the mark, but all she said was she'd understand if I refused the task. So, I did. She didn't ask why. I'm sure she knows why. She seemed almost pleased that I'd said no.'

'What about Meryl and Denys?' asked Patti, concerned. 'Have they withdrawn?'

'I don't know,' said Tim. 'We haven't spoken. But I wouldn't be surprised if all this has something to do with the last assassination. I want to find out who the target is.'

'Can I help?' asked Andra.

Tim nodded. 'There's no more word out about you in the Guild. The order to find you has been rescinded, so you're safe. I'd appreciate your help.'

'I'll get the girls to keep an open ear for anything they hear from clients,' said Patti with a sly wink at Andra and Tim. 'Not much gets by Patti's girls.'

'Someone's got a lot at stake,' said Tim with a frown, 'and I'm just curious enough to want to find out who and what.'

A Ahmud Ki ran his fingers along the arrow shaft, feeling the Aelendyell runes cut precisely and delicately into the wood, and ruffled the leaf formed the feathering. It was good that he kept the three arrows from his excursion to Elvenaar Forest. They were to serve a vital function in his plans of revenge. He passed the arrow to Meryl, who kneeled before him, her eyes fixed directly ahead, focussing on an unseen point beyond the Advisor. 'Three points of death,' he uttered softly, his voice amplified by the curve of the Deep Cave, and stepped back from the three assassins. 'You have the appointed day and time. You know your target.'

'Yes,' three voices responded in unison.

'Good. No one else must see your arrows. You are forbidden to speak to anyone about your task. You may not even talk between you. To do so is death. Understood?'

'Yes.'

A Ahmud KI's light sphere reflected on the neck chains

worn by the three assassins. 'On the appointed day, you will arrive separately, at your designated positions. When the hit is made, you return here. No one must stop you. If anyone accuses you of making the hit, that person, or you, must die. Understood?'

'Yes.'

'Hide the arrows.' Meryl, Denys, and Morris slid their arrows neatly inside their quivers. 'Go.'

As one, they rose from their knees, and filed from the Deep Cave, past Orrin, who stood waiting obediently near the entrance to the Maze.

A Ahmud Ki motioned for the Guild Master to approach, and said, 'They serve the Shadow's Voice, but you must watch, in case any one of them forgets their task. If so, the penalty of the Oath must fall. I hold you personally responsible.' Orrin nodded in understanding. 'Leave me,' the Advisor instructed. Orrin withdrew in the wake of the three assassins.

'And you advise that We hold a parade before the city population, to boost morale?' Thana asked, as he leaned back in the golden chair at the head of the King's Table.

'Yes,' A Ahmud Ki replied.

'If I may speak, Your Highness?' a lord tentatively asked. Thana nodded assent to Gerran. 'Your Highness hasn't been before the people since – well, since the Great Armies first marched from the Great City,' Gerran noted in his boyish voice. 'In fact, there's been no form of celebration, no games, apart from the parade of the Saviour that is, since then. The people are miserable after a long and wet winter. They need to see the Great King in all his glory in the streets.'

'You must consider,' Lord Kerry broke in, 'that the people have little to buoy their spirits. The Armies are locked in the pass at Central Gate, the Aelendyell no longer come, the Shaddites hole up in the Dwarven Mountains in fear of the Dragonlord, and the Targan ambassador stayed on her ship at Balos. They need to see someone important to keep their minds from mundane things.'

'My priests would enjoy a parade,' said Haephus quietly.

'Perhaps High Lord Surdrok could spare some warriors and Haardrishii to make the parade more impressive,' added Gerran enthusiastically. A Ahmud Ki grinned at the young Lord's naive concept of war.

Thana pressed his fingertips together, beneath his wobbling jowls, and considered the idea. A Great King had to lead by example. The new Chancellor and Royal Advisor said as much. Pomp and ceremony were important to status. The people expected it. The presence of the Great King would raise their hopes and increase his popularity. A parade was essential.

The Great King pushed away from the table and stood to command his lords. 'We have decided. A ceremonial parade must be arranged. Soon. We cannot disappoint the people of the Kingdom.' With a gracious smile creasing his fat cheeks, Thana turned to A Ahmud Ki, and said, 'The new Royal Chancellor will arrange the details.' A Ahmud Ki bowed, as Thana turned back to the table. 'Lord Gerran will see they are carried out exactly to plan.' The Great King waddled toward the door to his Private Chambers. 'As for Us, We are tired of discussion today. We dismiss you.'

Just as Tim went to step out of the alcove, to speak to Morris, Andra grabbed him, and pulled him into the shadows. They silently watched the assassin pass along the corridor and disappear down a set of stairs. 'Why did you do that?' Tim hissed, puzzled and angry.

'Did you see what he was wearing?'

Tim peered into the empty corridor. 'No. Well, clothes, but nothing unusual.'

'Around his neck. Inside his tunic.' explained Andra. 'A neck chain.'

'So what?' asked Tim, irritated by the riddle.

'Isn't that unusual to you?'

'No,' Tim answered, but he reconsidered. 'Well, in a way.

We don't wear chains, if we're on a task. They give us away. Too light reflective and noisy.'

'That's not what I meant,' said Andra, fighting for a reason to his own confusion. 'There's something familiar about the chain.'

'But you must have only caught a glimpse of it, if it's inside his tunic.'

'I know. That's what bothers me. I've seen a chain like it before. But I can't remember where.'

Tim shook his head. 'If you can't remember, then I certainly don't know what you're thinking of. I just missed a golden opportunity to find out who the target is going to be. Morris and I have always been honest with each other. I'll go to his room and talk.'

'No,' said Andra flatly. 'He won't tell you a thing.'

Tim stared with surprise. 'How do you know that?'

'His eyes had no expression. I remember now. Liam's were like that, in the parade. Exactly the same. That's what bothered me. I saw the chain, and I looked at his eyes because Liam wore a chain just like it. And that's how I know. But I don't understand the connection.' Tim moved uneasily in the shadows, suddenly tense, so tense Andra could feel it in the assassin's presence. 'What's wrong?' he asked.

'Everything,' whispered Tim. 'I think I understand the connection. But I still don't know why. Or who.'

Thirty One

Lord Rheims fussed over the black and green cushions, lining the royal carriage, where His Royal Majesty Great King Thana would recline, while the people of the Great City watched him pass. The shock of losing his position, as Chancellor to the Royal Advisor, numbed his feelings, but he compensated by zealously throwing himself into the preparations for the royal parade. After all, Thana wanted him to act as Royal Valet, so his years of experience as Chancellor were not to be lightly cast off, but he was driven with a renewed urgency to show his king that he was still useful, still needed. No one else knew how to pander to Thana's wants like he did, least of all the new Chancellor. His bony fingers prodded the cushions into position, while around him, a handful of boys and maidens giggled restlessly, bored with waiting.

Lord Gerran paced nervously through the assembled throng, checking each contingent was in order, and ready to begin. High Lord Surdrok begrudgingly released another fifty Haardrishii from Central Gate to ride in the royal parade, although he steadfastly refused to participate himself, informing Gerran, in short manner, that his responsibility was fixed to the Kingdom's security, and he had no time to waste on the Great King's whimsical frivolities. Gerran omitted telling Thana Surdrok's full message as a matter of tact.

Lord Haephus was speaking quietly to his orange-robed priests, whose incense burners hung listlessly from their hands, awaiting the command to be lit, so their fragrances could purify the path of the Great King through the common masses of humanity. The High Priest nodded courteously to Gerran, as the latter passed, but Haephus held the boyish lord in contempt for being foolish and naive. Why Thana never allowed Haephus to organize matters of state irritated the earthly representative of Teka. Instead, important public events fell into the incompetent hands of less masterful lords. He suspected Thana had other motives of interest in the youthfully handsome Gerran, but he was careful never to voice those thoughts beyond the domain of his temple.

The black robed Royal Assassins waited silently, and Gerran avoided lingering near their group, walking instead toward the castle gates, where gatekeeper Garth and his men awaited Gerran's command to open them. All the parade needed, to begin, was the Great King and his Chancellor.

'Will he be dressed in gold robes?' Milly queried, as she slipped on a fresh tunic.

'Peace, girl!' ordered Patti, laughing. 'If you don't hurry, you'll miss the parade altogether, you will.'

'Does his carriage have white horses? Is it full of jewels and furs and rich things?' the girl persisted, pulling on a rough pair of leggings.

'There wouldn't be much room for anything else in the carriage, given his size,' Jen chipped in.

'They need ten white horses just to pull him along,' added Tim with a wink at Milly. 'He's not called the Great King for nothing.'

'You be careful makin' fun about size, my young Tim,' warned Patti, glaring at the thief, 'or I'll think you might be sayin' such things about me, behind me back. And you wouldn't dare,' she threatened, waggling her index finger at him.

'I'd never dare such a thing,' replied Tim, with a touch of mock apprehension. The gathering laughed at his jibe.

'Since when's Patti begun to defend the Great King?' asked Jen.

'Him? He's mad. It's size I'm touchy about,' she chuckled. 'And you know how I prefer 'em big.' She winked at Andra, who smiled sheepishly when the others turned to laugh at him.

'Something you haven't told me?' inquired Tim, with a

teasing smile. Andra pushed his friend away, and laughed with the others.

'I'm ready!' cried Milly. She flicked her hair back and gave Andra a toothy grin. 'I wanted to see a parade when I came to the Great City. Isn't it exciting?'

'You can watch from my shoulders, Milly,' said Andra, and he tousled her hair, drawing protestation from the girl.

As they moved along the Maze's corridors, Tim drew alongside Andra. 'I haven't found out any more about the hit,' he half-whispered. 'I can't get near Morris. And I haven't seen the other two in The Maze, in the past days.'

'Where could they be?' asked Andra, slowing to his friend's pace, and allowing the others to draw ahead.

'Anywhere. It's easy to disappear for weeks down here. As you know.'

'They wouldn't strike in the parade, would they?'

Tim shook his head. 'Hardly. Daylight, and far too public for an action by The Hand. I can't recall any assassinations being made in daylight,' he said. 'No. There's something else afoot. They might be making a hit tonight, during the revelry, after the parade. I'm curious as to who demands so much importance from the Shadow's Voice this time. High Lord Nisus was an extremely risky hit, whatever the reason for it. You know what I can't understand about that one?'

'What?' asked Andra.

'Why the Royal Assassins didn't retaliate. The Hand's implicated in the murder of their leader, and they accept it without a murmur of complaint. It doesn't make sense.'

They emerged in the backroom of Detton Tomas' Inn of Dragons and joined the crowd. Andra recognised a handful of faces, thieves from The Maze, and he glimpsed Roy's heavy features before the thief disappeared through the front door. Most people in the inn were men, content to lean at the bar, or sit at tables, drinking.

Ribald comments greeted Patti and Jen as they entered, and Patti rebutted them, reminding the offenders to watch their manners in the presence of a child. Milly blushed, and threw Patti a fierce glare at being publicly labelled a child.

Tim led the way toward the door, into the street, and then around the back of the Inn of Dragons.

'Where are we going?' asked Andra, as they reached the bank of Dragon River.

Tim began to cast a line off a boat tucked in the green reeds. 'Across to Riverway Street,' he explained, as he helped the others aboard. 'The parade's supposed to follow the King's Way south, and cut across the Lower Bridge, and back up Riverway. There'll be less people that side.'

Satisfied, Andra clambered aboard the leaky rowboat, pleased to be in the open air, because he'd spent too many days, hidden in the bowels of the Maze. At last he was getting a daylight view of the Great City. He settled beside Milly, and watched Tim dip his oars into the blue waters of the river's steady current.

'When's the Great King coming?' asked Milly, with her usual effervescence.

'When he feels like it,' retorted Patti. 'He's the Great King. He does as he's a mind to.'

'When he's got 'is mind,' piped an old man, who was bent over his crooked walking stick, trying to make his way to the other side of the street.

Andra scooped Milly up over a wide mud patch and put her down on the other side. 'Why don't people like the Great King?' she asked.

'What makes you think they don't like him?' Andra queried.

'Don't you hear what Patti, and Tim, and Jen say, when they talk about him?' she replied. 'They make nasty comments about how fat he is. And that he's lazy. And stupid.'

'They don't mean them,' said Andra, without conviction.

'Yes, they do,' Milly insisted. 'They don't respect him. He's supposed to be the Great King, but they're rude about him.'

'Sometimes people aren't always what they seem.'

'What do you mean?'

Andra felt as if he was being backed into a verbal corner. Milly wanted an answer. 'You wait till he comes, and judge for yourself,' he said. 'I don't know whether he's good or bad.'

'If he's the Great King, he must be good,' declared Milly. 'There can't be bad kings. People wouldn't let them be king if they were bad.'

Great King Thana eased back into the luxury of his carriage and gazed up at the grey clouds, hanging low in the sky. It wouldn't dare rain on him. He ordained a royal parade through the Great City, and the weather was compelled to obey. After all, he was Great King, the One and True Descendant of Aian Abreotan, Eternal Ruler of the Kingdom. He ran his fingers across the warm fabric, lining the inner sides of the carriage, and its sensuous touch pleased him. The new Chancellor did well to suggest a parade before the people. A parade would be good for him, restore his faith in himself, and remind him of his potency as Great King. He needed to know who he was again.

There had been too many changes in his Kingdom, in the past year, too many political machinations in the past weeks, to make him feel comfortable or secure, and, although he was the Great King, he was frequently troubled with fears that he was not always fully in control of affairs. Rheims proved unreliable, and weak. High Lord Mara failed him in his war against the Dragonlord, and his successor, Nisus, was too ambitious, too desirous of Thana's throne. His assassination, though timely, remained uncomfortably mysterious. The rest of the lords were fools, too concerned with themselves to be of real use to a Great King. Gerran was a boy, Kerry a half-wit, and Haephus a religious idiot. The Royal Drycraefter said nothing to anyone, remaining unpleasantly aloof, as he always had, an attitude that infuriated Thana, but convention and history prevented him interfering with Waeron Ardath or his duty. He might as well not even exist. There was only the Royal Advisor. He had given Thana important advice. He encouraged Thana, reminded him of his position, and helped him to assert authority when the Lords were restless, and uncooperative. He was a gift, from Teka, to protect Thana against the Dragonlord. He held all the keys to the Kingdom's future and Thana's personal glory. As Chancellor, he would enhance Thana's power, protect him against exploitation or stupidity from the others, and spread his influence back through the Kingdom.

A spot of rain fell on Thana's sweating forehead. Broken from his reverie, he glanced to the side and realised his procession was passing along the King's Way. The ride in the carriage, drawn by its six white war steeds, was smooth. Behind the ranks of the leading mounted Haardrishii, Haagii war prisoners pushed large stone rollers to flatten the ridges and fill the ruts churned by winter traffic in the King's Way.

He made no effort to acknowledge the people lining the street. If he had, he would've been disappointed, because there were only curious children and women, old men, thieves of various trades, and occasional merchants and shopkeepers. Too many people, mainly the Kingdom's young men, were dead at The Rim Shield, or were gathered in the snow-filled valley of Central Gate facing the vast Haagii war machine. The Great City could no longer provide crowds for the Great King's parade.

Thana lifted his head to look at the solitary form of the Saviour, riding directly ahead of his royal carriage. The warrior's black Haardrishii armour had been exchanged for a special suit of plate mail, worked in dark green metal, bearing the royal griffin insignia on the breastplate. The Chancellor ordered it made before the parade. Thana felt safer than ever, being led by the prophetic incarnation of the Kingdom's saviour. The warrior was destined to meet and defeat the Dragonlord, and the Chancellor claimed he knew the whereabouts of Abreotan's sword, the final link in the fulfilment of the ancient prophecy. All was well. He would rule as Great King for a long time.

Thana relaxed into his cushions, oblivious to the care and labour of his ex-Chancellor, the insect Rheims, and he was reclining comfortably in that position, eyes closed against the threatening overcast sky, when three fatal shafts pierced his chest.

Andra was looking for Tim, who'd wandered south, along the winding Riverway, to see if the parade was approaching. They heard the distant royal fanfare along the King's Way, but the trumpets blared on only four occasions, the last, as close as Patti could guess, near the Lower Bridge. The sky darkened, and rain was imminent. A cold breeze kicked up along the street, and Milly snuggled closer to Andra to keep warm. 'How much longer?' she asked, for a countless time.

'Soon,' replied Andra. 'Soon,' but when he saw Tim running toward them he knew something was wrong, because a second person ran a short distance behind Tim, shouting, and the people he passed broke from the cover of the ramshackle buildings to run south, toward Lower Bridge.

Tim gesticulated toward the river. 'To the boat! We'll get there quicker!' he called, and he headed in the indicated direction.

Andra grabbed Tim's arm to get his attention when the party reached the riverbank. 'What's wrong?'

Tim glanced down at Milly, catching his breath, and looked across at Patti and Jen. 'They made a hit,' he said deliberately. 'The Great King.'

'Who made a hit?' said Andra, struggling to comprehend the magnitude of Tim's news.

The thief's eyes met Andra's, and the Guardian was puzzled to see his confusion mirrored in his friend's gaze. 'The Aelendyell,' Tim replied.

A Ahmud Ki waited patiently in the Deep Cave. Meryl and Morris were kneeling before him, their faces unemotionally etched into relief by the floating sphere of light the

Chancellor had generated. Their platinum neck chains glinted. Muffled footsteps came from the entrance to the Maze, and Denys appeared, moving swiftly through the shadows into the circle of light. When he saw A Ahmud Ki, he stopped and dropped silently to his knees. 'The Great King is dead?' asked the Royal Advisor quietly.

'Yes,' answered Denys.

'Are you certain?'

'I'm certain, Master.'

'Good,' breathed the wizard, and he smiled. He walked toward the tunnel, leading to the spring that fed Dragon River, and when he reached the entrance he motioned for the three assassins to rise and follow. As one, they obeyed his call.

Thirty Two

Much as he hated the pompous world of the Great King's castle, Surdrok had no choice but to attend the meeting, now Thana was dead. He reluctantly left Claarn in command at Central Gate, especially since the Haagii were increasing their attacks, as winter began to turn, but he consoled himself with the knowledge that the idiotic fat Thana was dead, and by the time he reached the Great City he felt almost pleased to be attending the King's Table under the circumstances. Without Thana's paranoid interference, the war against the Haagii and the Dragonlord might make positive progress.

Surdrok pushed open the door into the meeting room, before the servant could perform that duty, and he marched in defiantly, his bearing informing the attendant lords that he was the High Lord, master of the Great Armies, and potentially the most powerful man in the Kingdom, but he halted when he saw A Ahmud Ki sitting in the golden chair at the head of the King's Table.

'Welcome, High Lord Surdrok,' said A Ahmud Ki, rising with the others to greet the stocky warrior dressed in his black Haardrishii armour. Surdrok bowed stiffly and moved to the seat he rarely occupied since his rise from the ranks of the Royal Assassins, barely a year before. Much had changed in the Kingdom.

A Ahmud Ki waited for Surdrok to take his place. He expected no opposition from the High Lord, despite the man's surly attitude to everything. Surdrok knew A Ahmud Ki was instrumental in his rise to power, and that he owed the new Chancellor favours. They'd talked. The High Lord was a plain man, disinterested in political guile, and even if Surdrok ever did see a reason to oppose A Ahmud Ki the latter knew the opposition would be open and blunt – and predictable.

'Sit, gentlemen,' A Ahmud Ki instructed. The lords obeyed. 'There's no need to dwell on the Great King's death. Few of us here had little love for the man.'

A Ahmud Ki watched the lords' reactions to his statement. Rheims' mouth opened partially, but the rest were passively agreeing. Thana had not been loved, hardly even liked. Even the boyish Gerran was nauseated when the Great King stood too close to him in the palace.

'But his assassination leaves us with problems. That's why I called this meeting.'

A Ahmud Ki stood and briskly walked to the door, leading to the Throne Room. He tapped lightly. Two Haardrishii opened the door, and stood at rigid attention, while a third marched in, bearing a silver tray. The Chancellor reached for three bloodied shafts, resting in a red silken cloth on the tray, and held them up for the lords to see.

'These are the shafts taken from Thana's chest.' He turned them carefully, casting a cursory glance across the runes and patterns cut into them. 'Aelendyell arrows, skillfully crafted by Weapon Bearers from within Elvenaar Forest.' He handed the arrows to the closest lord, Lord Kerry, and continued speaking as the lords passed the instruments of death between them to inspect the markings on the shafts. 'There is no doubt who killed the Great King,' he said slowly, letting his words work with the vision of the arrows. 'The Kingdom has enemies within, as well as without. The Aelendyell are a selfish people, concerned only with their own purposes, their own fears. They would rather let the Dragonlord swallow the Kingdom, and its people, than lend their magic for its protection. They refused to give Thana the Orb of Radiance, and have since attacked him in his own palace, on the pretense of coming to negotiate. They've ended all diplomatic ties. They lock themselves in the security of their forests and sneak out to butcher the Great King through vengeful spite and hatred.' His eyes met Waeron Ardath's. The Drycraefter would never be convinced by this performance. Did it matter? He knew Ardath preferred to remain aloof, but would Ardath dare to oppose him, now that Thana was dead? He broke the stare.

Lord Haephus gently placed the arrows on the table before him. 'The Goddess Teka cannot sanction the murder of her anointed king. If this is how the Aelendyell choose to act, then I call for them to be outlawed.'

'Yes!' Gerran agreed. 'Who will they murder next?'

Waeron Ardath coughed to attract attention. 'Aren't we being presumptuous?' he asked.

A Ahmud Ki turned his gaze on the white-haired Lord. Had he misjudged the Drycraefter?

'What do you mean?' asked Haephus.

'I mean,' replied Ardath calmly, 'you're assuming the Aelendyell are responsible for this assassination.'

'We have the proof,' said Haephus, picking the arrows up.

'Three arrows,' Ardath blandly stated.

'Yes,' the High Priest asserted. 'Three Aelendyell arrows.'

'Shot by whom?' Ardath asked, with raised eyebrows. 'Who saw the bowmen?' The lords all turned to A Ahmud Ki for an answer.

'I did.'

The unexpected voice from the Throne Room entrance swung their necks toward the door. Standing in the entrance was Liam, in his dark green armour.

'Go on,' prompted A Ahmud Ki. 'What did you see?'

The lords listened attentively, as Liam explained. 'Three figures on the rooftops near Lower Bridge. They loosed the arrows. There was nothing I could do to warn the Great King. It was only chance that I saw them at all.'

'You recognised them?' asked Haephus.

'Yes. One lingered to see if the arrows struck true. He had long silver hair.' Liam glanced toward A Ahmud Ki. 'Like the Chancellor,' he said, 'and green clothing. They were Aelendyell.'

'Are you sure?' asked Waeron Ardath.

'Yes,' Liam confirmed. 'I've seen the Aelendyell in Elvenaar Forest. They were Aelendyell.'

Liam's declaration created a buzz of voices at the King's

Table. Waeron Ardath looked at A Ahmud Ki, and understood all too clearly the unfolding direction that the meeting was taking. He leaned back in his chair, and watched with an observer's eyes to see how the Chancellor would manipulate the others.

'I repeat my call,' Haephus directed to the Chancellor. 'The Aelendyell must be made to pay for this murderous attack. Teka must be avenged!'

'I agree!' said Kerry. Gerran and Rheims vigorously nodded support.

'There are no Aelendyell in the Great Armies,' said Surdrok, breaking over the anger of the others. 'They've never offered to help the Kingdom against the Dragonlord. They're not our allies. Therefore they, too, are numbered among our enemies. Outlaw them as a matter of military necessity, if for no other reason.' Mutual assent greeted his statement.

Only Waeron Ardath remained unconvinced. When the babble eased, he interrupted. 'There's the matter of a king,' he said with a theatrical shrug. 'Without a king, there is no Kingdom.' He guessed A Ahmud Ki's reply, before he asked his question, but he wanted to draw the Chancellor into revealing everything to the lords at the Table, if only for his own appreciation.

The more Waeron Ardath baited him, the more A Ahmud Ki enjoyed the Drycraefter's presence in the castle. Ardath was an excellent foil, a worthy adversary, more so because he had no aspirations to the throne. He was a necessary threat, keeping the Chancellor's wits sharp and prepared for doubt or opposition. He resisted the temptation to smile at Ardath's question, which came almost according to plan in his leading of the meeting, as he announced, 'Your king already stands before you.'

The lords lifted their eyes to the Chancellor. Ardath was fascinated to think that he misinterpreted A Ahmud Ki's methods of working for power. The Chancellor was being far more direct than usual, if he was claiming the throne. Then he saw A Ahmud Ki indicating the figure in the doorway:

Liam. All eyes rested on the warrior with the prophetically scarred forehead.

'The cycle of the Prophecy unfolds before your eyes,' said A Ahmud Ki with a deliberately measured voice. 'Thana's successor already prepares to take what is his, according to the Law of Abreotan. The new Dragon Slayer is the Saviour.' He sensed mixed reactions of disbelief, and understanding from the men at the King's Table, and he was prepared to weave a spell to enhance their compliance with his plans, but when he saw Waeron Ardath watching him he let the idea go, realising he needed their open acceptance of Liam for his scheme to work.

'What right has he to the crown?' Haephus asked, turning back to the Chancellor.

'Every Lord in this room could claim equal possession of the throne of a childless king,' said Rheims, with a rare glimpse of understanding.

'That was Nisus' claim,' Waeron Ardath added quietly.

Surdrok saw his opportunity. He stood stiffly and banged his fist against the table. 'I replaced Nisus. I claim Thana's throne!' he bellowed. He glared at the other lords, who stared open-mouthed at his declaration, but when he faced A Ahmud Ki the disdain on the Chancellor's face warned him he overstepped his mark. He felt vulnerable, when the Chancellor's grey eyes fixed him with their impersonal gaze, and wondered why he was foolish enough to think so bold a move could have ever succeeded.

'Your claim is denied,' A Ahmud Ki said with emphasised control, control that suggested to everyone else the Chancellor was restraining a greater threat to Surdrok than mere denial. The High Lord wisely sat, without further comment, leaving A Ahmud Ki to continue. 'According to the Prophecy, as the Royal Drycraefter correctly informed you at this table, the new king must bear Abreotan's sword. So, it will be. The sword will be found and returned to the Great City. The Saviour bears the mark of the moon, and soon he will bear the sword of Abreotan. He is your new king.'

After a pause, during which the lords at the Table

assimilated A Ahmud Ki's point, they stood, Ardath and Surdrok reluctantly, and politely bowed to Liam. The warrior remained at attention, as if fully expecting the honour the lords paid to him.

'In the meantime,' A Ahmud Ki concluded, once Liam had received appropriate homage, 'we have a former king to bury.'

Tim flicked a piece of gnawed bone across the room, into the blazing hearth, where it landed with a flurry of sparks. 'So you don't believe the Great King was killed by the Aelendyell?' asked Andra, between mouthfuls of lamb that Jen and Milly cooked.

'They don't work like that,' replied Tim, with a shake of his head.

'How do you know?'

'I know. Better than anyone in the Guild, I know.'

The firelight threw crazy patterns against the room's earthen walls. Andra remembered the night he stumbled upon the Haagii camp in The Vale searching for Flintok's pigs. He still wanted to leave the Great City and return to The Vale, to see his parents, and the beauty of the small valley nestled beneath the craggy Ureykyeu peaks. The Guardian inside him stirred uneasily, needing to protect the world he was trained and raised in. Tim's Great City was filled with too many mysteries, too many conspiracies, too many unknown dangers.

'Drink?' Tim held a carved wooden wine goblet toward him.

Andra shook his head and asked for water. A ladle was dipped into the nearby water bucket and Milly passed it to him, letting droplets spatter the earthen floor.

'Morris has disappeared.'

Tim's news rekindled Andra's interest. 'Since the Great King's assassination?'

Tim nodded. 'And Meryl and Denys. Three assassins.'

'Three arrows,' said Andra, comprehending his direction.

'You think they did it, don't you?'

'I have no proof, but the pattern fits neatly together. I've asked discretely, in the Hand, if there's been a hit on other assassins, but no one's had a task since the invitation I received from Death's First Hand.'

'But why Aelendyell arrows? And how?' As he asked the question, Andra remembered Freyar's gift. 'My -?'

'Not your bow, Andra,' Tim cut in. 'It's safely stored where I hid it. I went there first, fearing someone found it, but nothing's taken.' Andra relaxed, but the question irritated him. Tim responded, as if guessing his vexation. 'Rumours abound from the castle. The Orb on the wizard's tower is an ancient Elvenaar artefact, very sacred to the Aelendyell. I doubt they easily parted with it. One rumour is the Royal Advisor stole it. There was an Aelendyell deputation to the castle, very recently, and they were removed from the Great City by a force of the Great King's Guards. There's more than political positioning involved. Someone's trying to foster hatred between the two races. I think this assassination was set up by someone to make the Aelendyell look guilty.'

'The Royal Advisor?' Andra suggested.

'The Chancellor, now,' Tim corrected. 'Possibly. Although his appearance suggests he's part Aelendyell, so it seems odd to think he'd want to hurt his blood people.' Tim crossed to the hearth and poked at the wood with his dagger, stirring the flames. 'Death's First Hand asked for you today.'

The news surprised the young Guardian. 'Why?'

'She's been asked by the Shadow's Voice to provide four competent members of The Hand to join a party under the leadership of the Saviour.'

'Liam?'

Tim nodded. 'He's named Heir Apparent to Thana's throne. According to the popular prophecy, all he has to do is find Aian Abreotan's sword. Then he's the new king.'

Andra joined Tim beside the fire, confused by his friend's outpouring of information about events surrounding the Great King's murder. 'What's all this got to do with me?'

'Death's First Hand requests that you be one of the four assassins to go on the journey to find the sword.'

'Why? I mean, I'm not even a member of The Hand,' argued Andra.

'Two reasons,' Tim explained. 'Because I asked. And because of the scar on your cheek.'

Andra instinctively lifted his hand to his left cheek and ran his fingers along the crescent scar. 'Why the scar?'

'You know why,' replied Tim. 'She's superstitious. She thinks there's a connection between you, and your Saviour friend with all the moon markings. She's worked out that you're both from the same place, and she figures there's more than an accidental likeness between you.'

Andra laughed. 'I know how I got this,' he said, remembering the plunge into the marshes in his desperation to escape the Haagii. 'Sharp sticks make messes of people's faces.' Then he became serious. 'I don't know how Liam's marks appeared. They've come since he left The Vale.'

'It doesn't matter,' said Tim. 'Death's First Hand insists you go with me. Or me with you. I said we would.'

Andra stared into the fire, watching flames dance along a short chunk of timber, turning the black and grey wood to glowing reds and flaming yellows. 'I wish you'd asked me first,' he said with a note of disappointment.

'Why?'

'The Vale. Winter's nearly over. Another few weeks, and the Valley of Rivers will be passable. I could go home.'

Tim laid a friendly hand on Andra's shoulder, trying to show he understood Andra's longing to return home. 'I'm sorry, Andra. I forget. You make your own decisions. Your home's important to you. I understand how you feel. If I had a home, I'd feel the same. I just thought that you'd be keen to go with Liam on the single most important adventure this Kingdom's ever likely to see. Abreotan's sword is the stuff of legends.' Tim released his grip and moved to the room's centre, beside a low wooden table where their meal dishes were cluttered. 'If Liam succeeds in finding it, then I might have to reconsider my attitude to prophecies,' Tim said, with an ironic grin, and he laughed, trying to humour the downcast Guardian. 'The Dragonlord will have to reassess his own philosophies too. Nothing worse than a prophecy interfering with plans of domination.' He watched Andra's face for a response. 'On the other hand, if Liam fails -' Tim shrugged, and sat on the edge of the table. 'Well, perhaps you'll be safer in The Vale anyway.'

Tim's final comment struck a chord within Andra's pride. The Guardian lifted his head, a troubled expression lining his brow. 'I'm not running away, Tim Gaelus,' he said, setting his jaw.

'I never said you were,' Tim replied, but he knew Andra's conscience had been pricked. He had one card to play in his gambit. 'You want to go home to protect The Vale. That's noble. Your people would be proud of you. But I ask one thing, my friend. Is The Vale your only home?' The question puzzled Andra. In the flickering hearth light, he thought Tim's features were more Aelendyell than human, and he saw Terath, or perhaps Freyar staring at him. He blinked and the vision vanished, but Tim whispered a single word across the space between them. 'Hondgesella.'

'What did you say?' Andra asked; but he did not need an answer. Tim's word was already written deep inside his memories and he knew there was only one answer to the question Tim asked.

Thirty Three

Teka could hardly have provided a less fortuitous beginning to our journey, thought Andra. He pulled the black cloth, marking him as a member of the Hand, across his face, to keep out the biting breeze, and glanced up at the scudding clouds filling the dull morning sky. He gripped his horse's reins tightly as he touched her flank with his heels.

The mounted party, Liam at their head, his dark green armour glistening from the soft drizzling rain, wound between the priests Haephus ordered lined up to bless their passing out of the Great City. Behind Liam rode four Haardrishii, followed by three Chancellor's Apprentices, their bald pates covered by woollen caps, pulled down over their ears to keep out the cold and damp. Tim Gaelus rode beside Andra, and two more members of the Hand, Sasha and Jo, filled out their group. Six Haardrishii filed along in the rear, bringing the party to eighteen.

They headed west, passing between the incomplete gates of the half-built outer wall Thana ordered constructed months before his death. Work on the wall ceased with winter's onset and the dwindling labour caused by the on-going drain of the war. Andra gazed at the line of stone, and the rock piles awaiting orders and mortar, and wondered if the Great City would ever see the wall become reality before the Haagii swept onto the Plains of Ky.

Beyond the city, Liam settled his horse into a steady gait, and led them along the King's Way, toward Ky. They passed through the town, late in the afternoon, stopping to water the horses, before pressing on, toward Central Gate. With the advent of night, Liam's pace increased, but they didn't enter the sodden Central Gate valley until close to midnight, when all that lit their way were soldiers' campfires strung along the valley floor. Disgruntled soldiers, who questioned their purpose pushing through Central Gate at so late a time, stopped them on several occasions, but each time Liam resolved the matter.

When they climbed above the snowline, Andra felt a bitter cold set in. He followed Tim's example, and pulled the thick cloak, Patti provided, from the pack on his horse's rump to wrap himself in, but the cold wormed inside his cocoon, making him long for a blazing fire and sleep.

Just when he felt he could ride no further, Liam ordered them to dismount and shelter beneath an overhang, a short distance up the side of the valley, visible because of twin campfires burning beneath its rocky shelf. As he hobbled his horse and stretched a woollen blanket across its back and flank, he felt sorry to leave the animal in the valley on so cold a night. He patted the horse's white nose, before he followed the others up to the shelter.

The occupants were Haardrishii. Their black shields reflected the red glow from the fires. 'Not only do we have to travel with Haardrishii,' sneered Jo in a low whisper, as they entered, 'but we have to sleep with them as well.'

'Better than sleeping with Haagii,' Tim responded.

'Is there a difference?' Sasha asked.

The Haardrishii warriors sombrely greeted their fellows, and invited them to join them at the fires, but no such offer was extended to the Apprentices or assassins, who met defiant stares.

'We're not welcome,' said Sasha, as she slipped her pack from her shoulders.

'Is this all because of the code back in the Great City?' Andra asked, turning to Tim.

Tim led them toward a corner of the overhang, away from the Haardrishii, where he said, 'No. The Haardrishii are fighting a war. They resent the fact the Guild hasn't committed thieves to the Great Armies. They consider us cowards, traitors.'

Andra glanced at the black-armoured figures, sharing the fires' warmth. The Haardrishii were proud, like he had been proud as a Guardian, proud to defend their Kingdom from the enemy. 'Why won't the Guild support the Great Armies?'

he asked.

Tim dropped his pack and began searching for loose wood on the rock floor. 'At first, the Guild saw no reason to be involved. When High Lord Mara marched north against the Haagii, the Guild guessed the war would be quickly concluded. It didn't expect the disaster that followed. Since the Shadow's Voice appeared, Orrin has simply refused to let the Guild become involved in the war.'

'Don't you think that's wrong?' asked Andra. 'The Dragonlord threatens us all.'

Tim straightened. 'I've come on this errand for the sword. Does that answer your question?'

Sasha and Tim had a small fire burning before the assassins bedded down, huddling to share their warmth. Andra observed that the three Apprentices, a short distance away, wove their hands through the air and passed them over each other's body, before they lay on the bare rock, without covers or blankets, and went quickly to sleep, immune to the intense cold. Around the twin fires, the Haardrishii were settling into their bedrolls, except two, who remained seated, on watch to guard the shelter. At the firelight's edge, on the lip of the overhang's entrance, Andra saw one person staring into the sleet and the night's darkness, his hand resting on the hilt of a familiar sword, and his green armour reflecting the fires' dancing flames. 'When will you tell Liam?' Tim's whispered question startled the Guardian.

'When I have a chance to talk to him, alone,' Andra answered, 'but not yet.'

The giant of Tressel Deep was angry. The High Lord was relieving him of his leadership role and sending him on an errand to baby-sit a group of would-be warriors going in search of a lost legend. He hardly considered it a worthy challenge for a mighty warrior, when the Dragonlord's host, the enemy who humiliated him on The Rim Shield, sat waiting for the snow to thaw in anticipation of a full battle for Central Gate. He ached for the opportunity to meet the Haagii and dragons in combat to avenge the debacle of The Rim Shield. Now Surdrok was taking his chance for glory away. He swept his thick bear hide across his shoulders and motioned to Marella to join him. The woman leapt from her watchtower, landing agilely in the soft snow. 'We have no choice in the matter,' said Claarn. 'The short pig insists we go. And we must obey him, or be treated with dishonour.' The giant shook his red mane and spat with contempt.

'What about Artega?' Marella asked, reminding Claarn of the war dog.

'I've left him with Nessa. She'll see he's looked after.'

As the pair climbed out of the lower reaches, heading for the meeting point Surdrok described, Claarn cursed a black cloudbank descending into the valley. Heavy snow was coming. He surveyed the makeshift shelters and tents spread across the valley, behind Central Gate's western wall, already three-quarters submerged beneath snowdrift. Conditions were harsh for the soldiers. Too many had fallen victim to frostbite, losing fingers and toes in the snaps of freezing weather that flashed through the valley, and the daily Haagii attacks wore down their morale. He predicted the fighting, to come with spring, would be bitter and protracted, but only if the soldiers' hearts were in it. He really didn't want to leave. The timing was crucial. His only hope lay with Surdrok's determination to inspire the Great Armies with the news that Abreotan's sword was being retrieved, but if Surdrok failed Claarn did not hold much chance of the western wall keeping the Dragonlord's hordes at bay for long – not without him there.

Claarn and Marella's unexpected appearance in the entrance, outlined against the white snow, buoyed Andra's tired spirits. He rose from the small fire he was tending, and strode past Tim and the others, arms extended, overjoyed to see his old companions again.

Claarn stared open-mouthed at the approaching

apparition, long believing the young Guardian to have perished at the edge of Dragon Breath Plains. When he realised he wasn't dreaming, he roared with delight, 'By all that's impossible!' and vigorously embraced Andra, lifting the young man off the ground in a huge bear hug. 'By all the miracles of Teka!' he laughed, putting Andra down, and pushing him away at arm's length to scrutinize the black garb of an assassin. 'You were dead. I saw it myself!' Claarn declared, eyes wide beneath his wild halo of hair. 'I laid you down in the stinking grey dust, nearly done myself. If the villagers hadn't found us ... And you were dead.'

Andra grinned at his friend's exasperation. 'Not dead enough, obviously,' he laughed, lifting his arms above his head to demonstrate his existence. 'I return.'

'But how in Teka? And these rags. An assassin?' the giant queried, raising his eyebrows.

Andra was aware the others had gathered, curious to learn what relationship existed between the oversized warrior and an assassin. Even the Haardrishii, keeping a respectful distance, were fascinated.

'It's a long tale, one we'll share at a fire,' explained Andra, and he smiled at Marella, the dark-haired woman he admired on their journey through the Valley of Rivers. 'Some things are best told away from the wrong ears.'

Claarn burst into laughter, and clapped Andra heartily on the shoulders with both of his big hands. 'The young warrior's learned to be secretive,' he chuckled in a low voice as he finished laughing. 'There's hope yet.'

Liam stepped between them, to face Claarn. 'I take it High Lord Surdrok ordered you to guide us through the Haagii lines?' Liam asked, dispassionately.

The smile faded from Claarn's broad, bearded face. 'That's what we have been asked to do,' he replied, 'and then we have the pleasure of accompanying you to wherever it is your party's bound.'

'So the Chancellor wishes,' said Liam. 'We leave at your convenience, after the party is instructed about the purpose of this journey.'

'And you know this Saviour?' Marella asked, lifting her dark eyes toward the place where Liam was explaining the journey's purpose to Claarn, Tim, and two Haardrishii.

'He is – was like a brother. He travelled a short way with us in the Valley of Rivers, when you and the others were locked inside your cages,' Andra explained, as he pulled the leather drawstring tight on his pack.

'And he knows you.'

Andra looked Marella directly in the eyes. 'No. Whatever reason he has, he chooses to ignore my existence, as if his being a Guardian of The Vale was nothing to remember. I tried to speak with him, once, in the Great City, but he ignored me, almost let the Haardrishii cut me down. I doubt he recognises me now, especially in this assassin's garb.'

'I wouldn't have known you, Andra,' Marella smiled. 'Apart from your face, I see nothing resembling the warrior I met in the Valley of Rivers.' She leaned forward to whisper, letting her dark locks of hair swing close to his face. 'Are you really an assassin now?'

Andra leaned back. She was a powerfully attractive woman, her face strong, but high-cheeked and feminine, and although she wore a thick hide cloak and leggings to keep out the winter cold he remembered the tanned beauty of her athletic body from the journey through the Valley of Rivers more than a year past. But he also stood beside her on The Rim Shield, facing the Dragonlord's immense army, bathing their limbs in the blood and gore of battle, and saw the hungry warrior. She was complex, a person he hardly knew. 'Of course not,' he whispered. 'But I had to have a reason to be here.'

Marella tossed her head, to shake out her hair, and grinned. She glanced at the others making their plans, and stared at Liam, before turning her dark eyes back to Andra. 'The Saviour wears your sword. I remember Claarn telling me how he was obliged to hand it over to the Royal Advisor.'

'He's Chancellor now,' he said.

'Aren't you going to ask for your sword?' she asked, tilting her head to the side, an action Andra found enticingly beautiful.

'I can't, under the circumstances. Tim told me Liam believes it's his by right, given to him by the Chancellor because it contains magical qualities that only he can draw from it.'

'I saw you wield it in battle. The blade never stains with blood. You brought out its magic.'

Andra slowly shook his head. 'No. Nothing like Liam has done. There's already a legend about the sword in his hands. He formed a bridge across a lake and can create light. It was never anything but a sword in my hands.'

'But it was a gift from your father. Isn't that so?'

Her words made him feel like a traitor to his father. He looked down, to focus on the pebble beside his right foot. 'It was a gift, but perhaps I was never meant to use it. Perhaps this prophecy is true, and I was only meant to bear the sword to Liam,' he sighed. Marella touched his left cheek, and he looked up as an unfamiliar mixture of cold and softness thrilled him, while her fingers traced his scar. 'What are you doing?' he asked, trying to hide his blush.

'Claarn laughs about the prophecy,' she said in a hushed voice, as she withdrew her hand. 'He said to me that you bear as good a mark of a moon on your cheek as anyone.'

'Mine's just a scar. Nothing more,' he told her. 'You only have to look at Liam's forehead to see that he's marked by more than a stick wound. Have you seen the runes and ancient symbols? They're signs of magic.'

'They're signs,' Marella bluntly corrected.

Approaching footsteps broke their conversation, as Tim and Claarn came to squat beside them. The Apprentices were seated on prayer mats, in deep concentration, and beyond them the Haardrishii were organizing their gear. The original occupiers of the shelter were leaving, heading down the slope toward the western wall of Central Gate. Tim's assassin colleagues were scouting the valley for shelter for the horses, since there was a growing threat of snow in the darkening fog-bound afternoon.

'Well,' Claarn began, in his sturdy voice, 'seems we're in for a thief's role – sneaking around like rats on a riverbank.'

'I thought you'd be a natural for this,' Tim said facetiously, and ducked a sweep of Claarn's great paw.

'So?' asked Marella. 'What is to happen?'

Claarn glanced at Tim, hoping that he would explain, being the more fluent speaker, but the assassin looked away and began a tuneless hum. 'By Teka, you're nothing but a pack of trouble, Tim Gaelus,' Claarn growled in annoyance. 'Tell them the plan.'

A broad grin spread across Tim's countenance, a grin Andra associated with brewing wit in his friend, but Tim relented from his obvious intent to tease Claarn, when he saw Marella's stern glare, and outlined the outcome of their earlier discussions with Liam and the Haardrishii, running his finger across the dust and rock as he talked. 'According to Liam, the sword lies in an old castle at a place called Cennednyss. It's an Aelendyell word for birthplace,' he added.

Claarn closely studied Tim at the mention of the word's meaning. 'How do you know what the name meant?'

Tim smiled. 'An assassin has to be very intelligent, my large friend,' he said. Claarn's eyebrows knitted, as he suspected a jibe being made at his expense, but Tim ignored him, and continued his explanation. 'There's no easy way to get there from here. Between us, and Cennednyss, lie mountains, forests, and the Haagii. We can't go through the mountains. There are no known paths. We could try to cut through Elvenaar Forest, but the recent events with Thana's assassination, and the outlawing of the Aelendyell people, would make that more dangerous than the one we've chosen.'

'And that is?' Andra queried.

'To walk right through the Haagii lines and reach the northern spur of the Bitter Peaks.'

Andra wasn't certain he fully understood. Walk through the Haagii lines. The idea was ludicrous. The Haagii would recognise them and slaughter them before they made a thousand paces onto Axxon Plains. What was Tim's real plan?

'We leave as soon as it's dark,' Tim concluded. 'In the meantime, get some more sleep, if you've packed your gear. You'll need every ounce of energy you can find tonight.' Andra met Tim's gaze and saw in his friend's eyes the sharp edge of seriousness that belied his cheerful exterior. They really were going to walk straight through the Haagii army.

Thirty Four

Bruised rain clouds were melting into the darkening plain. Andra leaned a gloved hand against a wet rock and watched the rain spread slowly across the vast Haagii army, extinguishing unsheltered campfires, turning them into intransigent shafts of steam, white against the blue-black shades of evening. Perched below the snowline, on the western face of the mountain, they patiently waited for the night and the rain to settle on the broad Axxon plain.

When Tim signalled, they picked their way down precipitous slopes, following narrow half-paths, clinging to jutting rock faces, constantly aware that one thoughtless step, one ill-timed move, would be fatal.

Andra followed Sasha, but in the dark she frequently faded out of his sight, forcing him to reach forward and touch her to reassure himself she was there. She accepted his need, just as he accepted the tentative hand of the Haardrishii warrior who followed him in blind faith, each dependent on the other for their direction and their lives.

Andra felt more secure when they reached the fringe of the trees along the foothill ridges and valleys. He had no idea of the time they took to travel down the mountain, but he felt cramping weariness, as much, he conceded, from the concentration demanded on the descent as from the physical effort it involved.

Tim waited in a secluded clearing for the full party to assemble. The lack of moonlight made it difficult for Andra to see what was happening, but he sensed the other two assassins, and thought he heard Tim whispering. Then Tim whispered to him. 'The Haagii have spread through the trees. I've seen firelight at the camps. We'll have to move as quietly and quickly as possible, once we've disabled the nearest camp, but be prepared, in case we stumble on unlit campsites. Wait until we return.' The assassin disappeared into the night and rain.

Andra pulled his thick, black cloak tighter to shelter from the drizzle. Out of the darkness, a woman's voice called, 'Andra?' He took two steps toward a darker patch of air and stumbled into Marella and Claarn.

'This is going to be easy tonight in this weather,' said Claarn, with his deep bass rumble. 'Not even the Haagii like such weather.'

'I certainly don't like it,' retorted Marella.

Andra didn't comment. Under the umbrella of Claarn's oiled skin shelter, he was content to wait for Tim Gaelus and listen to the whispered banter of his friends. Someone tapped his shoulder. The three disengaged from their shared warmth, and Andra heard Tim talking to Claarn. 'I've given four Haardrishii and the Apprentices Haagii shields, and over clothing to add to our disguise. The Apprentice Peret can speak their language. He's our leader, if we're challenged. The rest of the Haardrishii can pass as the black-armoured soldiers, if we're observed.'

'I want one of those black devils at the end of my sword,' Claarn growled. 'The one who spoke to me at The Rim Shield preferably.'

Andra recalled the blond, tall, undeniably handsome and proud warrior who delivered the Dragonlord's warning to Claarn, and the giant's frustrated howl at being denied an honourable battle death. Something in the bearing of the Dragonlord's emissary convinced Andra he was no ordinary warrior, and perhaps more than a match for the giant of Tressel Deep. If Claarn ever got his wish, he might regret it.

The party reassembled, and Tim moved to the front to lead, as they twisted between trees, working past distant fires in the camps of cold, saturated, and sleeping Haagii. Word was passed, warning them to move quietly, as they circumvented unlit Haagii camps where their enemies were asleep.

Andra was aware of steady change. Patterns in the darkness disappeared, and the ground became less steep and undulating, as they entered the plain. Small points of light dotted the darkness, making the earth mock the blind sky with its tapestry of synthetic stars.

Three times, voices challenged them. Andra heard short interchanges between Peret, the Apprentice, and unseen Haagii. The guttural grunts and words escaped Andra's understanding, but his fingers tightened on the hilt of the short thieves' sword strapped to his side beneath his black cloak, expecting a fight to erupt. The incidents passed without violence, but the further they walked the less comfortable he felt. He heard another Haagii voice, although the exchange was brief before they were moving again, and as he edged forward, fingers touching Marella's back, he almost tripped over something heavy and malleable in the darkness. Reaching down, he touched a freshly killed body, face down in the mud. The trailing Haardrishii hissed at him to keep moving.

They passed as far from campfires as they could, except once when they were forced to walk between two, passing at the edge of their light's circle. Seven figures hunched over the sheltered fire, long hair wet and straggly from the rain, clothing sodden, and they all looked so miserable that Andra wondered how the Dragonlord could drive so unkempt and ill-treated an army without fear of rebellion.

Three lanterns swung toward them, their yellow light glistening on fragments of armour. Tim changed the group's direction, but the lanterns altered their path as well, deliberately converging. 'See them?' asked the Haardrishii behind him, breaking the silence. Andra nodded, before he realised the foolishness of his response. Feeling the Haardrishii's hand on his backpack, he shrugged to reply as best as he could without speaking.

Marella stopped, and whispered, 'Draw your sword.'

Andra passed the order to the Haardrishii and heard a faint sliding of blades in the gloom. The lanterns drew closer, and silhouettes he guessed to be the Apprentices in Haagii garments appeared within the first lantern's circle. The lantern bearer's black armour was spiked at the shoulders. Andra's stomach churned. The rear lantern dropped inexplicably and sputtered out. He heard a shout, and Marella moved toward the points of light. A second lantern went out, and whirling chaos erupted around the lead lantern. A sword blade flashed and cut down the lantern bearer. Two more figures fell into the light, daggers embedded in their backs. By the time the rearmost Haardrishii joined the others the scuffle was over.

'The night's about worn out,' said Tim, in a lowered voice, 'and the appearance of this little group suggests someone might know about us. We can't linger. Grab the lanterns. We'll risk using them, until there's dawn light. Expect trouble.'

Andra clutched his sword, as three Haardrishii lit the lanterns. Light splashed over the slain enemy, and glittered in puddles, and Andra glimpsed yellow hair beneath the dead warrior's cleaved and bloodied black helmet. Claarn touched his shoulder, and said, 'I would've liked the pleasure of slaying one of these.'

'Who did?' Andra asked.

'The Saviour,' the giant replied, with unmasked disappointment.

Andra peered at his short sword in the disappearing lantern light. It was a poor weapon. Thieves rarely used swords, so they carried ineffectual ones. He spotted the silvered hilt of the dead warrior's sword, in the puddle at his feet, and retrieved it. It was heavy, but it had definite quality of balance, marking it superior to the one he had. Satisfied with his find, he dropped the short sword Tim Gaelus gave him, and followed the bobbing lanterns into the night.

Predawn light filtered through the secretive clouds sooner than Andra expected. The campfires disappeared with the night, as the Haagii slept, and the drizzling rain eased to a wet mist. The lanterns were extinguished as soon as it was safe for those without night vision to travel rapidly.

First light revealed they had passed through the thickest enemy lines, and they were moving quickly across low hills, where larger distances separated the Haagii encampments. Although the camps were less numerous, the few scattered here were larger. In the distance, Andra saw the mountain peaks they were heading for, and his spirits rose as he realised they would be free of the Haagii threat in a short time.

Beneath the crest of a larger hill, out of visual contact with visible Haagii encampments, Claarn called the exhausted party together. 'The eastern spur of the Bitter Peaks lies directly ahead, less than half a day's walking,' he informed them. 'Forget your tiredness. Push it aside, until we reach the mountains, and then you'll be able to sleep.'

Andra studied Marella, and Tim. Both friends showed the signs of weariness everyone in the party felt. Then he spied Liam, standing behind them, staring. When Andra lifted his eyes to make direct contact with the warrior, Liam switched his gaze to the Apprentices, who still wore the ill-fitting Haagii leather armour and ragged brown cloaks. Andra speculated why his old companion had been staring at him.

Three crests further on, a shout of alarm came from the rear Haardrishii. Andra followed the direction of his pointing arm and saw a dark mass pour over a neighbouring crest, running toward them. 'Haagii!' spat the Haardrishii beside him. 'They've smelt us.' Andra looked for a defensible position, but there were no natural rocky outcrops, and it was too far, he judged, for them to run to a tree clump on the next rise. The others were preparing to make a stand. He pulled his new sword from his belt, and stuck it point first into the earth beside him, unhitched Freyar's bow, and nocked a shaft. He knew he lacked Aelendyell speed for firing bows, but if two less Haagii reached them, he'd be satisfied.

'How many?' he heard a Haardrishii ask Marella.

'Forty. Perhaps more.'

'Good. Two each,' the Haardrishii said, without emotion.

The charging Haagii reached the hill, and began their wild ascent, and as they closed, Andra loosed his first arrow at the leading warrior. The shaft went a touch wide, felling a Haagii beside him. He quickly strung his second arrow and fired, and this time the foremost Haagii grabbed at his throat in a vain attempt to remove the fatal shaft. His fellows pushed past, while he collapsed, rolling down the hill through the trampled green grass.

'Shot!' yelled Tim, catching Andra's eye, as he dropped his bow and hefted his sword. The Haagii crashed headlong into them.

The sword was heavy, but the first Haagii warrior toppled after Andra parried his thrusting weapon. He ducked a spear, tossed from short range, and turned to swing his blade across the back of a warrior to his right. The sword sliced neatly through the leather armour, killing the Haagii. The cries and shouts of battle ended as quickly as they erupted, the grassy hilltop strewn with dead and dying Haagii. Claarn and Liam stood, side-by-side, at the centre of the carnage, the giant grinning with pleasure, as always, after a battle, and the Saviour silent, untouched by everything, holding the sword of Cedwyn.

'Too easy,' said Tim, swaggering toward Andra, cleaning his dagger, 'though I don't go for this hand-to-hand fighting. It's decidedly unintelligent and unhealthy. I'll leave it to the Haardrishii and your kind, I think,' he declared, and laughed. 'I don't normally believe in giving an opponent an even chance.'

'The Haagii hardly had a chance against this party,' Marella chipped in.

They abandoned the hilltop and headed for the mountains. Liam replaced Claarn at the head of the party and led as he had from the Great City to Central Gate, walking at a brisk pace, as if he was unaffected by the weariness seeping through everyone from the night's excursion.

A while later, as he was talking with Andra, Tim pointed south to a wall of smoke. 'Elvenaar Forest,' he said sadly.

'I saw Wynwuduholt burning like that,' Andra muttered absently, as he looked toward the smoke pall rising to the rain clouds.

Tim pulled the Guardian aside to let the trailing Haardrishii pass. 'You mean the Border Woods,' he said. Andra's eyes widened, but the assassin read Andra's confusion, and whispered, 'You used the Aelendyell name. Don't. Not here.'

Andra understood what Tim was saying, but not why – unless Tim's reason was the same as Terath's, when he made Andra promise not to speak of Wudufaesten in the outer world. But what did Tim know of Wynwuduholt? He stared at his assassin friend, reading the traces of Aelendyell heritage stored in his features, until Tim sensed Andra's intention and clapped the Guardian heartily on the back. 'That's a good joke!' he laughed, and tousled Andra's hair. 'I like spirit!' He ran to join Sasha and Jo, leaving Andra to trail, shaking his head, as he tried to fathom his friend's odd behaviour.

By mid-afternoon, as near as Andra could guess, they were standing atop a ridge, surveying a tree-lined river that curled through the scorched ruins of a large town, before disappearing into the smoking fringes of a forest nestled beneath low mountains. 'That was Hall,' said a Haardrishii. They watched a Haagii troop wander through the devastated outskirts, and begin following the road northeast, toward the open plains. Across the river, more Haagii milled around burning wood heaps, occasionally dragging tree trunks from the forest to pile onto the fires, or grabbing firebrands, before heading into the blackened forest to set more of it alight. From his vantage, Andra could see fires raging at many points throughout the forest to the west, much of it already turned to ash, with great swathes of destruction scarring it in every direction.

'No Aelendyell live in Darken Wood,' said Tim.

'Why?'

'It's been human forest for a long time. The town of Port sits at its centre, on the mouth of Abreotan River, and humans spread through the wood very quickly. The Aelendyell moved out. There were no sacred sites in the wood.' Tim paused to gaze across the smoke strewn sky. 'I doubt there are humans there either, now,' he said, pointing toward a thicker column of smoke due west of where they stood. Beyond it, Andra discerned a fascinating deep blue smudge. 'That fire would be Port,' explained Tim. 'If it hasn't already fallen to the Haagii, it soon will.'

Andra watched the smoke twist and curl from the forest, and wondered what fate befell Spurl, after Milly and he left. The town could never have withstood the Haagii onslaught. Did the Haagii kill everyone? Or did they enslave the people they caught, like Thana held prisoners of war to parade through the Great City?

Lost in his thoughts, he trudged after the others, as Liam led them southward, along the ridge, into the hills that rose to become the northern spur of the Bitter Peaks. As he crested the first tall hill, a cold south wind whistled against his cheek and he tugged at his cloak, pulling up his hood to keep out the wind's icy fingers. A little further, and the first part of the journey was over. In the mountains, he could rest and sleep, and gather his strength for the next stage, with the Haagii threat safely out of the way.

Thirty Five

Ice glistened on the rock. Overnight fog had frozen wherever the frigid wind breathed, and coated the pools, caught in rocky recesses, icy mantles reflecting the weak sunlight breaking through the low ceiling of clouds. Andra stretched his tight shoulder and leg muscles, the ache of the previous night and day journey clutching his body. Weeks in the Maze had taken their toll on his fitness, despite Tim's training.

The first object Andra turned to, as he stood, was the sword he took from the dead warrior with the blond hair. He had little opportunity to examine it, before they scrambled, exhausted, into the mountain cave, the evening before, and collapsed into deep sleep. He reached for its silver hilt and held it up for inspection. It was a masterly wrought weapon. The silvered handle was decorated with an elaborate pattern to enhance a warrior's grip, and the pommel was worked into the likeness of a demon's face, wide-eyed, fanged, its tongue poking out. The heavy, broad blade was made from an unfamiliar metal, with a bluish tint, and alien symbols were etched into the blade's point. The sword wasn't a weapon Andra associated with the Haagii. Its bearer was likely to be highly trained and proud of its ownership.

He looked beyond the blade, toward a corner of the cave where he remembered the three Apprentices made their beds, and noticed Peret was hunched over something that gave off a faint glow in the cave's semi-darkness. Everyone else was sleeping, except a solitary figure huddled in a bundle of cloaks in the cave entrance. The Haardrishii always keep their watch, he noted.

The symbols on the blade were likely to be Haagii language, and he remembered that Peret could speak Haagii. He shuffled toward the hunched figure, trying not to disturb anyone else, but as he drew near Peret jerked around. The faint glow in his hands evaporated, and the

Apprentice stuffed whatever he held into the depths of his woollen clothing beneath the outer Haagii disguise. 'What do you want?' he asked defensively.

Taken aback by the Apprentice's fearful hostility, Andra regretted his decision. 'Sorry, I didn't mean to disturb you.'

Peret remained guarded as he acquiesced. 'You didn't disturb me. I was just surprised to see anyone else awake.'

Andra realised it would be pointless asking Peret what he'd been doing. Instead, he lifted the sword, and passed it, hilt first, to the Apprentice, saying, 'You understand the Haagii language, don't you?'

Peret took the sword and nodded. 'A little. By magical means.'

'Can you interpret the symbols on this blade?'

'Where did you get it?' Peret asked, running his hand along the flat surfaces. Andra explained how he exchanged it in the night, but Peret didn't appear to be listening. The Apprentice was tracing the symbols on the blade with his fingertips and concentrating on an invisible point somewhere beyond Andra's shoulder, an action that made the Guardian uncomfortable. Peret shook his head, as if freeing himself from an odd thought, and held the sword across his lap, in both palms. 'There are two languages here. The Haagii symbol is this one.' Peret indicated a simple figure. 'It says Turag, which means 'Slayer' in our tongue. The others are unfamiliar to me.' Andra waited for Peret to return the sword, but the Apprentice's eyes narrowed. 'I know who you are,' he said.

The statement caught Andra unawares. He tilted his head, as if trying to understand Peret's meaning, and though there was insufficient light to see he sensed a change in Peret's features, a return to the fear he encountered when he interrupted the Apprentice.

'You were dead. I saw you die.'

Suddenly Andra understood the Apprentice's reference. He saved Peret's life on The Rim Shield road. No wonder he was shocked. He survived the crossing of Dragon Breath Plains and was probably there when Claarn laid Andra in the grey dust at the desert's edge. 'I didn't die,' he explained quietly.

Peret shook his head, bewildered. 'But I saw. You were left behind. How could you have survived?'

Unable to truthfully answer Peret's question, he said, 'Luck of Teka,' with a false grin. 'A villager happened to retrace your steps. He took me to his home and nursed me back to health.' Peret maintained his stare, making Andra wonder whether the Apprentice believed his story. It didn't matter. He told Claarn and Marella a similar tale, and Tim would always be willing to corroborate it, if anyone asked. His oath to Terath bound him to the lie, and though he disliked untruth, he was learning its necessity in a world of unknowns. 'Thank you for trying,' he said, as he held out his hand to take the sword from Peret's lap. The Apprentice let Andra remove the sword, but he didn't alter his questioning gaze. Resolved to be unconcerned by the Apprentice's behaviour, Andra returned to his sleeping place, and when he reached his gear he glanced back at the Apprentice, but Peret was engaged in the process of waking his companions.

From the escarpment, they watched the enemy warriors winding through a narrow defile, directly below, trailing them. Claarn estimated close to a hundred Haagii, and probably seven or eight black armoured warriors. There were others scattered through their ranks, figures in odd dull-coloured garments, without armour, but shouldering short bows. There was also a taller man, wearing long blue robes. 'With so many, we'll easily lose them,' said Tim. 'They can't possibly keep pace with us.'

'They're a good distance behind, as it is,' added Jo.

'Who are the others?' asked Andra.

'The Dragonlord's assassins I'd wager,' answered Tim.

'And the one in blue?'

'Your guess is as good as mine,' said Tim. 'Though it seems the Dragonlord's gathered more than the Haagii under his rule, since last summer.'

Throughout the morning, they clambered through clefts and along paths perched above cliffs, heading roughly west, through the centre of the Bitter Peaks. The way was easier than the perilous descent they made the first night in the Andrakians, and there was no sign of snow on the peaks above them, but the air was brittle, and the constant rise and fall, climb and descent, was tiring. Several times, the assassins doubled back to check on their pursuers' progress, and confirmed they were rapidly leaving them behind, as Tim predicted.

Early in the afternoon, Sasha returned from her check to inform them she could no longer see the Haagii. Either they had dropped far behind, or abandoned the chase. Andra breathed easier with one less threat to trouble his thoughts.

No one in the party had been in the Bitter Peaks, which meant Liam was leading by intuition and good fortune, but his luck ran out. A massive landslide blocked the path. They followed a narrow valley, only to reach a dead end. The creek bubbling through the valley, apparently oozed between the gigantic rock fall to continue its downward journey, but there was no way over the blockage. The lengthening shadows of the waning afternoon were quickly darkening the valley. If they retraced their steps, it would be night before they reached the point where they entered. 'There's shelter from the wind here,' said Liam, 'and fresh water. We'll start again in the morning.'

Andra was pleased to rest. He unhitched his pack and bow, and, with others, searched the valley floor for firewood, and they soon had a substantial pile. Claarn kept the Haardrishii busy building a protective barrier beyond their campsite, using rocks and boulders. Andra joined his friend, and enjoyed the shared labour, as night crept rapidly up the valley walls. 'You think there's a danger?' he asked, as he placed another rock on the wall.

'I fear the enemy I can't see much more than the one I can,' replied Claarn stoically. 'A good warrior knows how to be safe.'

'At least we'll be warm tonight,' said Andra. He rubbed

his gloved hands together, to push out the chill settling in the mountains, and glanced back at the fire being kindled by the assassins.

Claarn however, was grumbling and shaking his head. 'A fire in enemy lands is a beacon for disaster,' he warned.

An arrow thudded into the huddled mass lying beside the fire, and a second found its mark, burying half its shaft into its target. The fire crackled, its flickering light creating wild dancing shapes across the rough campsite. No one moved, as if time was suspended. A third arrow whistled out of the darkness and struck another bedroll.

Andra tried hard not to shiver. He pressed against Marella for greater body heat and watched the flames of the fire leaping across the wood. If he'd been down there, he'd be warmer. He looked at the arrows jutting from their targets. He'd also be dead. Claarn's plan had merit, if they didn't freeze to death in the meantime hiding in the surrounding rocks.

A muffled shout came from further along the valley, and figures appeared at the edge of the firelight. Swords glinted, and spears hurtled through the air into the packs and empty bedrolls. The Haagii charged, but as they started to ransack the camp they halted, recognizing the ruse they'd blundered into. At the same moment, the shadows at the edge of the camp closed in, as the ten Haardrishii emerged from their cover to attack the intruders. Marella and Claarn ran to join the skirmish.

Andra nocked an arrow and peered into the wavering darkness at the firelight's extremity, obeying the order Claarn gave him earlier, when he laid his plans. A vague shadow ran to the light's edge and kneeled, taking aim. Andra hesitated. It was a long shot. As he tightened his bowstring, the kneeling figure released an arrow, and bounced to his feet. The impact of Andra's shaft spun the figure around before he crumpled to the ground. Andra fitted a second arrow to his bow and waited.

Another ran out of the darkness, but as Andra raised his bow he recognised Jo's gait. The assassin carried a bow and a quiver, but when he saw Andra's victim, he stooped to gather the weapons lying there. He turned to look in Andra's general direction, and Andra felt as if Jo could see him, despite the cloaking darkness. Then the assassin headed for the fight in the campsite.

The Haardrishii were outnumbered, but the Haagii were losing before their fierce, ordered onslaught. Claarn wielded his sword with passion, slaying his enemy at will, and Marella mirrored his path of destruction through the wilting Haagii, while at the centre Liam flailed the sword of Cedwyn with wild abandon, felling the Haagii with consummate ease. Andra stayed his urge to rush down and join his friends, but the Guardian in him stirred to the sight and sounds of melee.

As the surviving Haagii took to their heels, realising they were hopelessly over-matched, Andra saw a shadow at the edge of the firelight. The flickering yellow light touched sandaled feet and blue-green robes, trimmed with gold. The man had white hair, and a full flowing beard, and he held a twisted staff in his right hand, but he stayed, obscured by shadows, observing. Andra raised his bow and sighted the stranger along his arrow shaft, but as the retreating Haagii crossed his field of vision, the robed figure vanished into the darkness. Andra lowered his bow and waited until Claarn's piercing whistle signalled he should come down from his post and join them.

In the camp, the full extent of the Haagii attack was clear. Claarn was dressing a superficial wound on Marella's leg, and among the dead Haagii were two Haardrishii, one with an arrow embedded in his forehead. When he saw the bodies, Andra cursed himself for being too slow in reacting to the enemy archer. Jo was receiving attention from a Haardrishii for a deep cut across his chest. The assassin looked pale and short of breath. 'Where's Tim and Sasha?' Andra asked, studying Jo's gaping wound, as the Haardrishii cleansed it with creek water.

'Keeping watch,' Jo replied, and he winced as the

Haardrishii poked cloth inside his tunic to mop up blood.

Andra made his way to Claarn and observed the three Apprentices emerging from their hiding place, beyond the campfire. 'How's the wound?' he asked Marella.

The woman smiled. 'Puts character on the leg,' she replied. 'A day, and it'll heal.'

He looked up at Claarn and saw the lines of concern on his face. 'What's wrong?'

Claarn peered down, and looked toward the mouth of the valley, beyond the stone barrier they hadn't even used. 'I've a bad feeling about all of this,' he said calmly. 'The Haagii found us too easily. We could've gone several different ways from the entrance to this valley.'

'Our trail wouldn't be too hard to follow,' replied Andra, trying to ease his friend's thoughts.

'That's where you're wrong,' said Claarn. 'Tim and his companions weren't doubling back just to check if we were being followed. They were masking our tracks, to put anyone who did try to follow us on the wrong trail.'

Andra let the seriousness of Claarn's news sink in. 'Maybe they had a lucky guess.'

'Perhaps,' Claarn muttered. 'But now they've caught us in a dead end. And they know it. When we try to leave, they'll be waiting.'

Tim shifted his weight, and dragged his left foot gingerly across the rock, until he found new purchase, twisted ever so slightly to transfer his weight back to that foot, and inched upward, until his right hand reached the lip of the cliff. He tensed his shoulders, hauled himself up, and disappeared. A moment later, his head popped into view, and he lowered a rope to the rock on which Andra stood. 'Quickly!' Claarn ordered. Andra tied the rope through his belt, and he was half-lifted, half-scrambled up the vertical rock face to join Tim.

'Set up over there,' said Tim, as Andra unhooked the rope. 'Any movement at all, shoot.'

Andra crawled to the outcrop Tim indicated, and took position. From it, he could see further along the valley. Tim's idea to climb out of the valley, rather than risk retracing their steps into a Haagii trap, was proving sound. He could just make out Sasha, secreted in a clump of bushes on the edge of the cliff, where she was intently watching something in the valley, but from his lower position he couldn't see what held her attention. He loaded his bow and waited. Jo joined him soon after, bearing the short bow he collected from the enemy archer. Andra knew Tim had the second weapon. Breathing heavily, Jo settled against the rocks. 'Are you alright?' Andra asked the assassin. Jo nodded and focussed on the valley floor, but Andra glanced down at Jo's chest and saw the spreading stain on the man's tunic. 'You're bleeding again,' he said.

'It's nothing,' the assassin whispered. 'Give it time to heal.'

Slowly, the others climbed the cliff face, Liam after the assassins, and then the Apprentices and the Haardrishii followed, leaving Marella and Claarn to climb last, but as Marella began her climb Andra heard Sasha shout. She was pointing at the valley, to the far right of where he had been watching, and he saw a dozen Haagii running through the stunted trees, ahead of three black-armoured warriors. Behind them strode the figure in blue. He nudged Jo, and called a warning to Tim, before he took aim on the foremost Haagii. Marella was halfway up. As the Haagii dipped through the creek, and crested the near bank, Andra released his shaft. A Haagii warrior toppled backwards, but the rest continued, undaunted. Jo and Andra fired as the Haagii came into short bow range, and two more fell among the rocks. This time, the others faltered, staring at their dead companions, but a voice from a trailing Dark Warrior ordered them on. The three warriors in black armour crossed the creek. Andra lifted his aim from the Haagii, to the Dark Warriors, and fired. The shaft buried in the neck of one, and he staggered sideways to fall into the creek beside the dead Haagii.

When the leading Haagii reached the base of the cliff, they formed a half-circle around Claarn and began baiting the giant warrior, thrusting their spear points at him, taunting him to fight. Marella yelled to Tim to lower her back to the ground, but Andra saw Liam lean forward and speak to Tim, words that brought the assassin around to glare at the Saviour. The nearby Haardrishii closed in threateningly on Tim Gaelus.

Andra didn't have an opportunity to watch the confrontation's outcome, because the Dark Warriors were advancing to join the Haagii, and the white-haired stranger in blue was crossing the creek. Jo released a shaft at the Dark Warriors, but his arrow shattered harmlessly against the armour of its intended victim. Andra nocked another arrow and leaned over the edge. His shot dropped another Haagii warrior. Their attention distracted by the unexpected attack, the Haagii were caught napping by Claarn's lunge, and the giant's sweeping sword sent two more Haagii sprawling backwards, clutching their faces.

'Shift to there!' Andra shouted to Jo, and the pair of archers scrambled across the rocky outcrop to a more exposed position, that opened the base of the cliff to their fire. By the time they set up again, Marella was at the cliff top, waving her arms furiously at the Haardrishii, and the Dark Warriors were standing before Claarn, their swords drawn.

'If we shoot at the Dark Warriors from here, we might hit Claarn,' Jo said.

Andra reluctantly accepted his judgment. 'Then let's finish off the Haagii,' he said. The archers loosed their shafts.

Claarn saw two more Haagii fall from the enclosing ring, but he kept his eyes on the warriors edging toward him. 'I've waited for a chance to fight your kind,' he snarled. The Dark Warriors turned their swords in their hands, and silently stalked the tall, broad warrior from Tressel Deep. One lunged, but Claarn deftly turned his thrust, catching the warrior with a sharp kick to the chest, that threw him off balance. The second swung, and, although Claarn dodged, the point of the heavy sword scored the back of his left arm. Enraged, he roared, and his sword smashed against the plate armour of the second warrior, sending him sprawling at the feet of his Haagii followers. Simultaneously, two more arrows found marks among the Haagii. The first warrior struggled to his feet and charged, but Claarn judged the swing and met it with his weapon. The impact shattered Claarn's sword and the Dark Warrior's blade cut through his mail armour into the surprised giant's ribs. Claarn stared down at the hilt of the broken sword. The Dark Warrior raised his sword to strike again, but Claarn's broad arm flashed out and caught the warrior's throat in a vice-like grip. He flexed his fingers, crushed the warrior's throat, and dropped the lifeless body at the feet of his astonished fellow.

From the clifftop, Andra saw Claarn take the initiative and advance on the second Dark Warrior. The surviving Haagii panicked, and scrambled away from the giant warrior, who seemed so invincible even the Dark Warriors couldn't match his strength, but Andra's eyes rested on the blue-robed figure thirty paces from the base of the cliff, because the man was weaving his fingers in a rapid pattern, a motion Andra recognised as conjuring. Claarn dropped to his knees, clutching his chest. Comprehending the spell intervention turning the confrontation in his favour, the Dark Warrior lifted his sword. Andra fired. His arrow sped toward its target, but at the last instant the sorcerer turned, and the shaft struck him in the upper chest, just below the collarbone. With what should have been a mortal wound, the sorcerer stared out of the valley, straight at Andra, as if he was daring the Guardian to loose another arrow. Andra tried to fit another missile to his bow, but oddly he had no strength of will because the air seemed to be sucked out of the world around him. His head was spinning. He felt violently ill. Unable to move his limbs, he couldn't stop himself from pitching into a darkness that rose to swallow him.

"By the coming of spring, the beasts of the Dark Lord multiplied a thousandfold in the Kingdom. Overwhelmed by number, the Great Armies capitulated, the feared Haardrishii swept aside like chaff before a storm. Dragon fire turned towns to ash, and the Kingdom's rivers ran with blood. Driven before the merciless murderous hordes, the people escaped to the hope of the Great City, there to pray that Teka would not forsake her flock as the slaughterous wolves closed in, hungry with the bloodlust of their kind."

entry 1,905 in The Ancient Lore,
by Drycraefter Waeron Ardath

Thirty Six

A Ahmud Ki watched the dwindling aura, until Peret's features faded into the communication crystal. The wizard straightened his back and gazed beyond the amber sphere to the tapestry map of the Kingdom. If Peret's report was accurate, they were less than three days from Cennednyss – but the Apprentice had disquieting news. A Ahmud Ki rose from his stool and worked his spells to descend to the ground floor. As his feet touched cold marble, he was aware of Damon, who immediately abased himself before the master. 'It's my intention to walk in the gardens. I will appreciate a meal on my return,' A Ahmud Ki said, in indifferent fashion.

'It will be so, Master,' Damon obediently replied, and he waited, face to the floor, until the Chancellor passed through the wall.

There was a touch of sun on the rich green fronds of the garden ferns, and the sight made A Ahmud Ki shiver involuntarily. Winter was ending. Soon the Plains of Ky would be awash with sunshine, the dormant flowers in the castle gardens would bloom in brilliant colours, birds would start foraging in the foliage, and the Dragonlord's forces would renew their assault on Central Gate. Apprentices sat in a meditative circle, under a bower near the black tower, but A Ahmud Ki walked away from them, wanting solitude for reflection. He found a small cairn, someone built before a low rock stool, beside a bubbling fountain, to please a long dead Great King. He sat on the stool and stared at the glittering water, dribbling from the fountain into an algae-covered pool, contemplating the changing events unfolding in the Bitter Peaks.

The questing party had separated. Peret described encountering a Haagii force that trailed them through the mountains, despite the assassins' best efforts. They'd lost two Haardrishii, the two warriors Surdrok commandeered, and two assassins. A sorcerer led the pursuing Haagii. One assassin slew the sorcerer, but he fell victim to a spell that left him unconscious, useless to the party. The giant warrior Claarn was seriously wounded, as was a second assassin. When Liam ordered them to journey on, the warrior woman refused to abandon the disabled ones, so they left her to tend them. Peret also had garbled news about the assassin who slew the sorcerer. Apparently, the assassin was also the man who originally carried the sword A Ahmud Ki took from Claarn to present to Liam. He hadn't perished in the desert. Peret hadn't known he was an assassin. Curiously, he carried an Aelendyell bow, and his loss to the party was disconcerting because his archery proved valuable. If he hadn't killed the sorcerer, the skirmish may have been far more costly.

Fourteen was more than enough to reach Cennednyss, A Ahmud Ki reasoned. The Haardrishii were competent warriors, and the Apprentices could exercise their limited magic, if necessary, to protect the group. As long as Liam and Peret were there to claim the sword of Abreotan in Cennednyss, the quest would be successful.

But A Ahmud Ki's mind was teased by nagging doubt generated from Peret's report. The man, who first owned the weapon Liam now carried, who reappeared, months later, as an assassin carrying an Aelendyell bow, was becoming a worrying enigma, and A Ahmud Ki was curious to know who he was, and from where he came.

And he had a more immediate concern: Mareg. A Ahmud Ki felt the Dragonlord's presence, at the fringes of his magical consciousness, every time Peret communicated through the crystal. Mareg destroyed A Ahmud Ki's first crystal in an attempt to kill him, just before the battle at The Rim Shield. In rekindling the magical communication, he was risking another demonstration of the Dragonlord's sheer psychic power – except, this time, A Ahmud Ki was ready for an outburst from Mareg. He was almost daring the Dragonlord to attack.

Perhaps Mareg knew that. Perhaps he was content to sit at the periphery of his consciousness, to observe, and learn. Perhaps he was stalking his quarry, enjoying A Ahmud Ki's fear of another psychic attack. Not that he was afraid. The Dragonlord had made one thrust, and it was unsuccessful. He was confident he wouldn't fall foul of Mareg that way again, not while he knew what to expect. The Dragonlord must also realise he could replace communication crystal easily. Perhaps Mareg enjoyed playing cat and mouse as much as he enjoyed it. If so, he was content to be the mouse for a while, because he needed to learn what magic he could from the Dragonlord, even through accidental lessons, to measure the extent of Mareg's power.

There was a price. He knew why the Haagii could track the questing party through the Bitter Peaks. Mareg was using Peret's communications to monitor the party's progress, and the Dragonlord was passing his knowledge on to his minions pursuing Liam. A Ahmud Ki accepted the risk was a small price to pay for learning.

'By all that the gods preserve! Look!'

Surdrok heard the watchtower soldier's cry and followed his outstretched arm to the mouth of the valley, where the Haagii army was pouring up the long, muddied slope, like a vast black tide, toward the walls of Central Gate. 'Sound the alarm! To the wall!' the High Lord yelled. Four soldiers along the wall began beating on hollow, bell-like shields, setting up a clamour that echoed along the valley, to be picked up and repeated at the camps strung through Central Gate.

Soldiers scrambled from their hide tents, and from caves and clefts on the mountainsides, and ran through the slush and melting snow toward the wall, to take up defensive positions. Devis moved among their charges, organizing, deploying soldiers to positions for maximum effect. The tall, blond-haired longbowmen climbed both sides of the valley, above the wall, and settled onto the rocky platforms carved into the cliff faces for them. From their rooks, they could generate a devastating pattern of arrow fire to rain upon the charging Haagii, even on those pressed against the wall, because there was no cover in the valley. Behind the wall, warriors loaded catapults with rocks and flammable materials, and cranked the war machines into readiness. A hand-picked Haardrishii squad formed three ordered rows behind the main gate on horseback, preparing to repel any breakthrough, and everywhere men and women carried or wheeled barrels of spears and arrows into position to feed to the defenders.

Surdrok observed the advancing Haagii force from his vantage point and knew they weren't mobilizing a sortie. The battle for Central Gate was about to be renewed in all its bloody desperation, and he had no choice but to commit every soldier, every warrior of the remaining Wheels, to its defence.

The preparatory noise gradually diminished, until an uneasy quiet descended. The defenders watched the approaching enemy, the black mass running toward them, coming on in unnatural silence over the sodden ground, rapidly closing the distance. Strange black totem poles and banners swept forward in the rushing tide, and bearers held aloft crude ladders and scaling devices. A wave of sound broke over the defenders as the leading Haagii crested the nearest rise, screaming their battle cries, and they charged headlong at the wall.

The first arrows from the Longbowmen cut a swathe through the front ranks, but the Haagii tide poured over the dying and wounded, crushing them into the earth. Three more volleys took a terrible toll by the time the Haagii reached the defences, and then the Longbowmen switched their attention to specific targets in the enemy ranks; the bearers of scaling equipment. The rain of arrows had little effect. The ladders were being passed across a sea of hands, and even as a group fell beneath the onslaught of shafts, other hands took up the ladders and passed them toward the wall.

While the defenders on the parapets awaited the

inevitable hand-to-hand conflict, catapult operators launched their deadly barrage. Rocks arched over the wall and crashed among the tightly packed enemy, each crushing several warriors, followed by flaming missiles, their fiery cargo smashing into screaming and yelling victims. Ladders were thrust against the wall, but the defenders pushed them away, and for a short while the attackers' effort seemed futile. The trapped Haagii milled wildly, like market cattle caught in a furious slaughter, and their dead clogged the ground.

Then a surge rippled across the Haagii ranks, and their shouting rose to a crescendo. A flurry of arrows erupted from their midst, crashing into the defenders who were reaching out to push a new wave of ladders away from the wall. Dead and wounded soldiers crumpled on the parapet. Their positions were refilled, but a second rush of arrows greeted them, and again the defenders reeled from the ladders. Surdrok grabbed two Runners, and ordered them to pass word to the Longbowmen to concentrate their fire on the ladders, to discourage anyone from climbing, but as the Runners headed off he saw the Longbowmen were already training their fire on the ladders.

The low, continuous drumming against the gate maintained a steady, persistent rhythm. The Haagii were packed around the warriors operating the ram, their shields held high to cover the ram operators from the longbows on the cliffs. Their fellows were failing to scale the walls, so they had to force a breakthrough. The gate was thick, but it was slowly weakening. It was a question of time. Behind the gate, the Haardrishii sat on their mounts, lances lowered, patiently waiting.

Her hand brushed his cheek. He could feel her, beyond the line of seeing, but there was something wrong. She was worried. About him? 'Mirith?' he gasped.

'Andra?' she whispered. A veil covered his eyes, preventing him seeing her. 'Andra?'

'Mirith?'

Her voice was different. Something was being lifted from his face. There was dull light – torch light. Marella. 'How do you feel?'

His head was hazy, unable to keep a thought in focus, and his eyes stung. He rubbed them furiously. 'Lousy,' he muttered.

'Don't rub too hard,' Marella advised.

He wanted to rub inside his head, to bring his thoughts into sharper focus. He sat up, feeling dizzy.

'Easy, Andra,' she said. Her arms enfolded him, holding him steady.

'Where are we?'

'In a cave.'

'Where are the others?' he mumbled. He knew there were supposed to be others.

'Left us,' Marella said simply. 'There's only us.'

Andra felt Marella's grip ease. He heard a groan to his left. 'Who's that?'

'Claarn,' Marella answered.

'What's wrong with him?'

'He's dying,' she said softly. 'I think he wants me to go to him.' She withdrew.

Andra shook his head, trying to clear the fogginess that impinged on his thinking. Claarn is dying? Why? What is happening? He remembered a narrow valley, and a man in blue – the sorcerer – the Dark Warriors. Claarn was dying.

He fought the dizziness and struggled to his feet. Marella crouched beside Claarn's outstretched form, partly obscured in shadows thrown by a flickering torch. He moved awkwardly toward her, but as he approached, she turned, and he saw tears staining her cheeks. He glanced down at the giant warrior. Claarn's broad chest was stained with blood from sword gashes, and a similar wound ran from eye to jaw on the giant's right cheek. His eyes were closed, and his breath came in short shallow gasps.

'I tried to save him,' Marella said, her dark eyes flashing defiantly. 'The Saviour ordered Tim to leave him, but I

326

couldn't. He was just going to let him die. If you hadn't killed the sorcerer, he would be dead already.'

The sorcerer. The man in blue. Dead? The spell? After the arrow. He struggled to fit the pieces together. 'The Dark Warrior?' Andra asked out of his confusion.

'Tim Gaelus disobeyed the order. He used your bow, after you fell,' Marella softly explained, trying to control her passion. 'But he was too late to stop this. Claarn tried to fight the spell, but the Dark Warrior was too quick, too strong.' Andra bent to study Claarn's wounds. 'He's a powerful man, Andra, but these wounds would kill ten ordinary men,' Marella whispered, her sorrow rising.

'Where's my pack?' he asked.

She nodded to her right. 'Over there. Why?'

'Can you fetch it for me?'

Marella sniffed, and crawled to the pile of equipment, stored in the corner of the tiny cave, to retrieve Andra's pack. 'Here,' she said, passing it to him. He rummaged through the contents, pulling out foodstuff, rope, a cloak and other items, until he extracted a dirty rag, which he carefully unrolled to reveal a small pouch. 'What's that?' Marella asked.

'Healing powder,' he replied. He loosened the pouch's silver drawstring and inverted it, sprinkling blue powder into his palm. He leaned over Claarn and applied the powder to the warrior's wounds, emptying the last portion over Claarn's gaping cheek.

'What will happen?' Marella asked.

'He'll sleep. If he hasn't lost too much blood, it will heal his wounds,' Andra explained.

Marella reached for the empty pouch and held it up to inspect. 'Who did you get it from?'

'A friend.'

'Mirith?'

Andra was astonished to hear the Aelendyell girl's name on Marella's lips. 'You know her?'

Marella shook her dark hair. 'No,' she said. 'You called her name before you woke from the spell. Who is she?'

He recalled the Aelendyell beauty, and for a lingering moment he could see her braided silver locks and her naked form slipping through the deep blue river waters bordering Wudufaesten tun. She had his heart still. 'Someone special.'

Marella's gaze dropped to Claarn, and her eyes filled with tears, and in that moment the strong warrior woman seemed soft and defenceless. Andra reached out and enfolded her to his chest.

Thirty Seven

The bitter sea wind whistled from the foam-flecked ocean waves, carrying the stinging salt spray high above the rugged cliffs, into the caves and clefts overlooking the ruined castle of Cennednyss. Enormous waves crashed against a finger of rock that thrust out of the raging water, a hundred spans from the cliffs, launching spires of angry white foam into the air, which the wind obliterated, lashing the cliffs with the watery fragments it could fling across the gap. Atop the finger of rock, the shattered remnant of Cennednyss castle, a stone edifice that rose to a chaotic jumble of blocks and exposed floors, was in the advanced stages of decay. A stone bridge arched across the watery chasm between castle and cliff, a statement of defiance against the ravages of the ocean and its weather, and perched on the bridge, its great black wings wrapped protectively around its massive scaly body, was a dragon.

Andra, Claarn and Marella lay on their stomachs, pressed against the cold rock ledge, gritting their teeth, as they peered into the howling gale lashing the rugged coastline. Andra stared at the ugly beast sitting at the beginning to the bridge. Studying its snake like head, he saw the yellowing fangs protruding down the sides of its crooked jaw, and the ridge of scales, running from the middle of its forehead to disappear over the back of its neck. The dragon was too distant in the poor conditions to make out its eyes, but Andra had a creepy feeling the creature was watching everything, waiting for movement along the approach roads, so that it could satiate its blood lust, and burn with its fire. He remembered the attack on Wudufaesten tun, and the terror on The Rim Shield, when the black creatures swept in from the sky and burned everything at will. Arrows and lances couldn't penetrate their hides. Of all things the Dragonlord brought against the Kingdom, the dragons were the most fearsome – and now one blocked access to Cennednyss.

Andra felt a touch on his arm. Marella was motioning for him to withdraw. He took a last look at the black dragon, noting the long talons on the creature's powerful hind legs, before he slid carefully from the ledge and followed his friends into a tiny cave they'd discovered when they stumbled upon the ancient ruins. They felt their way into the darkness, until Claarn was certain light wouldn't spill out of the cave's mouth, before Marella fumbled with her tinder and a torch. Moments later, she wedged the burning torch into a crevasse to free her hands.

'How good are you at killing dragons?' Claarn asked quietly, looking at Andra.

'Let's say I've seen a few now, but never killed one,' he answered, a reply that brought a wry grin to the giant's face. Andra was conscious of the blue-red scar dominating the warrior's right cheek. The Aelendyell healing powder had served its purpose, but nothing would hide the brutal scar the giant warrior would bear for the rest of his life.

'I suggest we eat first, and then talk out a plan of action,' said Marella, and she began to remove gear from her backpack.

The cave was tiny, cramped. Smoke from the burning torch constantly threatened to choke them. Andra chewed a handful of nuts and seeds from his exhausted rations.

Claarn was fortunate to be alive. Five days before, he'd come close to death, and only Mirith's gift saved him from it. He slept for two full days, while Andra and Marella watched over him and sheltered from a wild storm that ripped through the mountains. When he awoke, he was renewed, full of vigour and energy, like Milly was when Andra rescued her from the Haagii, north of Spurl.

They never considered turning back, once Claarn was healed. Led by Liam, their party abandoned them, but the quest for the sword was theirs as well, and they knew too little of the Bitter Peaks to risk returning, or going a different way, so they followed the trail of the others, where they could find traces undisturbed by the passing storm, hoping to make up some of the five days' difference before, or after, Cennednyss. Andra figured Liam's party would've been forced to shelter from the storm's ferocity, so at most they had three days' travel to recover. As a smaller group, they could move faster through the mountains, and they had a minor advantage in following a path left by the party, rather than having to find an unfamiliar way. They found evidence the Haagii were still searching for Liam's party, but they never stumbled across Haagii as they travelled.

'How do we get past the beast?' Marella asked, after she swallowed a mouthful of water. Claarn shook his head.

Andra scratched his fingernail against a rock and queried, 'How have the others got past?' They sat brooding. 'Perhaps they haven't been in yet,' he suggested.

'The signs on the paths tell me they've come this far,' Claarn answered. 'I haven't seen anything to suggest they passed by.'

Marella leaned to the side, to retrieve a burnt torch. 'Someone else was in this cave recently,' she remarked. 'The torch is wrapped like the kind the Haardrishii carry.' She handed the remnant to Andra.

He turned it in his hand. 'Perhaps there's another way in.'

'Then we best start looking,' said Claarn, closing his backpack, 'and carefully,' he added. 'The last thing we need is that great ugly lizard breathing down our necks.'

Marella skirted the boulder poised on the edge of the cliff, and crouched behind a low ridge, out of the dragon's field of vision. She crawled toward a shadow she'd spied in a cleft, between two granite shoulders, near the ravaged cliff. It was an opening. When she reached it, she found the cleft had been fashioned from the rock by tools, and a flight of steps dropped into a squared tunnel carved into the cliff. She listened for sounds from the tunnel, but the wind howling in from the ocean drowned everything, so she made her way back to the cave, where they agreed to meet, and told the others what she'd found. They followed her out to the cleft.

The three warriors felt their way blindly down the steep, narrow steps, until they were sure they were safe from observation, before Marella lit a torch. The stairway walls were hewn from the rock, and Andra was surprised by the acute angle of the steps. He took care, being at the rear, not to miss his footing and stumble into Claarn, an error that would send them all tumbling to their deaths. As they descended, he noticed individual runes cut into the rock at regular intervals, but neither he, Claarn nor Marella, could decipher their significance. From below came a faint rumble, a distant susurration, like a great beast breathing, and before long the air in the tunnel was moving regularly, drawn in and out, taunting the flame on Marella's torch and threatening to extinguish it. The walls were damp, and great pearls of water droplets hung from the rock, reflecting the flickering torchlight. 'We're at the level of the ocean,' Marella whispered, as she paused. Ahead, three tunnels branched. 'Which way?'

'Where's the air coming from?' asked Claarn.

'The right,' said Marella. 'The one to the left climbs again. Straight ahead drops deeper.'

'Go right,' the giant instructed.

Marella followed the right tunnel. The passage rose slightly, as it twisted and turned, and every section was damp and wet, as though frequently drenched. The air movement dramatically increased, until the noise became a roar. Daylight seeped in, and Marella's torch guttered out, leaving them to feel their way in the limited light.

Around a final corner, the tunnel opened into a low cave. Andra pressed behind Claarn and looked past the stooping warrior's side to see surging waves thundering into the cave. The water level rose, rushed up furiously to within a hand span of the rock where Marella stood, hesitated, and was sucked back down by the retreating waves, until it was at least twenty spans below her. Barnacle-encrusted rocks were exposed, their marine secrets glistening in the pale light, until the waves surged in again, forcing the water rapidly upward. It swirled to the level of Marella's precarious

332

perch, and lapped over the rocky lip into the tunnel at Claarn and Andra's feet. 'We go another way!' Claarn yelled.

At the tunnel branch, Marella rekindled her torch, turned and headed down again, deeper into the cliff. They hadn't descended more than a dozen steps when they were confronted with a doorway, carved from stone, the door ajar. The flickering light revealed a symbol on the door – a sword, ablaze. Beyond the open door, the tunnel ran level for five paces, and dropped again. They passed through three doors in a short distance, all forced open and left that way, but the tunnel construction improved in quality. The walls were smoother, the ceiling higher, so Claarn no longer stooped. The steps widened, and the rate of descent decreased, until the steps disappeared, and they stood in a corridor, expertly crafted by stone masons of rare talent, wide enough to comfortably walk three abreast. Marella held her torch aloft, as they paused to admire the plain but precise craftsmanship. 'Dwarven hands shaped these walls,' said Claarn.

Andra heard the awe in his friend's voice, and it mirrored his feelings. He recalled Hanna and Bear's reluctance to enter the chambers they stumbled upon in the Andrakian mountains, but he could guess what was below the old highway the Dwarven carved through the mountain rock, and he wished they'd been more curious.

'I'd say we're well below the level of the ocean,' said Marella, turning to the others. 'This tunnel echoes. It's long. I'm certain it leads to the castle.'

'The others must've entered this way,' said Andra.

'And left as well,' added Claarn. 'Three days would've been enough time to explore and find the sword.'

'I still want to see for myself,' Andra argued.

'So do I,' said Marella, offering him support. Claarn twisted his scarred face into a grin, and the three friends began strolling along the corridor toward Cennednyss.

The corridor ran straight for a hundred paces. No doors opened into the walls, and no apparent seams or other discrepancies marred the stonework. Andra wondered what magic the Dwarven stonemasons employed to craft a flawless construction below the wild ocean. He remembered hearing melancholy in Hanna's voice, when she briefly mentioned her ancestors, and now he understood why. The Shaddite descendants lost so much of their heritage, in the intervening period since the Dragonlords of Abreotan's era wantonly destroyed the Dwarven Kingdoms.

The impact of Claarn's broad hand catapulted Andra backwards, and he nearly forgot to roll to regain his feet, as he tumbled. He heard the warning cry, 'Haagii!' just before a spear clattered along the stone floor past him, and warriors charged into their circle of light. Andra parried the sweep of the first Haagii's sword with his hand, pushing down on the flat of the weapon's blade, kicked out and up, and caught his assailant on the side of his shaggy head with his heel. The Haagii reeled backward, giving Andra a chance to draw his sword. Again, he parried a thrust from the Haagii, lunged, and slew the warrior. A second Haagii confronted him. Andra blocked his downward swing, spun and caught his opponent off-guard, slicing through his leather chest plate with a sweeping blow. Enraged, the Haagii lashed out, but Andra met his second attack with his own lusty swing, and as the swords clashed the Haagii warrior's blade shattered. Shock registered on his enemy's face as the Haagii realised what had happened, but a sudden blow from Claarn killed him. His useless sword hilt tumbled from his hand and rattled on the floor.

Four Haagii corpses lay on the blood-spattered floor. Marella was cleaning her blade. Claarn rolled over the last victim of his wrath and stared into the grimaced, leathery face. 'Seems we aren't the only ones down here,' he said. 'How many of these filth are we going to find?'

The flight of stone steps ended at a t-junction. Left and right, grey wooden doors lined the walls. The corridors were littered with broken furniture and pottery fragments. 'Now which way?' whispered Marella. Before Claarn could answer, a door banged at the far end of the left side corridor, and torch bearing Haagii warriors entered. Marella snuffed out her torch. The three companions withdrew down the steps, their swords ready, but the Haagii strode past the junction, unaware of their presence, and continued right. 'They were all heavily armed,' Marella observed.

'How many?' Claarn asked.

'Fifteen,' said Andra.

They waited, until a second door slammed, before they sneaked back up the steps. Marella struggled to relight her torch. 'I've only one torch left,' she said, as the flame grew.

'Use mine next,' offered Andra, 'although I've only got two.'

They listened at the door, until they were certain no one was behind it, and Andra eased it open. Steps led up. At the head of the steps, they found a door hanging crazily from one hinge, battered open. A dead Haagii warrior lay spread-eagled on the floor, an arrow shaft protruding from his chest. 'Tim's been here,' said Andra, as he inspected the arrow's feather and recognised one of his own arrows.

They discovered six bodies along the corridor, and they ascended two more flights of steps, before Andra halted, and motioned to Claarn and Marella that someone was around the corner. The warriors of Tressel Deep went to advance, but Andra shook his head, reached into his tunic and dragged out a small leather money pouch, which he upended. Three silver coins dropped into his right palm. He caught one between his fingers and flicked it against the opposite wall. It dropped with an audible clink. Boots shuffled toward the corner, and a Haagii warrior, spear dangling from his left hand, bent over to see what had made the noise. Andra brought the flat of his heavy sword blade across the Haagii's vulnerable head, knocking him unconscious.

Shouting reached their ears, as they entered the corridor, and a wounded Haagii warrior stumbled out of the darkness. Marella felled him. Ahead, thick smoke filled the air, reducing visibility, but they could discern more Haagii in the smoke. The corridor rang to the sounds of fighting.

Claarn's face grew grim and he headed for the battle.

Set on from the rear, the Haagii offered brief resistance, the vision of Claarn looming through the smoke causing the enemy to run. Andra and Marella slew several, but the rest pushed past to escape. Beyond the first Haagii, Claarn encountered a larger party. Thick smoke restricted his view, but it afforded the three warriors cover in return, and they wielded their swords with devastating effect, before the Haagii comprehended the rout occurring in their ranks. By then, twelve of heir troop were slain. The remaining Haagii bolted.

Andra saw black shapes near the smouldering pile of wood that was the source of the choking smoke and guessed them to be Haardrishii. The Haagii were trapping Liam's party in Cennednyss. He followed Claarn forward, but as he drew nearer dread gripped him. He recognised the cruel spikes on their shoulder plates, and arms – the Dragonlord's Dark Warriors: three of them. Claarn stopped. The two factions faced each other in the swirling smoke. Andra's eyes were weeping from the acrid fumes, but he concentrated, recalling the Guardian training under the Guardian Master. He was tensed, yet relaxed, disciplined, ready. The Dark Warriors advanced.

Andra had no time to consider Claarn or Marella. Face to face with a Dark Warrior, he projected his thought into the weight and balance of his heavy sword, meeting his opponent with purpose, determined that what he lacked in armour he'd gain through agility, but he was unpleasantly surprised by the strength behind the first blow he warded. The Dark Warrior nearly forced him to buckle at the knees. Recovery cost him a second blow. He rolled with the sweep of his opponent's sword and let it slice harmlessly through his cloak, and responded by bringing his sword sharply up, the point clanging against his opponent's breast plate. The Dark Warrior adjusted to the attack and flicked Andra's sword point away from his chest, followed through with the same motion, and Andra only escaped serious injury by jumping up and back. His retreat encouraged the Dark

Warrior to take the offensive, and Andra fended a flurry of attacking thrusts as his opponent drove him along the corridor. He knew he was losing. The Dark Warrior was too strong, too fast. One had nearly killed Claarn. He skipped back another couple of paces, to avoid a slashing cut, and slipped on a Haagii corpse. Seizing the advantage, his attacker lunged, but Andra rolled to the side, leaving the Dark Warrior's sword to gouge into the dead Haagii, and wedge in the corpse's ribs. It was a chance. He thrust his sword into the groin joint in the Dark Warrior's plate armour. The Dark Warrior dropped his sword, with a gurgling cry, and clutched the wound, as Andra wrenched out his blade.

More dark figures moved beyond the burning barrier. Claarn and Marella had forced through. Smoke was stifling Andra's lungs, making him cough, but he was intent on breaking through the barrier. Sword poised, he ran, and jumped. As he landed, he tumbled through a half-roll to bounce to his feet, ready to fight more Dark Warriors, but in the torchlight, he saw Tim's grinning face.

Thirty Eight

'Three days,' Tim replied, closing the door. 'We've searched the well thoroughly. Sasha nearly drowned yesterday. The water's deep, and there's absolutely no light down there. We've hung torches above the water, but they don't make a difference.'

Andra followed the assassin across the wide room. Rusted iron struts, that once held lanterns, projected from the cracked stonework, the floor was strewn with fragments of rotted wood, and doors hung from broken hinges. 'Hard to believe this was one of the finest castles in the Kingdom,' Andra said, half to himself.

'This room was probably a smaller dining room,' said Tim, as they passed through a doorway, and entered a short corridor. 'Those doors lead to sleeping quarters,' he indicated, and pointed to a flight of stone steps. 'Those lead to the castle proper. Or at least what's left of it. There's nothing much up there, except wind and roosting sea birds. The well's through here.' The door he pointed to was recessed in an alcove, and as they approached a Haardrishii emerged. 'Liam's ordered Sarich to stay on guard here,' Tim explained, acknowledging the Haardrishii warrior as they passed him to enter a small room.

Light radiated from a small sphere, floating half a span below the high ceiling, directly above a well. Andra recognised Peret the Apprentice and saw his companions peering into the depths. A rope disappeared over the low, carved wall ringing the well's perimeter. 'Where's Liam?' Andra asked, noting the Saviour's absence.

Peret glanced up at the sound of Andra's voice, and astonishment fleeted across his face. Tim, observing Peret's reaction, put a hand on Andra's shoulder. 'My friend's managed to find us,' he said with a grin. 'He's brought the warriors we left behind.' Peret nodded slowly, but he continued to stare. 'Where's the Saviour?' Tim asked.

His echo of Andra's question broke Peret's stare. 'He's climbed to the top of the ruins,' the Apprentice replied.

The rope in the well bounced, and strained, interrupting the brief conversation. Tim moved to take a grip, and Andra helped him to pull Sasha, wet and shivering, to the surface. Andra took off his cloak and wrapped it around the assassin. Her teeth chattered violently. 'That's more than enough for today,' declared Tim, looking directly at Peret. 'We're finding a warm, dry spot.'

'As you wish,' the Apprentice replied. 'We'll try later. It's your turn to swim next.'

Tim and Andra led Sasha along the corridor, into the dining room, where he wrenched open a reluctant wooden door. The air was musty, and Tim's torch revealed a long disused bed, and broken furnishings scattered around the floor. 'Perfect,' he said. He began gathering the wood and quickly had a small fire burning, leaving Andra to towel Sasha with his cloak. The smoke rose to the high ceiling and gathered in thickening clouds.

'This'll smoke us out,' Andra complained.

'Not for a while,' said Tim. 'By then, Sasha will be warm again. I'll get dry clothes.' He disappeared out the door.

Sasha huddled close to the fire. Her dark hair, cropped short for convenience, was jewelled with water, and Andra thought there was a touch of girlish innocence in her strong features, enough to make her pretty in the firelight, but he also remembered she was an assassin, one of the best in the business. Her full lips were discoloured, the cold turning them purple. 'Do you really think there's a sword in the well?' Andra asked, as he sat beside her.

She didn't face him, and he felt as if she was ignoring him, but she answered in a voice broken by involuntary shivering. 'There's no sword in the well.' Her tone informed him she'd searched the inky depths of cold, stagnant water thoroughly.

'Why are you looking, then?' he asked.

'Orders!' she snapped. 'The bloody Apprentice is adamant it's there. He says Master Ki – you know, that

Chancellor wizard – is never wrong.' Contempt filled her voice. 'Only, this time, he is wrong.'

'Why the well?'

'The legend says it's there,' said Tim, his calm voice interrupting to answer Andra's question. He dropped an old tunic, leggings, and a cloak beside Sasha, who stood, and began peeling off her wet garments. 'According to the legend about the moon warrior,' said Tim, 'the new king must have Abreotan's sword. And the legend says it lies beneath the waters of the well in Cennednyss.'

'The exact words?' asked Andra, curiosity aroused.

'The exact words,' Tim confirmed.

'I would have thought that casting it into a well wasn't really a good way of keeping it safe,' said Andra, as he rose from his sitting position to lean against the door.

'The sword's magical,' said Tim, watching his friend. 'Presumably water can't rust it.'

'I don't just mean that. It's not exactly a guarded hiding place, is it?'

Tim shook his head. 'No. Not now. But this castle would've been swarming with people in the days when the sword was first hidden in the well. It would have been guarded then.' When he saw Andra was unconvinced by his reasoning, he waited for the Guardian to speak, and when he didn't, choosing to lean against the door in thought, Tim prompted him.

'I don't know a lot about the legends, Tim,' he said slowly, 'but what I have heard means the sword is the most awesome weapon ever created. I would have thought its final resting place, especially if there were prophecies claiming it would one day be needed again, would be cleverly designed to keep would-be thieves from stealing it.' He glanced up with a broad smile. 'Present company excepted, of course.' Tim laughed.

The smoke in the room was thickening, and Sasha, dressed again, sat by the fire, soaking in the warmth. 'It's not in the well,' she mumbled.

'What about hidden panels?' Andra suggested.

'That's all we've been searching for,' Tim replied.

'By feel,' added Sasha, with a sneer. The dry feeling of fresh clothes hadn't softened her anger toward those who were ordering her into the water.

'We searched the well, after we arrived. We even picked over the walls and floor of the room where the well is, in case there were hidden passages, or panels to let the water out, or expose the sword somehow. No luck,' said Tim.

'Someone's either beaten us to it a long time ago, or we're being led a miserable dance,' Sasha grumbled. She held her long, slender hands over the diminishing flames. 'Fire's nearly out.'

Peret bent over the glowing crystal sphere and concentrated. The interview wasn't going well. Master Ki's anger frightened him. The wizard wanted the sword of Abreotan for the Saviour. It had to be in the well. Peret was going to find it, even if he had to dive in the well himself, because the sword was beneath the waters of Cennednyss well. He couldn't deny the prophetic words. They found only one well in the castle, but no sword beneath its waters: only skeletal remains of less fortunate seekers.

The Master also ordered him to keep close watch on the Guardian, Andra. Peret sensed Master Ki was becoming irritated by Andra's reappearances, and he wondered about the Guardian because there was an uncanny similarity between the Saviour and him. Peret remembered thinking, on The Rim Shield, that Andra was the Saviour, because he had a ragged scar on his cheek that coincidence wrought into a crescent moon. The Saviour's forehead markings were far more convincing proof, the magical runes clearly identifying Liam as ordained by the gods, but now Peret was less certain. Andra bore a charmed life. He came back from death in the desert, reappeared, disguised as an assassin, at the beginning of the journey to find Abreotan's sword, escaped a spell attack, somehow miraculously healed the dying Claarn, and stole past a dragon into Cennednyss. How? Was he just incredibly lucky? Or did a greater force protect the Guardian?

A Ahmud Ki's image changed. Peret blinked, trying to make out what was happening, as the crystal lost opacity, and grew sharper, clearer. Another face came into relief, and A Ahmud Ki's features faded, replaced by a strikingly similar face, high cheek-boned and handsome, but the eyes were oval, slanted, and there was no trace of a beard. The eyes burned red.

Overwhelmed by fear, Peret tried to wrench his eyes from the vision, but he was locked into another consciousness, trapped within the crystal by a mind exceeding his comprehension. The crystal's brilliance magnified a hundredfold, blinding the Apprentice's eyes. There is no sword. The thought words cut into his mind like burning brands. He tried screaming, but he couldn't hear above his own panic. The fool you serve has sent you on a pointless errand! the thought voice roared. Abandon the quest, human. I am your new master. There is no sword. The staring eyes were balls of red flame, burning into his brain like the words. There is no sword!

Andra sat up, engulfed by darkness. He felt for the hilt of his sword and clutched it in his fingers. The sleeping resonances of Tim and Sasha and Claarn filled the room. He listened. No one stirred. He crawled in the direction of the door, remembering that Tim slept hard against it, in case intruders tried forcing in. Always one step ahead, thought Andra. He touched Tim.

'What do you want?' a sleepy voice whispered.

Andra wished he had Aelendyell night vision. 'Outside,' he whispered. In the corridor, he lit and hung a torch in one of the rusted holders dotted along the decaying wall.

Tim blinked and rubbed his eyes. 'Night vision's a curse when people keep lighting things. What's this about?'

'I had a dream,' Andra replied.

Tim's left eyebrow cocked cynically. 'So did I. She was

beautiful. Can I go back to her now?'

'No. That's not what I'm talking about, Tim Gaelus,' Andra said with a shake of his head. 'I dreamed I was back in The Vale, with Erik, and Alain. Liam was there too. The way he used to be before the marks appeared on his head.' Tim yawned and leaned against the wall. His eyes closed. 'Are you listening?' Andra hissed.

'Go on. I'll pretend I'm awake,' Tim grumbled.

'If you don't want to listen -'

Tim's eyes snapped open. 'I'm listening. I listen with my ears. It's my eyes I closed. I don't tend to listen with them.'

Andra continued, when Tim's irritability appeared to settle. 'We were all standing by the creek. There's a creek runs through The Vale. The Guardian Master was there, except he was dressed in Haardrishii armour. He used to be Haardrishii before he came to The Vale.' Tim nodded absently, and yawned again, closing his eyes, but Andra ignored him. 'He was holding a stone, a black stone. He said he was going to hide it beneath the waters of the stream.' Tim's eyes opened slightly at the allusion to the prophetic words. 'He made us go and return the following day,' said Andra. 'He was standing on the other side of the bank holding a sword. It was shining with light. There were others standing behind him, all in armour, like Haardrishii, but so many I couldn't count. He pointed to the stream and ordered us to find the stone. He said whoever found it he would serve eternally.'

Andra paused to see if Tim was awake. The assassin squinted at him, and murmured, 'Go on.'

'The others started into the water. I tried to warn them, but they didn't listen. The water swallowed them all, except Liam. He just stood in the water, up to his waist, staring at me as if I didn't exist, like he did in the parade. I wanted to go into the stream, to find the others, but I couldn't move. When I did go, I walked downstream, away from them. There was a door in the earth. It looked like it went under the creek, except the creek was now a river. When I looked across toward the Guardian Master, all I saw was a warrior

343

in silver armour, like nothing I've ever seen. He had blond flowing hair, like the Dark Warriors, and he sat on a white horse. It had wings. He was smiling at me and nodding, as if he approved of what I was doing. He held a sword. It was burning.'

'What was in the door?' asked Tim sleepily.

'I didn't open it. I woke up.'

'Oh.' Tim yawned. 'I think I need to get back to sleep. Marella will be here soon, and she'll want someone else to keep watch with the Haardrishii.'

Andra grabbed Tim's arm, as the assassin went to turn toward the door. 'Tim! The dream told me where the sword is!' he said emphatically.

His urgency changed Tim's exhaustion to mild interest. 'Where?'

'It's not in the well,' said Andra.

'We've told you that. Tell me something new,' Tim mumbled, his interest disappearing.

'What are the words of the prophecy again?'

Tim shook his head. 'For the sake of Teka, Andra!' he protested.

'Say them!' Andra demanded.

Begrudgingly, Tim mumbled through the words. 'The sword of Abreotan lies beneath the waters of the well in Cennednyss. Or something like that. Satisfied?'

'Exactly!' laughed Andra. 'Beneath the waters of the well.' Tim screwed up his face to squint at Andra. Not enough sleep. His friend was becoming over-exhausted. 'Don't you understand?' asked Andra incredulously.

Tim nodded. 'I understand. Do you?' he retorted. 'I need sleep. So do you.'

Andra threw up his arms in disgust, grabbed Tim and shook him to make his point. 'The sword is not in the waters of the wall. It's beneath the waters! We have to find a place underneath the well!'

He watched his revelation dawn on the assassin's face. A slow grin spread across Tim's lips until he began to laugh, and he embraced the Guardian in an impromptu bear hug.

'Of course!' he shouted. 'Of course! Beneath the waters! It's so bloody obvious! By Teka!'

The pair pushed and danced with crazy delight in the flickering glow of the torch, laughing at Andra's wild dream realisation, until their noisy celebration woke Claarn and Sasha. When Claarn flung the door open, sword in hand, he couldn't believe the mad display in the corridor.

Thirty Nine

'There's something odd going on,' said Marella. 'A while back, the Haagii started pounding against this door, and we were certain they were going to break through. They tried heating it with fire to crack the stone, and failed, but perhaps they guessed the heat weakened it. It didn't. They kept pounding frantically, and then their pounding faded. The door cooled. They went silent on the other side. Then these appeared.' She traced her finger along one of hundreds of fine cracks, like cobweb, across the door face. 'We waited for the Haagii to break through, but they didn't, and there's been no sound beyond the door since.'

'Have you tried opening it?' Tim asked. Marella shook her head.

'If the Haagii are trying to sit us out, that's exactly what they'd be waiting for us to do,' said Claarn. 'Better we wait until we have to open it.'

'Maybe they'll give up,' said Andra, but neither he nor anyone else expected that to happen.

Marella left a Haardrishii in charge of the door, and joined Tim, who led her, and the others, up through the corridors and stairwells carved in the rock, until he came to the room where Liam slept. He knocked. 'Yes?' a voice called from within.

Tim opened the door, extinguishing his torch because a small lantern lit Liam's room. They had few torches. 'We've worked out where the sword is hidden,' Tim said in greeting.

Liam was studying the workmanship on the blade of Cedwyn's sword. 'Peret's informed me that there is no sword. It's a hoax,' he said, without emotion.

Tim glanced over his shoulder at Andra, who shook his head. 'How does Peret know that?' Tim asked.

Liam slipped his sword into its scabbard. 'The Master told him last night.'

'You believe that?'

Liam's eyes flared and anger flickered in his voice. 'If the Master says it's so, it is so!' he said with finality. 'Our task here is at an end.'

'What a choice,' Marella said. 'Fight a dragon, or half the Haagii army.' The wind whistled around the wall, where they sheltered, staring across the churning watery chasm, separating Cennednyss from the sea cliffs. The dragon still sat at the bridgehead, its massive form obscured by the dull daylight, driving rain, and its blackness. There was no sign of Haagii in the open, but above the road leading to the bridge, hidden somewhere beneath overhangs and shelters, there were Haagii camped, because curlicues of grey smoke twisted out of the rocks before the vicious wind disintegrated them.

'There's no real choice,' argued Andra. 'Either way we go, we'll have both on us.'

'I only want to get out of here so I can go back to the Great City and wring the neck of that fool who sent us here, for no reason but his royal whim!' snarled Claarn.

'I can't believe there's no sword,' said Sasha. 'All those pointless sessions in the stinking well for nothing!'

'There is a sword,' said Andra quietly.

The others turned to him. 'It was a dream, Andra,' said Tim gently, trying not to offend his friend.

'No. It's more than that,' Andra replied.

'Explain,' Marella asked.

Andra lifted his head. 'The Royal Advisor, or Chancellor now, says Liam's the one chosen to find Abreotan's sword. Everyone in the Kingdom believes that.'

'I don't,' said Claarn. 'It's a prophecy – nothing but a witch's dream.'

'Perhaps,' said Andra. 'But if it is, why did he go to so much trouble to send Liam to a place of great danger, only to pointlessly sacrifice him? That isn't logical.'

'Not a lot is logical about the ones who live in the castle,'

347

observed Claarn. 'The Great King was mad. So's the Royal Chancellor.'

'What are you saying?' asked Tim.

'We look for the sword,' said Andra, 'as my dream described it. We have nothing to lose, given what lies in wait for us, over there.'

The others stared at the Guardian. Tim nodded. 'We can't leave yet,' he said, 'but we don't have a lot of time, either. Our food's nearly gone, and the water. There aren't many torches left to burn.'

'But where do we start?' asked Sasha.

Andra paused to reflect, and replied, 'Back in the well room.'

Torchlight flickered on the stone, throwing their shadows into relief, as they searched every section of the room. 'Try this,' Claarn called to Sasha.

The assassin studied the crack Claarn found, using her thiefly touch to discern weakness or movement. 'Nothing. I think I checked this one before.' she sighed.

'Over here,' Marella said. Again, Sasha found nothing.

'That's every possibility,' said Tim, as he leaned against the low wall surrounding the well.

Andra looked at the wall, against which Tim leaned, and asked, 'What about on that?'

Tim glanced down. 'Doesn't make sense, Andra. The wall's not thick enough to open into a tunnel.'

'But it might hide a key or something.'

The group meticulously explored the low wall, fingers and eyes searching every nook and cranny. Sasha and Tim were kept busy, constantly responding to calls of discovery, none proving valid, until Marella's excited voice filled the room. 'Here! Here!' She pointed to a discoloration in a rock, and, when her fingers slid across it, the top layer opened, like a lid, revealing a very smooth, square panel of red rock.

'It looks like a —' Tim left his words hanging, as Andra impulsively pressed the rock. It depressed, and a loud click echoed inside the well. 'What was that?'

'Look here,' said Claarn, who was peering over the rim. 'There,' he pointed. Barely two spans below, a dark patch appeared in the side of the well, an opening large enough for a person to crawl into.

'Didn't you search the walls?' Marella asked Sasha.

'Not this high up.'

'Who's first?' inquired Tim.

'Shouldn't we tell Liam and the others?' asked Andra.

'I'll get them,' said Marella.

Tim was already clambering over the edge, down the rope they'd secured the first day they began searching the waters of the well. 'Don't be too slow, or we'll find the sword without the Saviour,' he called.

The vertical shaft was pitch black, and cold, as Andra inched down each metallic rung of the ladder, concentrating on finding the succeeding rung with his foot, praying that he wasn't about to tread on Tim's fingers, or have his own crushed beneath Claarn's invisible boots descending above. He was conscious of his breathing. Light flared below. When he looked down, and saw Tim's tiny face framed in torchlight peering up at him, he marvelled at the distance Tim descended in the time they were in the shaft. The light increased his confidence.

Moments later, he was in an alcove, beside Tim, facing a large metal door. 'This looks promising,' said Tim cheerfully, as they studied the bas-relief on the door, depicting three severed dragonheads, floating above a long, flaming sword. Runes surrounded the picture.

'Can you read this?' Andra asked.

'No,' said Tim.

Claarn's heavy footsteps approached, and Sasha joined them. 'Where's the handle?' Claarn asked, staring at the strange door.

'There isn't one,' explained Tim. 'This is a magical door.'

'So how do we open it?' the giant queried.

'Depends,' said Tim, rubbing his chin.

The assassins searched the door and its surrounds.

349

Finally, Sasha tapped Tim on the shoulder, and pointed at one rune etched into the door, above the tip of the sword. 'Worth a try?' he asked. She nodded. Tim stood back to watch, as Sasha traced her finger around the rune. The rune glowed, and, as Sasha straightened, the metal door slowly slid vertically into the ceiling, revealing a staircase, descending deeper into the earth.

'How did you work that out?' asked Andra, incredulously.

'Lucky guess,' Sasha replied. 'Nothing else was out of place on the door, or its surrounds.'

'Stop giving away trade secrets!' Tim hissed. He turned a blatantly false smile toward Andra, and added, 'He's only a pretend thief, remember.' Andra swung a playful cuff, but the assassin had already skipped to the stairs.

The stairway cut back on itself five times, as they descended. Tim led, and Andra was aware the assassin was moving cautiously, testing every step before he put his full weight on it. While Tim eased down the steps, Sasha's hands were nimbly skimming along the wall, searching expertly for aberrations that might lock or release trapping mechanisms. At the bottom, they faced a blank wall. Tim paused on the last step, studying the wall, before he gingerly touched the section of floor immediately before the wall. Nothing. He stepped forward, but motioned to Sasha to remain on the step while he approached the wall. Andra shared Tim's disquiet. 'No door at all,' growled Claarn. 'Now what?'

'I don't like it,' said Tim, gazing at the wall. 'The wall's a door. It's not fixed to the side walls. The obvious thing to do is put pressure on it, to see if it budges. There have been no traps, so far, but if the sword is beyond here there has to be more than a pretend dead end stopping us.'

'Let me try,' said Claarn. 'Get off the floor section.'

Tim obeyed Claarn's directive. The giant moved to the bottom step and drew his sword. With it, he easily spanned the gap between step and wall. As he pressed, the wall started to move. They heard a scraping of stone, and the landing fell away. Tim peered over the drop with his torch, and saw, several spans below, between the rock debris of the shattered floor section, iron spikes gleaming wickedly. 'Thanks, Claarn,' the assassin breathed.

'But how do we get across?' asked Claarn.

'Push,' said Tim. Claarn gave the stone a determined shove with the outstretched sword. The stone slid away with great ease, and a second floor section emerged from under the steps to fill the gap. The alcove revealed a doorway to the left, and a faint glow shimmered in the opening. 'Hope this floor's more substantial than its predecessor,' said Tim, with a sardonic grin.

Someone called from behind, and Andra turned to see Marella leading Liam and three Haardrishii down the stairs. Behind them, his hand cupping a soft sphere of light, was an Apprentice. 'Where's Peret?' Tim asked as Marella joined them.

'He refused to come. He still claims there's no sword, and that searching here is foolish.'

Liam pushed past Marella, Claarn and Andra, and stood on the new floor section, gazing at the light spilling from the doorway. 'Must be safe,' mumbled Claarn.

'If the sword lies here, I'm ready,' Liam declared, and he entered the doorway of light.

Beyond the doorway, a corridor extended thirty paces, but there was no need for a torch or the Apprentice's sphere because magical light exuded from the ceiling and walls, from the essence of the amber stone used in their construction. 'By all that is known!' gasped Claarn. 'I've heard the tales of Dwarven power, but I never dreamed I would see such a thing in my lifetime.'

Andra shared the giant warrior's amazement, as he gazed on the incandescent amber glow. He turned to Tim, who was walking ahead, beside Liam, talking emphatically to the Saviour, though Liam didn't appear interested in Tim's speech. Tim knocked Liam hard against the left wall, as a circle of metal flashed from wall to wall, waist-high, missing them both. Outraged by Tim's unprovoked attack, the Saviour kicked and struggled to his feet, and abused the assassin. Andra, Claarn and the others rushed forward, but halted before reaching Liam as Sasha pointed to a pair of cleverly hidden lines in the floor: a pressure plate. Tim pulled Liam around to watch as Sasha pressed the plate with her dagger. Again, an arc of metal flashed from left to right, a scythe-like blade attached to a silver rod fixed in the ceiling. It was easy to spot, if one looked up, Andra considered, but no one normally looked closely at the ceiling in corridors. Liam's churlish mood did not abate, but he indicated Tim and Sasha should lead.

At the corridor's end, another metal door barred the way, but this time an entire battle scene was etched into the face. Andra assumed the tall warrior at the centre, wielding a flaming sword amid a dozen dragons, was Aian Abreotan. Behind him, a dozen figures in black robes, with long flowing hair, were descending from a sky, beneath a quarter moon. Their features were unmistakably Aelendyell, although they were exaggerated at the cheeks and eyes to appear more sinister. Around the central piece, warriors were locked in the throes of a great battle, before a castle on a plateau on a wide plain. He recognised the place, but what caught his eyes was the creature Abreotan rode: a winged horse, exactly as in his dream. When he turned to Tim, he saw bewilderment staring back, and knew Tim was remembering the dream details.

Sasha found a camouflaged panel on the wall, like the one on the well, so the party retreated from the door, while Tim secured a rope round Sasha's waist, in case another floor section gave way. She pressed the stone, it slid in, and the metal door sank into the floor.

The circular room, beyond, was bathed in amber light, emanating from a central shaft, shining from ceiling to floor. Unlike constructions they previously encountered, the room was pure marble – walls, floor, ceiling – and around the walls, spaced at intervals, twelve in total, were marble statues of the same warrior, caught in different poses, each wielding a mighty sword. In the shaft of amber light, rotating slowly, one and a half spans from the floor, point extended upward, was a sword, its broad blade glistening.

No one spoke as they filed into the chamber, recognising they were privy to a legend. Andra's eyes were riveted to the spinning sword. Its blade wasn't the pure length of smooth metal he expected. Jagged spikes erupted at random, along its edge, giving it a vicious, evil aura. The hilt was amber-gold, and the pommel encrusted with multitudinous jewels. Suspended, the sword appeared too large for a person to wield, as if the real Abreotan had really been twice any living man in every possible way.

As Andra stared at the vision, Liam approached the light, his hand outstretched toward the sword hilt. Voices cried, 'No!' as the Saviour's hand reached the light shaft. Bright white light flashed, blinding Andra, and a fist of wind punched him backwards, onto the hard, slippery floor.

When Andra opened his eyes, Marella was leaning over him, her dark hair near his face. 'I'm fine,' he said, but as he struggled to his feet, the reek of burning flesh made him retch. The room still glowed amber from the central shaft, the sword still spun in place, but Claarn, Tim, and the Haardrishii were bending over a body. Andra pushed in, where the stench and sight made him retch again. Liam's arms were melted to the elbow stumps: flesh, armour, bone. His green-black armour steamed with heat, melted and twisted around his body, and the platinum neck chain was a liquid pool, sizzling on his chest and on the floor. Liam's face was scorched black. One eyeball was shrivelled to a black mess in a collapsed cheek, and the other twitched convulsively in its socket. Worst of all, despite his horrific injuries, Liam was breathing. His body stiffened repeatedly, his legs kicked, and drooling groans oozed from his blistered lips.

'What in Teka is that thing?' Claarn asked, looking at the shaft of amber light.

'A glyph,' answered the Apprentice, who stood apart from the group.

Liam shuddered twice, and died, leaving the survivors in

a hiatus of time, trapped in their thoughts, until Tim broke the silence. 'Now we have a real problem – a sword without a saviour.'

'How do we turn that thing off?' Claarn asked the Apprentice.

'I don't know,' he replied, moving to study the light. 'Only magic can work here.'

'So, work your magic,' said Claarn.

The Apprentice shook his head. 'Only Master Ki could work the magic required here.'

Claarn's anger was aroused. He spat on the floor. 'Then why didn't he come?'

Andra felt as if Tim was staring at him, but when he turned to the assassin he discovered he wasn't staring at Andra, but at the wall behind him, studying a series of runes and symbols. 'What is it?' Andra asked.

Tim didn't answer. Instead, he walked by Andra, grabbing his arm as he passed, and took him to the wall. 'There are four languages carved here,' he explained, as he pointed to various symbols. 'This one's unreadable. Probably something ancient from the time this was created. This one I think may be Dwarven. Some of the symbols are like Shaddite writing.' Tim moved along. 'These I can't read, but I'm sure they're Elvenaar. That's Elvenaar for sword.' Then he pointed to the last set. 'These are Aelendyell – well, virtually Aelendyell, though they're very ancient too. See how they're like Elvenaar writing?'

'What are you two up to?' demanded Claarn.

The others gathered. Marella pressed against Andra and he felt sensually aware of her, and guilty for feeling that way. 'What do they say?' Andra asked, diverting his thoughts to the runes.

'They must be about the prophecy,' Tim answered. 'The Aelendyell describes one who bears the mark of the moon. It details the return of the Dragonlords, and the need for a new king in the land. It says that, when he comes, he will be able to reach for the sword, unharmed by the light of fire, because he will bear the charm of Ethelreddor.'

A lingering memory rekindled in Andra's mind. 'Ethelreddor is the Elvenaar name for Dragon Forest,' he said, without pausing. He was aware of Tim staring intently at him. 'What's wrong?'

'How do you know that?'

'The Tree Keepers told me,' Andra answered. Then he understood. His fingers caressed his wrist. Only he knew about the bracelet he wore, hidden in his skin, part of his being. The memories flooded back. Ethelreddor. Marvin the Longbowman. Artega. Hyacinth. The Tree Keepers. Tree Home.

'Andra?' Tim was speaking to him.

'What?'

'Look.' Tim pointed to each rune set. A common symbol marked all of them – a crescent-shaped moon – like the scar on his cheek.

There was no turning back. Whatever path fate had marked out for him, he was now destined to discover. He rubbed the invisible band around his wrist and turned toward the amber shaft of light where the glittering sword rotated in its orbit. He glanced across to the dark, deformed corpse that had been Liam, and felt the pang of brotherhood that bound Guardians through their training in The Way.

Claarn's huge hand rested on his shoulder. 'Teka go with you,' he said.

Andra smiled. He understood his path. He patted Claarn's hand. 'What will you do if I become your king, old friend?' he remarked, but before Claarn could reply, Andra strode toward the amber light. He hesitated at its edge, shut his eyes, and reached in. His fingers closed around the cold hilt, and his entire body flowed with energy, tingling, as it did when he passed through the Aelendyell glyph protecting Wudufaesten tun, but he felt none of the wild untamed power that marked his passing through the magical field.

When he opened his eyes, the amber glow of the glyph had evaporated, replaced with a white radiance, shining from the heart of the sword, lighting the chamber with its brilliance. He saw the Apprentice face down in supplication on the floor, and the wide-eyed astonishment of the three Haardrishii. Beside them, Tim and Claarn, Marella and Sasha were laughing with joy.

Forty

Three dragons circled below the clouds. Surdrok studied their black shapes, wings spread, long snaky necks, tails twisting lazily, as they drifted on air currents, above Axxon plain. The Haagii massed in the valley had gone silent, as if awaiting a signal, and their front ranks had retreated from the foot of the wall, leaving a mound of dead piled five or six deep from four days of incessant, bloody battle. Surdrok never imagined such unremitting slaughter was possible. His army had been steadily depleted by successive Haagii attacks, but the daily losses the Haagii suffered never seemed to diminish the vastness of their army. Eight times, the Haagii smashed through the gate. Eight times, the Haardrishii repelled them, at a terrible cost. Now the gate no longer existed, shattered by constant ramming and burning, and holes in the defence walls were plugged with corpses.

Surdrok saw the signal the Haagii awaited. One dragon wheeled, stooped, and its cry, as it plummeted toward Central Gate, made the hair rise on the nape of his neck. It swooped toward the centre, where the remnant of the gate was, at a speed defying Surdrok's comprehension, and released a jet of flame that seared the stonework, exploding with awesome force, over the parapet and through the barricade of bodies. Those caught on the parapet screamed, as flames engulfed them, and Surdrok watched soldiers leap from the wall, into the mud and slush, to escape the dragon fire. The dragon flashed through the valley, between the mountain cliffs and was gone.

A roar erupted from the enemy, inspired by the dragon's pass, and the Haagii charged toward the breached gateway. Surdrok tried to rally the defenders one more time, but as he surveyed the renewed assault brewing along the valley he saw the second dragon stoop and sweep across the plain, and he knew Central Gate was lost.

Andra lifted Abreotan's sword, letting it light the base of the stairs. Dark water lapped against the step. 'It's flooded!' Marella gasped. 'How?'

Tim Gaelus pushed past and descended to the water. He dipped in his hand and lifted his fingers to taste the liquid. 'Salty. It's seawater,' he said. 'Somehow it's found its way into the corridor that runs below the cliffs.'

'The sea cave,' Andra said.

'You didn't close the doors on the way down,' Sasha muttered.

'No matter,' answered Claarn. 'The Haagii followed us down anyway.'

'That's why they went quiet after all the furious pounding on the lower door,' Marella realised. 'They were drowning. The seawater was pouring in. It extinguished their fires.'

'That eliminates one problem,' said Claarn, with a philosophical shrug.

'And one exit,' added Tim, ascending the steps. 'Guess which way is out for us now.' They looked at each other, understanding Tim's message. The only way out was across the stone bridge – to the dragon.

'Who opened the lower door to let the water in?' asked Sasha.

'Perhaps it finally collapsed,' suggested Tim.

'Or the Haardrishii opened it,' said Marella.

'In that case, they're drowned,' said Claarn.

His blunt statement stopped the conversation. Tim glanced at the three Haardrishii warriors standing silently behind Claarn, wondering if they felt sorrow for their fellow warriors who may have drowned in the flooding waters. 'If they did,' said Tim, 'the odds aren't looking good for us.'

'We have the sword,' said Andra. He didn't quite know why he said that, although holding the sword filled him with a secure sense of power and authority, a degree of confidence he had never really felt before, except perhaps the day after he was initiated as a Guardian: but even that experience paled in comparison. Then, he felt important, almost brash about his new status in the village of his childhood. Now, holding a legendary weapon, whose possession proclaimed him the new king, the bane of the Dragonlord, he felt strong, in control, superior, but calm. It wasn't at all how he felt when he became a Guardian. It was more like the balance of self, the harmony the Guardian Master spoke of when a Guardian truly accepts and becomes part of The Way; the inner understanding only the self can appreciate when it has recognised the path of life it is destined to follow. Already, he controlled the sword, and it controlled him. They were becoming one – an entity – a power. The light generated on his thought came from within the sword, and also from him.

'Where's that Apprentice?' Claarn growled.

'Gone to find Peret, I imagine,' said Tim. 'I suggest we do the same.'

The party ascended the corridors and stairs, past the sleeping quarters and the well room, until they reached the room the Apprentices shared. Tim pushed open the door. Peret rose, tucking a crystalline sphere inside his smock, and the other Apprentices rose and looked away. When Andra stepped into the room after Tim, however, all three Apprentices dropped to their knees and abased themselves. 'You could get used to this,' Tim laughed.

Andra smiled at his friend, and crossed to Peret. 'Don't kneel,' he instructed the Apprentice. 'We've got to plan an escape.'

The Apprentice raised his eyes to meet Andra's stare, and asked, 'How can I help, Your Majesty?'

The request amused those with Andra, and Claarn bellowed with laughter. Tim joined in and clapped the astonished Guardian on the shoulder heartily. 'You'd better get used to that as well, my friend – Oh, I mean, Your Highness,' the assassin chuckled. Andra lifted a hand, as if about to box Tim across the ear, but the assassin waggled his finger before Andra's nose and warned, 'That's hardly seemly behaviour for a person of royal standing, Your

Majesty. You have a servant, kneeling before you, who seeks your royal guidance.'

Andra glared at his friend, who withdrew to stand beside Claarn, still chuckling, before he looked down at Peret. Was he really going to have people dropping before him like this? He couldn't imagine Claarn doing it. Or Tim. Or Marella or Sasha. What was the point? 'I asked you to stand up,' he said to Peret. The Apprentice stood, but averted his eyes, which made Andra feel decidedly awkward. 'We're all that remains. The lower passages are flooded. The only way out is to cross the bridge. Have you got any suggestions?' Peret shook his head. Andra lifted the sword, letting its light glow faintly. 'What can you tell me about the sword's powers?'

Peret glanced at the other Apprentices, before shaking his head and replying, 'I'm sorry, Your Highness, but I know nothing of the sword.'

'What about your Master Ki?' asked Tim. His unsolicited question surprised Andra, but it shocked Peret, who subconsciously placed his left hand across his smock where the communication crystal lay hidden.

'Would your master know?' asked Andra.

Peret nodded. 'If there's anything to know about the sword, Master Ki will know.'

'Ask him,' said Tim. He stood beside Andra, as he gave his order to the Apprentice. Peret hesitated, looked at Andra, and back at Tim. An expression of hate crept across the Apprentice's face, but disappeared.

'Can you ask him, Peret?' Andra repeated. The Guardian didn't understand Tim's purpose, but made the request of Peret out of loyalty to his friend.

The Apprentice shuffled, looking trapped. Claarn edged forward, and the imposing bulk of the warrior from Tressel Deep decided Peret's mind.

'Yes, Your Majesty,' Peret whispered, 'but I cannot do so, while everyone is present. The spell requires utmost concentration.' He threw another sharp glance at Tim, a glance Andra observed, and he tried to catch Tim's eye, but the assassin was oblivious to his attempt.

'We'll leave you alone,' Andra said.

'Ask him what ideas he's got for shifting dragons,' Claarn chipped in, over Andra's shoulder.

The party withdrew, closing the door to Peret's chamber, and prepared to wait while the Apprentice set to work. 'What was all that about?' Andra asked of Tim, while Marella lit her last torch.

'That Apprentice hides more than he tells,' Tim cryptically replied.

'So do you,' said Andra. 'That didn't enlighten me at all. How did you know he could communicate with his master?'

Tim leaned casually against the wall, and replied, 'I'm an assassin. It pays to know everything and everybody. Backpacks and pockets tell more stories, and reveal more secrets, than people care to be known about them.'

Sasha smiled as Tim finished, and the assassins winked at each other, but Claarn growled, 'If I find out you've been in my belongings, my sly friend, I might do the same for yours. And I'm a lot less subtle about it.' Andra laughed at Claarn's benign threat. 'Of course, Sasha can go through my goods whenever she wishes,' the giant added, with a leery grin. His lewd comment brought a sudden sharp kick to his shin from Marella, causing the giant to wince, and everyone to break into merriment.

When he gathered his breath, Andra returned to questioning Tim. 'What did you find in our Apprentice friend's pocket?'

'A curious crystal sphere,' Tim replied.

If he hated anything, it was learning that events were outside his control. A Ahmud Ki picked up the communication crystal, tempted to throw it against the wall to express his anger, but he restrained his impulse, and kicked his stool over instead, before ascending to the Meditation Chamber, where Berak N'eth's amber glow bathed everything.

Peret's news was completely unforeseen. The wrong warrior held Abreotan's sword. Liam failed. Why hadn't

Peret obeyed his instructions and accompanied the Saviour to the place where the sword was found? What interfered with his plans? Or was it who?

Doubt and confusion ran like wildfire through his mind, as he put on his red Ithosen robe and settled onto the prayer mat. He cupped his hands and concentrated on emptying the turmoil of questions from his head. He couldn't block out his concern. The wrong warrior wielded the sword, a warrior over whom he had no control. The prophecy he set out to fabricate was inadvertently fulfilled, and he unwittingly contributed to it. Was Liam's failure an accident? Or was there a power moving currents of time and people, beyond his control, toward destinies promised by seers and wise ones? Was this Andra, this unknown warrior with an uncanny knack of disappearing and reappearing, the Chosen One spoken of in the legends, the Saviour of the prophecies? And if there was a greater power directing it, how could he, A Ahmud Ki, control that power, and make it his own?

Berak N'eth was with him, and in him: of that A Ahmud Ki was certain, because the God of Power lifted him above the mortal realm, allowing him to learn greater magic than anyone. Only one being was greater – Mareg Dru'artha Sutnavanistra – a Dragonlord. And A Ahmud Ki aspired to that power. He knew the magic of the Dragonlords, the Fifth Ki, was within his grasp, hidden, but accessible, beneath him, in the heart of the monolith on which the castle sat. With that power, even prophecies would fall. Berak N'eth had marked him for greatness. When he met the god, face-to-face, during his Ithosen initiation, he knew he was chosen for greatness, and his mentor, Karrilyon, admitted as much. The Targan witches knew. But why had Berak N'eth remained silent all these years? Why had his god forsaken him? He was A Ahmud Ki. He commanded respect and fear in this Kingdom. Berak N'eth should be pleased. He was the seed of power, the inheritor. Why was Berak N'eth silent?

Small matters nagged him too. Central Gate was falling. The defenders had already been driven back from the first and second walls, and although they were grimly holding the third and final gateway that opened onto the Plains of Ky, it was only a matter of time before Mareg's dragon hordes poured toward the Great City.

The Orb of Radiance would turn the dragons from the Great City, but the Haagii armies weren't affected by its magic – unless he altered the Orb's purpose – but that strategy would risk opening the way for the dragons to enter the battle. It was hardly an alternative. The sword was essential now. Wrong warrior or not, the bearer had to bring it to him, so he could fathom its functions, its powers, and use them to boost his own. If the prophecy was as real as it seemed to be, the sword was the Kingdom's sole hope of salvation.

But one of Mareg's beasts squatted on the bridge out of Cennednyss, barring the exit, defying A Ahmud Ki's people to escape. Filled with frustration, he rose from the mat and incanted a spell to descend to the tower's lower levels.

On the ground floor, he found Damon sweeping away broken pottery shards. 'Leave that!' A Ahmud Ki barked. Damon dropped to the floor in supplication, forehead pressed against stone. 'I want every text you can find on dragons!' A Ahmud Ki tersely instructed. 'I want them now!'

Andra clutched the jewelled handle of Abreotan's sword and stared across the windswept gap separating Cennednyss from the dragon. Haagii warriors moved among the rocks, black shapes with ragged cloaks fluttering in the wind, as rain-burdened clouds blocked the sun, casting their gloom over the world. A storm was brewing. 'We could wait until they give up and leave,' said Tim, in Andra's ear.

'They won't leave,' Andra said calmly. 'They know why we're here. Peret admitted that much. If you were the Dragonlord, and you knew about the prophecy, you'd want this sword at all costs, wouldn't you?'

Tim paused. 'Yes,' he answered.

'I'm only surprised he hasn't sent a bigger army,' said Andra. He continued to stare across the bridge at the black creature, hunched like a preying cat. It could breathe fire. Its massive jaws could rip armour off a dozen warriors at once. The talons on its smaller front legs were razor sharp, like eight huge scythes. It could fly. Fast. High. He held the sword.

Fleeting images from the tapestries and carvings he glimpsed of Aian Abreotan's legend passed through his mind. The sword could flame. It produced light. He studied its ragged-edged blade, its sharpness. Peret's Master Ki had only one piece of information relating to the sword: a saying – 'He who wields the sword will know its powers.' What were its powers? How would he know them? Cedwyn's sword, the sword Malcolm bequeathed to him, the sword Liam carried, was easy to wield, and blood never stained its blade, but the glyph protecting Abreotan's sword destroyed Cedwyn's blade along with Liam. Abreotan's sword was lighter than any weapon he'd handled, as if it was an integral part of him, not a mere extension. The moment he came into contact with the sword, it flowed into his being, and he into it. What were its powers?

'Take my shield, Your Majesty.' A Haardrishii was holding out the familiar black shield, embossed with the Great King's royal insignia of the green rampant griffin.

Andra looked up. He didn't even know the warrior. 'What's your name?'

The Haardrishii seemed surprised to be asked. 'Byrtnoth, Your Majesty,' he replied respectfully, and bowed his head.

'Do you believe in the prophecy, Byrtnoth?'

Byrtnoth raised his eyes. 'Before I saw you take the sword, I would have said no,' he replied, 'but what I see now is the truth. You are the new king. You bear the sword every warrior would give his life to wield but once. My life is your life.'

'Thank you, Byrtnoth. Thank you for your offer. I won't forget it,' said Andra, 'but keep your shield. The sword is my protection.'

Andra studied his companions huddled against the crumbling ruins of Cennednyss. If he asked them to go with him against the dragon, they would. He knew that. Tim grinned at him. That assassin always seemed to know much more than he let on. He already owed Tim his life too many times. He hardly knew Sasha, but already he appreciated her practical nature, and her cynicism. Marella was strikingly beautiful, her dark hair whisked by the breezes eddying around the stone, and a warrior worth nothing less than absolute respect. And there was Claarn, the giant who yearned to fight a heroic battle. Perhaps, today, he would get his wish.

Andra's eyes rested on the three Apprentices. If he was destined to be king, they were men he had to understand. They served the one person he already saw as an enigma in the Kingdom: if he was destined to be king. 'Wait here!' he ordered 'If it is The Way, we will meet on the other side.' He didn't wait for protests, or wishes of fortune, but held Abreotan's sword in both hands, point upward, and strode onto the stone bridge, toward the dragon.

The vicious wind pulled at his tunic and leggings, whipping his cloak violently around his body, and threatened to push him from the arch. He unknotted the cloak, and let the garment tumble away, spiralling downward, in the taunting wind, toward the raging waves. A voice rippled through his senses, chanting in rhythm to his pace across the bridge. I am you. You are me. We are one. He rolled the hilt of the sword in his hand, felt it tingling, felt energy flowing through him, filling him. He was the sword. The sword was him. What were its powers?

The black creature, at the end of the bridge, lifted its brutish head as he approached, and glared at him from huge red reptilian eyes, and its ugly jaws opened, exposing rows of glistening teeth. Two upper and two lower fangs jutted over the lip. The dragon shifted its weight, its scaly body moving slowly, its long snaking neck extending forward and down, bringing its head in line with the advancing warrior, so that Andra could see the scales sliding as the beast breathed in. A ball of fire erupted from the dragon's jaws, enveloping him.

Claarn and Marella sprinted onto the bridge determined

to avenge Andra's death, followed by the others, but as they closed the distance they were transfixed by a vision of Andra, unharmed in the raging flames, defying the dragon's fire.

Andra clutched Abreotan's sword and willed the fire to pass around him. He could hear and see the fire, as it wrapped about his body, but he felt no heat, no pain, only the pressure of the breath driving the flames. Then it passed, and he was facing the creature again. He was the sword. The sword was him.

The dragon lifted its great head again, exposing the glittering ebony neck scales on its underside, and extended its wings. Tim put a shaft to Freyar's bow, and the arrow whistled toward its mark, only to shatter uselessly against the dragon's hide. The dragon's head snaked down at Andra, jaws gaping, but Andra judged the speed of the attack, braced, and swung Abreotan's sword with all his strength, to meet the dragon, feeling the shock of impact as he struck. It was nothing like the impact he anticipated. The dragon recoiled with a gaping wound in its jaw. It flashed out its snake-like tongue, licked the bleeding cut, and hesitated, as if surprised by the ferocity of the small human's attack. Andra seized his opportunity. He leaped and pointed the blade directly at the dragon, channelling his being into the body of the sword. The blade erupted in flame, and a bolt of raw energy shot from its tip, hitting the dragon's massive chest, ripping through its scaly armour, exploding its heart. The creature twitched and stiffened, stretching up to its full height, towering over Andra, as if it was determined to take flight, but its black wings folded and collapsed, and the huge body crumpled against the rocks, shuddering, great hind legs stretching out and in, its tail thrashing angrily in its death throes, until it lay motionless.

Andra never saw the dragon fall. Overcome with unfathomable exhaustion, his energy spent in the magical attack, he teetered forward two steps, as the dragon rose over him, and collapsed face down on the bridge.

Forty One

They travelled, without rest, due east, through the heart of the Bitter Peaks, battling the lashing rain and freezing winds brought by the storm, moving with grim purpose along the mountain trails, and through the narrow valleys. The storm was a blessing, masking their trail from pursuing Haagii who still had courage to follow them after watching Andra slay the dragon at Cennednyss. They were certain the Dragonlord would want the sword now, its reality dramatically unleashed in their escape from his trap. Time was against them, but for once foul weather was a boon.

Just over a day from Cennednyss, Tim led them onto a ride, overlooking the vast expanse of Elvenaar Forest that stretched north and east between the Andrakians and the Bitter Peaks. Andra could see the ocean waters to the south whipped by passing squalls, and in the middle of the forest, less than half a day's travel east, was a solemn grey lake. 'Gnornung,' said Tim. 'It's the ancient lake of Elvenaar souls. It's sacred to the Aelendyell; a place of pilgrimage. The Royal Chancellor and Liam pilfered the Orb of Radiance from an island there called Heolstorcofa.'

'Do we go that way?' asked Andra.

'There's no other choice,' Tim informed him.

No cave lent shelter to the weary band, but Claarn found a cleft in the mountain leading to a trail that descended into Elvenaar Forest, and as the grey daylight dissolved into the inky night they set to making themselves warm and comfortable, wrapping in their cloaks, and huddling. A fire was out of the question, lest it signal their whereabouts to the Haagii.

Andra stood alone, staring across the dark land to the horizon, where sky and earth were almost one. He clutched the hilt of Abreotan's sword, remembering the sheer drain he felt as he, or the sword – he was unsure which – slew the dragon with a bolt of magical energy. Had he really conjured the sword's power?

'What are you contemplating?'

The immediacy of Tim's voice startled him. He forgot how well his friend could see in the absence of light. 'My world's changing,' he replied. The Guardian he'd been was no more. He was entering metamorphosis, but he wasn't sure he was ready for it.

'Change is the only certainty, Andra,' said Tim. 'My world has changed more times than I care to relate. I'm sure it will change again. Uncertainty is all I can be certain of.'

'In The Vale,' Andra responded, 'the certain was all we knew. Sun-Call, the roles of the Task Masters, the Council, the Guardian Master: these were the things we shared, generation to generation. They were ancient institutions and ancient practices. Only the faces changed. I knew nothing of this greater world, of a Kingdom, of Dragonlords, of Abreotan's sword or prophecies. Two days ago, I was only another thief, a poor one at that. Now, I hold the futures of every one of us in the sword. Am I really the one chosen by destiny?'

Tim put an arm on Andra's shoulder. 'You were the only one who could take the sword, Andra. You wear the charm of Ethelreddor. No one else does. There's only one such magical item in existence. You are the chosen warrior to succeed Abreotan. Never doubt that, my friend. Even when the burden of that responsibility threatens to overwhelm you, remind yourself that you, alone, were chosen, and you cannot give that burden away to anyone.' Tim lifted his arm and, as he walked to the campsite, he whistled, and the whistle of a hunting nighthawk replied from above the cleft: Sasha on watch.

For a long time, the young Guardian contemplated the darkness. He drew Abreotan's sword from his belt and clasped the hilt in both hands as he concentrated. He wanted the sword to emanate warmth. Slowly, gently, the blade glowed – dull red that brightened to red-orange – and heat radiated to his arms and face, though the light barely illuminated more than an arm span. A tingling sensation filled his hands. Satisfied, Andra carried the weapon to his friends to share its warmth, pleased he'd discovered another useful function of the sword.

Of its own volition, the sword dipped and smashed the Haagii blade. The shaggy haired warrior recoiled, stunned by Andra's speed, and ran. Andra checked how the others were faring. Tim was nocking an arrow to Freyar's bow, and Marella stood over the bodies of three Haagii, her blade dripping blood. She looked up at Andra, and smiled, waving the Dark Warrior sword Andra had given to her at Cennednyss, after he'd taken Abreotan's weapon. Claarn grabbed two Haagii warriors by their hair and threw them hard against the face of a rocky cliff. They collapsed in a shower of dirt and stones. The surviving Haagii scrambled up the slope, sending small pebble avalanches spattering down in their wake. A parting shot from Tim brought down a Haagii as his companions fled to higher ground. 'That should discourage them,' the assassin shouted, and grinned as he shouldered the bow. 'They're not likely to follow us into Elvenaar Forest anyway.'

Regrouped, after staving off the attack, the party followed Tim and Sasha's lead down the winding path, toward the first stand of trees bordering Elvenaar Forest. Andra glanced to the north, where a wall of thick white smoke rose from the perimeter of the forest. As at Wynwuduholt, the Haagii were trying to burn the Aelendyell homes, destroying forests in pyrrhic madness. How much they'd torched already, he couldn't guess, but he knew the Aelendyell, in the depths of the forest, would be hard at work preparing their magical defences to turn back their Ealdfeond.

Tim stopped them at the first tree. 'We're entering Aelendyell lands and that means we're trespassing,' he warned. 'Since the late Great King outlawed the Aelendyell, we may well be treated as their enemy. If you see an

Aelendyell, say nothing and do nothing. Leave your weapons alone. Don't make any show of resistance, or force. If we're stopped, I'll do the talking. I speak the tongue fluently. Elvenaar Forest is a risk, but I'd rather reason with an angry Aelendyell than the Dragonlord's army.'

The forest twilight filled Andra with belonging, as he entered. The mountains were stark, rugged, cold, and whatever beauty the ancient Dwarven had seen in the mountains escaped Andra, but he understood why the Aelendyell worshipped their forests. The forest atmosphere was fascinating. He could smell its essences, drink its closeness, its mystery, and the elmoaks, their roots and boughs covered with lichen and moss, the ferns, the pebble-strewn creeks, were familiar friends. His thoughts flashed to Mirith and Terath, and Wudufaesten tun, and he wandered through memories while he followed Tim and Sasha along the forest's trails.

Aelendyell shadowed their progress all day. By midday, Tim was leading them through the trees, a few paces from the southern shore of Gnornung. A chilling breeze rippled the lake's surface, and every time Andra glimpsed the grey water through the forest cold shivers touched him. He imagined the lake to be a bright crystal blue, as if he'd seen it before, but his eyes saw only the lake's deadness. They crossed a swinging vine-bridge, over a wide river, flowing from Gnornung toward the sea, and pushed on, along paths and trails, deviating to avoid tuns and villages. Whenever they digressed, Andra was aware the Aelendyell dogging them closed in, until they were visible through the trees, but neither group attempted to communicate.

As night filled the forest, Tim brought them to a halt. 'No fire,' he said loudly. 'No wind or rain is likely to reach us, because of the thick canopy, so we'll be relatively warmer in here than we were on the mountainside.'

'Why no fire?' Claarn asked, disgruntled at the prospect of spending another miserable night without the basic element that gave both warmth and cooking.

'If your enemy were busily burning every patch of a

forest you cherished as part of your own being, would you appreciate unwanted guests lighting a fire in the heart of your lands?' Tim asked, anger sparkling in his voice.

Claarn shook his head and grumbled. 'Thank Teka for the sword then,' he grunted, and glanced at Andra.

Tim's voice rose in reply beyond the ring of trees surrounding their camp. Andra focussed on the Aelendyell words, trying to translate what was transpiring, and heard references to worold-buend, their party, and the Haagii, and the word draca featured at one point in the interchange, but Tim, and the invisible Aelendyell with whom he was communicating, spoke too rapidly, so much of the meaning escaped him.

When Tim joined his friends by the glow of Abreotan's sword, two Aelendyell accompanied him. Andra saw they carried bows and swords, identifying them as Aelendyell Weapon Bearers. He also noticed they didn't look at anyone in the circle of the sword's incandescence. Their wide almond eyes were staring at the sword, features fixed in wonder. One lifted his eyes to Andra and studied him. The young Guardian imagined Terath's face. The Aelendyell people saved his life when he should have perished on Dragon Breath Plains.

Without thinking, Andra smiled and said, 'Hondgesella.' The Weapon Bearer's jaw gaped. His companion glanced at Andra, held his gaze, and the two melted into the night, leaving Andra to wonder what he'd said wrong. He turned to Tim for an explanation, but the assassin carefully, almost imperceptibly, shook his head, warning Andra not to ask.

'What was that all about?' interrupted Claarn. 'What frightened them off?'

'They've had very little contact with your – our people, Claarn,' Tim explained. 'They're naturally very suspicious. When they saw you and the Haardrishii, they were preparing to kill us, as revenge for what happened in the Great City when their emissaries sought the return of the Orb of

Radiance.'

Claarn's eyebrows knitted. 'They could try,' he growled in challenge. 'They'd learn what a true warrior can do in battle.'

'Difficult to fight with a dozen arrows in your back,' said Tim.

Andra heard the icy reality beneath the assassin's retort. The Aelendyell could've ambushed them any time, through the day, and efficiently. Claarn was a mighty warrior on a battlefield, but the Aelendyell were masters in their forests.

'What did they want?' Marella asked, trying to direct the conversation away from an argument about fighting prowess.

'They wanted to know why we dare to invade their forest, when the Great King's law made them outlaws, and us their enemy.'

'And?' Sasha prompted.

'I told them why we were here,' said Tim, in a matter-of-fact tone. 'At first, they didn't believe me. Then I pointed to the glowing sword. They came to see for themselves.'

'What significance is it to them?' Claarn asked.

'Abreotan's legend has a part in Aelendyell lore. The Dragonlords nearly destroyed the entire Elvenaar culture, before Abreotan drove them away, and slew the dragons,' said Tim, and he paused to gaze at the sword, as if considering what else to say. 'This weapon has Elvenaar magic worked into it. The Aelendyell understand a little of its power, but no Aelendyell can wield it,' he explained. 'They do know that, without it, the new Dragonlord cannot be stopped.'

'What happens now?' asked Marella.

'We sleep,' replied Tim. 'We're safe here. The Aelendyell have posted watches around the camp, and the two who came here are already on their way to their tun, to speak with their Elders.'

'So, we're trapped,' said Claarn.

'No. In the morning we'll have permission to travel through Elvenaar Forest.'

'Why are you so sure of that?' asked Marella.

'Because Andra bears the sword,' Tim replied gravely.

The Aelendyell Elders watched from a flat outcrop of rock, a line of green and grey merging with the forest hues, as the party passed below them, and Andra was conscious they studied him closely as he passed. He expected the Elders to demand to inspect the sword, but they didn't. They remained distant observers, content to witness the sword pass safely through their tun.

Thirty Aelendyell warriors accompanied them during the morning, and through the afternoon, as they journeyed northeast, toward the foot of the Andrakian Mountains. Tim constantly chatted with the Aelendyell, and the more Andra saw his friend in the Weapon Bearers' company – his ease with the Aelendyell, his uncanny familiarity with the forest, his confidence – the more he was convinced that Tim hid secrets about his identity, and it made him wonder how often Tim frequented forests rather than city streets. Tim told him, on the night they absconded from the Great Armies' camp, he knew very little about the Aelendyell; that he was raised as a waif in the Great City by Patti, ignorant in the main of his quartercast heritage – but observing Tim in Elvenaar Forest, Andra doubted the truth of his friend's tale.

Other Aelendyell appeared and disappeared throughout the day. Most came to stare at Andra, and the sword, although none tried to speak with him. They stared because he was already a legend. Tim recounted his slaying of the dragon at Cennednyss to the Aelendyell, with whom he spoke, and the story spread rapidly, drawing them out of their villages and tuns to gaze at the new Abreotan, the new king who was to inherit the lands of the humans living beyond the forests.

Andra was relieved when the last Aelendyell escort withdrew, as the party began an abrupt ascent out of the forest, into the Andrakian foothills. The more attention he attracted in the forest, the greater humility he felt as the inheritor of Abreotan's legendary strength. He reminded himself constantly of the words Tim shared the night before they entered Elvenaar Forest – that a great responsibility rested on his shoulders, heavier than any sword, and he had no choice but to bear that responsibility and see it through, as a Guardian should. If he was to be the new king, the warrior chosen by destiny to confront the Dragonlord, acceptance was his only option. Such was the nature of The Way. Removed by time, distance, good and bad experiences, so far from his birthplace and home in The Vale, he stumbled upon his path as the Guardian Master promised he would. He carried the burden, but within himself he had found his purpose. He was the sword. The sword was him. One step on the path – and though the path's destination was unknown, at least he knew its direction.

Forty Two

No word from Peret. His last communication came before the warrior, Andra, was meant to face the dragon with Abreotan's sword, but since then he hadn't called or responded. Eight days had passed.

A Ahmud Ki closed the volume on the bench and rubbed his hand across his finely-cut beard. At least I have one inherited blessing from my bastard father, he considered. Aelendyell can't grow beards. They have no facial hair. Pleasingly, the beard marked him apart from the people he despised.

So, why hadn't Peret communicated? There were obvious possibilities. Peret was dead – but, even if he was dead, another Apprentice would've filled his role. He'd lost the communication crystal sphere. Possible: clumsy, but possible. The crystal had been stolen. Could he trust the thieves? Maybe the dragon killed them. The dragon.

A Ahmud Ki approached a pair of ebony poles, rising vertically from the tower's marble floor, and ran a hand over the structure. The work was complete. The portal had taken enough time, when he first constructed the tower after Great King Thana – that poor, idiotic, incompetent, fat, dead excuse for a king – made him Royal Advisor. His map study during past months gave him the knowledge to operate his portal with greater effectiveness than any Targan sorceress could dream of a portal being used. He could travel to Targa, to Ranu Ka Shehaala, wherever he chose. He had the knowledge now.

Why hadn't Peret communicated? If this Andra, this Guardian who usurped Liam, had Abreotan's sword, where was he now?

A Ahmud Ki slapped the pole furiously and stormed to the centre of the room. There were too many variables, too many pieces, too many unknowns. Mareg lurked at the periphery of his communication crystals, listening, gauging his every move. How did he tune in to the crystals? What power enabled the Dragonlord to access his magic? The Fifth Ki?

And Central Gate. Surdrok had failed. The Haagii and the dragons had crushed the South and East Wheels' resistance, and Mareg's hordes were pouring toward the Great City, so how would he stop them now? The sword? Where was it? He had controlled Liam. The spell in the platinum chain ensured that he, A Ahmud Ki, not Liam, would rule the Kingdom, once the sword was retrieved from Cennednyss. Liam was meant to be a puppet, a shell of a king. This Guardian, who took the sword in Liam's place, was a different matter because he wore no chain. A Ahmud Ki had to counter that. If there was to be a new king, if the sword was Abreotan's sword, if his warrior could bear it back to the Great City, despite the dragon squatting before Cennednyss, despite Mareg's host massing on the Plains of Ky, then he had to control him. He had to forge a new chain. But where was this new king? Why had Peret failed him?

Horses thundered toward them, along the road, the riders spurring their mounts and closing the gap at a furious pace. The hooves clattered over the wooden bridge and came on between the huts and outbuildings of Hillswater.

Claarn stepped out to meet them. The leading rider reined in and dismounted in the one motion to stand before the giant warrior. 'I am Devi Karl,' the Haardrishii gasped. 'The Chancellor sent mounts and orders to speed you safely to the Great City.' Claarn estimated thirty to forty Haardrishii formed the escorting party. He pursed his lips and whistled. Figures emerged from different buildings along the street, returning their weapons to scabbards and quivers, and Andra strode into sight, slipping the sword over his shoulder into the back scabbard fashioned from leather scraps in an abandoned forge where he'd hidden.

The Haardrishii troop turned in unison toward him and

watched until he stood beside Claarn. Devi Karl bowed his head and dropped to one knee. The Haardrishii contingent dismounted, following their leader's example. 'We serve you, Your Majesty,' said Karl. Andra, taken aback by their courtesy, paused before asking Karl to stand. 'My Lord,' said Karl, 'horses are provided.'

Andra looked at the horses. 'Thank you,' he said. 'Where are the villagers?' When they arrived in Hillswater, late the previous afternoon, they found the village deserted, except for chickens, pigs, and other domesticated animals. Doors were ajar, woodpiles overturned, furniture scattered. The village showed signs everywhere of sudden evacuation.

'The Haagii are pouring through Central Gate,' the Devi explained. 'The last defence fell two days ago. The Armies have withdrawn to the Great City, to defend it from the Dragonlord's hordes, and High Lord Surdrok ordered every village cleared and the people to flee to the Great City.' Devi Karl caught his breath, and added, 'There's very little time, Lord. We must leave. Even now, we will need to move fast to regain the Great City before the Haagii completely encircle it.'

Andra clutched the reins as his horse galloped across the Plains of Ky toward a distant black dot. They'd left the road, riding due east to avoid the advancing Haagii army, and, as much as he wanted to survey the land they crossed, his limited equestrian skills forced him to concentrate on staying mounted. He prayed there were no runnels or creeks to jump. 'To the north! To the north!' a Haardrishii shouted, as they crested a low ridge.

A dark smudge appeared on the near horizon, and behind it, smoke columns spiralled skyward, from burning farms and villages overrun by the Haagii. Shapes broke free of the smudge and headed toward them. 'Riders!' Claarn yelled, and dug his heels into his horse's flanks. Andra urged his mount forward, and they followed Devi Karl down the southern slope of the ridge, and cut east again, across its face.

Each time they glimpsed the pursuing riders, the distance between had diminished. The pursuers were on fresher mounts, horses that hadn't been ridden non-stop for the good part of a day. They couldn't outride them.

Tim spurred his horse, until he was alongside Karl, and Andra heard them shouting to each other, before Karl nodded. They wheeled to the southeast, heading for a tall ridge.

As the party passed over the crest, Karl ordered them to rein in. The Haardrishii formed a broad line, swords drawn, pushing Andra, Claarn and their fellows to the rear, and they waited as the closing rumble of the pursuer's horses climbed the far side of the ridge. When the enemy horsemen rode blindly over the crest, they were met head-on by the Kingdom warriors, and the ambush threw them into chaos. Swords rang, and the air filled with the cries of bloody conflict and the whinnying of horses. The enemy horsemen weren't Haagii, but strangers, clad in lightweight chainmail and scarlet garments. They wielded lances and short swords, and they were agile, expert horse riders, but the Haardrishii were too heavily armoured, too well trained, to be troubled.

The encounter ended as swiftly as it began. Unable to reorganize, or match the Haardrishii's ferocity, the enemy riders fled, leaving their dead and dying on the field. The Haardrishii weren't without casualties. Five black-armoured warriors were dead. Their fellows hoisted the bodies aboard their horses and attended to the three who received major wounds.

Within moments, the band was galloping northeast again. The only compensation Andra had, in his desperation to stay mounted throughout the furious ride, was when he saw the pale, grimaced faces of the Apprentices who were clinging to their horses between pairs of supporting Haardrishii. He, at least, was not alone, and not the worst.

They were too late it. Between them, and the Great City, was a dark field, studded with burning fires, as if the night sky had fallen to earth. 'Teka curse them!' Claarn growled, as he clambered down from his exhausted horse and rested a hand on the heaving ribs of Andra's mount.

Tim steered his horse toward them, silhouetted against the purple and blue streaks of waning twilight. 'This is where we started this whole escapade,' he said, whimsically. 'This is turning into an impressive beginning for a legend, Andra. All we have to do, now, is gallop through the Haagii ranks, and into the Great City.'

'Sometimes you're a fool,' Claarn grumbled. The day's wild riding had worn the giant's temper to a brittle state. He walked away, searching for Marella and Sasha.

'Something I said?' Tim asked, and grinned.

While they rested, Karl organized his Haardrishii, assigning four to each of Andra's companions. Karl and eleven of his men were to protect Andra, to ensure he and the sword made a safe dash to the Great City. Marella and Claarn were to take their Haardrishii with them, the Apprentices and their Haardrishii bodyguards formed the third group, and the rest, defending Tim and Sasha, made up a fourth party. His plan was simple. On a signal, the four groups would race on different paths through the Haagii encamped between them and the Great City, creating as much confusion as possible. Four independent charges would deprive the unsuspecting Haagii of any opportunity to coordinate their capture. A little luck won't go astray either, thought Andra, as he listened to Karl's instructions.

They galloped into the midst of the Haagii. Andra clung to his horse's mane, aware of the Haardrishii pressed around him. If riding during daylight had been difficult, riding into darkness, Andra decided, even with campfires lighting part of the way, was lunacy. He saw nothing in their initial rush, only heard surprised cries and shouts, as their band rode, sometimes between, and sometimes through, Haagii tents and groups. His horse leapt again and again, clearing invisible obstacles, and he nearly fell every time, remaining in the saddle only because firm Haardrishii hands pushed him back as he began toppling. He heard a cry to his left, and was aware of a gap appearing at the edge of his vision. He glanced sideways and saw a rider-less horse. His horse lunged, and he instinctively grabbed at the reins. Whatever else happens, I must not fall, he reminded himself, not in the midst of the Haagii, not with Abreotan's sword. He tightened his grip.

The world unexpectedly reeled before his eyes, as his horse tumbled from underneath, and he flew through the spinning night to land heavily. He scrambled to his feet, his shoulder and left knee smarting, and wrenched Abreotan's sword from his back scabbard, as shadowy figures closed in menacingly. He willed the sword to flame. A tingle sparkled along his arms, and bright flames burst from the weapon's blade, startling the encroaching Haagii, forcing them to shield their eyes against the light. Seizing the advantage, Andra swept the sword in a broad arc, slicing through the leather breastplates of three Haagii, who fell, and their companions staggered back, terrified by the warrior's fiery weapon.

He saw and heard confused melee to his left. Knowing his Haardrishii escort would have stopped to aid him, he bolted through the terrified Haagii toward the centre of conflict. Swarming Haagii warriors, who'd witnessed the disturbance and run to help their own people, hopelessly outnumbered Devi Karl and his men. The Haardrishii formed a nucleus, back-to-back, desperately warding thrusts and cuts made by their encircling foe.

Andra charged into the fray, flailing the flaming sword, relentlessly cutting through Haagii, as he pressed forward to join the Haardrishii. For every warrior he slew, others fled in fear when they witnessed his fury and prowess, and the sword's magical fire shining white in the darkness. No emotion, no hate, no trepidation touched him, as he waded through the carnage he created. The weapon was lightweight, almost wielding itself against Andra's foes.

When he reached the Haardrishii, he took a place beside Devi Karl, and, wordless, they set to slaying the Haagii who dared to oppose them, as they edged toward the outer perimeter of the Great City. Riders closed on the spirited fight from two directions, and he prepared to meet their onslaught, but into his sword's circle of firelight came Claarn, Marella, Tim and their escorts, shouting, and leaning forward to scoop their embattled friends aboard their steeds.

Hearing a distant cry from the battlements, A Ahmud Ki paused on the path from the palace to his tower, wondering what provoked it. The Haagii army had swept toward the Great City from Central Gate for six days, steadily encircling it, their numbers swelling, until Haagii spread in every direction across the Plains of Ky.

Tents and shelters sprang up everywhere. Dark riders moved through the encampments, their numbers increasing daily, and for the past two nights the plains were alight with campfires. He never envisioned the assembly of so vast an army possible, even under Mareg's rule, yet here the Haagii were countless in number – an army fifty times larger than the entire Kingdom could have mustered before the tragic debacle at The Rim Shield. Peret had spoken of an ocean of Haagii, pouring from the valleys of the Fire Mountains on The Rim Shield, but A Ahmud Ki put his soul-numbing description down to overactive fear affecting the Apprentice's imagination, especially with dragons in the sky. Now, he knew otherwise. Mareg's earthly power could wipe the Kingdom, and every inhabitant in it, from existence. And the Dragonlord hadn't yet revealed even the tiniest portion of his true power. Feet ran on the gravel in the darkness toward him. 'Master Ki! Master Ki! You must come at once! You must see!' called Damon, panting. He dropped to his knees before A Ahmud Ki.

'What must I see?' the Chancellor asked, coldly, annoyed to be begged to go somewhere he hadn't intended going.

'I can't describe the vision, Master. You must see for yourself,' the Apprentice insisted.

Damon was never demonstrative in his emotions, so his agitation had to have foundation. A Ahmud Ki succumbed to his servant's urgency and followed the Apprentice into the palace. Damon led him to the castle's outer wall, and they climbed the gate tower to the highest point on the battlements.

When they reached the top, A Ahmud Ki saw a dozen Royal Guards pressed against the wall, staring down, and with them were Lords Surdrok and Kerry. Damon ushered him to a space, beside the others, from where A Ahmud Ki gazed over the Great City spread below the plateau in the cloaking darkness. Clouds blocked out the moon and the stars, and the only lights twinkling on the Plains of Ky were the lights of a hundred thousand Haagii campfires. 'There, Master. See?' said Damon, pointing into the night.

A Ahmud Ki followed the Apprentice's direction toward a point, southwest of the castle, where the incomplete outer wall of the Great City's defences ran its ragged course. The campfires flickered harmlessly, but his eyes were drawn to a different light, a shining amber flame, moving through the darkness, larger, brighter than any campfire, racing toward the Great City. He focussed, concentrating on the light, as it approached the edge of the Haagii lines, before he cast a spell to enhance his vision, letting him see what the eyes of those watching with him could not see. The amber flame enveloped a sword, held aloft by a warrior clinging to the back of a companion, as their horse leaped the low outer wall and thundered into the Great City streets. Behind the glowing sword, other horses were bearing warriors of the Kingdom to safety from the pursuing Haagii.

A Ahmud Ki shook his eyes free of his spell and turned to the amazed viewers on the tower parapet. 'Behold!' he announced, with calculated deliberation. 'The new King is among us,' and, for the first time in days, he smiled.

ABOUT THE AUTHOR

Australian writer, Tony Shillitoe, entered the fantasy field in 1992-3 when Pan Macmillan Australia published his popular and successful Andrakis trilogy. He followed the trilogy with a stand-alone coming-of-age fantasy novel, *The Last Wizard*, which was short-listed for the inaugural Aurealis Awards Best Fantasy Novel in 1995.

From 2002-2008, Tony published two more fantasy series – the Ashuak Chronicles trilogy and the Dreaming in Amber quatrology – with HarperCollins Voyager Australia, and *Blood*, from the Ashuak Chronicles, was shortlisted for the Aurealis Awards Best Fantasy Novel in 2002.

Tony branched into Adolescent/Young Adult novels in 1999, with the publication of *Joy Ride* by Wakefield Press. Tony's second teenage novel, *Caught in the Headlights*, a HarperCollins Angus and Robertson imprint, was listed as a notable read for Older Readers in the 2003 Children's Book Council Awards, and subsequently appeared on Premier's Reading Lists around the nation.

Tony has written and published short stories, scripts, poetry, professional writing course books and ghost-edited a variety of projects. More information about his work and life can be found at his web site The Phoenix Rises: http://www.tonyshillitoe.com.au

BOOKS BY THE SAME AUTHOR

FANTASY NOVELS
The Andrakis Trilogy
The Waking Dragon
Maker of Kings
Dragonlord War

The Ashuak Chronicles
Blood
Passion
Freedom

Dreaming in Amber
The Amber Legacy
A Solitary Journey
Prisoner of Fate
The Demon Horsemen

The Last Wizard

STORY ANTHOLOGIES
Tales of the Dragon
The Red Heart

TEENAGE NOVELS
Joy Ride
Caught in the Headlights
In My Father's Shadow
The Need